LA CHIMÈRE
OF
PRAGUE

A NOVEL

Rick Pryll

First Printing: 2020
Foolishness Press
4619 Water Oak Road
Charlotte, NC 28211
www.rickpryll.com

Although some of the events and locations are real, the novella is a work fiction, and is not meant to accurately represent the actions and conversations of historical figures. Any resemblance to actual persons, living or dead, is entirely coincidental.

Cover art: *Loutka*, Oil on Canvas, 30 inches by 24 inches, © Holly Spruck HMCAS 2020. All rights reserved.
Cover art: *The Beast*, Ink Blob Print, 14 inches by 14 inches, © Holly Spruck HMCAS 2017. All rights reserved.
Frontispiece: *Hundred Spire Town*, Pen & Ink on Paper, 11 inches by 7 inches, © Holly Spruck HMCAS 2020. All rights reserved".

Cover Design and Interior Format

PRAISE FOR

LA CHIMÈRE OF PRAGUE

"Once you're fully engrossed in Joseph's character it's impossible to put the book down. Some of Pryll's prose balances on the brink of poetic." — Asher Syed, 5-star review

Praise for Part I, "The Chimera of Prague"
"Move over F Scott Fitzgerald because someone just captured a time period and feeling better than you." — Avid reader, 5-star Amazon review

"One of the most exceptional books I have ever read. The style is unique - perfectly balancing literary prowess against a determined unpretentiousness. The imagery is sublime, the tone informal. It is written beautifully, but is rarely (if ever) preoccupied with the prose. It's rare to find a book - or indeed an author - that is able to hit all the sweet spots like this does." — Katherine Parsons, Goodreads 5-star review

"Rick Pryll doesn't conform to the tried-and-true writing form. In a time when authors want to copy the fad or compete against the modern literary giants (think Tom Clancy, Dean Koontz, and Stephen King), his writing is a refreshing diversion." — Mark Smith, Goodreads review

"Not your run-of-the-mill novel. At times I wanted to reach through the pages and shake him, tell him to get it together. Other times I found myself cheering him on. Either way, the fast-paced nature of his thoughts kept me turning the pages for more." @HoldThatPage, Goodreads review

"This novel is not merely for world travelers or diviners of personal truth. It is a message for all of us to be bold, brave and to know through this text, that we are not alone." — Bibiana Krall, author of Volga Black

Praise for "Homecoming"
"Subtle characterization, lyrical prose, terrific pacing. Quiet but compelling." — Morri Creech, poet, 2014 Pulitzer Prize Finalist for The Sleep of Reason

CONTENTS

To Holly

ACKNOWLEDGMENTS

Let me start by saying thank you to Holly. I am so lucky to have the privilege of watching you grow and evolve as an artist, as a wife, as a mother to our kids. I love you. I'm only trying to keep up with your brilliance.

Next, I will thank my kids. Promise me that you will always go after your dreams, no matter what. You swear too much, now go to bed. Dammit. ;)

In the time of the pandemic, I want to thank the universe for the blessings my furry companions bring: LiLi, the aggressive lover; Maggie Mae, the shy one; and Roxy, the editor dog laying (or is it lying?) on my feet under the desk.

I want to say thank you to my biggest supporters. I know I can always count on you. Linda and Chris Ostrom, Sabrina and Steve Brown, Liz and Steve LeBoo and our ArtPop Fairy Art-Mother, Wendy Hickey. To all the helpers: Kathy Kerrigan, Heather Sangster, Sandy Fluck, Kim Killion and Jennifer Jakes. Hats off to the teachers (my continual source of inspiration): Ilona Karmel, Sarah and Morri Creech, Julie Funderburk, Kathie Collins, Paul Reali and Jessica Peterson. To my writer friends: Tracy Sumner for all the craft books, Bibiana Krall for making me promise to read the whole thing out loud barefoot in my backyard, Landis Wade, C.S. Smith, Hope Smyth, Bonnie Ditlevsen, S. Craig Renfroe, Charles Israel and Sarah Fitzgerald. Let me thank my lucky stars for CharlotteLit and Charlotte Writers Club. Last but not least, all the readers and reviewers out there: thank you.

For the cover art, the ink blob beast (head and body), for the line art, I have to say thank you one more everlasting time to Holly Spruck HMCAS.

EPIGRAPH

"It is not a question of better or worse. The point is, not to resist the flow. You go up when you're supposed to go up and down when you are supposed to go down. When you're supposed to go up, find the highest tower and climb to the top. When you're supposed to go down, find the deepest well and go down to the bottom. When there's no flow, stay still. If you resist the flow, everything dries up."

— Dr. Honda, from Haruki Murakami's The Wind-up Bird Chronicle

AUGUST

MOVING, 2.8.98

CHANGE IS GOOD — BUT it isn't easy. I leave my fairy-tale flat behind. I take the chance. I might never be able to come back.

In the small bathroom mirror, next to the standing shower I'm going to miss, I look into my face. To see what I can see. Brown eyes, black hair that could use a trim, grubby stubble. The smudged tortoiseshell glasses. I push them up on my nose.

I packed up last night. I cleared the bathroom. I wrapped the cooking utensils that I'd bought with my mother when she'd visited. Need to take my reluctant collection of books from the kitchen. Need to pack my clothes from the bedroom. Three boxes, two to four hours tops. I get the keys to my new place at 7:00 p.m. My two buddies will get here around six. With a car and a little luck, we'll be done in an hour. One trip. Get it over with.

I think of Karina. I have to give her a chance. I should be patient.

The new place will be better. I'm excited to move. I hope the phone is not a party line. I hope the hot water is hot. White tile and clean porcelain, one of those sit-down bathtubs with the shower wand. That's a step in the wrong direction. I pray the neighbors aren't fucking assholes.

She'll do it. I can't put pressure on her. I can't be the one to ask. Already out on an osier limb.

I didn't go to the CzechTek Festival at the Old Ironworks near Dobríš this year. I attended last year in a different village. A crazy weekend of no sleep in a chlorophyll-green field and three free stages of blindingly white pulsating techno music. It's a bunch of artists, a group called Spiral Tribe. A mélange of squatters and travelers, with all kinds of vehicles, a massive generator in a huge field. Hard hard house tracks thump at the heart of it. Tents and fires all around. It touched my Seneca soul — the one-sixteenth of it anyway. The festival is going on right now. I could escape this gray city under its gray sky, I suppose.

I'd love to see raven-haired Karina out there. Yeah? And then what? I mean, first, what're the chances on God's viridian earth? Second, what would this yellow-belly do if I did see her?

She wears a gold cross on her Modigliani neck. I thought Bohemians weren't religious — more like they weren't allowed to be religious for a time. Czech religion goes way back. Izabela wore a gold cross on her neck too. It danced on my sternum.

Izabela's long gone. On Thursday, she canceled our date. That's okay. Let her sink herself into her boyfriend, the Czech-French wunderkind. I hope she gets what she wants. Why does it sound sarcastic if I say it?

I can't imagine what people think. Love's a crazy thing; we act like idiots. Is that what this is? Love? Izabela? I played the fool. Karina? No more chasing.

I've had a good run here: my mom came to visit, the super-model from New York stayed with me for a few titillating days, my afternoons with Izabela, my nights with Ilona. Ah, Ilona. My sad-eyed waif. Sharpish tongue. It all happened here, in this space, maybe because of it. This storybook apartment, these windows, the medieval courtyard. You can almost hear the harpsichord soundtrack. The kitchen table creaks. The shelf holds my books. The wardrobes hug my clothes. It morphs into memory. Legend.

A year after Rachel and I split, I left New York City. That was different. It was desperate. I was dying there. I worked for a bank in midtown. I walked home at night to my apartment in Alphabet City. In the heat of summer, I traversed 3.1 miles of sizzling urban blocks in my gray Hugo Boss suit, jacket draped over my forearm, my shiny yellow tie loose, a scuffed leather laptop bag slung crossbody. Summer sweat dampened my collar. It ran in rivulets down the knuckles of my spine.

The walk kept me from remembering what I'd given up. Given up so easily, my cozy little nest with the girl in the John Lennon mirrored glasses. My marriage. My ex. Those feline eyes hidden behind the reflection. She said she loved me; I didn't love myself enough to believe her. How could she love me?

In the hollow weeks after she'd left, I walked home from 50th Street, down reddish-golden 2nd Avenue. The day drained away. I crossed blinking 42nd Street and the more orange 34th into coral brick Murray Hill, near where my Rachel and I had our first New York apartment together the summer of the garbage strike: the days of Hooker's green and black, stinking heaps of refuse as high as the street signs. All that filth reminded me somehow of the sparkling white snow cliffs the plows would leave in the parking lot of Fay's drugstore in my hometown, in Western New York. Boyhood versions of my younger brother and me would climb and dig tunnels while my mom shopped for day-old pastries and palettes of no-name soda: lemon-lime, orange and grape.

Through Union Square — though that was more west — down to 14th Street, through the East Village by Tompkins Square Park. I hoped to see Lenny Kravitz in bell-bottoms and a skin-tight vest, or Allen Ginsberg in khakis, a white button-down and a thin black tie. I kept my eye out for the high-foreheaded extra from *Seinfeld* I'd seen there once. I tried to forget the way my voice sounded the time I ran into Rachel, twenty-five years old and already my ex, in a bikini top and cutoffs. She was sunbathing with a book on the grass near a drum circle. She'd packed her novel in her canvas tote. I cried out to her. Desperation was there. That voice, that forlorn *screak* in my voice; that's why I had to leave Manhattan.

Work here has been different, though. I made some significant progress on Friday. The fault tree logic opened up to me. I need to solve the real estate thing too. It's a simple database to track the properties that Identity Partners have either sold or rented to expats. It stores knowledge of what Prague has to offer. If I have enough of a database to show by the end of the week, I can make rent this month. Prove to these real estate guys that they should give me more work.

As far as Karina goes, we'll see. If she's interested, she'll open up. We'll build trust out of nothing. Like new land.

Organizing, 4.8.98

Out my window, the sky is cerulean blue with big puffy clouds. Clouds that have depth. Shaded masses. Flat bottoms. Elephant gray. Upward-facing torsos of yellow and blue. Clouds that backstroke in synchrony across the bowl of sky. They slant into the distance. Clouds that suggest a foreground, a middle ground, a background; a beginning, a middle, an end. I slept for a long time. I'm exhausted.

I'm barely out of bed.

Furnish the new flat. Populate my new life. Make it feel less dead. I don't have money right now.

No pot to boil water in. No coffee. I'm bitter. I'll go to the library. That'll cheer me up.

Václav Havel

I chose a book on Václav Havel. I knew he was the current president, and that he'd been a playwright, but not much else.

Turns out Havel had been at the presidential helm for three years before Czechoslovakia dissolved, from 1989 to 1992, then was elected as the first leader of the new republic in 1993. He was also a poet, an essayist, a counterculture intellectual, known to zoom down the long corridors of Prague Castle on his red scooter. Imagine.

I dig in. Who was this guy really? Foremost, a playwright. A dissident during the Communist years, starting from his time as a student at Czech Technical University, continuing through the Prague Spring of 1968, all the way until the Velvet Revolution of 1989.

Born on October 5, 1936, it seems Havel grew up in the relative luxury of a middle-class family. His family owned Lucerna Palace, an entertainment and shopping complex just off Wenceslas Square. Could he have been personally embarrassed by the family's wealth? When the Communists disenfranchised the bourgeoisie, was Havel secretly relieved?

A heritage of prosperity and advantage had both shaped and betrayed him. His early years centered on the cultural life of the Czech Republic, but discrimination prevented him from gaining admittance to the school of his choice: the Academy of Performing Arts. As an artist, he transformed this experience into fuel for his work. His genre became absurdist theater; he wrote and published three plays between 1963 and 1968.

Okay. I get that. But how did he become political? When did that start?

Here it is. Havel's career as a political dissident began in 1956. He was invited to speak at the Writers' Union conference for young artists. A chubby, blond young man with blue eyes, he spoke the truth, openly criticizing the Union. He objected to the continued oppression of literature. He pointed to the unfair practice of ostracizing poets, authors and playwrights who didn't follow the strict code of the Communist regime, who didn't comply with the Communist-approved brand of art and literature called *social realism*.

Was Havel the only hero? Far from it. I'm discovering that there were more than a few. In 1968, the Slovak Chairman of the Communist Party, Alexander Dubček, ushered in a new brand of Communism. It was considered dangerous by the leaders in Moscow, especially Leonid Brezhnev. Over four months, Dubček began a wave of reforms to bring about political liberation and democratization, cultural openness, ultimately allowing another political party besides the Communist Party to exist. His "socialism with a human face" granted citizens freedom of speech, freedom of the press and increased freedom of movement. This was the Prague Spring.

Problem was, these changes weren't favorable for everyone. Think about it from the perspective of the Soviet Union.
Must have seemed like things were getting away from them.
In response to the threat, Moscow enacted the Brezhnev Doc-
trine to justify the enforcement of the Warsaw Pact, a treaty I
need to dig into more later. If any member country began to slip
ideologically away from the Soviet Union, the Pact members
reserved the right to intervene — up to and including the use of
military force. Which they did, exactly once, in August 1968.
In Prague.

On August 20, 1968, 400,000 Warsaw Pact troops and tanks
rolled into Czechoslovakia.

Photos of that day are stunning. A tank in front of a paint
store. Pedestrians surrounding it, a man on a bicycle. You can
almost hear the shouting. "Why are you here?" Soviet tank
commanders, goggles up on their foreheads, look down on the
citizenry. Another photo: A body laid out on a mattress outside
the scaffolding in the front of a building as a woman in a skirt
and matronly heels passes by. A man in a scooter helmet looks
askance at the camera. In the background, a young boy can't
help but stare.

Imagine your city being overrun by a foreign army. It's
demoralizing. Crushing. It's a day most Czechs want to forget.
A day for staying alive. Imagine watching the tanks rumble past
your second-story window as you listen to the sounds of war —
a small group of soldiers with machine guns ramming through
a barricaded door to try to get to the radio headquarters. Hours
earlier, Prague had been waking up to a beautiful summer day.

A picture of a tank rolling over a vehicle that had been posi-
tioned as a barricade. The sullen faces of the Czechs standing
around, one waving a Czech flag.

It's all about intervention. Politicians need to realize that you
can't change the will of the people with force. Batons don't
change minds; they harden hearts.

On that day, Chairman Dubček was arrested and transported
to Moscow, where he remained for four days. Oh to be a fly on
those walls. Upon his return to Prague, he announced that he
would resign. I imagine everyone knew what that meant, that

he was forced to quit.

Let me get back to Havel. What was it like to be a writer living under Communism? Although his plays were highly regarded and critically acclaimed, they were banned from the theaters in his own country in 1969. He wasn't allowed to travel abroad to see his work come to life on stage. It's been said, however, that Havel's blacklisting had an ironic and positive side effect: it forced him to focus his talents on writing political commentary.

I come across an example in the book: an open letter Havel wrote in 1975 to Chairman Husák,Dubček's replacement, questioning how the success of an administration should be measured. He asserts that the reason people in his country don't rebel — why they comply with the current regime — is fear. He warns against "the path of inner decay for the sake of outward appearances." From the moment he sent that letter, he carried an emergency kit wherever he went, expecting to be arrested on the street. It contained toothpaste, cigarettes, razor blades and a fresh pair of underwear.

Havel continued to ramp it up when he wrote *The Power of the Powerless*, a damning arraignment of totalitarianism that became his most famous piece. The illegal essay spread throughout the former Soviet bloc nations via the *samizdat*, a form of dissident publishing that consisted of little more than a typewriter, carbon paper and the courage of those who dared to read the text and then pass it on. This one essay inspired leaders of the Solidarity movement in Poland and beyond. Havel's words, directly and indirectly, led to the fall of Communism.

It gets even more trippy. In response to the 1976 arrest of the Plastic People of the Universe, a psychedelic rock group in Prague, Havel and his fellow artists were spurred into action. Seeing how the musicians were treated — and the publicity achieved by the trial — they were inspired to form Charter 77, a human rights organization mobilized by a manifesto that criticized the government for failing to implement human rights provisions. This document laid the foundation for the 1989 Velvet Revolution.

Havel was imprisoned three separate times for his activities. The longest stint was from 1979 to 1983, when he was convicted of subversion to the Republic. While in jail, he was allowed to write a single letter to his wife each week; this collection of letters is now known as *Letters to Olga*. I find a worn copy and flip through it. You can hear his voice.

...I didn't understand the cult of tea that exists in prison, but I wasn't here long before grasping its significance and succumbing to it myself (I, who used to drink tea, if at all, only once a year, when I had the flu)...

The cult of tea — priceless.

What is striking about his letters is that they are at once self-absorbed (oh yeah? look who's talking), even petty, and yet there is something noble about contemplating tea while being held in prison. Havel, it seems to me, shows himself to be a man of enormous moral strength. He struggles to preserve his dignity and identity. It's heroic. I have so much more to read now.

The poet-president hosted interesting characters in Prague Castle: Frank Zappa, the Rolling Stones and, maybe most notably, Lou Reed. I read in an anecdote that Havel once commented to lead singer of the Velvet Underground, "Did you know I am president because of you?"

I'll see if Markéta can go shopping with me today. She's my friend Patrick's wife and is like a sister to me since Pat convinced me to move to Prague back in September 1997. Has it been that long? Dark hair. Piercing eyes. She thinks she's a witch. Like a divining rod, Markéta focuses me on the essentials.

I ordered some stuff for the desk from Patrick's office yesterday too. Folders and a rack. I need to get organized.

I was here with Markéta alone. It didn't occur to me. I do better. I love Patrick and Markéta too much. Nothing stupid can happen.

Settling, 5.8.98

Laubova 10, Prague 3 is an area called the Vineyards. If this flat had a style, we'd call it *hezky česky* ("nicely Czech" or "pretty Czech"). Kitsch. Retro. A throwback to a time before the Velvet Revolution. Like many expat flats, it's partially furnished. Ugly mismatched plates in the cabinets. Metal utensils with plastic handles in the drawers. *Partially furnished* sounds good, but it's actually just an assortment of spartan things, leftovers, unwanted stuff.

Including furniture. The kinds of furniture that you hate at first, but before you know it you're attached. The expat life in the Czech Republic is like camping — it requires a suspension of any need for glamor that one might harbor. It's not chic. In response, one develops a taste for *dobrodružství*, adventure. A determined resourcefulness complemented with a tireless sense of humor.

But then reality catches up. You remember the things you had, the things you left behind. Stupid stuff. The leather couch. Man, I thought Rachel and I had it made. It's depressing. I shake it off. I remember the English-language collection librarian who smiled at me. I head to my happy place.

The Warsaw Pact

I said I'd do a deep dive on this, and here we are: the collective defense agreement known as the Warsaw Pact, signed in Warsaw on May 14, 1955, formally known as the Treaty of Friendship, Cooperation and Mutual Assistance. What a title, who wouldn't sign up for that? What started it all was the Paris admission of West Germany into the North Atlantic Treaty Organization (NATO). So the Warsaw Pact was really the first step in a systematic plan to bolster Soviet control over Communist satellites, a plan laid by Nikita Khrushchev and Nikolay Bulganin after they came to power in 1955. The Soviet Union and seven Eastern Bloc nations (East Germany, Poland, Czechoslovakia, Hungary, Romania, Bulgaria and Albania) all signed the agreement. Albania withdrew in 1968. East Germany withdrew to allow for the reunification of Germany in 1990.

It's helpful to remember that the Soviet Union, or the Union of Soviet Socialist Republics (USSR), was already a collection of fifteen nation-states created in 1922 by Vladimir Lenin. While it existed, the Soviet Union was the largest country in the world and included Armenia, Moldova, Estonia, Latvia, Lithuania, Georgia, Azerbaijan, Tajikistan, Kyrgyzstan, Belarus, Uzbekistan, Turkmenistan, Ukraine, Kazakhstan and Russia.

Thus, the Warsaw Pact was really a collection of twenty-two nation-states. Members of NATO numbered fifteen in 1955 after the admission of West Germany. They were Belgium, Canada, Denmark, France, Greece, Iceland, Italy, Luxembourg, the Netherlands, Norway, Portugal, Turkey, the United Kingdom, the United States and West Germany. But wait. Aren't the names the United Kingdom and the United States indicative of collections of nation-states, not unlike the Soviet Union? Fair question. The full name, note, is the United Kingdom of Great Britain and Northern Ireland, which at one point had colonies around the globe. Hence the statement "The sun never sets on the British Empire." By 1955 though, Winston Churchill and the crown, Queen Elizabeth II, had granted India and Pakistan independence, for example. But the British Empire still maintains colonies in Africa and the Caribbean Sea. What about the United States? Since 1897, Puerto Rico, arguably an island nation-state unto itself, has been a part of the United States that is not represented by a star on the spangled banner. Not to mention American Samoa. Perhaps the approach of counting nation-states breaks down in this regard.

The librarian who smiled at me is not here. Today it's some Czech guy. He frowned at me. I got it. The American guy, barging in here, threatening to steal away his captive librarian crush. All in my head, of course; no evidence of this charming romance anywhere else.

I could go back and research the populations of each of the member states to try to determine the size of each consort. I am not that depressed. Not yet anyway.

Describing, 6.8.98

Bedhead. I grope for my tortoiseshell glasses on the floor. Morning on Laubova Street. Spectacles balanced on my nose, the picture comes into focus. From the vantage point of my futon on the floor, the naked walls creep up and over, a dingy white stucco. A single plastic globe hangs from a wire near the center of the ceiling. To my right, a particle board wardrobe towers over me. Light wood grain, beachy, tall and empty. My suitcase is a heap on the floor to my left. Other than that, the room is empty. White three-panel wooden doors with faux-antique lever handles and large keyholes. In case anyone wants to peep. The panels are ringed in black soot. The floors are European oak tumbled hardwood parquet, covered with a thin veneer of polyurethane. In one corner I have stacked a couple of stories and my journal. Slumping next to them, a black leather pouch. It contains a black rollerball pen, a Ticonderoga number 2 pencil, a sharpener and an empty ballpoint.

On the floor by the futon, a secondhand lamp salutes and a book reclines. I'm rereading *Doctor Zhivago*.

The bedroom is four meters by four meters (thirteen feet by thirteen feet). It has three windows opening out onto Laubova. Underneath the windows is a rectangular white radiator, by my head.

I stretch. The V-neck T-shirt and the striped cotton pajama bottoms were a gift from my mother. I barefoot across the entry hallway to the water closet to pee. I don't close the door — no one's here. If *water closet* seems like a quaint euphemism, it's not. It's a closet with a toilet. No sink. Just a toilet, a toilet brush, and a roll of toilet paper languishing on the tank.

I wash my hands in the kitchen sink, then fill the red tea kettle with city water and set it on the gas stove. I take my place at the table, journaling longhand while the water heats up. From my perch at the white rectangular kitchen table, I look up. Through the two large windows, the Žižkov Television Tower dominates my view.

It looks like a prop from the 1980 *Flash Gordon* movie, even though it was built between 1985 and 1992, an example of Czech high-tech architecture. At 216 meters (708 feet), it's taller than the Washington Monument. The bottom half is composed of three vertical silver tubes connected with space-aged rounded rectangular boxes arrayed at angles. Lined with windows. The top half puts one in mind of the grip on a disposable ballpoint pen, a textured section in stark white, topped with the red and white stripes of an oversized antenna. Like an anachronistic alien intruder, it is set behind a squat stone building. All the buildings in this part of the city are colored in soot from the roadway below. Most startling about this piece of grotesque art are the ten gigantic metallic babies with barcodes instead of faces. They crawl upward and downward.

I stand and step around the table to open one of the windows; they're huge. The windows are doubly encased. The inside panes swing into the flat; the outside panes open wide to the street. No screens. The windows have smears at the edges. Around the table are four chairs, all wood, two matching, two misfits. Like me.

Three meters wide by three meters deep (ten feet by ten feet), with ceilings three meters high, the kitchen — except for the wall on the left indented by the water closet — is a cube painted white.

The linoleum floor is yellow and patterned, scabby tiles grouted in orange. In the center of the wall opposite the entry is a chunky refrigerator. Next to it, on the right, the wall is partially tiled in white, with white grout. Lined along it are cabinets, a sink and a small gas oven with a four-burner cooktop. The red tea kettle whistles. I take it off the heat. I pull a chipped Polish pottery mug from the nearest upper cabinet, white with dark brown highlights. The drawer pulls and the cabinets knobs are white plastic U-shaped atrocities. The upper cabinets are tiny and have a huge space above them. I spoon in a measure of instant coffee, add hot water, stir. I leave it swirling on the tired Formica countertop and step back. The lower cabinets are the right height and ugly. I turn around to settle back in at the table and continue to describe the place, scalding my mouth and tongue at intervals.

My glasses slide down my nose. I push them back in place. One lens has a smudge. I think of Lars's smudgy glasses at Ingrid's memorial. I can sit still no longer.

I set my pen down, drink the last sip of coffee and get up from the table to put the chipped mug in the shallow sink. I step out into the entry hallway and pad toward the apartment door on the left. I turn left again into the washroom. Crowded in this room are a small basin beneath a mirror, a short tub with the dreaded shower wand, a washing machine and a folding metal drying rack.

I turn on the hot water knob, and the tankless heater next to my left shoulder clicks on. Whoosh. I pull a gray facecloth off the drying rack — it's new, washed in the machine last night. It's stiff. Once it hits the stream, it softens. I stow my glasses on the shelf beneath the mirror and wipe my face, my neck, behind my ears. I ring out the facecloth and place it on the towel bar. Turning off the hot water, I twist the cold-water knob and run my toothbrush beneath the trickle, then apply the toothpaste. As I brush my teeth, I watch my blurry self in the mirror.

I replace my glasses on the bridge of my nose, the white foam at the corner of my mouth coming into focus. I spit, rinse with a mouthful of water from the Bohemian cut-crystal highball on the mirror shelf, spit once more. I wipe my mouth on a stiff gray hand towel on the drying rack. I hang it over the towel bar. I floss, rinse with a capful of mouthwash. I'll need to shave before I head to work. Today's Thursday. I plan to get there by 10:00 a.m.

Music makes the place feel less lonely. It accompanies me. I dress for the day beside the ghost of Blanka. I wonder if she died here. Her son, my landlord, left her nameplate on the door. I wonder what she was like. In my imagination she's a salt-of-the-earth hippie intellectual. Bohemian stacks of books strewn about the floors and tables, long hair gone gray, flower-child frocks. Decadent beads draped to her navel.

I cut across the entry hallway to the living room, adjacent to the bedroom. A shelf stereo system on a small antique table with a polished wooden top and iron legs painted black — an old sewing machine table. Blanka smiles. She approves.

I press the Play button.

A telephone sits on the floor near the entryway. I have hooked up the answering machine. Neither apparatus has a home. I'll need to find a table to perch them on, something unique, something Blanka. The angular mustard-plaid couch. A light red chair that could be the throne on the *Flash Gordon* set. The living room is in the corner of the building, two windows along Laubova and three more along Ondříčkova. The flood of daylight is swallowed up by the dingy white walls.

Dressed for work, the worn Coach saddlebag slung crossbody contains my laptop and my journal. I leave the apartment, closing the door behind me. I jangle the keys in the lock, check that it's locked and stow the keys in my bag. The hallway is empty. When I moved in, I saw the old woman who is my neighbor to the right of my flat — she sniffed at me and my friends. Without so much as a good day. I was surprised by the negativity. I'll charm her yet.

There are four other doors on the fourth floor. The hallway is painted yellow; it's meant to be cheerful I suppose, but it's sad. It could do with a sponge and a bucket of hot soapy water. The hallway floors have not been mopped in ages, the ceramic tiles are gritty with filth.

A winding staircase descends in sections of eight steps, cornered with square landings. Central to it is a small elevator. I swing the door open, pile in, close the door behind me. I press the button labeled 0. The stuffy elevator clanks and whirrs. Two sides are glass. I watch the floors going by as I descend, the car banging and jerking.

I push the door open and enter into the dimly lit entryway. I step up two steps across a hallway and down two steps into the foyer. Brown metal mailboxes line the left wall. I depress a white button on the right wall and hear a pop. A buzz echoes. Leaning my weight against the heavy door, I expose myself to the cobblestone sidewalk of Laubova. I hang a left, head to the metro stop named after George of Podebrady and make my way to work.

I managed to spend 2000 CZK (68.97 USD) on furnishings for the flat and another 300 (10.34 USD) on groceries. Another 300 on drinks last night.

I got a skillet for 195 CZK (6.72 USD.) Pillowcases, black and white, a black fitted sheet. A dish rack, a pitcher. Oven mitt, a matching apron, colored navy and white.

A cute blond cashier checked us out yesterday. She exchanged words with Markéta. On the way to the car, I asked Markéta what was said.

"She asked how long we were married." Markéta frowned at me. "I told her we were friends. Idiot girl smiled at that."

I asked her how the cashier could tell I didn't speak Czech. Markéta looked at me.

She opened the trunk and I dropped the stuff in. "She asked me how she could land an American."

"Wait here. I have to go back." I smiled.

"If that's what you want." Markéta felt sorry for me. I hate that.

Expecting, 7.8.98

I love this kitchen. A real hangout kitchen.

No Ilona tonight. Not going to happen. I'd rather do nothing. I could read more *Doctor Zhivago*. Have a quiet night. Work all weekend; fine by me. See what Pat and Markéta have in mind.

I enjoy my coffee in the new apartment. I decided last night — I'm on an austerity budget. No books, no CDs, nothing that costs more than 100 CZK (3.45 USD.) I've been spending too much money.

I have a great apartment. I have paper and a pen. I'm healthy. My family's healthy. I have friends. I should invite them over: a housewarming. That'd be fun.

I want my money back from my mother. I lent her money at the beginning of April. I thought I didn't need it at the time. I was wrong. I needed it shortly thereafter. If you look back, I had my panic attack about money just after I'd made the loan. That's the thing about lending money: you can't demand it back when you want or need it. Sometimes you have to wait. I shouldn't do that anymore.

Nurturing, 10.8.98

Today is the third day in a string of cloudless hot days. From this chair, the matte silver and the plastic white of the Žižkov Television Tower vibrate against the saturated blue sky.

Friday was weird. It started with me bringing a small payment to Patrick at his office. Awkward, but it had to be done. I owe him and Markéta money. I hate borrowing money; I love paying it back. It's a token, a step in the right direction. Now if my mother would pay me back — think of it this way, karmically speaking, I'm clearing the way for her.

On Friday night we decided to go for a spin. We started at Roxy, where DJ Loutka was playing his typical depressing hard house. I danced too much, of course; the music was just what I needed. Ljuba, the emerald-eyed snake girl, was there with her boyfriend. I danced with her while he went off to get us soft drinks. I danced close to her. Her stiff red hair whacked me in the face, the smell hitting me hard: apple shampoo. Her boyfriend came back and handed me a cola. I took a sip, the taste on my tongue stunning me. It reminded me of another night, a long time ago.

INFERNO

Earth has four layers: the crust, the mantle, the outer core and the inner core. Each has its purpose and function.

This is how terra firma is formed. Deep below the ocean, in waves of convection, rocks melt. They form hot gas bubbles. The bubbles rise. They expand. Heat and pressure build up in lava chambers. Once the pressure is stronger than the surrounding rock, fractures open. Magma oozes to the surface. It cools and solidifies. The color meanders from glowing orange to patent-leather black. At the intersection of superheated magma and surface air and water, ash, pumice and volcanic glass are formed.

In a small grotto, deep in the woods in Western New York

State, behind a thin veil of a waterfall, an orange and yellow flame burns. Seemingly impossible, it's as if the flame emits directly out of the rock. This phenomenon can be found in the Shale Creek Preserve, within the Chestnut Ridge Park. Geologists have determined the macro seep has some interesting properties that allow the flame to stay lit. First, while most natural gas is primarily methane, the gas in this location is primarily propane and ethane. Second, the amount of gas produced here is as much as a kilogram per day.

Typically, for the carbon structures in shale to be sublimated into the components that create natural gas, rock has to be heated to 212 degrees Fahrenheit. How is it possible for gas to be produced in such quantities without the additional heat energy? One theory is that there's a catalyst present that allows the rock to break down into gas at lower temperatures. Could it be love?

After their escapade at Nu Lake, Dani has a dream. She sleeps on the couch downstairs at Joey's house. Waves of his father's snoring crash over her. In the dream, they're at the track. She recognizes the surrounding terrain: Javelyn High School. She stands outside a chain-link fence, holding a pile of Joey's clothes. They smell like cinnamon. Joey is inside the fence, readying himself to run the 400-meter race. A track of cinders. Dani hears the crunch of the runners' spikes. Joey wears a black singlet. Orange nylon short shorts glow against his legs. Joey's coach/dad is inside the fence. Hugging a clipboard, Big Joe positions himself between the track and the young woman; her view is obscured. He puts his orange windbreaker back to her. He spits, looks over his shoulder and mutters, "Women weaken the legs."

A diagonal arrow. On the back of his windbreaker. In black. Hash marks slash the shaft. His shoulders are dusted in ash. His black ball cap too. Dani cranes her neck. The gun goes off. She yells; it comes out as gibberish. She screams, *"Tköyënöhtôni!"* She wakes up.

Her eyes barely open, she writes it down in her dream journal, then goes back to sleep. She reads it again in the morning with a cup of coffee, one cream and one sugar, sitting across the table from Margaret, Joey's enrobed mother.

Cheektowaga, New York, was named by the Seneca tribe; it means "land of the crabapples." A nightclub called Special Place In Town (S.P.I.T.) rises up from the earth near the Buffalo-Niagara International Airport. An odd coincidence delays the club owner from obtaining his liquor license. He has the same name as a felon convicted of vehicular manslaughter; one moonless night, on the side of the road, a young man was killed.

While the owner petitioned the liquor authority to clear up the confusion, he opened the club on the weekends for teenagers. Liquor license in place, he renamed the club Inferno. His little experiment had been such a success, he continued to host minors on Sundays.

Unlike an eternal flame, it was a brief phenomenon, a magical playground. A dance club fitted out with a state-of-the-art sound system and light show. It closed for good in 1987, just a few months after our story.

Behind the club, Joey and Dani find a place to park his cousin's Canyon Red Ford F-150. He backs in, strategically placing the bed snug under a row of crabapple trees. Beyond the trees, endless fields of sweet corn. They get out. Joey touches the patch on the front bumper. A sticker has been removed.

A warm autumn evening, Sunday night. They don't have school the next day. They get in line. Not many places have lines around here. Except communion on Sundays.

Teen night; no alcohol. Small gaggles of kids congregate around the parking lot. Peppermint schnapps, California coolers, other questionable choices are in abundance. Joseph and his girlfriend don't drink. A dance club on the seedy side of town is all the excitement they need.

She wears a plaid skirt, tiered, youthful. Mid-thigh. Equilibrium. A solid black waistband. A black tank that showcases her thin shoulders. Silver drop earrings reflect the light of the full moon, 98% visible, at the entrance. They remind Joseph of the crystal that hangs in the window of her bedroom. Shoots geometric rainbows around the room.

A hammered silver bangle on her wrist, like a cuff. Black

leather clutch, chrome zipper. Everything looks good on her wrist, he notices. He holds her hand.

Joseph needs to vent. The superheated dancing energy. He rehearses in front of a mirror in his bedroom. A black T-shirt, faded blue jeans. Too much cologne. He cleaned up the stubble high on his cheeks and on his neck. Planned carelessness. Unlike his hair, freshly updated at the barbershop, militaristic, high and tight, except for the dark lock in his eyes.

From the mantle of the parking lot, the club throbs. The sound system bass booms through the gravel parking lot in waves, flowing out of every orifice like magma. They feel the music in their chests; a catalyst. Electricity arcs across their connection. Joseph bobs his head. His girlfriend bites her lip. She hyperextends a knee.

The surly bouncer waves them through.

Inside, the club pulsates. Like the chambers of a beating heart. There are four levels, people dancing everywhere. Joseph grabs Dani's hand, and they ooze through the crowd toward the inner core. There's a stage to one side. It's not set up, so people climb up and dance along the edge. The song winds down, synthesizers and a fracturing beat. They all know the next one: "You Spin Me Round" by Dead or Alive. The lights flash.

Joseph and his girlfriend dance close together. She looks down, raising an arm, her lips ducked. Joseph mouths the words, moves his hips. He focuses on Dani. She has attracted more than his own attention. He smiles, keeps her nearby.

It's easy, like water flowing downhill, dancing with her. She moves like a flame. She constrains her moves. Joseph's bobbing his head, so close over her shoulder, their bodies fit together. Like they were made for each other. Her body heat roams over him like the arcing lights.

A large African American guy, heavyset, gets after the beat. His moves aren't exaggerated, they're compact, like Dani's. They're right on time — instead of looking like a lumbering giant, he looks like a landslide; big, powerful, under control. He rocks out. A macro seep. Joseph follows along, like he's at home, watching MTV, trying to pick up the moves in his bedroom mirror. Next to the landslide is an Asian American kid: thin, wiry, all muscle. He wears a bucket hat low over his eyes. He snaps moves off. Girls sprawl in a booth nearby, sitting this one out.

Suburban white teenagers. A lot of feathered hair. Stone-washed denim with pleats. They smell of Dentyne, peach schnapps and Boone's Farm Strawberry Hill. These kids have last names that end in *-ski*, names with more consonants than vowels.

The previous song cools and solidifies. "Bizarre Love Triangle" by New Order. Dani turns her back to Joseph and dances into him, sweat at her temples. She radiates heat. She leans her head back against his shoulder. Joseph hasn't seen this side of her before.

The lighting engineer goes heavy on the strobe. Glimpses of Dani flash. Synthesizers trill up and down. She smiles a series of strobe smiles. Sweet. Salty. Wholesome. Hungry. Green and purple shadows. She bathes in dark light.

Their hips bounce with the double bass line, rocking left and right. Joseph feels pressure in his pants. Dani looks at him for a second, eyebrow raised. She puts a hand on his chest, kisses him, then casually pushes him away. She dances free.

The drum beat and synthesizer of Prince's "When Doves Cry." The lights are hypnotic. Joseph is close. Her buffer. She forgets everyone else. Her desire overwhelms. She steals a kiss. She tastes his tang. Before she's able, Joseph mouths over the bass.

"Help me button my shirt!"

"What?" Dani hollers over the din.

"My shirt!" He pantomimes. His fingers flicker.

Dani winks. They push through the throbbing crowd. Like bubbles of overheated gas.

Re-entry stamps stain their wrists. The surface of the night is crisp; a veil of moonlight. They parked on the outer crust, the tailgate facing a grotto of trees and empty fields. Cricket song overtaken by the rush of a landing jetliner. Dani's hand in Joseph's. He steps on a crabapple. It pops. A subtle sour scent floats up.

He unlatches the tailgate. "Here. Let me help." He lifts her. The truck bed is warm. Dani's breathing shifts.

"Your shirt, the buttons," she teases. He has no buttons on his shirt.

The club thumps. The high falsetto. The Bronski Beat's "Smalltown Boy." Splashy snare. Joseph kisses Dani, then pulls his shirt over his head. Her eyes close. She feels the air on her lips. She spins. He balls up his shirt. She lifts her hips. Her underwear on the wheel well. He places his shirt under her head. Through her tank he feels her heart. More insistent than the synth bass.

"Crabapples. Smell?" Joseph whispers. The superstition. Say your lover's name as you toss the crabapple pip into the fire. "If the pip pops, happily ever after."

"If it doesn't?"

Joseph sweeps an arm. He quotes, "'I prithee, let me bring thee where crabs grow; and I with my long nails'" — he wiggles his fingers above her face — "'will dig thee pignuts; show thee a jay's nest and instruct thee how to snare the nimble marmoset;...'"

Dani rolls her eyes. She loves it. Does he have to be so smug?

A pumice disk, the moon dappled gray. City lights drown out the heavens. If she uses her rods and cones, she can make out the stars. "We have to be *careful*." She reaches for her clutch, unzips it and pulls out a condom. There's no way the moment gets past her. She tastes the foil. She kisses him. Grease, mud, a rotting smell, sweet. He slides his boxers down. She rolls the condom on.

The skirt around her waist. He sets his weight on her. He looks her in the eyes. Something he hadn't noticed before. Is it sorrow? Is it age? Her birthday in two months. He doesn't know what he's going to get her.

She centers herself under him and nods. He can see her thoughts. *Will the pip pop?* Reaching her chin up, she kisses the doubt away, guiding him into her. Together they move their hips. The moon reflects in her earring, moonlit highlights cascading over her, her ear, her neck, her hair, her cheek, her nose and the touch, the kiss, the taste, the warmth. He presses into her. She arcs into him.

Together they create new landforms of trust. She hopes they won't crumble into the sea. She kisses his neck, she savors, whispering in his ear, "Joey."

Her panties back on, her clutch in hand, she touches the corner of her mouth.

Joseph assembles himself. He'll get her talking on the ride home, he decides. See what's on her mind. She tightens her topknot, adjusts her skirt on her hips. She holds out a tissue. He smiles. He places the item. She drops it in the trash can outside the entrance. They show their wrists. As if they just stepped out for a swig of wine cooler. Nobody's the wiser.

The song is "Push It" by Salt-N-Pepa. Joseph can barely contain himself. They find their way to the outer core. Joseph lifts Dani up. He surges up. The crowd cheers; it doesn't matter whether it's for them, they enjoy the attention.

Low smoke floods the room, seeping into everything. The sweet acrid odor. The creeping vapor carves up the crowd. It makes each individual more vivid.

Dani crouches with her legs together. She hops down. Joseph follows. They wade into the haze as the strobe comes on. They are lost in a labyrinth of fog.

They squeeze curfew. They run out to the truck, nervous giggles. Dani slams the door shut. Joseph rolls down his window. Both seat belt. Joseph steps on the accelerator and the wheels spin, shooting gravel into the grass.

Twenty minutes to get home. Joey floors it.

The engine screams as they fly down the road. Joey swerves.

"Getting home on time is one thing, getting home alive is another." The panic in Dani's voice. She hates it when he acts like this. "Joey!"

Across the yellow lines. Oncoming lane. Dani looks at the speedometer — the needle is past eighty. It reaches for ninety. She looks at her boyfriend. He is blank, pale, gone. He's more desolate than a moonscape. She looks out her window. Telephone poles whizz by.

He slows. They turn off Route 33. He turns to Dani. "Do you want to talk about it?"

"How you almost killed us?"

"What you were thinking about. Back there. I could see the gears turn."

"No gears." Dani eyes flash. She asks about the quote. "Pignuts? Monkeys?"

Joey smiles. He tells her. Shakespeare writes about crabapples more than once. To most, Joey says, it's just rotting fruit. Crushed underfoot. "On his island, to Caliban, it's treasure."

Joey eases into the gravel driveway and puts the truck in park. He turns. She stares out the window. The willow trees droop in the moonlight.

"Treasure, Miss Daniella, or just rotting fruit?"

Where does he go when his face freezes over? "You're annoying." She swings her eyes to Joey.

"I'll kiss thy foot." Joey leers.

"It's both."

He gets out and comes around to open her door. Tears in her eyes, she slides out. She hugs him. "I want both."

The overhead light flickers on. It illuminates the gravel, the garage. His mother's robe at the kitchen window. The robe is baby blue.

Mr. Friend-zone watched us dance. Ljuba, her boyfriend, me. I took my cola and went to stand with him. Mr. Friend-zone with the mousy gray hair. He asked me if I'd seen Karina. I told him I had. Karina had been planning to drive to Amsterdam. On the way out of town with her bumper dragging on the cobblestones, a hose broke. It dismantled the entire trip. She would've had fun. She didn't invite me. She deserved her mishaps.

It's not going to work out. I'll nurture a friendship instead of an end-ship.

Later, Pat, Markéta and I walked over to Marquis de Sade. Rumored to have been a brothel during the time of the first Republic, just after World War I, it's considerably tamer now.

High vaulted ceilings, velvet couches, red velvet drapes over the side entrances. Tasteless art that is supposed to be provocative. Pat and I get beers. We nod our heads to the music.

In the low lighting, in the center of a large group at the intersection between two couches, I see a large round man. One woman in the entourage is dressed in green, a shimmery dress hugs her outline. It ends abruptly mid-thigh. Her dark hair makes her pale skin paler. She's practically translucent. A short man with a shell necklace talks to her. He's standing with his feet apart, knees locked out. He holds a tall drink. She turns her head and laughs.

The woman in green is familiar. I have seen her somewhere. As I approach, I see that the man is, in fact, our least favorite Californian. A young woman sits next to Bertrand. She looks at me. Is that a smirk? Bert stands up. I excuse myself from my friends.

I shake Bert's hand. The young woman, her hair the color of straw and bare knees, reclines on the couch. She watches me with a grin.

"Joseph! My talented friend." Bert smiles. "Can I get you a drink, or maybe something a little more interesting?" Bert winks at the young woman. He lowers his voice. "She's new to the group, not one of ours yet. I could introduce you."

I wince. "I'm fine, Bert. Any interest in our idea?"

Bert's smile vanishes. "There is. I have a contact who's looking for something a little less morally ambiguous than Czichs. com — sent him our plan, haven't heard back."

A short man with a thick neck approaches. Bert offers his ear and nods. He stands up to his full height. "Excuse me a moment." Bert and his thick-necked accomplice step away.

The straw-haired young woman slides over and pats the velvet sofa next to her. I sit down. I introduce myself in Czech.

She smiles, her mascara hiding her brown eyes. "Call me Šárka. What you are doing here, Joseph?" Her shoulders twist. Her mouth hangs open. The question lingers. She reaches for her drink and bites the stir stick.

"Freelance. I'm a consultant," I answer. She tugs at the hem of her miniskirt. Patrick and Markéta watch me; Pat's teeth show all the way to his bicuspids. Markéta shakes her head. Pat points his chin at me — I pretend to ignore him.

Šárka presses her elbow into my ribs. "No, no. I don't mean that. How do you know Bertrand?" She brushes her hair over her shoulder, lowering her eyes to my collarbone.

The heat from her gaze warms my skin. "Bert? We're colleagues. We're seeking funding. For an idea."

"You are pornographer?" Šárka leans in. "You don't look like pornographer, Joseph."

I swallow. I note her scent. It's something like air-dried linen with a hint of ozone, the smell on the wind right before it rains. "No. I'm not. Are you?"

Šárka smiles. "Too shy. Too many freckles to be pretty on camera. Scars. I'm better with numbers than naked bodies. Bertrand needs an accountant, no?"

I laugh. "An accountant? Love it. You approve of the business?"

Šárka leans away. "I don't judge. People make up their own minds, right and wrong. Sex on camera for money, why not? You Americans have problem with that?"

I shouldn't take offense. My skin's thicker than that. But still, I feel it. The sting of pride. I try to excuse myself.

"Stay. One drink." Šárka flags a waitress. "Do you know how hard it is to find someone to talk to? Tell me about your friends over there. They seem lovely." She orders me a beer — she can tell what my order was back over with Patrick and Markéta. For an attractive young woman, it's surprising — to be aware. To be considerate.

The waitress brings me a heavy glass mug with a handle. White foam halfway up the side — much quicker service, might I add, than I would have gotten myself — I engage. How old can she be, twenty-five or twenty-six?

"Call me a puritan, but pornography is not legit. I couldn't live with it." The woman in green looks at me. I need to keep my voice down.

Šárka adjusts her clear bra strap. It doesn't fit under the thin strap of her halter top. "You don't look at pornography?" Šárka smiles. My face goes blank.

"Looking at it and making money off it are two different things." I take a sip. Delicious, crisp foam. I wipe my mouth with the side of my hand.

Šárka squints. "Looking at pornography doesn't take advantage of the woman?"

I smile, caught in my own logic. It's an out-of-body experience. The more she talks, the more I forget how beautiful she is. "I concede. You said you don't judge?"

Šárka drains her drink. The ice rests against her teeth as the clear liquid seeps past her pale lips. Her tint matches her skin tone. It's refreshing. "I try not to judge. I try to understand. I don't know anything, but from experience, Americans are predictable. Maybe you are not so predictable, Joseph?"

I touch my glasses. I credit her. I tell her about my friends. I say that Patrick is smart and Markéta, she's intuitive. "I'm an amalgam. Of the two. You?"

Šárka rattles her glass at the waitress. I would never. Maybe if I spoke impeccable Czech. "I don't care about fairy tales. No time for lies, there is so much truth."

I'm about to blurt out to her that I am a fiction writer. I am not a writer. That dream is dead. "At least I don't have to figure out a way to ask you out. We could never date. You would hate me. Shame. You are pretty."

Šárka's gin and tonic, garnished with a wedge of lime, arrives. "Na zdraví. Cheers." Our eyes meet, our glasses clink. We each take a drink. I smirk at the awkward silence.

"Thank you for the compliment. You save me trouble. I'm stupid enough to say yes, rather than hurt your ego." Šárka pauses. A mole on her neck. It wouldn't look bad on camera.

"How do you learn about emotions if not from books and movies?"

"I read — nonfiction. Emotion in history, biography, no?" Šárka watches me.

"What about art? Fashion? Frivolous?" I sip beer. Šárka's nose is straight. The tip turns up.

"Not frivolous. Necessary. Art is a rational pursuit. We cherish writers and poets here. Fashion goes too far, but I love it." She squeezes the lime over her drink. She drops the wedge in.

"Maybe the one irrational thing I enjoy."

My mouth runs before I can stop it. "I have a friend who models."

"A friend?" Šárka lowers her voice. She eyes the girl in the sparkly green dress. "Aren't models vain? I can't imagine you would be satisfied with a dull model."

I laugh. She sounds like my friend, Aneta, the earthy sprite. "I'm vain. Are you not vain?" I scan her halter top, her miniskirt.

"I know my outfit doesn't discourage boys. I don't care. I will not be young forever. I hope to be fat crazy lady one day. With no teeth." She smiles. Straight white teeth.

Bertrand and his minion come back. "Looks like you two hit it off."

I stand up. "Contrary. We want nothing to do with each other. Isn't that right?" I hold my hand out. She obliges. Hers is cool and dry, such long fingers, such slender nails.

Šárka's taller than me. All legs. Taller than Karina. "Mortal enemies. Pity. He's cute." Šárka addresses Bert, "I'm here for job."

Bertrand has a quizzical look on his face. I slap him on the shoulder. "Careful, Bert. I think we just found your secret weapon — in the end, we'll all end up working for Šárka."

"It's nice from you, but ... I would not hire a dreamer," she says, her smile cold. I strut back to where Patrick and Markéta sit.

Markéta is the first to speak. "Porno?"

I meet Markéta's eyes. "It's all my fault. Czichs.com was my idea."

"You don't control the planets."

I smirk. "The most attractive woman on his team is his accountant."

Pat chimes in. "Too tall. Too skinny. Too much makeup. I bet she's bony."

Markéta closes her eyes. She pats his hand. "Nice try, husband."

I sigh. "Too symmetrical. It's annoying." I finish my beer, wipe my mouth, "Let's get out of here. Too many shady people."

Working, 11.8.98

Bertrand has set the goal for 404 in an email to Dash, Avi and me: achieve venture capital in one month. That's a long time, but I have stuff to do. Don't expect anything. Open yourself, open your mind to all possibilities at once. I wonder if Šárka got the job.

Working on the fault trees yesterday for Patrick, it occurred to me that I'm a fault tree. We all are. My existence is a sum of all these tiny existences, these tiny facts that come together to form me. If one of these facts fails, like if I get tired or I don't eat enough, the fault ripples through the entire system. If I get strung out on a girl, or if I lose patience with a wife who is grieving her mother's death when I need her to be loving and appreciating me, then that fact changes the rest of the tree. I decide to cheat on her, not so much a decision as a reaction to a stimulus — an opportunity presents itself. I make my choice.

Last night, I worked on the real estate database for the Identity guys. I'm a database too. I'm a collection of facts stored for future reference. I pull from memory, I read from my hard drive. The disks spin. The plates whirr. Like the DJ's turntable. I access memory. Sights and sounds, tastes. Feelings. Sensory data conjures up the emotions of past experiences. In creating a database, I structure information to be stored. I create order in the universe. I reduce entropy. I keep chaos at bay.

I don't like going to Prague grocery stores anymore.

Yesterday I ran down to the local on the corner. I walked in and squinted. All fluorescent lights. The floor was greasy white construction tile. Black grout. Grimy. I grabbed a forearm basket. Loosely organized shelves. Each week, almost daily, items changed places. A woman in cheap white sandals with white socks wore a smock, a basket over her arm. She removed rotten fruit. Cardboard boxes and filthy green plastic trays stacked in the aisles. I couldn't tell how she chose — most of the fruit looked a little sad. My theory is that this is the way fruit actually looks. I had grown up with the American version: everything polished, genetically modified to look bigger, brighter, more wholesome. Maybe. Or maybe this was just sad-looking fruit.

I grabbed some undersized bananas. I snatched a carton of the long-life milk. Fresh whole milk was the good stuff. I grabbed the strange, unrefrigerated box. Durable milk. Tastes like it was taken from irradiated cows. The milk was stacked on a pallet in the middle of an aisle. I got a plastic tray of pretzel sticks, thinner than a #2 pencil, longer than a middle finger. I got six small rolls out of a yellow plastic bin. I used one cellophane bag as a glove. I placed them in another cellophane bag. I got the cheap Czech rolls today. Since I wasn't flush. I grabbed a tub of spread butter. My hand hesitated over the horseradish one. I got the chive flavor. I liked to dip the rolls directly into the spread. It's so easy. Tasty. I saw a Czech construction worker do it once.

I took my forearm basket to the front of the store. Fresh from her break, the checkout woman was ripe with the smell of stale smoke. Heavy mascara. No lipstick. She spoke Czech to someone. I couldn't tell who. She asked a question, not looking at me. She didn't change her tone. She repeated. Then she looked at me like I was an idiot. It's a question for me? She realized I didn't understand. She rolled her eyes. She proceeded to ring me up quickly — the Czech version of quickly, which was not quick.

Everyone is suspicious of the American, me. The lady at the deli counter, the customers in line behind me, the checkout woman. They keep an eye on me.

She wasn't putting anything in a bag so I grabbed two from the pile next to me. The checkout woman sighed. Exasperated. It dawned on me. The question she'd asked at the beginning of our transaction was if I wanted to purchase bags or not.

As I packed up my two bags, my hands shook. The rotund Czech woman behind me in line clucked her tongue. I pulled a wad of cash out of my pocket. I forked over a hundred-crown note (3.45 USD). I held out a handful of coins. The checkout woman rolled her eyes again. She pecked out the coins.

I saw the Snickers after I'd already paid. I stopped cold. I set the bags down and put the candy bar in front of her. I pulled the coins out of my pocket again and held them out to her. She wagged her finger at me. That special way Czech ladies have of wagging their fingers. I left the pile of coins on her counter and put the Snickers in a bag. I strutted out of there, a bag in each hand, thinking I didn't do much in the way of improving Czech-American relations.

Out on the street, I exhaled. I had just survived an interrogation. I paid way too much for that candy bar. Because fuck her, that's why. Fucking Snickers lady.

Measuring, 12.8.98

Zero. That's how much excess cash I have. I have to pay rent on the 20th, which is next Thursday.

I've been forcing myself to work uncomfortable hours to get the job done. It's good for me. Keeps my mind off what I don't have. Keeps me focused on creating. I clean dishes at home. One small good thing. Add order to the universe.

I have to talk to the work guys about the hours. I've used up the eighty hours we budgeted. There's some ways yet to go. We need to populate the database in order for me to test more. I need to create a few more reports. I know I can solve problems, not easily of course, but at least I know how to get started. The trick in this particular case is to use queries to update the numbers and a module to call the queries. First you initialize the variables. Calculate phi, sum across phis, which is labeled as P. Compare P to the target value (0.05, 0.5, 0.95) and then split the x in two. Throw away the negative value. Repeat until forty tries or our tolerance is met. Whichever comes first. See? I told you I can do it. Faith and patience.

The last thing I have to do is come up with a design for 404 without a name. Working with Avi is not easy. He likes to have his ego stroked. Am I like that? I like to work with smart people. He's creative for sure. He has an eye. But I don't know how smart he is. Being from Cooper Union and all, I assumed he was, but I'm not sure. He could have done a campus tour of Cooper Union for all I know.

I learned I won't have an equity stake of 25%, I'll have something like one-ninth, or about 10%. Better than nothing. The salary is what I'm after anyhow. I don't care about cashing in.

I'm not trying to get rich here. I'm trying to get along.

I need a job where I can feel productive, where I feel useful. Working for Patrick and the guys lately has been satisfying. I come and go as I please. I knock work out. It's great when I don't have any distractions. I keep myself busy with the fault trees, with the databases, with the business plan for Bert. I journal. I scribble here and there. Something to dabble with when my mind wants to play with something that's not numbers. Once I stop chasing the big whatever — like I'm chasing Karina now — things go well. It's lonely. Not unbearable.

She'll slip through my fingers once again; this time for good. Worse. I'll get her, only to find I don't want her. Why is that?

Walking, 13.8.98

Last night I watched the movie *Platoon* with Ljuba and her boyfriend in the basement of Terminal Bar. The red-headed flirt tickled me in the ribs. Right in front of her boyfriend. Her eyes flashed. He didn't seem bothered. At the end of the movie I shook his hand. She kissed me on the lips.

I stepped out the door. Cobblestones. The tangerine nimbuses of the streetlights. Like beads on a string. The night's necklace. I headed for Old Town Square.

A blind alley curved away. I followed it. I found the passage by Chapeau Rouge. It goes through the courtyard behind Týn Church.

Above the buildings, against an indigo sky, a vast figure appears. One moss-green pointy hat, two, puncture the frame. Light blue highlights. They crown a bright ochre visage with dark eyes.

The Church of Our Lady before Týn is probably the most iconic feature of Old Town Square. Built in the fourteenth century in the Gothic style, the twin eighty-meter-tall (262.5-feet-tall) towers are each topped by an array of eight smaller spires, two layers of four. The northern tower is named Eve, the southern tower Adam.

Prague is known as *stověžatá*, a wonderfully compact Czech way of saying "city of a hundred spires." Could it really be a hundred? I looked it up. The count is well over five hundred.

Understated. I like that.

The spikes raked the navy sky. The movie spurred something in me. The character Chris stares down two conflicts: one with his platoon and the other with himself. I can hardly compare my expat existence here to Vietnam. That was a soldier in an unwinnable war. This? This infatuation with Karina? This is a chimera.

Bereft of purpose, I obsess over an elusive young woman.

I emerged by the statue of Jan Hus. A reformer long before Martin Luther nailed his demands to the church door. For his beliefs, Hus was burned at the stake. Even this late, nearly 1:30 a.m., people roamed throughout the square. A drunk slept on the bench at Hus's feet.

I continued past the Astronomical Clock. It tells more than just the time. I turned left up my old haunt, Železná, Iron Street. I steeled myself past my old fairy-tale flat. The place I had when my mother came to stay. The thick wooden door in the archway. I continued in the direction of Wenceslas Square.

What's my purpose? Why did I come here? I dug my hands in my jacket pockets. As if I could find an answer in there. I didn't come to Prague to find a woman. I came here to shake up the path I was on. A predictable trek, a couple dead ends. A failed first marriage, a soul-sucking career in corporate America, the pipe dream of writing a novel. Could an old magical city in the heart of Europe fix that for me?

I passed by the market at Havel Square. It has been here since 1232; it's silent now. I wound through the square where crowds would flock to see the sword swallower tempt fate.

I materialized at the base of Wenceslas Square. Near Můstek, where money changers gouge tourists. I sauntered by the Baťa shoe store, where Izabela would meet me in front of the window display. She wore wedges and a short skirt. She stands there in the twilight. She dangles from the strap of her purse.

I climbed to the top of the square. Underneath the balcony where Václav Havel — at the tender age of fifty-three, a former political prisoner and a playwright — promised to tell the Czech people the truth.

On the far side of the median, I stood over a bronze cross.

It slithered out from underneath the cobbles. Installed in the weeks following the Velvet Revolution, a memorial to Jan Palach. A student at Charles University, he self-immolated on this spot in January 1969 as a protest against the invasion of the Warsaw Pact tanks.

I stopped a moment beneath the statue of Good King Wenceslas. I looked up. The National Museum sits at the top of the square, if not the top of the city. I breathed in the night.

I went down into the metro, Muzeum, and made my way across the station, past the movie posters. The newsstand was shuttered and locked. To the stairs. I cut through the park and ambled up past Radost, velvet couches and vegetarian cuisine. The name means joy. That's a stretch. Sunday nights they host an English-language open mic called Beefstew.

Something to do with fire. Jan Hus was burned at the stake for his belief that no one could buy his way into heaven. Jan Palach doused himself in petrol and lit a match. Covered in flames, witnesses say, he jumped a rail and ran. A human meteor. His suicide note was titled "Torch no. 1." In it he sought to "awaken the national conscience."

Awaken the conscience. That was it. That was my purpose.

Stop ignoring what happened. That was tactical. For survival. Now, I need to *remember*.

The night chill refreshed my lungs. Nearly two in the morning. I lurched along.

At I.P. Pavlova, I turned left. Pavlov, as in the dogs. I panted. I walked up the hill in the direction of Peace Square. The Church of St. Ludmila loomed large up the hill.

The grandmother of Good King Wenceslas, she was killed by her own daughter. It's a peaceful spot, especially in the dead of the night with the facade of the church lit from underneath. A neo-Gothic Roman Catholic church built in the late 1800s, it's young as far as churches go. The twin spires on either side of a tall gable. A central stained-glass Oculus. It dissected me.

I could've waited for the night tram. As much as half an hour. From there, I could've been home, rolling over in bed, in less.

I strolled along the right side of the church, past my favorite hot-dog stand in Prague. The heated spikes upon which the hot-dog rolls impale. Past the square and up the hill toward George Street. Almost home.

The next stretch was lonely. I talked to myself.

"Why, Ingrid? I need to know. It seems pointless. Did you do it? Why come back here just to do that? It doesn't make any sense." I threw my arms out. I felt alive. "It's not like you to not make sense. 'Tisn't." I needed to find Naked Pete. He'd have answers.

Quarter past two in the morning. I spoke to the night. The bricks listened. The cobbles absorbed. Hands out of my pockets. A little out of breath.

I told Karina it's not her. I pointed at her. I pointed back at myself. I told her it's me. I told her I needed time. To figure myself out. I told her she wouldn't want me now anyway. I mimicked her valley girl Czech, "Jako prostě, you're beautiful. Everyone will see what I already saw. I see what the butterfly will look like before the metamorphosis is complete. I did it with Dani. I do it with you." I repeated the last sentence. I dug my hands back into my pockets.

I passed the Green Line metro stop. Nightingale Street was empty. The traffic light blinked. Before me appeared the Church of the Most Sacred Heart of Our Lord, a stumpy brown structure with a massive transparent clock sitting on top of it, like an all-seeing eye. The coffee-colored block is spangled with a pattern of white bricks.

I faced the speckled church, squaring my shoulders. I held my arms out wide. I submitted myself to the wadjet.

A lane veered off to the left near the entrance, Laubova Street. Down the block, at the end, I found the blue tin sign on the wall, number 10. I entered the building from the street.

I disrobed, put on my pajamas, brushed my teeth. I collapsed onto the futon.

"Goodnight, Blanka." My voice echoed around the empty flat. I smirked at myself. I squeezed my eyes shut.

Tingling, 14.8.98

The key to the door of today — keep it simple. Go to work at Patrick's office. Don't chase Karina. Simple. I have to go to

Terminal Bar today anyway.

The regularity thing works except that I get bored. Forget about the girls for now. I need to concentrate on me. Blanka and Ingrid nod.

How does raw feel? A tingling sensation inside my elbows, my chest feels light, like my heart has stopped. A good hard run would cure all of this. Maybe I'll do that right now. That's a great idea. It'll take me a while to get to work.

At this point, as messed up about Karina as I am, it's my own fault. She's done nothing to make me this insane. Of course she hasn't. The constant throughout this spring and summer has been my desperation. Stress. Ever since Ingrid, Izabela, Ilona and about five others, ever since the divorce from Rachel.

I'll be alone until I learn how to be comfortable alone. No one's truly comfortable alone. Maybe a few. I'll get better at it.

My name is Joseph. I'm not crazy. I'm not lazy or stupid. I'm having a hard time coping with the position in which I find myself. I trust that I'll make it through. Somehow. I have faith. I have faith that I'll fall in love again. Someday. Because of this faith, I take the next step forward. I'll continue.

Choosing, 16.8.98

On Friday, I went to Terminal Bar at 2:30 p.m. Karina didn't appear to be there (she must have been at lunch, I see now...) I figured she was gone for the weekend. I went back to work and left for home around seven. I made dinner. I called my American friend Brad. Brad with his ponytail and his Czech girlfriend. She's from Olomouc, Agata (October 14). They came over. Brad practically discovered Agata, on a visit to her small town. She must see him as her big break. Her chance to get to Prague. Brad suggested we get some stuff and some movies and we hang out. Perfect.

Oh yeah, the date thing. Name Days here are almost as important as birthdays. I have been slipping. I used to be good at it. I have the calendar on my fridge. Blanka's (December 2) fridge, forgive me. Every day is someone's Name Day. Wish the person a Happy Name Day, buy them flowers, give them a little present. It comes from the feast days for the Roman Catholic saints. In the Czech Republic, it would seem cruel to give a baby any name that didn't have a Name Day. They're important. Everywhere I've lived here, I've attached a calendar to my fridge. I study them. I record Czech people's Name Days when I first mention them in my journal. Let me get back to that.

We went to Terminal Bar to rent a movie. Karina's (January 2) there. Blue-black sleeveless velvet dress to the floor, slit to her knee. Scoop back. Black suede platform sandals with a block heel. To waitress at an Internet café? Her hair was up in a loose bun. I walked by, stunned. We picked out movies and Karina came back. I felt underdressed. She seemed bored.

I wonder... Of course! She came back to see what I was doing. I want to believe that. I went and talked to her. She mentioned Roxy. I'd already started down the path with Brad and company; I was committed. I decided to stay with the sure thing. Rather than chase after a ghost. She would've left early anyway.

Yesterday, we had to go back to return the movies. I thought maybe she wouldn't be there. She was. I was there with six friends. Markéta (July 13) put her arm around me and kissed me full on the lips. I gave Pat a big fat hug. Karina saw it. Can I please stop my obsession with this girl?

Why this girl? Why am I like this? Is it because I'm alone? It's okay to be alone. The answer is that I have no control. Allow yourself to be surprised, Joseph. It's the joy of life. Faith means less stress. Trying to control something you can't control. Don't push. Don't chase. Ingrid laughs at me.

I'm here. I'm alive. I have faith. Faith's all I need.

Demanding, 17.8.98

Monday morning. 11:30 a.m.

I hate the hour or two I spend every morning trying not to obsess about things. I'm too lazy to get up and be done with it. I think about Ingrid. I have to find Naked Pete. Simple as that. I get up to leave him a message. Why doesn't he answer his phone? Now I'm up.

For the next few days I'll get up at 8 a.m., I'll do my normal stuff, I'll go to bed at a regular time. I think this is the way out. I can demand money from my mom. I need it.

I can't demand anything from my mother. I know she feels guilty. She feels guilty that she had to borrow money from me. She feels guilty that it didn't work out with my father. She feels guilty for other reasons too, one big one that I can think of. She probably thinks that I don't know, but I've known for a long time. You don't have to be an ace student at math to count the months between your parents' wedding anniversary and your birthday.

That's enough about that. I'm not going to demand anything from my mother. That's final. I'd rather starve.

I cleaned the kitchen last night. It was painless.

Karina and I keep missing each other. By this much. I hope we make the connection soon. We both deserve it. Our day's coming. I can't wait. I want it now.

I went to Letná Park to enjoy the last bits of summer, to read a book. I made my way-from the tram stop, a brisk walk up under a canopy of trees, and sat in a grassy meadow at the end of the beer garden. I wasn't the only one who thought to come here. There was another guy scribbling in a notebook, a couple on a blanket. I couldn't look directly at them. Before I could even crack the book, I noticed all the yellow. Had I known that Prague had dandelions? Had I seen them before, growing between the cobbles, pushing through the cracks in the asphalt? I picked a bunch. I wove them into a crown. It took me a minute to remember how to weave them so they'd stay together. It reminded me of home.

I put the crown on. I read.

NU LAKE

The principle of intrusive relationships. An igneous seam stabs across a vein of sedimentary rock. The cooled magma formation must be younger than the surrounding sedimentary rock.

Rocks forged hot are dark, or mafic; rocks molded cold are lighter, or felsic. Mafic magma has a higher viscosity, it oozes and flows; the result is basalt. Much of the ocean floor is basalt. Felsic magma is found in special convergent zones; because it's stickier, it forms steam caps that erupt. The most common type of felsic rock is granite.

In 1954, between West Main Street Road and Pearl Street Road, off Wortendyke, construction began. One man in a cheerful yellow bulldozer cleared the beatific deciduous forest. The machine knocked down old trees. Wide continuous treads called swamp tracks roamed over. The machine piled trees like refuse. The man soaked them in gasoline and burned them unceremoniously. Smoke curled overhead, a shadow of progress. Another man in a jolly yellow excavator gouged away. A third man in a giant blue dump truck with tires eight feet tall hauled dirt. A massive crater was carved out of the earth. A corruption, an intrusion. The cup of earth was laced with cement, filled with water. By 1965, Nu Lake, that's what they named it, was considered the most exciting recreation resort in Genesee County; folks converged there in long-finned cars, on bikes with banana seats. They swam, camped, fished.

By the early 1980s, Joseph hikes the back way to the lake from his house less than a mile away. The resort in disrepair. The snack shack boarded up. No one swims, camps or fishes. Nu Lake isn't "nu" anymore.

Revelers stream to Darien Lake, an artificial lake of similar vintage a few miles up the road. The owner installed rides and games. Reinvented it as a theme park.

Joseph stands at the corrupted lake's edge. It was overgrown now in milkweed, cattails, Queen Anne's lace, dandelions. Iridescent oil, blankets of algae spangled with beer cans. A fat bullhead dozes at the bottom. He smiles, he dreams.

A rural Western New York allegory of jet-age hubris. The folly of Nu Lake puts Joseph in mind of a legend he once heard. An old woman, a Seneca, living on the reservation in nearby Indian Falls, told it to all the kids:

When the Earth was very young, Mudjekeewis the Mighty kept the west wind for himself. He gave the other three to his

sons. He gave Wabun the east wind; to the turbulent Kabibonokka, he gave the northwest wind. He gave the south wind
to the lazy Shawondasee. Shawondasee left the comfort of the
northland.

"Farewell, brother," roared the fit northwest wind. "In your
hot land, I'll lend you my cooling breath."

The lazy Shawondasee gave no answer. He plodded to the
southland. He built a shelter of live oak and kudzu. In an emerald tangle, he lay on a bed of Eastern white pine straw too small
for his girth, railing against his curse. He did not feel the fragrant airs. He longed for the north. He sighed for its sage hills.

For a year, Shawondasee, too lazy to follow the migrating
birds, the winds of his brothers, lay in his lodge. He got fatter.
He sighed.

The next spring, he looked northward. Behold, a slender
maiden. She stood in a grassy meadow. Her garments waved an
emerald tangle. Her hair was yellow as gold.

Shawondasee whispered, "Tomorrow." Each morning, he
murmured, "Tomorrow, I'll win her for my bride." He didn't
move.

Summer came. Maiden's head white as snow. He exhaled
short, rapid sobs. The air filled with silvery fibers. The maiden
vanished.

Fast-forward a couple years. It's a cool September evening.
Joseph and Dani are parked at Nu Lake. The mafic ooze of early
fall. The moon is waxing gibbous, 93% visible. Near full poten-
tial. Wind out of the lazy south, seven miles per hour, gusts
up to fifteen. Dani stays the long weekend with Joseph. Her
parents trust their Capricorn to keep her feet on the ground. No
milk for breakfast. Joseph's mother sends them out to the Quik
Stop. They detour.

The parking lights glow lava orange. Bryan Adams sings low,
a song called "Heaven." The emergency brake digs into Joseph.
His lips granite, her lips basalt. The collar of her dusky blue
fisherman's sweater. A glimpse of her collarbone. A long denim
skirt, the look of a Bohemian fortune teller. A navy-blue silk
peony in her hair; a small rhinestone. She smells good. Joseph

traces lace. He wishes he was cool enough to remove Dani's bra with a finger snap.

A relationship forged of stolen moments. A cream-colored cowlneck sweater, shiny gray parachute pants, silver zippers. His crow bangs hang in his eyes. Joseph could be in an a-ha video. Joseph reinvents himself, baggy art T-shirts with black jeans and black canvas slippers. He knows his girlfriend doesn't care for the new look. Today he wears what he used to wear, like a month ago, the ebb and flow of fashion when you're seventeen. It's not an olive branch; it's Iroquois, a bough of white pine.

Dani's game. She read a tattered copy of *Fear of Flying* in the tenth grade, a stolen gift from a friend; she knows a thing or two about zipless. Hardly, she smirks, with parachute pants...

Joey flicks a handle. She lays back, the seat too short for her length. Her heart brims. He climbs out of his tight pants. She holds out the condom to him. His teeth rip open the foil. He rolls the ring into place. Joey eases over her like kudzu. He cradles her head. The music fades. "Is This Love" by Whitesnake comes on. Her skirt shimmied up, panties in a bunch. She levers herself into him. She's lodged there, carved into him. An intrusive relationship.

He levitates. Their bodies converge, muscle to muscle. She whispers, "I love you." She chants, "I love you." She moans, "I love you." She calls out. It's all he can take.

He craters into her. She absorbs. They rock. The instant expands in the lush night by a dark abandoned lake.

He exhales, "Whew. I can't. Catch. My breath," his damp eyes beatific.

Her breath grazes his neck. "It's okay." She brushes a dark lock. She studies his face. "It's okay."

She promised. The thistledown meadow in the hot, lazy sun. The cicadas thrum. Joseph, the dandelion ring. Has she kept it? She wants to be sure.

"I better get this thing." He reaches down with a hand and secures the rolled edge of it, guiding it free. He sighs. She comes up to her elbows, supporting herself. Her collarbones pool the light, her hair highlighted in silver. The silk peony is intact, riding high. The song is "Photograph" by Def Leppard. In his mafic moments, Joseph rails against this trite crap. Music worth listening to gets no play on the corrupt airwaves.

They hear a dim roar. It gets louder. It surrounds them. The lovers are stunned.

A vehicle erupts from the road, barreling at the van. High beams glare hot. It slides to a stop. Dust surrounds the tires, glints in the veins of light. Joseph holds his hand up to shade his eyes. Is it a truck?

The vehicle arcs violently away from them. The driver slams it into drive. The vehicle careens over roots and grooves in the dirt. Lights swirl around the inside of the van. The engine revs erratically. A sticker on the front bumper — the Confederate flag.

"I'm scared," she says.

"Me too." Joseph doesn't look at her. "Cover yourself. Stay low." His voice breaks. He wants to protect her, but what can he do? One clunk on his head and it's over. Then, who knows what?

The truck migrates away from them. It turns around. The driver squares the headlights on the van. A cone of light stabs their eyes. Joseph scans, then looks back at Dani. The faint glow of the dash. A glowing purple shadow stamped into his vision.

Dani wriggles her underwear up. She straightens her sweater. She drapes her skirt.

Joseph's pants around his ankles. He feels ridiculous. He shakes. He tries to get his sweater over his head.

"Can they see us?" she says.

"I don't know."

"Who is it?"

"Get in front." He looks out. He sees movement. "We gotta go."

She tumbles into the front seat. The moment craters. She turns the radio off. She sobs.

His hands shake. He's in the driver's seat now, pants up, no shoes. He holds the key. Does he recognize the square headlights, the dirty felsic truck? Could be anyone. The rebel flag throws him off. Could be his parents, or hers, but that wouldn't make any sense.

She looks out the window. The lights approach. She screams.

He slams it into gear. They go too fast in reverse. Adrenaline pumps. Reckless, maybe, but justified. He slams on the brakes, throws it into drive. The front wheels spin in imported sand. They catch. The van hurtles forward, headlights glancing off a tall pine. It suffocates under vines. Headlamps flash off a chain-link fence. The van clunks up onto the asphalt. Wortendyke.

He drives slowly. He keeps looking in the rearview, hoping they won't be followed. They're in shock. "Who the hell was that?" she says.

"I don't know." He has a pretty good idea. He hopes he's not right. He thinks of her dad. Her dad would throttle Joseph if he knew.

In the mirror, he sees the lights from the truck turn in the opposite direction. He stops at the corner of Wortendyke and Route 5. Main Street. To the right, a green steel bridge crosses over the ominous Tonawanda Creek. The crick, they call it. The turn signal clicks. Maybe the truck is gone. He leans over to nuzzle Dani's neck. She giggles. "Just drive."

They turn. They don't notice the crick as they pass over it.

The lights in the Quick Stop parking lot are alien. They turn everything a weak green color.

Joseph jumps down from the van. He grabs his shoes, checks his garments. He plods around to the passenger side. Parked next to them is a red truck. Square headlights. Stars and bars on the front bumper.

The truck sits empty. Dani gets out and checks herself in the side mirror. She takes the peony out of her hair and tosses it onto the seat of the van. She turns to Joseph. He's frowning. They walk together into the Quick Stop.

Joseph grabs a carton of 2%. He makes for the cashier. Tripp blocks the aisle. His real name is Lawrence Junior; no one calls him that. Tripp's shorter than Joseph, a year younger, tends to show up at odd moments. He lives on the reservation in Indian Falls but, like Joseph, he's not full-blooded Seneca. On the plus side, he freely lends his truck to Joseph. It returns with a full tank.

"Windows on your mom's rice-burner were steamed up pretty good. If I get my lights right, I can *make out* what's going on in there."

Dani blushes. Joseph steps in front of her.

"Helpful, Tripp. Thanks for the information." Joseph leans in. "You scared the shit out of us. I suppose you'll tell Aunt Peg?"

"I figure sleeping dogs lie. You a sleeping dog, Little Joey?"

Dani can't help herself. "You're an a-hole, Tripp."

"She's right, Tripp. You *are* an a-hole." Joseph smiles. He pulls his wallet out of his front pocket. "Borrow the truck tomorrow? I'll swing by, help you remove the symbol of hate, you ignorant a-hole." He listens to one country song and now he's Ku Klux Klan? How's the rest of the basketball team in Indian Falls feel about that?

"It ain't racist."

"Read a book, Lawrence."

"Ooh, Mr. Mudjekeewis, acting tough. Book smart, life stupid. Come over in the morning, I'll consider lending you the keys." Tripp continues, "Hey, Dani, don't you have a friend for me?"

"No. You'd have to be a gentleman." Dani can't help but feel sorry.

"Around here, it's hard to change anybody's mind, you know?"

Outside, Tripp pulls out. He toots the horn and whips the bird. Joseph shouts, "Shawondosee!"

Dani bites her lip as she gets in the van. She looks at Joseph, one eyebrow higher than the other.

"It's nothing, some Injun legend an old bat told us when we were kids. He called me the mighty west wind, the one who gives away the other winds. I got it wrong — he's Kabibonokka, the turbulent northwest wind. Shoot!"

"You both remember the names."

"Read Longfellow in tenth. *The Song of Hiawatha* tells the same story. Tripp remembers it from when we were kids."

"He's in tenth — couldn't he have read Longfellow too?"

Joseph smiles with one corner of his mouth. "Tripp goes to Indian Falls. Native American stuff? He won't forget that."

"You know who would like Tripp? My friend Autumn, remember her? Works at the drugstore?"

Joseph turns the key. Dani fiddles with the radio. She finds the country station. Joseph looks over.

"What's that noise?"

"The Oak Ridge Boys, not that you care. 'Little Things' — listen. You might learn a thing or two." Dani rolls down the window. She tosses the silk peony out. She sings along.

I sat there reading in the meadow while these two lovebirds tore at each other on the blanket. All I could think was that they'd better be using protection. A group of young people left the beer garden. They weren't boisterous. In their midst, a tall woman, hair the color of straw. I set the book aside and stood up, wiping grass from my jeans.

The tall girl came across the meadow. She spoke low to me, out of earshot of her friends. "So now you are king? King of Prague?" She snorted a giggle.

"Alas, I am but a fool." I removed the crown of dandelions. I bowed. She's wearing a white shirt with a collar, denim capris. How dare any length of pant try to cover those long legs?

"The fools embody wisdom. It's why we keep them at court."

I held out the crown to her. "For you. I knew you were coming. I've been waiting."

Šárka (June 30) curtsied in front of me. I checked to make sure her friends weren't watching as she bowed her head.

"I dub thee, Queen of Summer." I held the crown above her head.

Šárka rose into my hands, the crown glowing against her fair hair. She adjusted her bangs. "Who'll be my king?"

"One very lucky dude."

Before I knew what was happening, Šárka kissed me. I opened my eyes, her head still so close to mine. Our noses next to each other. She looked me in the eyes. "Dreamer." Her smile was all mischief.

She rejoined her friends. She laced her long thin arm through the crook of one of her friend's arms. She looked back at me. She reminded me of something, someone, so natural and free and wild. Was it my mother? I touched my lips. The crown fit her perfectly.

Preying, 18.8.98

I had lunch with Markéta. She freaks me out. She asked me to name three animals. I was game. I said deer, rabbit, squirrel. She told me the first is how I imagine people see me. I didn't like where she was going. The second, she said, is how people actually see me. And the last? It's how I see myself.

"Interesting." She chewed, her cheek bulging with bread. "All prey."

She asked me if I was seeing anyone. Ha. I was stunned. I got stuck. A picture of Ilona (January 22) at my place late at night flashed through my head. I thought of Karina, the meadow sunlight appearing and disappearing between her long legs as she walked along beside me. I pictured Izabela (April 11) standing outside the Bat'a shoe store at the base of Wenceslas Square, waiting for me. I started to stammer. I laughed. I said no. Markéta nodded. Her eyes dropped to the table.

I wanted to open up to her, but I couldn't. I'm sorry, Markéta — you freaked me out.

Takes me back to a time when I had just arrived in Prague. Markéta took me out for tea. At a real teahouse. She was telling me a story about her ex-boyfriend, a time before she knew Patrick. He was an artist, obsessed with her. She was animated, the way she told the story. She had a confused look on her face. She stopped cold. The lights went out. We sat on the floor on pillows in the dark for a few full seconds. I looked up at the woman running the place. She walked to the front door and checked to see if power was out everywhere. The lights popped back on. Markéta continued with her story. As if nothing happened.

"After we broke up, he made a sculpture of me. He was no sculptor. He asked Patrick's permission, as if Patrick owned

me or something. It was odd. My ex is an odd man." Markéta
paused for emphasis. She sipped her black tea, the only kind
she drank. "Patrick agreed. I went. I modeled for him. Nude. It
wasn't anything sexy. He had me sitting, hunched over."

To this day I wonder about that sculpture. I wonder where it
is. I sipped my tea.

Markéta lowered her eyebrows. "You struggle with demons.
It's okay. Pick your battles." Ingrid nodded violently. In my
head.

I'm going to see Karina today.

Flinging, 19.8.98

I had lunch with Karina. Perfectly cut bangs, her hair is
lustrous. Shiny. Makes you want to touch it. She was on a
photoshoot. Her hair was freshly done. The color's better than
before. She has perfected the chocolate raven color.

She didn't get into the school she wanted; I hardly think that
matters at this point. Finish out her program, some kind of business thing. Keep with the modeling stuff. She wore a black
sleeveless hoodie and mustard-yellow capris. I commented on
how good she looked. She said the designer let her keep a couple outfits.

She has problems with her ex, the big dumb golem.

She told me she's been invited to Italy. That English teacher
of hers. He wants to take her to Florence. She said she doesn't
think she'll go. She was lying.

She told me she'd be at Roxy. She wasn't.

She's phlegmatic. I don't think she has the ability to love anyone right now. She needs to love herself first. Only she doesn't
know that.

I could align myself with her friend, the gray-haired mousy
fellow, Mr. Friend-zone. He's known Karina for a long time, he
probably wants more; he's my connection. Snake-eyed Ljuba
(February 16) too. If I want Karina, I know how to get her attention. What I need to figure out is this: do I want Karina?

I'm reminded of what that earthy sprite Aneta (May 17) said
to me, after Kentucky Buck's book party. Karina's plastic. She
lures me away from what I'm really looking for. I have to look

away. No more plastic.

Plastic People of the Universe
I stopped off at Terminal Bar. Karina wasn't there. I signed up for a computer and drank a soda in the front room until they called my name.

I opened up a browser and navigated to InfoSeek. I typed in "Plastic People of the Universe." I'd read that Havel had been spurred to political action from watching the way this band was treated. I had to know more. My search brought up a bunch of weird stuff. One article about the band.

It seems they started one month after Russian tanks rolled in and ended the Prague Spring. They were supposed to represent the foremost of Prague's underground culture. They were harassed. They were arrested. For playing music?

The band was heavily influenced by Frank Zappa and the Velvet Underground. Their name comes from the first song, "Plastic People," on the album *Absolutely Free* by Zappa's band, The Mothers of Invention.

I tried another search, this time using AltaVista and the song title. Nothing. I would see what I could find at the library. I needed to hear that song. I searched one more time for the lyrics. Check this out:

Watch the Nazis run your town
Then go home and check yourself
You think we're singing
'Bout someone else?

There you go. I went back to my previous search. I wanted to read more about what they did to get arrested. In the results, I saw a link to a photo of the band. The caption read something like 21 February 1976 on the Charles Bridge, the Second Festival of the Second Culture, organized by the Plastic People of the Universe. I clicked on the link. The photo started to download.

I waited five minutes. The photo didn't load. I could see horizontal bands of it where it had started. I couldn't use the computer during this time. I tried to flag down a waitress. No luck. I canceled the download. I went back to the article. Who were these guys, the musicians?

Bassist Milan Hlavsa was credited with forming the band. He would be the analog to Lou Reed in the Velvet Underground. Another guy by the name of Ivan Jirous, an art historian and culture critic, became the manager and artistic director of the band. The muse. To keep the analogy going, Ivan was the Plastic People's Andy Warhol. Ivan populated the band further with Josef Janíček (guitar and keyboards) and Jiří Kabeš (viola).

Ivan believed that the band should sing in English. He invited Paul Wilson, a Canadian teaching in Prague at the time, to teach them English lyrics. Wilson became their lead singer from '70 to '72. During this time, they only played two songs in Czech, both heavily borrowing lyrics from a Czech poet, Jiří Kolář. Hence, combining musical spirit with literary thought. Wilson encouraged them to perform in Czech. The group gained saxophonist Vratislav Brabenec soon after that. Brabenec introduced them to the banned works of Egon Bondy; his words dominate the lyrics of the first album.

The PPU, as they called themselves, became the center of a collection of dissidents and political activists. But the band wasn't political. In an interview I found, Brabenec says his acts were cultural activism more than anything else. Their fans fueled the flames of activism in general.

Okay, here it is. They were arrested in 1976. They were convicted of "organized disturbance of the peace"; their prison terms ranged from eight to eighteen months. But hang on, their "license" to perform music had been revoked in 1970 — I think I saw that. Let me go back. It was true. The Czech Communist Party had originally given them permission to perform as a cover band. They played mostly songs from the Velvet Underground and the Fugs. The Party revoked the band's professional license in early 1970; it meant they couldn't earn money from their performances; they couldn't use any state-owned rehearsal spaces (sounds pretty dreary — maybe not a bad condition anyway) or any state-owned equipment. The license was reinstated around 1973 or 1974, only to be revoked again a few weeks later. The re-revocation seems to have been in response to their album *Egon Bondy's Happy Hearts Club Banned*. Ha. One song concerned constipation. Another listed all the drugs Mr. Bondy, a hypochondriac, ingested. Who's Egon Bondy?

Back to InfoSeek. I felt like I had to give it one more chance. It seemed like the results were better from AltaVista, though. Neither were great. Too bad Yahoo search wasn't better. Wouldn't it be nice if there were like a better, faster — ah, never mind. Here it is, Egon Bondy.

It's a pen name. Fascinating. His real name was Zbyněk Fišer, a philosopher and a leader of the Czech underground. He was a close friend of Bohumil Hrabal. Of course he was. He criticized both capitalism and socialism, particularly the corrosive brand of socialism called totalitarianism. He was a believer in a sort of pure Marxism. He was prolific: thirty books of poetry and twenty more of prose. He was most fond of his philosophical works. He was considered a revolutionary philosopher and poet, a true literary hero. Why the pen name?

I would get to that, but first I found an interview with Bondy/Fišer. He talked about the work of Martin Heidegger, a leading mind behind phenomenology and existentialism. I had studied it in school, I knew about eidetic variations: this is a chair if I sit it in, but if I use it to reach a book on a high shelf, it can also be seen as a step stool, etc. In this interview, Bondy/Fišer made the point that at first people liked existentialism; later they came to fear it. So true. The idea that you have a responsibility to make decisions *and* that you have to live with the consequences of your decisions didn't sit well. I totally got that. Bondy/Fišer pointed out that Sartre later simplified the concept: "We are cursed to freedom," he said. So interesting. I could go on and on. But back to Plastic People.

Back to the pen name. Fišer first used Bondy in 1949 when he was part of an anthology of surrealism. All the contributors took Jewish pen names as a protest against the rise of anti-Semitism of the time. Bondy had been the name of several prominent Jewish people in Prague over the years and was used by Karel Čapek in his 1936 book, *War with the Newts*.

A couple more tidbits. Long-haired and mustachioed young men in Czechoslovakia were referred to as catfish. I love that.

And this. During the time that their professional license was revoked, the band still found ways to perform. At the Union of Artists, whenever Ivan Jirous was asked to speak, he would present slides about Andy Warhol and have PPU "demonstrate" Velvet Underground songs. The slides would last ten minutes; the "demonstrations" would last hours. They played at remote venues and for private occasions such as weddings. One story is that a divorced couple decided to remarry just for the chance to have PPU play.

They were truly underground. Locations of their gigs were kept secret until one day before the performance. Didn't stop the police from finding out about them though. At a March 1974 performance in Budovice, the police showed up. They beat fans with batons. The PPU never even got to play at that one. They started to call themselves the Second Culture. They planned festivals. After the Second Festival of the Second Culture in 1976, twenty-seven musicians, including all the Plastic People, were arrested. Over a hundred fans were interrogated. PPU's equipment, tapes, films and notebooks were confiscated. Paul Wilson was deported. The indictment claimed their music was vulgar and the message was anti-socialism, that the lyrics were nihilistic and decadent. The trial was held six months later, drawing international attention. All but the four Plastic People and Jirous were set free. Brabenec in particular was subjected to interminable interrogations and physical beatings.

Václav Havel's 1976 campaign to support the musicians after their arrest evolved to become the human rights organization Charter 77.

After they were released from prison, the band continued to meet up at Havel's summer cottage to record new music, their numbers swelling to eight members. When Brabenec went into exile in Canada in the 1980s, the band asked Havel to write songs for them. He guided them to texts and influences, but it seems he never really wrote anything. Havel hailed the band's "special mystical, magical flavor, a very Prague flavor."

Back in Canada, Paul Wilson established a recording studio with a Czech name. He called it "God's Mill." A little presumptuous but optimistic and positive, I suppose. Through diplomatic

channels, Havel arranged for PPU's recordings to be smuggled
to Wilson. Wilson released the material in North America and
Europe.

I take off my glasses and hold them up to the light. Smudges.
I think of Lars at the memorial for Ingrid. Pear-shaped Lars. I
guess he wasn't seeing everything clearly either. I run my spectacles under hot water, then dry them, rubbing the lenses with
a microfiber cloth. I put them back on. With new clarity, I see.
I have friends. I have freedom. I live in a mystical, magical old
city.

I deserve better. I need to see beyond the surface.

Warming, 21.8.1998

I hosted the housewarming last night. I've been dreaming
about it since I moved in. Yesterday, I did it.

I went to Tesco, a British company that has a department store
on National Street. A brand-new gleaming grocery store in the
basement. I inserted a five-crown coin into the buggy handle,
liberating it from bondage. I got the coin back at the end when
I re-chained the buggy. I proceeded with the buggy to the flat
downward people-mover. It's the same as an escalator, only the
belt never turns into steps. The wheels of the buggy are mag-
netized. I rolled the thing onto the silvery belt and the wheels
stuck, couldn't be moved. It was exciting to take part in this
engineering marvel — only I couldn't shake the feeling that
human ingenuity could've been better spent.

At the bottom of the people-mover, I appeared in the fruit and
vegetable section. It was clean, well lit. The employees wore
nicely fitted uniforms. Bright blues, yellows and reds. I grabbed
a multi-colored set of bell peppers. A head of lettuce. A chain
of vine-ripened tomatoes; on the small side but c'mon, they're
vine-ripened — they must be good. I found a clear box of fresh
cilantro. I had looked it up in my phrasebook before I left the
flat. It would go nicely on the tacos. For those who don't have a

severe allergy or a mild predilection against it.

I headed to the butcher. An overly eager young man in a spat-tered lab coat stood behind the counter. He was deflated by my ability to fulfill my needs without consulting him. I found 1,000 grams (2.2 pounds) of freshly ground beef chuck. I made for the spice aisle. I came away with cumin and coriander.

Tortillas. I got the soft flour ones, the smaller size. The soft corn ones would be more authentic. It's a preference thing. I thought back. All the good Mexican restaurants I used to lunch at down near Wall Street when I lived in New York City. The thing that made those places stand out, the thing that made you tell your co-workers about the place, was the fresh tortilla chips. Made right there on the spot. An amazing little surprise for my guests. I would need flour, baking powder and lard. Salt I had.

I found the dry goods. A quick consult with my phrasebook confirmed that I had chosen the white all-purpose flour, not any of the nearby pretenders in similar sacks. The tougher one was baking powder. The straight translation, *prášek do pečiva*, is different from the actual name. It sent me all over the store when the ingredient I needed was right there by the flour. The whole time. Lard was easy.

I purchased three plastic bags with blue loop handles. They were 20 CZK (0.67 USD) each, an extravagance. I have piles of the forgotten bags back at my flat. No matter — this was my housewarming party. My guests were in for a treat.

The receipt was a kick in the solar plexus. Nearly 1500 CZK (46.15 USD)? Ingrid cackled at me. Unwise selections. I was obviously overpaying — for 1500 CZK, I could treat everyone to a hearty meal at Kojak's, beers and desserts for all. That's not what I was thinking as I forked over the cash — I was thinking about impressing my guests. If I could pull this off.

Brad and Agata didn't show up at the agreed-upon time. I played around with the flour, baking powder, lard and water to make my own tortillas. I made two. For a roller, I used an empty beer bottle. They needed to be rolled thinner. They needed to bake longer. They weren't a total flop. I made a good mess of it.

I went overboard. The more I made, the better they got; I focused on the thrill of cooking a meal for friends. That part was good. Once my guests arrived — Brad and Agata, Pat and Markéta, Jiří (April 24) — they didn't appreciate it. I'd spent all that money. I heard Pat say to Jiří that they should meet at the pizza place after. Jiří shook his watch on his arm. He gave Pat a weird look. I tried to brush it off.

Can't buy my friends.

I cleaned the place up after they left. It feels good to make a mess. To clean it up. To make this place my own.

I put on my pajamas. The place didn't feel warmer. It felt more empty. I went into the water closet. Someone had taped a slip of paper to the wall. It said:

"There are times when we must sink to the bottom of our misery to understand truth, just as we must descend to the bottom of a well to see the stars in broad daylight."
— Václav Havel

I love that. I will add more.

Slipping, 24.8.98

I went to Terminal Bar yesterday. Karina was not there. It's just as well. I was thinking about her when Ingrid came into the picture. I started wondering about that night. How could it have happened? One minute she's sitting with a group of friends, drinking, smoking. The next minute she's gone. She slips. She grasps. She tumbles. I can't let myself think about it too much. My imagination is too vivid. My stomach pitches. Poor Ingrid. I miss her. I still haven't heard from Naked Pete. I should call my mother.

St. Vitus Dance

It attacks children between the ages of five and fifteen. Twice as common in girls as it is in boys. It first presents as a halting gait, involuntary limping, unsteadiness in the legs. Then the hands and arms. Spasms. Rapid, involuntary, jerking motions.

Tics. Shoulder rolls. Frenzied gesticulations. As if from demonic possession. Unexpected twists. Then the face.

An eye-roll, a grimace, a sneer. The tongue pokes out, not like she's trying to stick her tongue out at you but like she's trying to taste something foreign on the bottom lip. The head snaps down. No rhythm, no pattern or repetition. Next come the feet. She reaches down like she's looking at the bottom of her shoe. She stomps. The legs give out. She careens out of the frame. She comes back sideways. She catches herself. Barely.

It looks like a dance. A dance to music that we cannot hear. The maneuvers might make sense, one thinks, if we could just hear the music.

Tongue fasciculations. Spontaneous contractions of muscle under the skin. Spasms. Rapid, irregular and undirected arm motions. Uncoordinated gestures. Muscular weakness, stumbling and falling, slurred speech, emotional instability and difficulty concentrating or writing.

Twitching. It can occur in any voluntary muscle group, but it is most common in eyelids, arms, legs and feet.

Puts one in mind of Tourette's syndrome or Parkinson's disease.

It's St. Vitus's dance, an old-fashioned term for Sydenham's chorea.

In the late Middle Ages, people in Germany and countries such as Latvia celebrated the feast of St. Vitus, a fourth-century Sicilian martyr. They congregated before his statue. They danced. Vitus is the patron saint of dancers and of entertainers in general. He is also the patron saint of Bohemia. The huge Gothic cathedral towering above the Prague Castle is the St. Vitus Cathedral. It was believed that dancing before the statue on his feast day would bring a year of good health.

It's good to dance. Inferno, Roxy, so many great nightclubs. Dance all night. His feast day is June 15.

Processing, 26.8.98

Let me start from the beginning.

Last night, I met Izabela and her boyfriend Kamil (March 3) at Little Glen's jazz club on Carmelite Street in Prague 1. A dingy little place with dirty yellow walls and mismatched chairs, a nice painting of a chess game to the left of the bar. The shelves behind the bar are dug into the arches — the whole place is arches dug out of arches. They serve a brunch menu all the time, strangely satisfying on a Tuesday night hanging out with people who I should probably not be hanging out with. I get a beer, I order eggs and Czech farmer's bread with klobasa. I watch Izabela fuss over her boy. She sits a little too close to him on the bench. She picks a piece of lint off his shoulder. She kisses his cheek. Kamil enjoys the attention. He keeps an eye on me.

Kamil has dark hair and skin the color of wet sand. He's half-Czech and half-French. He should only get half a Name Day. He doesn't speak much English. He's short, thick. Played soccer. He works for Eurest, the company that supplies most of the cafés in Prague; they both do. Izabela is a receptionist; Kamil is one of the entitled sales guys.

I know where I stand with Kamil. He thinks Izabela and I are friends, maybe he thinks I'm gay; he figures I'm harmless. Ultimately, I am harmless. I just get to fuck Izabela every once in a while.

I sop up the golden yolk from the plate with a piece of bread. Izabela looks up over my shoulder. I turn. Naked Pete has a beer in his hand. He walks in my direction.

"We need to talk." Naked Pete's voice is gruff, like he hasn't spoken for a while. He coughs and says it again.

I stand up. "You don't answer your phone?" I look back at my dinner dates. "Izabela, Kamil, my friend Peter."

Naked Pete nods. They don't get up. I shift on my feet. "Excuse me. I'll be back."

I get a whiff of Naked Pete. I blink the tears back. Gamy. We grab a couple of bar stools near the front window. The other patrons lean over their beers. I sit down, remembering that I left my drink at the table. Just as well. Purple half-crescents under

Pete's eyes.

"I had a dream about Ingrid." Naked Pete's bloodshot eyes bore into me. I turn to face the specials board, white chalk on a blackboard. I focus on one of the words written there. *Borůvka.* Blueberry.

"I need to talk to you about Ingrid." There's a catch in my voice, a sudden rope of phlegm.

"Let me finish." Naked Pete slaps the bar. I smile at the bartender, a muscly Czech lad. He watches us. He shakes his head.

Pete says, "Been drinking, didn't expect to see you, listen to me. Can you do that?" He turns to me. His beery breath on my face. At least he still has his clothes on.

"Go on," I whisper. I lead by example.

Naked Pete inhales deeply, gestures with his beer. "Ingrid came to me in my dream. Ingrid! She was so beautiful. I was happy to see her. I lay on her couch. She stood above me." He sets his beer down. "Her blue pants. You know the ones. She said that Ilona needed me, she said you were tied up, that's what she said, she said, 'Ilona needs you. Joseph is tied up.' Like that." He held his hands straight up on the edge of the bar. As if to measure his memory of the dream. In a raspy whisper, "Can you tell me what it means?"

I scan his bewildered face. His glassy eyes focus behind my shoulder, his mouth hangs open. He half laughs. He brings his focus back to me. I look away.

"I don't know." I shrug. I feel like a bad friend. "Have you talked to Ilona?"

"I have, mate. I have." Naked Pete stands, removes his coat and places it over the stool. He sits back down on top of it. "Have you?"

"Not since a week or so." I can't look at him. He stares at me. He seems less drunk. A lucid moment.

He leans into my ear, burps, then whispers, "She's pregnant, Joseph." He slaps me on the shoulder.

Izabela comes over. She hands me my mug of beer. "We're going. I'll call you, Joseph. Goodnight, Peter. Na shledanou. Dobrou noc."

I sit, frozen, holding the half-beer. My expression blanks. I raise up a hand.

A moment passes before I set the beer down and look at Naked Pete. "I need to go. This" — I wave my hand between us — "is not over. Go home. Take a shower. Answer your fucking phone."

Naked Pete smiles. "I miss Ingrid. She'd let me stay at her place. She'd know what to do."

I pause for a second, then turn to my friend. "She's still here." I pat Naked Pete's chest. He dives in for a hug.

I grapple with him. His whole body shakes. He wipes the sides of his eyes with the backs of his grubby hands. Naked Pete reaches for his wallet.

I motion to the barkeep.

"Already paid. The other guy who was with you."

Fucking Kamil.

I process the news as I walk.

I almost run right into someone. Short, dirty dreadlocks. Ruddy face, either sunburnt or drunk or both. "Would you like a tour?" British accent. He's standing outside the monastery. He hands me a brochure. I take it and walk away, dazed. I make excuses. I stuff it in my back pocket.

I get on a tram, then switch between the tram and the metro at Peace Square. Karina stands by the hot-dog stand, my hot-dog stand. Of all the luck. She talks with another young woman. Karina is tall and her friend, she's taller. Young, hair the color of straw. Wait — I know her.

I greet them.

Karina answers, "Ahoj. Hele, do you know Šárka?"

Šárka answers for me in English. "We met. One of Bert's business colleagues. Nice to see you again, Joseph."

Karina's cool facade disappears. She turns back to me. She touches the collar of my jacket. "Šárka is a school friend of mine. She finished, but I, few years more. Hele, Joseph, I have good news for you. Jako, great news." Karina smiles an impish smile. I'm confused by the attention. Šárka smirks.

I meet eyes with Šárka. "I could use some great news." She squints.

"Remember Guillermo? Last spring? He got me photoshoot.

THINK magazine. Jako prostě, they pay." Karina flicks the zipper pull on my jacket.

I look at Šárka. She shrugs. "That's great. Remember us little people who believed in you. Before you were famous."

"Little people?" Karina laughs. "You are big American, how you say, podnikatel, no?" She turns to Šárka. She leans into me. The flip of shiny black hair sends a dizzying cloud my way. Cedar and something more animalistic. The word *ambergris* jumps to my mind.

Šárka answers, "Entrepreneur."

I frown. A compliment? I pivot. "Šárka, did you get the job with Bert?" My arm snakes around Karina's waist involuntarily.

Šárka smiles through her eyebrows. After a brief hesitation, she nods. Her hair shakes.

"We should celebrate. I want to hear more. Photo shoot, new job. Can't now — I have some business."

Karina pouts. "Tak, pity. Another time." She stands up straight. She straightens my collar.

I adjust my backpack. I look into Karina's eyes. A sly smile steals across her rosebud lips.

I say good night. Karina turns to Šárka, who is lingering. She says good night.

"Tell Bert I said hi."

Šárka laughs and turns to Karina. Karina blinks. They cross the street. They head for the tram stop.

I walk away. I realize: no steady job, I have no money, and here I am. An attempt to slay loneliness ends in this? It was hollow sex, nothing like love. Sex is not free. My actions have consequences. I have said it before. I don't pay for sex. But hell, it's not true. I pay. Believe me, I pay.

The Infant of Prague

On the metro, I sit across from a couple of clubbers. I pull out the brochure.

The Infant of Prague is found in the Discalced Carmelites'

(barefoot Carmelites) Church of Our Lady Victorious. The brochure says he once belonged to St. Teresa of Avila.

This image of Jesus is forty-three centimeters tall (nineteen inches). He's made mostly out of waxed wood. He's mounted on an ornate silver pedestal, adorned with diamonds and crowned in gold. In his left hand, he holds a golden orb. Symbolizes kingship, it says. In his raised right hand, he holds his palm in a blessing gesture. Since 1713, his vestments, some of which have been donated by "very wealthy and aristocratic" families, have been changed regularly by the Carmelite sisters. The outfit he wears the Sunday after Easter, pictured, is especially fine. A cloak made of ermine, worn to commemorate the anniversary of the coronation of the statue in 1655. The other vestments are sewn with gold thread, studded with gemstones, made of silk and lace designed specifically for him.

It says that although it's not clear exactly when the image of the Infant was created, consensus suggests it's during the Middle Ages, most likely around 1340. Older than the Charles Bridge. The origin story is printed here: a monk in a desolated Spanish monastery, somewhere between Seville and Córdoba, dreamt of a little boy who insisted that the monk should pray. The next day, the monk prayed for hours. He realized what he needed to do. He began carving the image.

The statue seems first appeared in Prague in 1556, when a Spanish aristocrat married a Czech nobleman. It had been presented to her by her mother, Dona Isabella, who had received it as a gift from St. Teresa of Avila herself. It was the aristocrat's daughter who donated the image to the Carmelite friars in 1628. From the moment the image arrived in the Church of Our Lady Victorious, devotions were offered to it twice a day. Novices are required to make their vow of poverty in the presence of the Infant of Prague. That stopped in 1630, when the sisters and the friars were transferred to Munich in light of the disturbances in Prague from the Thirty Years War. By 1631, Sweden occupied Prague. The Carmelite friary was plundered. The Infant of Prague was tossed behind the altar on a heap of rubble. It lay there for seven years, its hands broken off, until Father Cyrillus found it. He prayed before it daily until one day he heard a voice say:

Have pity on me, and I will have pity on you. Give me my hands, and I will give you peace. The more you honor me, the more I will bless you.

Since then, the Infant of Prague has remained here in the city, in the Church of Our Lady Victorious. In 1889, a yearly nine-day celebration was instituted that includes a procession held in the statue's honor. It attracts millions of pilgrims.

That boy with the dreadlocks was a pilgrim.

Fuck. I'm the infant of Prague. I need to be a man. It's not about avoiding mistakes; what makes a man is how he deals with his mistakes. What are you going to do, Joseph?

I have no love in my life at all. I have nothing. I need help. I should call my mother. I'll end up telling her about the money. I'll make her feel guilty. Not an option right now.

I'm a real mess. I don't cook. I don't run. I don't journal. I don't meditate. What's up with me? I don't love myself. Right now, I need to.

It's after nine when I get to Laubova. The door slams a little too hard behind me. It's not that late. I dial her home number — she doesn't have a cellphone.

"Yes?"

I tell her it's me.

"Joseph, um, hi. I don't think I can talk to you right now. I mean, my parents are expecting a phone call."

"Ilona, I know. I talked to Peter."

Ilona's voice is low, angry. "I don't know whose it is."

She tries to be strong. "Ilona, it's okay. We need to talk about it."

"No worry."

"I'm probably the last person you want to see right now, but with Ingrid not being here…" I catch myself. My voice cracks. I twist the rectangular plastic receiver on my ear. Dirty dishes pile up in my sink. I take a deep breath. I ask her to tea. "Please?"

Ilona reluctantly agrees. The teahouse on Wenceslas Square. This Friday. What'm I going to say?

SEPTEMBER

Listing, 31.8.98

S HE BLOCKED ME. I SQUEEZED Ilona. I tried to kiss her cheek. She turned.

(I had journaled this first line on Saturday morning. I didn't write the date, which isn't like me. I couldn't continue. I skipped Sunday in a daze. Now it's Monday morning and I can't sleep. I'm forcing myself to get it down the way it happened.)

We passed the movie theater, the Divadlo Archa. The teahouse is tucked back in a passage. It has a little garden. Nestled in the center of Prague. How can it have a little garden?

We picked a low table near the back. No one was around us. We'd be able to talk.

I held out my hand, to help lower her to the fl oor. As if she was nine months pregnant. She looked at me.

We sat on pillows. She curled her legs around to one side. The proprietress came over. Ilona ordered the herbal tea. I got the green jasmine. Without considering how she might feel about that. The proprietress returned shortly with a tray. She knelt to deliver two small porcelain cups without handles.

I resolved not to speak until Ilona started. Looked like she may have made the same resolution. She picked up the cup in both hands. She puckered her lips and blew across the surface of the steaming tea. Her big brown eyes were on me, the whites so clear.

She looked out the French doors into the proprietress's small urban garden. Ilona exhaled. "I lied. It's you."

I took a sip of tea. I wanted to smile — I knew it — but I wasn't *that* stupid. "I know."

"You know nothing, Joseph." She pointed out that she could be with a different guy every night. Ilona accused me of not caring. "The other girl, what's her name?"

I hadn't expected this. I didn't *not* deserve it. "We never talked about it."

"We talk about nothing." Ilona took a sip. "No need." She told me Ingrid had set us up.

I blinked. "Wait — what? You talked about me?"

Ilona cocked her head. In her best impersonation of Ingrid's brogue, "Ah, yer grand." She paused, smiled, her nose crinkled; she caught herself. I was unable to look away. Her eyes. She said that I didn't pay attention to her. She said it wasn't my fault. "No, wait. Sorry." Ilona wiped the edge of her eyes with a paper napkin. "It *is* your fault." Ilona told me I should have checked. She said, "'Tis not on woman." That contraction was Ingrid all the way. She told me she should have asked more of me. She said she was tired of having to be the strong one. "I want fun too, like all you fucking Americans…"

I listened. The way the light from the French doors fell on her. I enjoyed being here. With her. I had to focus. She's right. Of course, she's right. I have protection at my place but I'm not careful. That's my fault. It must be damned annoying to see freeloaders like me in her country. Finding ourselves. Blowing through money like it doesn't matter.

"Tak. English!" Ilona admonishes herself. She rolls her eyes, takes a deep breath. "You are lost. It's okay." She tells me she knows I was married. I didn't remember if we had covered it. She knows about the divorce. She's heard the stories. "One day, good boyfriend, nice husband, maybe good fodder. No matter." Ilona looked me in the eyes. She told me what she needed. "Few of days. Peter say me to stay to his place. You ever saw his place?"

I take a sip of my tea, scald my mouth, wave my hands in front of my face like a lunatic.

"Ježíš a Marie, Joseph. Not cute." Ilona smiles. Her watery eyes glint in the sun. She asks me to stop. She has something to say. "I not love you. That was drunk Ilona." She wipes her tears. "I worry." She cups her hands in front of herself. It's like she's pointing to herself with all her fingers.

Out of breath, I say to her, "Stay at my place. I can stay with Naked Pete, I mean, Peter. It's the least I can do."

"The least I can do. Ha!" Ilona finishes off her tea. She gets to her feet.

"When?" I drain my cup. It's too hot. I make a face. I gasp.

"Tak, no questions?" Ilona is furious. With me, but it's more than that. She can't believe she let her guard down. "I think you are romantic man. With me, no. I am ugly to you."

It's going to sound corny. The timing isn't great. "I've never seen you look as beautiful as you look right now." It was true. She didn't have to believe me. "Ingrid wouldn't have put us together if we didn't need each other — do you think?"

"Ty vole. Now you talk like Peter." Ilona folds her jacket across her belly. "Leave the dead died."

We walked back to my place. She wanted to hear more about how I thought she was beautiful. I thought about telling her about my mother. It wouldn't have been fair. She was under enough stress. I couldn't pile on. I had to accept my half of the burden. She absorbed each compliment I gave her; there were a few, knowing I was right, that in the afternoon sun of a late summer day, wearing a light coat and walking to the tram, she was strikingly beautiful.

She came up. The first time she's come here sober. We sat on the floor in the living room. We used my phone. We made arrangements. When she settled the receiver in the cradle, I just blurted it out. "I have money. You don't have to worry about that."

Ilona told me it was covered. I believed her. I knew nothing of the Czech public health care system.

We made a shopping list. It should have been awkward, listing maxi-pads and herbal tea, chocolate pudding cups and *pretzliky*, but it wasn't. I think it might be lonely for her. I could send Naked Pete over to check in, maybe. I told her I would change the sheets. I would tidy up for her. She said she'd bring some schoolwork. She'd make good use of the time. We worked together.

The phone rang. I looked at Ilona. She frowned at me.

"Go on." Ilona starts to step out of the room.

I tell her I know who it is. I tell her I don't need to answer. "She'll call back." Why? Such an idiot, Joseph, c'mon, man.

Ilona frowns. "I take messages from all your woman."

"You're going to need more paper — let's put that on the list. So many woman." I feign adding to the list. I smile. She shakes her head.

"Who do I call if, you know, if something goes wrong?"

"My sister."

Wait. Ilona has a sister? I hold the pen out for her. Ilona rips off a corner of paper. She writes a name on it, a phone number. She doesn't show it to me.

"Nothing bad will happen. But, if — under the tea tin, I hide this."

"Is she as beautiful as you?" I call into the kitchen.

Ilona comes back. "She has two children. My nieces." Ilona pauses. She shakes her head and looks at me, folding her lips against each other. "No need to call her. You are not charming." Ilona holds an accusatory finger in my direction.

"Emergency only." I nod.

Ilona left. She had a shift at the Thirsty Dog. I thought I would meet her there, after a few phone calls. I stayed here. I kept it simple.

Realizing, 1.9.98

I didn't party last night. It was a good move for me. It was one positive thing. I have to do my thing. I have to clean up my mess. Maybe start with the dishes?

I was thinking, which is dangerous. I was thinking we could keep it. We're not in love but maybe it would be just the thing. A shared sense of purpose. It's not my choice, of course. I haven't talked to Ilona about my feelings. She doesn't know about my mom. Would it be unfair to spring it on her right now? I can't decide if I should talk to her about it, or if I should let it go. We aren't quite there in our relationship.

Maybe we need to fast-forward the pleasantries. We hopped into bed quick enough. We need to pick up the pace on the emotional side.

I want to be done with journaling. I want to get on with my day. There you go. A perfect example of my problems right now, on a small-enough scale that we can examine it. I want to be done, I want to move on; what I need is to slow down. Nothing else coming is better than what's already here. That I can't slow down, that I can't abide is proof: I'm lost. Thanks, Ingrid. I hear you. Loud and clear.

Spending time with Ilona, I get to know her better. She's lost too. She thought about keeping it, but c'mon, what sense does that make?

Reaching, 2.9.98

It's 10:30 a.m. I got home this morning at 1:30 a.m. I'm tired. I have to go to Patrick's office today. I can't allow myself to shut down. I need to keep moving. I should stay positive, although I'm not positive. I checked in with Ilona last night. She's okay. She appreciated my call. I hung up before I could fuck it up.

I may get hurt. I'm hurting, the way things are. I have guilt. Guilt is a ton of bricks; all you have to do is set it down. Maybe I'm tired. I know I can do better.

Something's upside down right now. I don't know what it is. Something's backwards. It's confusing. I can't ask my mother for the money she owes me. That's annoying. I could go to New York City, but I don't know. I have no friends there anymore. They all chose Rachel. Here, at least I have friends.

I'll lay low. The thing to do is to try to make it to Patrick's office for lunch. Go to lunch with these guys, if possible.

It's September already. It's the end of the summer. The weather has been beautiful. My life has been strange. I don't know what's good or bad anymore. Is this the way it's supposed to be?

I went back and read some of my journals from last month. I found the entry from 16.8 — don't push, don't chase, have faith.

Doing, 3.9.98

The invitation came by email. Tad, a college buddy, apologized for the unconventional invite, and then immediately took it back. The apology, I mean. He said that nothing about this wedding, if he had his druthers, would be conventional. Yeah, right. He's marrying a Spanish Catholic woman, Sofia. Just chaffing under the yoke of it. I can't afford to go to Barcelona. Unless I could take Karina. I almost immediately forgot about it.

Karina's blown me off too many times. I've blown myself off too many times.

She slams the door in my face; I give her the chance. I'll give it one last try this weekend. After that, I need to let it go.

That Phil kid, Karina's Phil, he introduces himself to me. I don't know why he did that. I guess he figures we are comrades. In the chase for Karina. He introduces himself to me, asks how long I've been here. He asks me if I teach English. No, Phil, I don't teach English. He tells me he thought that all Americans taught English, like he does. No, Phil, not all Americans here teach English, like you do.

I didn't come here to teach English. It seems beneath me. I would teach fault tree logic, databases, coding, the things I care about. Teaching English (*See Dick run. Run, Dick, run.*) to make beer money? Nah. That's not me.

Am I crazy or does it seem at times as though Karina's disappointed when I leave Terminal Bar? Yes, it does seem that way. She likes having me there. A humble failure, an honest one, is far less embarrassing than a crass success.

It wouldn't be worth anything if it was easy.

I tried to soft boil an egg. Two minutes is not enough. Let me check the cookbook right quick. The cookbook says three and a half minutes for medium to small eggs, like I have. I did two minutes; the results were gross.

Humble failure?

Cooking, 4.9.98

Glorious day yesterday. I woke at 7:00 a.m. I decided to jump into my day and sure enough, it worked. I journaled, I worked, I meditated. After my egg disaster, I carried on, unthwarted, and made tomato sauce. Two tins of tomato paste, two cloves of garlic (use more next time), two fresh tomatoes, one onion (more than enough) and too much sugar. I got worried that the paste was too strong. I dumped a bunch of sugar in. I went too far. It's the second time I've been caught in that trap. My sauce will be better next time. I journaled about cooking. I remembered the smells in the kitchen. It took me back.

FALLINGWATER

Thunder crashes. Joey's house shakes. Windows rattle in their frames.

Dani slips. Her flip-flops are soaked. The Sunbird Express slants in the driveway. She ducks under the breezeway. It is propped up on four beams. A copy of the *Batavia Daily News* hovers over her head. A daypack slung over one shoulder, a white paper sack in her hand. Her selections are deliberate: frosted cinnamon roll for him, salted pretzel bagel and cream cheese for her. Sweets for her sweetheart. For her, salt.

"Joey, you home?" she yells into the house. Her voice is drowned in the rush of the rain. It drums the roof, it splatters windows. She drips on the kitchen floor, clad in her Penn State T-shirt and matching navy-blue skort. Barefoot. Her black string bikini swims underneath her outfit. The plan had been to soak up some sun at Nu Lake. Her topknot is drenched. She reworks the day's blueprint.

The kitchen is avocado. Wallpaper yellows on the walls. Dark walnut cabinets boasting oil-rubbed copper fixtures thirst for an update. The breakfast dishes laze on the counter. The pungent odor of an unwashed bacon pan hangs in the air.

She sets the bakery bag on the kitchen table. She hears footsteps overhead.

"You have to see this," from the loft. She circles around the table. She angles to her left and climbs the unfinished stairs.

From the bottom step one gets a sense of the place. His father has been working on it for the past five or six years. Tongue-and-groove knotty pine panels. They climb up the walls to the cathedral ceiling. It takes full advantage of the space it is given. The finish is natural and bright. On less rainy mornings, it reflects the sun in a honey haze. An open, airy expanse at the top of the stairs. Rain washes against the oversized windows.

She carries plates up the stairs. Each with a napkin tucked underneath. A stage-like platform faces south. No shirt, barefoot, Joey. Olive-drab cargo shorts hang from his hips. The shorts have buttons and strings — the buttons are fastened, the strings hang loose.

Lightning flashes. He spreads his arms. He closes his eyes. He counts, "Six, seven, eight..." Thunder crashes, windows rattle. Pastries jump on the plate. She cradles.

"Eight miles away." He jumps down and sits on the side of the stage. The floors are not finished. The chipboard floors are rough underfoot. The two-by-twelve plank casing is a great perch. She hands him a plate. She sits next to him. "How long have you been up here?"

"Look, you can barely see the back fence." He points out across the backyard, two evergreens, one small and one large. A set of twin willows weeping beyond. The fence is a wire affair, designed to keep the boarded thoroughbreds in the meadow.

They have been studying architecture. Separately, each at their own high schools. They share a fascination with Frank Lloyd Wright. He wants to tell her all about his latest discovery. It's a theory. It speaks to him. A house, however humble, is more than a structure to provide shelter from the elements. A house is a habitat. It has a direct impact on its occupants. It sets a tone, it guides what happens within its walls, it sees everything and divulges nothing. It soaks up the light as the sun passes over it; it absorbs the night, with or without the moon. It changes color to fit each of the seasons. When a storm passes, inside or out, it is a shell of stoic calm.

He takes a bite of the cinnamon roll. He nods at her selection. He speaks through the roll, "Wonder how long it'll last."

She takes a bite of her pretzel bagel. A dab of cream cheese sticks to the corner of her mouth. He sets his plate down and turns to her.

"Let me get that." Has he forgotten that they are here, together alone? Alone together? He dabs at the corner of her mouth. Her bottom lip is dry. He's close enough, in the overcast light, to see the faint vertical lines cracked in the vermillion of her lip. He remembers.

He kisses her.

She holds her plate underneath their kiss. As if she could catch the crumbs. Her eyes are closed, she focuses on his lips. Exploring the sensations sparking in her limbs, she keeps the plate level, then sets it next to her. His lips pull away. She opens her eyes. His eyes are closed. He remembers the kiss, storing it away. He opens his eyes.

"Should we, you know, do it, right here? Under the storm?"

"Is this all we are now?" She doesn't know where it comes from, this anger. "You don't love me. You love the storm."

He panics. Yes, now that they've done it, they have to keep doing it, anytime they are alone. Isn't that how it works? Why did she come here? His confidence is swept away. Washed out by the downpour.

He plays it cool. He takes a bite of the cinnamon roll. His left thumb gets iced. He holds it out. His cheeks bulge. She doesn't hesitate. Her tongue is warm and soft against his skin. He can't concentrate.

His thumb wet, he touches her cheek. His fingers wrap into the curls at the nape of her neck. He guides her mouth to his. He kisses her lightly. She licks the icing off him.

Lightning pulsates in a burst of three. Like camera flashes. She stands, touches his naked shoulder. She drops the skort to the floor and flashes him. Her black Body Glove bikini bottoms. The high hip accentuates her athletic curves. Thunder rumbles. She tucks a curl behind her ear, kicks the skort to the side. She pads downstairs.

Her hip presses against the cool Formica. She drinks a tumbler of water. It is cool on her throat. Not cold. She reaches into the freezer and shakes three ice cubes free. She knows it's confusing. She's confused too. Full of hormones. She wants to split herself on the sky. She fills the glass again and heads back. She takes one cube in her hand. At the top of the stairs, he sits on the perch, smiling. He has stacked the plates, gathered the napkins.

She hands the water to him. He drinks deeply, gasps for air. He drinks her in. Wearing a T-shirt over her bikini, her skort in a pile, he can't take his eyes off her legs. She puts the hand with the ice cube behind his neck, like she's about to hug him. He jumps. He howls. He nearly topples the tumbler.

Dani shows him. An ice cube melts in the palm of her hand. "Think of anything we could do with this?" Mischief in her smile.

Joseph is in shock. "I can think of one or two things."

"We'll do both. Something to look forward to. An ice promise." Came to her out of nowhere. She's pretty proud of herself.

She plunks the cube in the glass at the end of his arm. She challenges him. "Let's make something."

He leads her down the wooden staircase into the kitchen. Their connection is palpable. Electric.

She leans against the counter. She asks what they should make.

He holds up a finger. He goes to the deep freeze in the garage, coming back with a package wrapped in brown butcher paper and yellow tape. Written in grease pencil "Venison backstrap, 1986." He pulls the slow cooker from a lower cabinet.

The lights flicker on and off.

He grabs a bag of raw, unpeeled carrots, a sweet Vidalia onion and four large red potatoes from the pantry. He places the ingredients on the counter. He surveys the spice rack. Cumin, yellow mustard, thyme, garlic powder, black pepper and, of course, salt. He collects the soy sauce and Worcestershire bottles from the cupboard, a lime from the refrigerator. He begins.

"Grab a bowl," he directs. She hands it to him. He follows no recipe. He's showing off. It wasn't long ago he made something like it. His mother guided. His confidence rebuilds.

He measures the wet ingredients, a cup, two cups, a splash. He adds spices. One cascades over the other. Colors overlap. Dramatic falls.

"Chop those, please?" he points with the knife. She dices an onion. The delicate bones of her wrists. He whisks the marinade with a fork. She hands him a whisk. He sets the fork down in the sink and takes the whisk bashfully. She flips the hem of her shirt at him. He whisks faster. The high arch of black bikini bottom on her hip. The fleshy curve of her butt disappears out of view. He wants to grab her, lift her onto the kitchen counter, take her right there.

Joseph questions himself. Do you love her? Do you love her enough? How will you know? He cuts.

She raises an eyebrow. She rinses a carrot, stalk and all. She caresses the carrot under the lukewarm water. He is mesmerized.

"You like that?" She measures the thick end between her fingers. Folds her fingers around it. She glides it under the water. "What about this?"

His mouth hangs open. He's affected. He sets the knife down. He wipes his hands on his shorts. The chopping will have to wait.

She snaps off a sheet of paper towel. "Or this." She enshrouds the carrot. She dries it. As if it is a sacred talisman. "You like?"

She taps the skinny end on her bottom lip. The air left in his lungs leaves abruptly. Devious is her smile. She steps closer to him.

His hair is messy, maybe a day out from being washed. His lips are the shape of a recurve bow, unstrung. His eyes are semi-sweet dark chocolate. He's lean and muscled, indentations under shoulders, forearms like rocks. Striated with veins. "Put a shirt on," she says. "We're cooking."

He brushes his hands together and withdraws into the laundry room. He finds a shirt, the one with the shrunken sleeves. It accentuates his shoulders. She loves that. He comes back into the kitchen. He gets close to her, leaning the small of his back against the counter. He folds his arms. He wants to say to her, "I want to taste you."

He nuzzles her ear, tries to kiss her neck. He misses, kissing her shoulder. He steps around her to scoop up the orange matchsticks and place them in the slow cooker. He nestles them around the roast.

She kisses him on the mouth, then stops for a second. She looks in his eyes as she reaches behind him. She replaces the glass cover over the slow cooker. She has already set it to low.

He wants to slide his hand along her back. He wants to find the ridge of her swimsuit bottom. He wants her hand to guide his hand beneath the tight stretch of fabric. She eases his two fingers inside her. Her hips meet his hand.

She wonders what he's thinking about; his mind a great inward sea. He scoops her up. He starts for the stairs.

He slows down. He maneuvers her through the narrow space. Her arms around his neck. His eyes dart around to each obstacle — the post, the railing, the half-wall. He stays true to her, he moves his hips to climb the stairs, he swings her slightly when they get to the landing. Something moves in her. A tectonic shift.

He carries her, the light now changed to a split-pea color, into his room.

The bedroom sports a fresh coat of Pittsburgh Paints Antique White. She read in a recent issue of *Architectural Digest* that a limited and organic color scheme pleases the eye and opens the mind. A Bohemian vibe. He replaced the closet door with a seventies-inspired hippie shawl. A local flea market find. The bed is colored earthy neutrals. Natural light cascades through diaphanous sheers installed on each window.

The room's decoration is piled on, Boy Scout sash displayed

on a boat cleat, cross-country trophy perched high atop his dresser. A baseball given to him by his grandfather.

He drops her on his bed. It's rough, maybe he shouldn't have done it. "I love you," he says.

He sits on the edge of the bed next to her. He flops back, putting one arm under his head. The storm has passed. It's followed by a wicked wind. The black walnut tree outside his bedroom window is licked and churned in the movement of air. The leaves make a slow-motion rushing sound. From above they look like paper dolls.

She rolls over on top of him. She sits up as she lets her hair down. She removes her bikini top from under the Penn State T-shirt and flings it across his room. He watches it arc. He smiles at the rebellious flight of it. She leans down and kisses him.

He is buried in her, her hair all around. He reaches up her shirt. He feels the warm skin of her back. He wishes he could feel her skin against his. She tumbles over, pulls him on top of her. She grinds her hips against him. She pulls into him. She imagines him inside her.

She stops. "The door." She hides her eyes in the crook of his neck. As if to become invisible. He holds her. She sighs. She feels a cataract of desire and guilt, parallel ridges of hunger and shame. He reverses off her, one arm crooked beneath his head. He winds his fingers in the hem of her shirt.

A savory aroma permeates the house. She comes back from wherever she just went.

"I want to taste your roast." She blinks back tears. She folds her arms into each other.

He holds her bikini top. "Any idea who belongs to this?"

She snatches it from him. She turns her back and slips her shirt off. Her naked back in his room. Her spine. Her bikini bottoms. She smiles to herself. Her eyes are wet. He echoes her. He remembers.

She slips her shirt back on. On the landing she steps into her skort.

The lid of the slow cooker is covered in condensation. He lifts it. A billow of steam escapes. The wind has subsided. Midday is overcast. The air is heavy. A great day to hunker down inside, with or without the moon, waning gibbous behind the cloud cover, 84% visible.

"Grab a spoon," he says. She tries two drawers. He holds the lid over a paper towel. He ladles up a spoonful of the au jus. He blows on it. "Here, try this…"

It's too hot. She waves a hand in front of her mouth. She nods. She lets the flavors sort themselves out on her palate. A wry smile spreads.

"Give me that." He snatches the spoon. He scoops a spoonful into his mouth. It burns his tongue. He's not about to let it show. The flavors are there, like the members of an orchestra tuning their instruments; there's no harmony yet. He checks off the tastes. What's missing? Black pepper, maybe?

"It needs more salt." She springs it on him with glee. He puts the spoon down. He sets the lid back in place. He grabs her. She repels. Brief shouts escape her.

"Could you two be less gross, please?" It's his brother, Sam. He sets his fingerless, crocheted bicycle gloves on the kitchen table. He goes to the fridge.

"You rode your bike in the rain? What an idiot…" Joseph snorts. Dani smacks him on his shoulder. He pours salt from the shaker in his hand. He adds a pinch and a half to the roast.

"At least I made money today, slacker. What'd you do?" He drinks orange juice straight out of the container.

Joseph and his girlfriend look at each other. She shrugs. "Not much," she says. "You know, hung out." Joseph nods, swallows, blinks.

Joseph's little brother gasps. He closes the top of the orange juice. "Your shirt is on inside out," he says to Dani. He glides into the living room. The television pops on. Dani and Joseph look at each other. They laugh. She brings her finger to her mouth: "Shh."

The roast cooks. She grabs the newspaper. An article in the Arts section. She reads:

600 million years ago, a great inland sea covered what is

now southwestern Pennsylvania. Over millions of years, a thin slice on the timeline, layer upon layer of sediment settled and hardened, forming cyclical beds of Pottsville sandstone, shale and limestone. The tectonic plate that is North and South America collided with the African plate 300 million years ago. Beds were smashed upward into long parallel ridges. The slow-motion grinding crash created the terrain consisting of ridges, plateaus, steep slopes and dramatic gorges.

A swift stream, named Bear Run, is fed by Appalachian springs. It drops 1,430 feet in four miles. From the western slopes of Laurel Hill ridge, to the Youghiogheny River, downstream to the Monongahela River. Water passing Bear Run winds its way to the Allegheny River, on to the Ohio River, down to the Mississippi River and right on out into the Gulf of Mexico.

He bustles over the counters. He moves dishes to the sink. She reads at the kitchen table. Her boyfriend cleans. Why is it such a turn-on? His mother taught him well.

"Joey, listen to this." Her voice is full. She reads out loud:

The softer limestone and shale erode. They are washed away. They leave behind sandstone. Ledges form. Water runs over. Breathtaking waterfalls and cascades form over centuries.

The most dramatic falls, near the stream's source, is the site where modern architecture gained worldwide acceptance. A photograph on the cover of LIFE Magazine in 1938. It featured Fallingwater, a house perched above a mountain cataract. Architect Frank Lloyd Wright's masterwork. Fallingwater became America's most famous house.

Without the LIFE Magazine cover, you might not know Wright's name. Before creating Fallingwater — at the age of sixty-seven — he was on the brink of losing his house and studio, Taliesin, in Wisconsin. The art world was ready to forget him — a backward-looking romanticist who did not stay true to anything, including his own rebellious ideas. With this one house, Wright reversed his fortunes.

He went on to create dozens of houses across the U.S. and

several buildings, including the iconic Guggenheim Museum in New York City. Today he is considered to be one of the premier architectural geniuses of his time. Maybe of all time.

The concept embodied by Fallingwater is revolutionary. Wright sought not to build a house in a place where man could admire natural beauty; his idea was to build a house that was natural beauty. His idea was to build an organic house that extends the landscape and — if possible — makes it more beautiful.

The concept was clear in his mind from the start. Wright had nine months between agreeing to do the project and presenting the plans to the client. He only needed two hours.

The day the client was to arrive, Wright finally sat down at the drafting table.

More than one witness has corroborated the story; they say it was a marvel to behold — the determination of a man who knows what the design is before a single pencil is sharpened. The master draftsman captured his concept in graphite, on vellum, in one magnificent try.

The design was bold. To realize Wright's vision, breakthroughs would be required. A house with no walls to obscure the falls. Windows that vanish into thin air. A staircase hovers over the swift Bear Run. A boulder that could not be moved? Make it into a fireplace. Beams sweep around an existing tree. They said it couldn't be done. They said the ground was too unstable to support it; Wright proved them wrong. In a muted palette, without a single element taken from a foreign source, earth tones abound.

Joey is over her shoulder. She gloats, "I picked the colors for your room."

"You might have suggested it." He gets back to cleaning. He would have to read that article later.

She flips to the crossword puzzle. It's a syndicated item, a *New York Times* crossword puzzle from a week earlier. Her favorite. She grabs a pencil from the junk drawer. That drawer's location she knows.

He scrubs the bacon pan. The way his backside twitches under his shorts...

He feels her eyes on him. He turns. She averts. She taps her chin with the pencil. She can't believe her eyes. Her mouth hangs. "What's a six-letter word for shirt fastener?"

He turns. "It does not say that."

"It does."

Joseph wipes his hands on a towel. He leans over his girlfriend's shoulder. She points the eraser at the clue for 9 down.

In unison, they say, "*Button.*" They laugh. She pencils it in. She uses the drafting lettering she learned in her favorite class. She thinks how a button is useless without a buttonhole. A buttonhole when the button is missing is left wanting.

I had a glorious day here by myself. It was nice. I didn't get all lost in the supermarket of life. I got out of circulation. I made noise on a tape. I hung a poem in my bathroom. I cooked. I worked all day long. I had grilled chicken from the place around the corner. I froze the bones for chicken stock. I went to the supermarket. I didn't get all lost.

Yesterday was Karina's half-birthday. That'll get me nowhere. If it was her Name Day, I could do something with that. I have no idea what to do with Karina but walk away and see what happens.

I should go to Barcelona alone. I should attend Tad and Sofia's wedding alone. I'm better like that. The whole date thing would suck unless I take someone I'm comfortable with. Karina's not it.

I should get a book on mushroom identification. Karina and I have been flirting with the idea of mushroom-hunting. It'd be nice: get out of Prague, spend some time together. Wait and see. What if she brings Phil?

Houby

It's the Czech word for mushrooms. In the Czech Republic, late summer/early autumn is the peak season for mushroom-hunting. Czechs head into the forest, basket in hand. It isn't just a hobby — it's a national passion that families celebrate together. Knowledge is passed on from generation to generation — which ones to avoid, which ones to eat, which ones to save, which ones to pickle, which ones to use in soup. Head to the woods and you'll see whole families involved in the search. You don't have to go far. You'll see them on the trains, baskets overflowing.

Common wisdom says a warm day after rain is a good day to look, whereas the day after a cold night is unlikely to yield much. On a day that is overcast, success can almost always be had.

Some claim that mushrooms grow with the waxing moon. A symbol of purity, youthfulness and enchantment. This theory is unproven. Nor is it true that mushrooms rise early. The morning is simply the best time to find them.

It is said that the first mushrooms to learn are the poisonous ones, such as the *Amanita* family. This family causes nearly 90% of all fatal mushroom poisonings. It contains many of the deadliest fungi on earth — the death cap (*Amanita phalloides*) and the destroying angel (*Amanita virosa*). On the other hand, the toadstool fly agaric (*Amanita muscaria*) is maybe the most iconic mushroom. With its brilliant crimson cap dotted with white spots, it's used on Christmas cards and in art as fairy dwellings.

Mushrooms are ingested orally. They can be dried or frozen. They can be made into a tea, or included in soups and salads. In order to protect public safety, the local police departments accept specimens to properly determine whether or not they are poisonous.

"Magic mushrooms" are the ones containing an hallucinogenic alkaloid called psilocybin. In the Czech Republic there are two variants found. Named for the two regions that make up the Czech Republic, they are *Psilocybe serbica* (also known as *bohemica*) and *Psilocybe moravica*. They have long slender cylindrical stems, typically light colored and round caps with dark gills. They can be found on the floors of deciduous forests or in grassy meadows on woody debris. They have a distinct sweet and spicy smell.

Psychedelic mushrooms have similar hallucinogenic effects to peyote or lysergic acid diethylamide (LSD), including changes in visual and auditory perception, changes in mood and behavior and changes in body temperature, appetite and sleep. Users report intensified feelings and sensory experiences — mixed senses, like the ability to hear colors or see sounds — and spiritual awakenings or connections. In extreme cases, dry mouth, excessive sweating and panic may result.

In the cases where poisonous mushrooms are ingested, initial symptoms — occurring within six to twenty-four hours after ingestion — include abdominal pain, nausea, vomiting, cramping and diarrhea. If the poisoning is bad enough, the person may collapse or stop breathing. If the poison gets to the liver or the kidneys, death can result within forty-eight hours.

Which one am I? The poisonous toadstool, waiting in the waxing moonlight to paralyze you? Or am I the wholesome one, the one with notes of wood and butter, the one that will take your potato soup to the next level? Wouldn't you like to know.

Reasoning, 7.9.98

The faucet's dripping. It's been dripping. For a long time. It drives me mad. Now it stops. That's worse. I didn't touch it. I could fix it. I should fix it. I will fix it. All I need is one of those screen things.

Water again. Hmm.

I have to get it fixed before Ilona stays here. She's coming tonight. That's the plan. She'll stay here tonight. She has an appointment for the procedure tomorrow. She'll stay for a couple of days after that until she's ready. We left it open-ended.

I'll clear out. I'll change the sheets and pillowcases, I'll wash the dishes and stock the house. We agreed that it would be best if we didn't see each other. I suggested it anyway. She didn't respond one way or another. It'll be cleaner this way, I figure.

I'll pack a bag and go stay with Naked Pete. No problem. I'll use his place as a crash pad only, no need to spend too much time there. I'll focus all my energy on work in the meantime.

I'll see Karina on Wednesday.

How do you let an obsession go? The thing to do is to replace it with another obsession. I don't want to be obsessed with anyone or anything. At all.

The fastest way to speed her arrival is to stop waiting for it. The fastest way is to occupy myself with other things. Let her go.

I can't chase Karina; it turns me into a ghost.

Brad and Agata are back together. To the detriment of both. The only thing worse than not being in a relationship is being in a relationship that doesn't work. I should appreciate what I have; instead I pine away. I'm completely free right now. Except for my little mess with Ilona. Big mess. I need to figure that out. I need to savor that.

Thinking, 8.9.98

I journal. Naked Pete's resort by the bay. Ha. Ilona was right — this place stinks.

The first thing I did when I got here was wash the dishes. It helped me to get my mind right.

I wasn't supposed to see Ilona, but I didn't get out of my flat fast enough. She caught me in the middle of changing the sheets. Right after I finished journaling yesterday, I found a hardware store. I managed to communicate to the shopkeeper that I needed a screen for the faucet. I replaced the screen and the gasket. No more leak. Time leaked away. I had to hustle if I was going to be out of the flat before Ilona arrived. I changed the pillowcases. I stripped the bed. She knocked. I felt it in my heart.

I opened the door. There she was. Book bag over one arm — I grabbed it from her — duffle bag over the other. She was wearing a black T-shirt and a pair of jeans. I invited her in. I set her book bag on a chair in the foyer. She proceeded into the kitchen. She sat down in a chair with the duffle slung over her arm. I took it from her and placed it on the bed. She followed me into the bedroom. With no chair to sit on, she crouched down on her haunches. She didn't say a word. I told her I was finishing up. I would be out of her hair straight away.

I looked at Ilona. I wondered, Had I appreciated her throat before? She has a long thin neck. I stole looks at her smooth forehead, glances at her suprasternal notch.

She saw my stack of papers on the floor. I meant to put them away. She leaned across. She picked them up. "Okay I read this while you are away?"

I nodded. I told her they were nothing, scribbling, loose thoughts. She smirked. I got the corners straight. I applied the fresh top sheet. I added back the duvet and fluffed the pillows. I held out my hand to help her up. She let me. I led her into the kitchen.

I showed her what I had laid in. All the stuff she'd asked for. She nodded, distracted. I was proud of my shopping. I was proud of my attention to detail — she was unimpressed. I guess she had bigger things on her mind. When I paused, she said one word. "Tea?"

I showed her the box of herbal tea I had procured. Exactly what she'd told me to get. She shook her head. She pointed at the tea kettle. She stepped around me and got two mismatched teacups from the cupboard.

I put the water on. My hands shook. I hoped she didn't want to talk too much. I didn't know if I could take it. She turned back to her book bag, dragging out heavy textbooks. One in English. Geology.

As we waited for the water to boil, I flipped absently through the geology textbook. I read a paragraph. I kept one eye on Ilona. She looked out the window at the television tower.

This was geology? It was deep. Huge. Sweeping. It was, I don't know, sensual. I thought it would be dry, technical. It read like poetry. Maybe it was my state of mind.

The water boiled. I got up and poured it into the two cups,

then dropped the tea bags in. I set the egg timer. I thought of my mom — she'd bought the egg timer when she visited. She'd said I needed to keep track of time. I brought the cups to the table. Ilona sat with her legs crossed Indian-style on the chair. Everything about her was physical. She was aware of her body. She sat on her haunches in the bedroom. The way she sits here, in the kitchen. The timer dinged. Ilona snapped out of her daze.

I wrapped the string of the tea bag around a spoon and back on the tea bag itself, squeezing the water out. I set the spoon on the table. I took a sip and burned my tongue.

Ilona shook her head.

I didn't want to tell her about my mother. I couldn't do that to her. Not today. I might tell her, maybe later. The only other option had been to tell her before; that chance was gone now. I couldn't tell her now what had happened to my mother. Before she and my father had been married. I couldn't tell her that my mother had probably considered it. This information might devastate Ilona right now. I decided to swallow it.

I couldn't take the silence. I babbled. I told her that Peter would visit her each day to see what she needed. I told her it would be fine, we would do whatever we needed to do. She took a sip of her tea. She set it down, looking at me. Her slanted brown eyes locked onto mine. "Come with me."

I knew what she meant. She didn't have to say more. This was a change in the plan. It wasn't what we had discussed. I held her gaze for as long as I could, then stared down at the table. I leaned forward onto my elbows. "Okay." What else could I say?

I wake up at Naked Pete's place. I get ready to go with Ilona.

That's why the kitchen sparkles this morning. I needed to keep my hands busy. I processed the information. I agreed to go with Ilona to do something I wasn't sure I could abide. I hadn't talked to anyone about this. Not my mother certainly, not Pat, not Markéta, no one. Not Naked Pete. Pete must have smelled my coffee the instant I wrote that in my journal. Or maybe he read my mind. He came in.

I took a break from journaling to talk to Peter. He was stunned by my frankness. I told him about my mother. I told him that I wasn't sure it was mine and at the same time, I didn't know if I could go through with it. Pete asked me, "What would Ingrid say?" I knew he was right. He encouraged me to support Ilona, whatever decision she made. "That's how it works, mate."

I wrap this up right here. I'm dressed now, I didn't shower but ran a cloth over my face. I'm about to head out the door, catch the tram and pick her up at my place. I have no idea what I'll say.

I have to love myself.

I haven't thought about Karina once this morning.

Dreaming, 9.9.98

When I got to Laubova, Ilona couldn't stop talking.

She had read my stories — all of them. Okay, this is where I have to admit that I've written a couple more.

"They are good. You must know." She told me that she can see what I'm doing. She told me that I'm working my way back. Is that what I'm doing? "You have to keep going." Ilona wore sweatpants and a T-shirt, a flannel shirt over top. My flannel shirt.

I reminded Ilona that I'm not a writer. I reminded her that the dream is dead. Should not have said it that way. Stupid. Insensitive. She didn't seem to notice.

"Not for anyone else. Write for yourself."

We were on the tram. Ilona sat in front of me. We sat in the singular seats at the back of the tram. I leaned forward, resting my chin on the handle behind her seat. Write them for myself. Of course.

"This girl, this woman, Daniella. Is she alive?"

I looked at Ilona. I nodded.

"Where is she?"

I shrugged. "Married, I think. Somewhere in America."

"Learn from what happened to you. The past is in the past." Ilona paused there, as if she'd heard herself. "We're going to be okay."

I should have been the one comforting her, not the other way around. I nodded, gave her a weak grin. The shocking realization was this: Ilona got better looking every time I saw her. Her eyes were tender — I used to think of them as sad. Her neck arched. Her smooth eyebrows. Just like me to fall in love after the fact. It was already too late.

Ilona got up. I followed her. We walked a couple of blocks. I knew to wear sweatpants and a T-shirt. I wore my running shoes. Ilona called them trainers.

We entered a building. It didn't feel like a hospital. I half expected there to be a crowd outside. If this was the States, people would be picketing. Ilona and I would be confronted with horrible pictures of procedures gone wrong. Placards saying awful things. If this was the States, Ilona and I would be accosted by shameless pro-life zealots. Zombie nuns. Little old men in windbreakers. Preachers in holier-than-thou collars. They'd shout horrible things at us from behind metal barriers, spittle collecting at the edges of their mouths. The filth, the bile. They think they can say anything. They think they're justified. Here? None of that. It was a peaceful Tuesday.

We sat outside a small window. We were the only ones. It felt more like a pharmacy than a hospital. Ilona continued, "The stories are not finished. You have pieces of dialogue, you have scenes, like the one at the falls, the one with the car, but something's missing. I don't know the words."

Ilona was right. I wracked my brain. I tried to remember.

Ilona smiled at me. "Figure out what's missing, finish each piece, see where it leads."

A nurse came out. I stood up, Ilona stood up. I leaned in to hug her — she stepped back. She squeezed my hand. I squeezed hers. She went through the door. The nurse closed it behind her. She smiled at me behind her surgical mask.

I opened up my backpack. I'd brought *Doctor Zhivago* and a bottle of water. I'd brought a notebook and my black leather pencil case. In case I had to take notes.

I tried to read my book, but my brain wouldn't focus. I read the same paragraph a third time. I looked up. In the chair where Ilona had just been sat Ingrid. She wore the blue pants, a cigarette in her mouth, about to light up.

"You can't do that here." Did I say it out loud?

"Hell, I can't. Who'll stop me?" She lit her cigarette, inhaled.

It glowed brighter.

"Fuckin' did it this time, didn't you, Joseph?" Ingrid sits back in her chair. She looked good, her round cheeks, her pale blue eyes.

I nodded, squinting.

"Didn't tell her about your mother... Recipe for some sleep-less nights, I reckon." Ingrid took a drag, exhaled.

It was strange to hear my voice. "I missed my chance. The teahouse was my opportunity, I suppose."

"The teahouse, you dimwit. Of course. A čajovna is a Czech woman's kryptonite — didn't you tell me that? A gem, that one. A real nugget. You're a bloody lady's man, aren't you now, Joseph?" Ingrid flicked her ash into space. The place didn't burn down.

I looked down at my hands. She softened, "Ah, yer grand. You showed up..."

There'd be no coming back from this. No reset button, no unringing the bell. I wondered if I'd ever be able to tell my mom. I told her everything. But this?

"'Tisn't about you. Your part was done ages ago. Now it's Ilona. Focus on her. When she's healthy and back in school, take the time to figure out what it means. Might help."

"Wait, Ingrid. What happened to you, was it... Did you..." I woke up. A sturdy Czech nurse sat next to me, where Ingrid — where I thought Ingrid — had sat. She smiled at me. *Doctor Zhivago* fell to the floor. She waited for my eyes to focus. She removed her mask. Her scrubs were rock-flour green.

"Dobrý den, pane." The nurse greeted me. She called me sir.

I asked if she speaks English.

"Bohužel." She tilted her head. The word for *unfortunately*. It's one of my favorites. She said it in a lilt.

I raised my finger to her. I dug in my backpack. Groggy from my little nap. My head swam. I handed her the notebook and the black rollerball pen.

She wrote. In Czech. She pantomimed the instructions. She put her hands together like a prayer. She put them alongside her face. She closed her eyes. Rest. Got it. She held up one finger. One day. She clenched her fist. She scrunched her face. Cramping. To be expected. Got it. I figured that Ilona would know all this. I paid attention just in case.

The next one was indelicate. This is a woman who dealt in indelicate stuff; she's not about to hold back. She touched her crotch. She flung her fingers. There may be some bleeding. Got it. The next one was either no sex, or no tampons — not sure which, clear on both. I had stocked the flat with plenty of maxi-pads. She wrote in her Czech script on the page. She drew two dots — one small, one about a centimeter (0.39 inches) in diam-eter. Beneath the dots she wrote the Czech word for red with an arrow to the Czech word for purple. She draws a box around the whole thing, dots and colors. Beneath that she writes, *sražen-iny*, which Ilona translates for me later as clots. Okay, got it.

At the top of the page she wrote her name and phone num-ber. If we had questions, we're supposed to call her. I nodded vigorously and in my best Prague accent, I say, Yes, of course, understood. The Czech nurse appreciated the attempt. She dis-appeared behind the door. I got *Doctor Zhivago* off the floor. I stowed the notebook and the pen. I stood. The door swung open.

Ilona was pale, stern. She didn't meet my eyes. I reached to grab her elbow. She pulled away. I held the door for her. I led her out of the waiting room.

I hailed a cab. Ilona would not climb up into a tram. Not on my watch.

Back at the Laubova flat, I guided her to the mustard-plaid couch. She stood. I grabbed pillows and the duvet from the bed-room. She curled up silently. I headed to the kitchen. I made her the herbal tea she likes. I set it on a stool by the sofa. Okay — that's it. I leaned in to kiss her on the forehead. I caught myself. Leave her be, I decided. I wrote her a note — I told her the time I left. Peter was supposed to check in on her at 6:00 p.m. I asked her to call Peter's flat if there were any issues. I paused for a second. I wondered if I should hang out until she wakes up. I asked Ingrid. She told me to go, she said I was grand. Ilona needs time to herself.

Asking, 10.9.98

In the rush to capture my adventure with Ilona in the journal,
I forgot to mention: I got a chance to talk with Peter. It was late
at night. I was reading my book. He'd been out drinking.

"Love what you've done to the place, mate." Naked Pete
wobbled on his feet.

I'd resolved not to drink that night. I put the book down on
the dusty sofa. I took two beers from the crate by the fridge. I
opened them, handing one to Pete. We clinked bottles.

"Were you there, the night Ingrid died?"

Peter's eyes bulged at me. I got him mid-swig. He coughed.
He let the bottle down. Tears came to his eyes.

"Should've been. Fuck. She might be alive."

"Wait — she came to Prague to get back her job at the Thirsty
Dog. But that night, she was meeting you, right?"

"She was. Spoke to her. I was going to meet her and some
other people up at Vyšehrad. I left the flat, missed the tram,
stopped to grab a beer. A few beers later, I caught the tram,
rode over there. It was dark. Damned dark. I walked up the
hill, I looked all over. I couldn't find them. I woke up the next
morning under a bush. Dragged myself home, slept it off. I was
pretty proud of myself. I hadn't lost my wallet or my keys."

Peter stopped. He took a long pull. Tears streamed.

"You wouldn't have been able to save her." I could see his
pain.

"Should've been there. I'm a proper cunt. I don't know how
to fix it." Peter wiped his face with his big fists.

I set my bottle down. I asked him how he ended up in Prague.

"Long sob story, mate. No need. Thanks for asking."

I took a big drink. I held the beer in my mouth. I let the car-
bonation fill my sinuses. I swallowed. The heady rush. "Try
me."

Pete sighed. He told me he woke up with a screaming headache in City of London Police station in Broadgate. "Said
goodbye to me ma and me da, took what I could carry and left
for good. I ain't never going back. Can't."

I asked why.

"Nothing for me there, mate." He studied to be a London cab

driver. It's a prestigious position, in London, to be a proper cab driver. Takes years of study. Years of practice.

I perked up. I'd read about it. "Been shown to change the size of a man's brain," I tell him, learning to be a London cab driver. That's what I'd read.

Pete was glad I knew about the Knowledge. Memorize over one hundred thousand landmarks, know the roads to get from any point to any other *and* be able to recite the route without hesitation. "I wanted me green badge," he said. "The brain didn't change none." He never learned it. Never got the chance — fucked it up before he could get a year behind him. Pete picked at the label on his bottle.

I asked. I was curious.

"Police record." Pete asked if I'd read that too. Can't have a police record and be a London cab driver.

Drunk and disorderly? "Hardly a felony, or whatever you call it in England."

"There was a fight." He told me he was charged with common assault.

Peter went on to tell me about the fight. He and his Knowledge friends had gone out after a day of studying the streets of London on scooters. At the bar, he ran into an old school friend who'd laughed when he heard Peter was working on the Knowledge. Little plug of a guy, dirty upper lip, a few stray curls at the back of his neck. Face like a teddy bear. He said he was surprised that anyone would think Peter was smart enough to try something like that. Peter invited the friend outside. For a chat. Peter took a couple of swings, didn't connect. The old friend got a hold of the back of his shirt. He pulled it up over his head. Beat him pretty badly. A hockey move. Peter had worn a rugby jersey that night.

"Never fight with your clothes on. It's a disadvantage, mate."

That's it. Naked Pete was not there when Ingrid died. One less chance. I couldn't let it go. I had to ask.

"I reckon we'll never know. That's not the Ingrid I knew. Don't fit my image of her." She did have her days, he pointed out. I nodded.

I finished my beer and took the bottle to the kitchen. When I came back, Peter had gone to bed. I put a flat sheet on the dusty old sofa and settled in myself.

Can I be okay with never knowing?

I got paid yesterday. They gave me 5000 CZK (172.41 USD). I spent the first 1000 CZK (34.48 USD) on razors, toilet paper, laundry soap, food, smokes, more food. Stick to food. Remember that I don't have any money. Go from there.

I have enough to pay last month's rent. I have about 4000 CZK (137.93 USD) after that. Oops. I have to come up with 8000 CZK (275.86 USD) in the next ten days. That's if I don't eat.

Karina's not going anywhere. Terminal Bar. Neutral territory. I don't get her full attention, but I get snatches.

I got new pens from Patrick's office. I meant to go buy some. I didn't have the opportunity. I'll buy *Illusions* for Karina today. Give it to her Friday or Saturday. Too bad it's not her Name Day.

I like to be near her. I don't speak Czech. Which reminds me. I should study...

I can't stop thinking about Ingrid.

I rollerblade alone. I swim alone. I'm alone right now. Get over it, my dear boy. It's not *that* difficult. On the contrary.

Deciding, 11.9.98

Where to start?

I'm back at my place. Ilona's staying with her sister, Božena (February 11), and exactly as I guessed, she's a beautiful woman. Let me go back to the start. Let me tell it.

Ilona had called Naked Pete's place. It was just past 7:00 p.m. the day after the procedure. Peter checked on her the first day. He failed to check on her after that. I picked up the phone.

"Joseph, I'm fine, but…" Ilona paused.

"Is the apartment on fire? Did you flood the place in tea?" I cracked jokes. Emotions must be in the vicinity. She wasn't going to laugh. She did what Rachel used to do. She did what Ingrid did. She rolled her eyes.

She said she wasn't lonely. "Joseph, can you?" Ilona's voice was thick. Had she been crying? Why didn't she call earlier? Ugh, Naked Pete. I'll ring his neck.

"I'll be right there."

The cobblestones were greasy. The sky pressed down. I wore a rain jacket with the hood up. I stopped to get a bottle of Bohemia Sekt. Bubbly wine. One glass, I told myself. She could say no. Be humble, I reminded myself. Ingrid nodded. In my mind.

My keys rattled in the lock. I figured she could hear me, might meet me at the door. I walked in. She wasn't in the foyer. Not in the bedroom, not in the living room. Or the kitchen. The door to the water closet was open. A Czech radio station played low on the stereo in the living room. Advertisements in Czech. I set the Bohemia Sekt on the floor. I stood. Blanka, where is she? The bathroom door was closed.

I knocked on the door. No answer. No movement inside. I opened the door and saw the blood, Ilona slumped on the floor. Her hand leaned on the small washing machine. Her feet dangled above the tub. Ilona, no!

I shrieked. I cried. I think I called for help. She was breathing. I was relieved. Let me tell it.

A gash on her head. Blood in her hair. I covered her torso with a towel. I remembered the indelicate nurse and checked for blood anywhere else. There was none. I wrapped her head in one of my new towels. I tried to wake her up, calling her name. I turned on the water in the sink. I splashed her face. She groaned.

She crinkled her eyebrows. Naked, the skin on her arms and legs — the skin on her belly — was damp. I hugged her to my body. I was able to get her upright. Her legs weren't there. With her face in the crook of my neck, she took one big breath in, pulled back, opened one eye. Then the other. Her legs straightened.

I breathed into the towel on her head, "We need to get you to the living room." I grabbed my robe off the hook and swung it around her. First one arm, then the other. She moved a foot. I held her close. She collapsed into me. Her eyes were not in focus. She tried to look at me. She didn't see anything. Her head fell back. I kept her legs moving. I guided her into the entryway, through the door, to the familiar parquet pattern. I carried her. She rested her towel-wrapped head on my shoulder. Was that a smile?

I set her on the mustard-plaid couch. She had moved the pillows and the duvet into my room. It meant she'd slept and read her books on my futon. That made me happy. I should call an ambulance. I should call her family. Her sister.

I grabbed a pillow and edged it under her poor cut head. I rushed to the kitchen and took down the tea tin. The slip of paper underneath it. I read the slip of paper. I walked back to Ilona, remembering her finger. I had to make a deliberate decision here. This decision would have consequences. Only for emergencies. Okay. Was this an emergency? I decided to check her head. Maybe sleeping wasn't the best thing for her right now.

"Ilona, you need to wake up. Talk to me. I need to check your head. Ilona?"

Sweetly, "Oh, Joseph." In Czech, she continued, "It's nice you came. My head hurts." She squinted at me. Reached her hand up. She uttered a universal ow.

"Let me take a look. I think you fell. You scared me." I moved around the side of the divan. Her hand reached up over her head. She found the side of my neck, my chin, my cheek. "I read your stories again, Joseph." In English, she continued, "They make me like you." Then in Czech, "My little poet." The word for poet is *básník*. She dragged out the long "a" sound. Like she was singing. She rubbed her thumb along my jaw.

I unwrapped the towel from her head. I said, "You really must have hit your head. You're being nice." Her hand retracted from my face. She smacked me a good one. She pointed her bony finger at me, then rested her palm on my cheek again. Tender, then firm, then tender. She'd have me trained in no time. Like a lapdog.

The spot on the towel was light red. A good sign. To keep her with me, I described what I was doing. "Your hair is wet. You weren't down long. Maybe you fell as I was coming up the stairs?"

"I smelled like cabbage. Is that the word?" She wanted to

clean up, she told me. "You were quick."

She was responsive. She remembered. Good signs. "Let's just get a look at this nasty cut on your beautiful head." I parted her hair. Her long hair. I remembered the day. After her shift at the Thirsty Dog. How it fell down her shoulders. Onto her tight white T-shirt. I isolated the cut, I felt around it with my delicate fingers. Minimal swelling. She wasn't pulling away.

In Czech, "No, Sir Doctor." Or was it Mister Doctor? Didn't matter.

The cut was a straight line. Less than a couple of centimeters. It looked worse than it was. All the blood. "I'll clean you up, stay here, don't sleep. I'll just be a minute." Ilona pulled her hand away from my cheek. I had forgotten it was there.

I got a bowl of hot water, the first-aid kit, a clean towel, a clean washcloth. I set it by the sofa. I had a decision to make. Screw it, I need to call her sister. If I was her sister, I'd want to know.

I sat on the floor in the living room. Ilona adjusted herself on the sofa. She smiled at me. The sound of the ringer was like the sound of the telephone in the Pink Floyd movie. After the third two-ring ring, "Ano?"

A female voice. All my Czech escaped me. I asked, "Božena?"

My Czech returned. I introduce myself. A friend of Ilona. Did I detect a smile? The way she said in Czech, "Yes?" The Czech phrasebook in my lap was almost helpful for the first time. I read from the script, "We've had an accident." In a jumble of Czech and English, I said, "She's okay. A small cut. On her head. No ambulance needed." I wanted her to know.

Božena did not hesitate. "Kde jsi? Adresa?" I told her the address. "Moment. Budu tam." She told me she's coming. I hung up the phone.

I dipped a corner of the washcloth in the bowl of hot water. I dabbed at the blood in her hair. The gray washcloth turned pink and brown. "Tell me if I'm hurting you." The part in her hair revealed her scalp. So pale. The sight of it made me feel vulnerable. A flash of an image through my brain. The fontanel of an infant crowning. I quelled a flood of emotion.

"You are gentle when you want to be." Ilona told me her sister's English was good. She told me not to be fooled. She told me to speak English to her. "You can tell her. Everything." Ilona said she's close. She'd thought about telling her before. Ilona blinked.

I continued to clean her up. Most of the blood was out of her hair. I tore open the alcohol wipe from the first-aid kit. I had a square of gauze. "This might sting."

Ilona braced herself. That same stern face from the clinic. I dabbed the alcohol wipe along the part in her hair, the length of the cut. She sucked air through her teeth. Her body stiffened underneath my robe. The cut wasn't deep, thank goodness. The ibuprofen I was about to give her would help with the swelling.

"What would Ingrid say if she could see us now?" I covered the cut with the gauze square. I applied firm pressure. Ilona smiled.

"Božena will be here soon. She lives near Florenc." One metro stop away? Why hadn't Ilona told me? What else didn't I know?

I want to write more but I have to get to work. Tomorrow's Saturday. I can take my time. I can finish the story.

Puzzling, 12.9.98

Let me finish the story about Ilona and Božena. Where was I? Oh yeah, the sister was on her way over and I was cleaning the wound. Funny, it reminds me of Dani, the day at the county park. We took a first-aid class together. Might have to write that story.

I wrapped Ilona's head in a clean towel. It held the gauze in place. I got her a glass of water and two of the Czech ibuprofen, the bright orange ones. She gave me that sad smile. That's how I knew she would be okay. Her spark was back. I let her rest. I waited for her sister to arrive. I put the Bohemia Sekt in the fridge, Blanka's fridge. I put the tea kettle on. I made myself a note to come back to the first-aid story. The tea kettle whistled. Ilona fell asleep. There was a knock on the door.

Božena stood in the doorway, looking me up and down. Jeans and T-shirt, not expecting company. I walked around the flat in my bare feet. Hippie Blanka would approve. I adjusted the tortoiseshell glasses on my nose. The look on Božena's face was skeptical. Worried. I remembered what Ilona had told me. I said, "Come in, Ilona's resting." I told her I wanted her to see the cut on her head. I wanted her to tell me if we should call the ambulance. I said it all in English.

She responded with a vague smile. In Czech, "Where is she?"

I responded in English. I waited for her to make the change. It's funny: when you want a Czech person to speak Czech with you, when you try your best, they respond in English just to spite you. When you speak English to them, their natural response is to respond in rapid-fire Czech. Just to spite you. It's probably not spite. It feels like spite. I continued on with her, bold with the knowledge that Ilona had shared with me. Unless the joke was on me. It could've turned out that way. I wouldn't have put it past her.

"She's on the couch." I waved Božena into the flat. I touched the plaque with Blanka's name on it, sending a prayer to her. I closed the door. Once inside, she paused, her arm crooked in her handbag.

She was pretty, lighter hair than Ilona's, thicker in the body than Ilona, but firm. Shapely. If I had to guess, her job would be practical. Technical. Nurse? Paralegal? I led her across the hall to the doorway looking onto the living room. She held her ground. She stood near the row of hooks. My jacket, my hoodie. My rain jacket drips. Božena scanned the place, trying to figure me out. At the doorway to the living room, I waved her in. She kicked off her shoes and lined them up next to Ilona's. Mine were splayed on top of each other. She hooked her bag on a hook and socked over, standing behind me on her tiptoes. She looked over my shoulder. I was a human shield. Ilona snored. She had a frown on her face. Božena gasped.

In Czech, she whispered to me, "Is she okay?"

I turned my chin to her and nodded, once, twice, three times. Is she okay? Am I okay? Are we going to be okay? I remembered the tram, what Ilona had said to me.

Božena turned, noticing that we were in front of the kitchen doorway. She tapped me on the shoulder and tilted her head toward the kitchen. I followed her in.

The kettle was hot. In English I said, "Would you like some tea?" Božena stood next to a chair at the table. I grabbed two cups from the cupboard. "Please, sit."

She folded one leg under her bottom. In Czech she said, "Don't you have something stronger?"

I slipped. I answered in Czech, "Of course, I have." I opened a cabinet door, then shook my head. In English: "Red wine? Beer? Bohemia Sekt? Maybe a plum brandy?"

Božena smiled. In English: "Slivovice. You are good Czech man."

"No. I am American," I responded too quickly. She knew I was American. She lobbed me a compliment; I wasn't gracious enough to accept it. She waved it off, picking up one of the mugs and holding it out to me. In Czech: "Let's talk." Would I have the nerve to tell her?

I poured her a plum brandy. I placed the bottle on the table between us. I made myself one of Ilona's herbal teas. Božena reached across, splashing plum brandy into my cup. I smiled and nodded at her. In English she said, "Be good Czech man, Yoselle."

She held out her cup. We clicked. I met her eyes. She approved and took a sip. I showed her I am trainable. I can be her golem.

She set her cup down, fingering the rim. In Czech, she spoke slowly, "She fell in the bath, yes?"

I was stunned. How could she know that? I squinted in disbelief. Was this female intuition, Czech female intuition, or straight clairvoyance? I did my little trick with the string and spoon, setting the tea bag aside on a saucer. I took a sip. She continued in English, "She didn't say you about the *aneurysma*? There is reason she didn't speak you about that."

My head started to swim. It was a drop of slivovice. I really am a lightweight.

I dove in head first. "There's something I need to tell you. Ilona and I, we... Wait, no. She, Ilona, she had a procedure." I stopped there and looked in Božena's eyes. The final piece of the puzzle clicked in. Božena almost smiled. Then sadness poured in. It was quick, like a cloudburst. It flooded in and was gone. She took a good mouthful of plum brandy, swallowed. In

Czech, she said, "Of course. She didn't tell me about the procedure. She didn't tell you about the aneurysm. Did you pay?"

Božena tipped more into her cup. She cocked her head at me and waited.

In English, "It didn't seem strange to you that you didn't have to pay?"

I frowned.

Božena poured again into my cup. "She tricked us. While she sleeps… She's a crafty one. Always has been." The word for crafty I would have to look up later. I smiled and smiled when I got it translated. But wait, I still didn't know how the two are related.

Božena flicked her chin at me. She saw my confusion. I was a little bit disappointed in myself. In my lack of curiosity. I took a drink. It was like I was tasting truth for the first time. She continued in a combination of Czech and English. She was excited to explain it to me. She half whispered, leaning in, "Maybe you are thinking that you could have had it. You couldn't. She couldn't. It would have killed her. The first time she collapsed in the bath, she was eleven or twelve. Same thing, cut on her head. When she saw her lying there, our mother screamed. I can still hear that scream." Hospital, stitches. The emergency room doctor told their mother she needed to see a neurologist. She was scared, their poor mother. But she did as he asked. Tests, more tests, weeks go by. Božena splashed more brandy into her cup. "Until, boom, it happened again." Back to the emergency room, back to the neurologist. They did a CT scan. They did a spinal tap. The doctor told them it was an aneurysm. It was inoperable. Their mother cried and cried when she heard. Božena took a drink. "Ilona soothed my mother, she must have been twelve or thirteen." The neurologist told them Ilona would never...

Božena paused there. She stood, releasing her leg from underneath her. She sat back in her seat. I took it in. All this stuff about my mother, it never mattered. For Ilona, this was life or death. Her decision wasn't a decision at all. It was self-preservation.

Things switched to claymation. Božena finished her drink. She used the toilet. She washed her hands in the kitchen sink.

She asked me to show her Ilona's wound.

I gently woke Ilona, who she sat up. She smiled. She spoke Czech with her sister. It was too fast for me. It was between sisters. It was none of my business. It was probably half about me anyway. Best not to know. I unwrapped the towel and lifted the gauze.

Božena was dismissive. "Yoselle, this is nothing. You should have seen her that first time. It was nine or eleven stitches." Ilona interjected, "Eleven."

Božena continued in English, "Tak, eleven stitches. Blood everywhere. I thought she was dead." Switching to Czech, "Do you remember Mom's scream? Of course you don't. I do. Jesus and Mary." Ilona smacked me on the leg. She pointed her bony finger at me. Božena prattled on. The look in Ilona's upturned eyes.

Božena, was she the oldest sister? I don't know. Information in this situation seeped and oozed. She was acting like an oldest sister; let's go with that. Božena took over. "Yoselle, call us a cab, then pour me another drink. One for the road." Was that her American accent, there? Nasal, pinched. Is that how she thought I sounded? In Czech, without missing a beat, "Get dressed, young lady. Gather your things. You're coming to stay with me." She thought I didn't catch this next part, but I did. Božena spoke rapidly out of the side of her mouth, "Although if it were me, I would stay here. This boy smells good, I got a whiff of his jacket in the hallway. I almost collapsed myself… You know, the husband, he smells like feet. These Americans, maybe they are on to something with all the stinking soaps and deodorants and colognes."

I did as I was told. I called AAA. I ordered a cab. I poured plum brandy. Ilona packed her clothes and her books. We clinked cups. Božena winked at me. Did she wink at me? It's fuzzy. Ilona came into the kitchen dressed, her hair pulled into a tight ponytail. No bandage needed. I stooped to gather her things. I handed her duffle bag to her and her book bag to Božena. It landed on her shoulder. She said, "Oof." I didn't kiss or hug either of them. I will hug each of them next time.

Finishing, 14.9.98

I think maybe, like in the end of *The Tin Drum*, you talk about the horrible things with lightness and grace. The author describes the scene, wallows in the details rather than the big picture; he takes us there. Then it dawns on you, the reader. All the details tie back to the big picture. That's the magic. I need to think about that as I finish these pieces. Finish them for myself, Ilona said. Wise for a young woman. The nostalgia floods in. I don't have a tin drum to drum on; where's my magic come from?

My heart tells me to try it one more time. My head tells me to forget it; if it happens, it happens. My heart responds, Yeah, but what if it doesn't? My head replies, Well what do you think? Oh, I forgot, you're the heart, you don't think. I have to do all the thinking for the both of us, don't I? My heart says, Oh, yeah, heh, I get it.

Brad and I watched *The English Patient* yesterday. Agata is back visiting her parents. I didn't know the story was based on a novel by Michael Ondaatje. You know I can relate to an unfulfilled promise... Count Almásy's a Fire sign (Aries, perhaps Leo), Katharine Clifton's Water (Pisces). Who says it can't work? Who says it has to end in tragedy? Who made up this notion of star-crossed lovers, destroying each other (and themselves) for love? I don't care if Shakespeare himself proposed the impossibility of it, I don't buy it.

Think about it: water can douse the fire, especially the spark, but it doesn't have to be that way. The water could get excited by the fire, like boiling water, like steam. The steam engine, in fact. We can be an engine.

That's more like a cooking fire, that's more like a long, controlled simmer, more like Sagittarius. More like my brother, Sam. The spark would have to be pretty powerful to boil water. Pisces is the fixed modality; it means she can really dig in. Oh boy. It's not gonna be easy to get her to boil over.

Complaining, 18.9.98

This nothingness. It could be endless. Life's going to be gobs and gobs more of this.

I'm cold at night. I want that fixed. I want a girl in my bed. Maybe not right away.

What am I complaining about?

My mother called last night. She wanted to know how to give me money. I gave her my account number. I gave her the routing number. She's paying me back. I'm stunned. I tried to figure out — the entire conversation — how I was going to tell her about Ilona. I couldn't do it. She could tell. I was distant. I heard the concern in her voice. I reassured her. I was okay, I loved her. I told her I appreciated the money. I told her that I would use it to go to Barcelona. She told me to say hi to the Williamses for her.

With help from my various employers, I might make it. I'd like to go to Barcelona with enough cash and enough time to enjoy. Maybe not party as hard as everyone else because I'm broke, but whatever, be there and then come back and enjoy the hell out of the following week with Dudley and Benny here in Prague.

Tomáš Garrigue Masaryk

The librarian with the pretty smile was there. Maybe that's why I decided to ask, just to have a chance to speak with her. That's not it. It was Šárka's fault. I set aside *Dr. Zhivago*. I went in search of history, in search of truth. I went for a biography.

I started in Czech. She replied in English. She said something like, No, of course, you can borrow. She asked me for my passport.

I started with TGM. Tomáš Garrigue Masaryk was the original philosopher-president, who founded Czechoslovakia in 1918 and served as its first president.

For the decade leading up to the founding of his native-born land, Masaryk bounced around Europe, stirring up support for his country's independence. He sought backing from foreign governments, expatriate Czechs and Slovaks. In 1917, he traveled to a dangerously unstable Russia to recruit POWs in Russian camps. With them he formed the first Czechoslovak

Army.

Prior to 1918, the regions of Bohemia and Moravia were known as the Czech lands, a part of the Austro-Hungarian Empire. When the Austro-Hungarian Empire collapsed at the close of World War I, an opportunity presented itself.

Masaryk was born March 7, 1850, near Göding in Moravia, a predominantly Catholic part of the Austro-Hungarian monarchy now known as Hodonín, Czech Republic. He died September 14, 1937, in Lány, Czechoslovakia, at the age of eighty-seven. He'd retired from political life two years before. By grace, Masaryk was never to see the Munich Agreement or the invasion of the Nazis.

His father, Josef, was a Slovak employed by the imperial estate as a coachman. He hailed from nearby Kopčany, which was then part of Hungary. Masaryk's mother was a maid and cook in a Germanized Moravian family. As a young man, Masaryk trained to be a teacher and briefly apprenticed as a locksmith before joining the German Hochschule in Brno in 1865, at the age of fifteen. He obtained his doctorate in philosophy at the University of Vienna in 1876. For one year, he studied in Leipzig, where he would meet a Brooklyn-born pianist, Charlotte Garrigue. Proving to be a match for him intellectually as well as romantically, her influence on his beliefs is evident. Among the books they studied together was John Stuart Mill's *The Subjection of Women*, which Masaryk later translated into Czech. He married Charlotte in 1878 and together they had five children. They lived in Vienna until 1881, when they moved to Prague and Masaryk took up his post as professor of philosophy at the University of Prague. After the wedding, Masaryk added her maiden name to his name; he is often referred to as T.G. Masaryk, or TGM. Beneath his statue just outside the gate of the Prague Castle, the three letters are emblazoned.

He was a neo-Kantian, influenced by English Puritan ethics and the austere teachings of the Hussites. For their part, the most radical of the Hussites believed in the Bible as the sole canon for Christianity. They favored stripping away anything that had no basis in the Bible, including superfluous holidays, the veneration of saints, the sacraments of Confirmation and the

Anointing of the Sick, among others.

Masaryk developed a critical standpoint on the self-contradictions of capitalism. One of his first major works was on the epidemic of suicide in modern civilization. Later, he risked being judged as unpatriotic, as he unmasked two medieval patriotic Czech epic poems as forgeries by a nineteenth-century Czech poet. Similarly in 1899, he opened himself up to public criticism. He took on the systemic anti-Semitism he perceived in the press. He proved two Jewish men were innocent of involvement in a "blood libel" ritual murder case, known as the Hilsner affair, a series of anti-Semitic trials.

I had to look it up. A blood libel is an anti-Semitic canard that claimed that young Christian children were being sacrificed for their blood by Jewish people. Conspiracy theories are nothing new.

The stress on Masaryk and his family during this time took its toll. He was accused of splitting the national cause. In response to his spirited defense of Hilsner, some claimed he was more in love with the cause of the Jewish nation than the cause of the Czechoslovakian nation. He was denied publication. He and his family were isolated. They were threatened in letters. They were publicly abused on the streets.

Neo-Kantianism was the dominant philosophical movement in Europe from the 1870s through the First World War. The movement had the express intention of a return to the philosophical tenets of Kant: doctrines of intuition, perception, subjectivity and transcendental philosophy, as well as accounts of the philosophy of science, ethics and religion defended by various leading figures.

To get a flavor of the neo-Kantians, I looked up Kant. Kant believed that the rightness or wrongness of an act could not be judged by the goodness or the badness of the outcome. In other words, moral worth only comes when you do what needs to be done because you know it is your duty, regardless of whether you want to do it or not.

In 1918, Masaryk traveled to the United States to meet with President Woodrow Wilson. He made his case for an independent and democratic nation to be carved out of the crumbling

Austro-Hungarian Empire, one that would constitute a federation of the Czech lands and Slovakia. At the time, Masaryk held a visiting professorship at the University of Chicago. It was in Chicago on May 5, 1918, mere months before he would be elected the first president of his new country. Some one hundred and fifty thousand Americans — representing the largest concentration of Czech and Slovaks in America — turned out in the streets to hear him speak.

At Masaryk's behest, Czechoslovakia was recognized as an Allied power on June 3, 1918. Its borders were demarcated as Masaryk had outlined. On October 18 of that year, U.S. President Woodrow Wilson signed the Washington Declaration, which became the founding charter of Czechoslovakia. Independence Day came soon after, on October 28. On November 14, 1918, Masaryk was elected president. He was re-elected in 1920, 1927 and 1934.

Although she was an active participant in political life, Charlotte Masaryk remained behind the scenes for most of her life. A lifelong advocate for women's rights, she decided against joining her husband's Realist Party and instead joined the Social Democratic Party in 1906, mostly for its feminist platform. She saw to it that her daughter Alice was among the first Prague girls to be admitted to university; Alice later became an internationally renowned sociologist. Charlotte consistently reminded her husband of the criticality of including women in all aspects of the ongoing national revival. When Tomáš was forced to flee the country at the onset of World War I — in the company of his daughter Olga — Charlotte steadfastly refused to know his whereabouts or the whereabouts of his writings, for fear that the Austrian Police would get the information out of her during an interrogation. Her daughter Alice was interrogated for two weeks and held under arrest for another eight months in a Viennese prison. By 1918, Charlotte could no longer enjoy Tomáš's political victories. Four years of war, the loss of her son Herbert, a post-impressionist painter, to typhus in 1915 and the conscription of her son Jan into the Austrian Army led to a deep depression and a heart condition that proved to be too much for Charlotte. She died in seclusion in 1923.

A marriage between a Czech and American? Was this a sign? Does Karina know about this? I wonder. How did I not know this until now? What else don't I know?

Fading, 20.9.98

After-party. It was in somebody's loft apartment. One group — including the flat occupant — was in the kitchen. It was too bright there. In the living area, another group of six people. Here the walls were all white and the lights were dimmed. Heavy drapes against the wan daylight. Awkward posts chopped up the space. It was painted white. Under the slope of the roof there was a low couch and coffee table. I sat in an armchair at one end. Ester (December 19) sat on the arm of the chair next to me, too close. I knew Ester, I'd danced with her. We'd not spoken more than a few words. Her tight plaid pants bulged full of thigh right next to my ear. I dared not look. I could smell my own sweat. I endeavored to keep my arms at my sides. I was there with Agata and Brad, I rode over from the club in Brad's car. Ashtrays, cups of wine, glasses of water, bottles of beer, a *THINK* magazine and a week-old *Prague Post* on the coffee table. Flecks of ash stuck between the glass and the wooden recess in which it rested.

Brad introduced me.

I stood up, a little formal. I shook the hand of Gracie, who gave me a shy smile. Her eyes darted away. She knelt at the coffee table, in front of where Jacques sat. Jacques stood up from the couch. He held my hand, looking into my eyes. I met his gaze. I was ready to be offended.

"Patrick, the nuclear physicist guy? That Patrick?"

"Yep." I waited for the judgment to enter his face. He looked like a musician, wallet on a chain, rings on every finger; Jacques was clearly not a nine-to-five type person. In a dimly lit room, he wouldn't look out of place with sunglasses, a top hat and big bushy hair down to his bony shoulders. Gracie is tan with sandy brown hair, young, athletic-looking. She has no accent, which means she has a New York accent, which means she could be from anywhere. I'd have to wait to decide. She's not short and she's not tall. Pretty eyes, but I couldn't tell you the color. I was afraid I might fall right in.

Brad prompted from his corner of the couch, "You work together, right?"

I told them we'd met at school, become friends. We'd stayed in touch after school. When I first came to Prague in 1993 to visit, it was Pat who'd invited me. When I came back in 1997, he gave me a few odd jobs to do. "Human reliability, sensor visualizations, boring stuff."

"Boring? Human reliability sounds interesting to me." Jacques. Of course, that was Jacques.

Agata lit a cigarette, inhaled, held the smoke in. She spoke in a strained voice, "Joseph is *básník*, poet. Isn't that right, Joseph?" Agata the agitator. She exhaled smoke in my direction.

I wouldn't go that far. "I've written bad poetry in the past. Haven't we all?" I tried to deflect. I blinked at Agata. Gracie stole a glimpse of my profile.

Brad said Jacques's a painter. He said Gracie's the literate one. Brad stabbed out his cigarette and sat back, draping his arm over Agata's narrow shoulders. "Never written a poem. Bad or otherwise."

Agata leaned back into Brad's arm. She looked at him, "Můj malý filmaři, ano?" Agata's voice's husky and accented. The willowy body, the long fingers, her smooth face, her clear eyes. I understood her to say something about Brad being a film-maker. The ponytail was the tell. She held her cigarette away and kissed him. I felt a twist in my chest. The meat of her lip at the corner of her mouth glistened. That little white connecting place, what do we call that?

I cleared my throat to hide the desperation on my face. I looked at Jacques. I asked what he painted.

"Humans being unreliable." Jacques stuck a cigarette on his ear. He leered at Gracie. He smiled at me and she rolled her eyes.

"Jacques's talented. He's not funny." She patted Jacques's black jeans on his knee, sending him a fake smile. She turned back to me. "Let's hear more about this bad poetry." She put her head on her hand. Her elbow tipped the ashtray. Jacques stabilized it.

I smiled at the challenge. "Do you write?"

Gracie accepted the parry. She told me her older sister writes. She'd had a couple pieces picked up in *Optimism* here and a few lit mags in the States. "I waste my time on men, alcohol, techno and other empty pursuits."

A writer and a painter. "We should be friends." I wondered if we could be. I didn't know many writers or painters. Jacques nodded, smiled.

I met Gracie's gaze. There was something there. Something was missing too. Her pupils were large, the black bullying the brown. What a strange look she gave me, her chin in her hand.

Jacques spoke, "Wouldn't it be amazing if we could predict when a human would be unreliable?" Jacques jostled Gracie's ribs with his knee. She absorbed it. Her gaze fell to the floor.

I responded too fast; could they hear it? "That's kind of the point." I told them I got to meet with the guy who wrote the textbook on human reliability. Within minutes, I had the answer. "Tell you the whole story over a beer," I said. I figured it would go nowhere. Like most early morning conversations after dancing all night. Fade to black. We'll not see each other again.

The Judith Bridge

This whole saga started with me crossing the Charles Bridge, an old stone bridge built in the fourteenth century. What existed before that?

The first bridge, made of wood, seems to have been built in the tenth century. It was destroyed in 1157. How does a bridge get destroyed? By a flood, of course.

King Vratislav II built the first stone bridge spanning the

Vltava from 1160 to 1172. His queen had urged him to build it. He gave it her name, Judith. The Judith Bridge was 514 meters (nearly 1,700 feet) long, 7 meters (23 feet) wide at its waist. It consisted of twenty-seven low arches. The upkeep and the maintenance of the bridge were taken over by the Knights of the Cross in 1253.

In 1342, two-thirds of the Judith Bridge was wiped out by a flood. The king at that time, Charles the IV, was forced to build the Charles Bridge in its place.

On the Old Town side of the bridge, facing the tower, off to the right behind the statue of King Charles the IV is a staircase. It leads down to where the boat tours arrive and depart. Down here you will find some remnants of the Judith Bridge. A stone visage of a bearded man with an open mouth. This is said to be the face of the builder of the Judith Bridge. Rather than being decorative or symbolic, it gauges the depth of the river. To this day, the pillars of the Judith Bridge remain at the bottom of the river, some of it built into the foundations of buildings on both sides. The Malá Strana tower belonged to the Judith Bridge before it was built into the Charles Bridge.

The Monastery of the Knights of the Cross with a Red Star, the only order of Czech origin, was originally built in 1233 and became instituted as an independent order just four years later. The monastery served as a hospice. It housed the keepers of the bridge. The knights collected tolls and duties. They protected the bridge. The buttress of the monastery contains the last remaining arch of the Judith Bridge, preserved beneath what is now the Charles Bridge.

I am a keeper of the bridge. The bridge keeps me. My former arches are preserved in my foundation.

Flood, 21.9.98

There were five people in the room. I was alone with my thoughts. This is yesterday. Sunday evening. Ponytail Brad's flat is less than a city block from my place. I haven't been home since Friday morning.

The air was hazy. Either that or there was a film over my eyes. Possibly both.

I sat on a low gray accent chair in front of Brad's television. It has high sides. I felt like I was submerged.

Relax. Watch the movie. It was like being on a plane; they show the movie to take our minds off crashing. We'd watched movies the whole weekend. The sun had set. I'd worry about the things I need to worry about when the time came for me to worry about them. Our weekend was shedding altitude. The seatbelt sign was on.

I got up and shook Jacques's bony hand. Gracie bounced up. She gave me a hug bigger than she is. I shook Brad's hand, staring at the strand of gray above his ear. Agata stood in front of me. She pecked me on the lips. Ester looked in my eyes. Her copper hair was asymmetrical. In typical Ester fashion, she said something Czech. She said, "It's like stroking a snake with bare feet." It'd make sense to me later.

On Brad's street there was one streetlamp. One that worked. I limped home. The cobblestones were uneven. The trees rushed and swayed in the wind. Spindles of light and dark swam over me. I crossed Ondříčkova. It was empty. Prague, this beautiful old city, its magic at rest. On duty over Žižkov, the television tower — matte silver and white like a rocket — pretended he wasn't watching me cross. On the far side of the boulevard, a Do Not Enter sign caught my eye.

My eyes, my head, my tongue. I wanted to rest. Pick up where I left off Friday morning. I keyed the locks. My fear was tangible; the keys, locks, a door that might not open. I tasted metal in my mouth. It tasted like blood. The door opened.

The entryway light broke the day after I moved in. I'd fix it if I had ten minutes to figure out how to fix it. I kicked my shoes off in the dark, the linoleum gritty under my feet. I knew the purple-gray dust gathered in corners. I didn't sweep enough.

My sock was wet. There was a puddle on the floor. In the foyer.

Hold it. Let me rewind a couple of days. The nights gave way to a chill. Summer was coming to an end. I haven't had to use the hot water heater for anything except showers and dishes. I liked to sleep in a chill — sleeping in heat suffocates me; I'd wake up drenched. I'd feel like I could drown in swirls of blankets. The chill developed into cold. On Thursday night, before the present of this story, I attempted to heat the flat.

The landlord — his name's Horáček — he showed me. In a blur. The day he handed over the keys. A couple months ago. It was hot outside, I didn't need the heaters to be on. He led me from radiator to radiator, bedroom, living room, kitchen. He showed me the numbers on the dials. He showed me switches that turn on or off. His rudimentary English echoed in the empty flat. He waved me into the bathroom. He pointed to a new water heater hung on the wall. It's the size of a briefcase. It has a pilot light, he showed me, and knobs: one for heat and one for flow. His plumber friend installed it. Horáček tried in English; I listened. I nodded. He pointed in through a cut-out on the face of the unit. I took a look. I didn't see anything. I nodded. He continued. I understood nothing.

Last Thursday night, Friday morning: dark, quiet, cold. I reached for the switch on the radiator. It was located at the head of my futon on the floor. I switched it on. I turned the knob to 7. I listened. A couple of drunks passed on the street below my window. I recalled what Horáček showed me. He flipped the switch. He turned the knob to 7. He held a hand to his ear. The water heater across the hall kicked on. I got to my feet. I tried the radiator in the living room. Flip, twist. I listened. Church bells rang somewhere. Chimed again. From across the hall, I heard nothing.

I went to the water closet. In bare feet. I sat to pee. The gray tiles in the little room were ice cold. I lifted my feet. The problem had to be with the water heater.

I looked into the black tube. I didn't see anything. I stood on one foot. The other foot throbbed. I stubbed my tired cold toe in the dark.

Pilot light was out. I heard a faint hiss. Damn it. Thick
wooden threshold — my pinkie toe curled up in defense. On
the heat knob, embossed in white plastic, was a flame. I twisted
the knob the way it didn't want to go. Nothing. I twisted the
knob the way it goes easily; the hissing got louder. I twisted it
back. I was desperate. I pressed the ignition with my thumb.
It clicked, thick-thick-thick-thick. I let go. A blue flame with
an internal halo, an inner aura, lighter blue, appeared. I turned
the heat knob slowly. Blue flames rumbled from within. A hot
bellow warmed my face. The flow knob was marked on the
periphery: a waxing triangle in one direction, a waning triangle
in the other. I twisted.

The scale on the heat knob, like the knobs on the radiators,
went up to 7, a sacred number. I like 7, but I prefer 3 — 3 is
magic. I turned it to 5 and leave it. The blue grid of flame stabilized. If the heat's high and the flow's low, my water would
be scalding. If the heat's low and the flow's high, the water
would come out cold. To feed the various heaters, in addition to
the faucets, I concluded, medium heat and above-average flow.
Whew.

I returned to the futon. I flipped the switch on the radiator. I
turned the knob to 7. Nothing happened. I put my face in the
pillow. My arm reached. I fell asleep.

Friday night we rented a pile of movies. We spun. We watched
movies into the morning. We talked. Brad and Agata on the
couch. Jacques straddled Gracie on a chair that makes a pair
with mine. Morning became afternoon; we tried to eat, we spun
more. The day's light gave way. The colors of movies jumped
around the room. It lit up our fronts.

I engaged. I felt empathy for fictional characters — more than
I feel for real ones. The flick I liked best had no dialogue, no
music; it was a tapestry of sound. Bed springs creaked. Bed post
thumped. Kettle hissed. A boiling pot rumbled.

The colors? They were velvet, silk, they were chamois, tulle.
The credits rolled. I congratulated myself. I hadn't thought
about my late rent, my cold flat, my stiff futon nested in dust on
a hardwood floor, the pinkie toe that made me walk funny.

I stood in the hallway of my flat on one foot. I stood on one foot *not* because I stubbed my toe. My sock was wet. I turned on the light in the bathroom. There was a spark behind the cover. I pulled my hand away. My sock needed to be wrung out. The first thing I appreciated was the thick threshold. It stemmed the tide. It leveed the water's reach into the hall. I saw now that the floor in the bathroom tilted toward the washer and the tub. I felt off-kilter.

In the trapezoid of light cast out of the bathroom, my shadow was spindly. Like tree limbs. I heard a sound. Bells tinkled. Was it real? Was it sleep deprivation? On the floor in the hall-way, against the opposite wall: my laptop, the phonebook, the *Prague Post*. The puddle has drowned half the population of Prague 1 through Prague 10. It has swamped the news.

I pulled off both socks. I grabbed the laptop's soft case. In both hands. I said, "No, no, no, no, no, no." I hustled the case and its contents to the high, dry cushions of my mustard-yellow plaid couch.

The stiff Communist cushions. I knelt. I unzipped the soft case. I felt dampness within. Beads of water dropped as the top zipped back. They dripped onto the black hard casing that was my computer.

I asked the landlord if he minded pets. He did, he told me; his wife was allergic. My kitten-having friends were disappointed; I couldn't take one. Deathly allergic — his wife — Horáček explained. He inherited the flat. His mother died, he went on; the inheritance belonged to his wife too. I accepted it. I silently cursed the miserable wife. Brad took the cat.

I held the computer above my head. I shook it. Water ran down my arms. I set it down on the cushion. I got a towel. I dabbed at what I could see, I spread the towel, picked up the computer. I folded the screen away from the keyboard. The screen, the keys — they were dry. I took a deep breath. I released the stays to the innards; like the screen, the keyboard flipped up. Inside: floppy drive, battery, hard disk. Each individually contained. Each component sat in the black tub of the laptop. Each com-ponent bathed.

I turned it over. The water drained onto the towel; it left a damp stain. I reached a dry corner flap of the towel into the corners. I set the computer down. My laptop. My databases. My fault trees. My fault. Dissected. Desiccated. Dust. I closed my eyes.

Options formed: 1. Get help. Go back to Brad's. Call my landlord. Find a neighbor. 2. Stop the hemorrhaging. Turn off the water. Determine where it's coming from. Listen. 3. Clean it up. 4. Go to bed.

Have I mentioned that I'm Aries? It's a Fire sign. I'm the spark. The blue pilot light. Water puts me out.

Bed's where Brad and Agata were, where Jacques and Gracie were. Creak, creak, creak. Thump. Thump. Bed's where Horáček and his allergic old lady were too. My neighbors. The whole damned building. Creaking, thumping. I needed to get my head together. I needed to face my fears. I opened my eyes.

I stepped out into the hall. The light was crepuscular. I heard music inside a door. I knocked. I knocked again. The volume weakened. The peephole was a cyclops. It looked me over. I hadn't slept in two nights. I heard movement within. Shuffling. A grunt. The noise came closer. The shuffling ceased. I looked into the peephole. I gave it my best in Czech: I have a big problem. Water. My place. I don't know. I don't speak much Czech. Water problem. I live in the flat over. Please. I need help.

The door opened. A hunchbacked woman, her head no higher than the doorknob, reached out with her cane. Her chin surpassed the door's edge; she wedged herself between the door and the frame. She spoke. She squinted. She opened her eyes. She repeated. She cursed. This part I understood. She said, "Shit."

The cane retracted. Her head set. The door shut. I listened to the memory of what she said. I discovered a word I know. Spectacles. There was a sound at the door adjacent. I saw a flash behind the peephole. I waited. The distant uneven shuffle got louder, closer. When she opened the door again, the adjacent door cracked. A woman's voice called to her.

Couldn't tell what they said. I tried to catch it; it's too quick. The door in front of me banged, bumped. It closed. The adjacent door opened. A woman my mother's age showed her face. She spoke to me in German. I responded in Czech. I said the same thing. She interrupted me. She asked me where. I stepped back from the door. I pointed up the stairwell, at a diagonal. The woman asked a question. I tell her I didn't understand. She said it again. "Can you wait? My husband's on his way." I told her I can't wait, I told her big water problem can't wait.

She came out into the stairwell. She followed me up the stairs. I pushed through my door. She looked into my bathroom. She looked at me. She said that I must learn to speak Czech. She said if I have a place here, I should speak Czech. Not this pub-Czech. She touched my arm. She patted. As if I knew her.

She asked me what she should do, what we should do. I held a finger to my lips. I said, "Shh." We listened. I expected to hear: drip…drip…drip. I expected to hear: burble…babble… booble. I didn't hear anything. I felt it. It expanded. The water was coming for me. I pointed to the end of the washing machine drainage tube; it lay on the floor, submerged. She picked it up. Nothing. She opened the hatch on the front of the washing machine. It was empty. She shook her head. She looked from the tub's spout to the faucet over the sink to the water heater. On the wall beneath the water heater, gray streaks weeped over pocked white plaster.

She looked under the unit. She touched pipes, rattled around, turned to me. Her fingers were wet. She pointed to one of a cluster of silver pipes snaking around in there. She said, "Bad." I didn't know how to say, "Stop it," or "Turn it off." I couldn't think. I went into a nosedive, a tailspin. Shit, the water heater? Did I break it? Why'd I have to fuck around with the stupid thing? In the middle of a cold night? Why couldn't I manage to find a warm body to sleep with? Could I afford to fix it? How much could one of these things cost, anyway? I couldn't afford to pay my rent. I'd be responsible; I'd own up to it. I'm not responsible. I did drugs; I mean, c'mon. Drugs? That's not me. What about my computer? Water and computers, water and sparks, did not mix. That's my career splayed out on the couch; soaked, open, beyond hope. I'd buy a new computer, I'd fig- ure it out. My fucking pinkie toe was killing me. A part of me reached for the undertow; a part of me wanted to fuck up so bad that I would never have to worry about fucking up again. Fuck it, right? Relax. Don't struggle. Lay back and enjoy it. Worry. Guilt. Fear. The big three. Not enemies. Friends. The ones you could count on. Let them envelop you; let them take you down. Crash and burn. Dead. *Smrt.*

My voice. In Czech. It sounded stupid. I said: Water. No water. Yes? Is possible? Water. Then no water? You understand? The woman in my flat shook her head. She mumbled. I repeated. She walked out. In the stairway, she turned. She waved for me to follow.

The elevator was small. She spoke to me in Czech; as if I understood. In the stairway, in my flat, I underestimated her girth. I plastered myself against the cool wall of the elevator; I didn't want to touch her with any part of my body. She went on and on. I nodded. I said repeatedly, "Hm-hmm. Hm-hmm." The elevator went down. Down past the floors where people live, down past the building's foyer. I hadn't been here before. She opened the door.

She led me past stalls walled in concrete blocks. The stalls doors were homemade; splintering wooden frames laced with wire. Wire woven over itself. I wondered how much he'd charge me for a stall down here. I've smelled worse.

The woman watched me. My fingers wrapped into the corners of the rusted wire lattice. Could she see my thoughts? She came back. I gripped rust into the webs between my fingers. The woman put her hand on my arm. She stroked with her thumb. She was someone's mother. I couldn't look at her, but I knew. I let go. She led me to the end of a row of stalls.

We stepped over a low concrete wall. This row of stalls was without doors. She pointed to the numbers written above. 24, 25, 26, 27... She asked me which number's mine. I told her 27. In English. I said it in Czech. I sounded like a moron when I said numbers in Czech. But 27! Isn't that great? It's 3 cubed. It's 3 to the third power. Magic to the magic power. When I saw the number above the door, when I viewed the rental for the first time, I knew; it's an omen. 27. I wanted to tell this woman about it. She wouldn't care.

She walked through the opening. She pointed to a curled yellow note taped to the side of the entrance. The note bore a name.

I flattened the note with my fingers. My hands were striped. Thin lines between my fingers, over my knuckles. Lines drawn in rust. Corrosion. I liked the way it looked; like dried blood.

Printed dot-matrix, the note said, "Blanka Wankeova." The same name was tacked to the front of my door upstairs. Beneath the peephole. On a brass plaque. I liked the name from the first time I saw it. Blank Wank. Another omen.

I said to the woman, as I entered the stall, I said, "Yup! That's it. That's my pad. Blanka Wankeova. Number 27. Ha ha!" She turned to me. She stood in front of a blue lever on a sweating pipe. She pointed to me, to my chest. She was emphatic. She poked at the air inches from my chest. She closed the valve with the other hand. She walked out past me.

I followed her into the elevator. I thanked her again. She looked at me. I explained. I was "away" for the weekend. We were drinking. We were enjoying ourselves. I told her I came home, big water problem. She snorted. Water problem. She said the name Horáček. She said the name Blanka Wankeova. She said the word *dead*. She said something about *Kapitalismus*, something about money. She complained about English tenants. I didn't correct her. The elevator stopped not at her floor, but at mine. She pushed the door open. She said: No big water problem. This is karma.

The water had stopped. I could tell. I felt it. I turned on the kitchen faucet. Water gushed, thinned, trickled, dripped. I went back to the foyer. The puddle reached the far wall where my computer was swamped. It was a sign — my computer, my life work, washed away. The wispy purple-gray dust balls were matted, stringy, black. My shoes were on my feet. Gritty footprints straddled the puddle, walked down the hallway, stepped into the kitchen. It's not like I could afford a maid.

I kicked off my shoes. No socks. I stepped on the thick threshold to the bathroom. I reached in to grab my towel. It hung on a cold radiator. I tossed it into the puddle. Right in the middle. I swiped it back and forth. The water swam around it. The towel got heavy. I picked it up. I held it against my T-shirt and jeans. I skipped to the kitchen sink. I tried to ring the towel. It was big and heavy. My forearms wrenched; the towel yielded a drib-

ble. I untwisted and tried again. The effort sent a wave of the
drug through me. I felt chills along the bony edges of my arms.
My hands tingled. I twisted again. I grunted. I held my breath.
Twisted. I dropped the towel. Head rush. I wobbled.

I was on my futon now. The jeans I wore on Friday to Brad's
place. Less than a block from mine. The same T-shirt. The front
of the shirt was wet, the front of the jeans were wet. I was under
the blankets. I gave up. My blankets were getting wet. I turned
over. Now my futon got wet. I put my face in the pillow. I held
my mouth open. My tongue touched the pillow cover. It tasted
like sweat. I squinted my eyes shut. I screamed into the pillow.

I changed my clothes. A clean T-shirt, a clean pair of cotton
shorts. I hung the saturated towel on the radiator in the kitchen.
It dripped into a plastic bowl. A stack of towels. I set them on
the couch. I started at the edge of the puddle. The linoleum
floor warped. The new curve kept the water in a smaller area.
I dabbed at it with the corner of a towel. I ran to the kitchen. I
wrung the corner out. I went back with another corner. I
wrung it out. I went through two towels. The puddle looked
the same. I had four towels left. Good thick American towels.
These things weren't cheap, I'd have you know. Who cared
about that right now? I haven't started on the bathroom yet; I
heaped wet clothing. I spread saturated towels over radiators. I
couldn't imagine being done with this mess. I couldn't
imagine lying down in a dry bed. I couldn't imagine trying to
sleep, much less sleeping. I tried not to think about it.

The doorbell rang. I opened the door. The woman from
downstairs, maybe her husband? It wasn't. It was someone
else. Medium height, slim. Hair in a hasty ponytail. I'd say no
makeup, but I'd be wrong. She said she was Mrs. Horáčková.
My landlord's wife. Sweatpants and a sweatshirt. White socks.
Those white shoes they called house slippers. They looked like
off-brand Birkenstocks. In one hand she held a bucket and a
mop. The bucket was heaped with towels. In the other hand
more towels; a whole stack! I had no idea what to say.

She looked me over. Did she know I'm behind on my rent?
I stepped behind the door. She came in. She smiled at me,
frowned at the mess, smiled at me. Would she try to collect? I

closed the door.

She dug right in. Her towels were thin, old, faded. She threw the whole towel in, twisted it around, flipped it over, wrung it in the bucket. Water dropped out when she twisted. Like a downpour. She snapped the towel flat in the air. She tossed the same one back in. She caught me watching her. I clutched a thick American towel. She handed me a stack of towels. She asked me a question. I didn't understand. She tried German. I shook my head. I felt guilty. I set my stupid thick towel aside. I tossed a shabby one in instead. I picked it up. I ran to the kitchen. I wrung out a corner. I hustled back. She passed me in the kitchen doorway. I bent to the last two teaspoonfuls in the hallway. She set a soup pot next to me. She twisted her hands. She pointed. Into the pot.

She kicked off her house slippers. She removed her socks. She hung her shoes and socks on the coat rack. She pulled the elastic bottoms of her sweatpants up her calves. She had nice feet, slender ankles. She wiggled her toes at me.

Mrs. Horáčková took her bucket. She waded into the bathroom. I heard a gush. I heard a snap. Pause. Gush. Snap. Pause. I smiled. I picked up my towel. I wrung it in the pot. It pinged and then it tinkled. The timing wasn't quite right. I held it. Gush. Snap. Pingly little tinkles. Gush. Snap. Again. Gush, snap, pingely and a tinkles; gush, snap, ping-ely and a tinkles; gush, snap. Mrs. Horáčková giggled. Gush, snap. Gush, snap. Ping-ely and a tinkles, gush, snap. Gush, snap, ping-ely and a tinkles; gush, snap, giggle. This time it was me.

The puddle was a slick spot. The floor needed cleaning. I stood up to see if I could help in the bathroom. She was wiping the corners with a dry towel. I watched her. The way she moved. Quick, efficient and somehow sexy. She stood on her bare feet. She poured a full bucket down the tub's drain. It was a seconds-long symphony. I stood in sheer ecstasy. The sounds ran up and down my arms. The last glug and gurgle echoed in the kitchen.

In German, she said to me: Not bad. I responded in Czech. I said, Not bad at all. She blinked at me. She pointed to the water heater. She said, It's new. She shook her head. She frowned. She shook her fist at it. She smiled at me. She adjusted her ponytail. If she knew that the rent is late, she didn't let on. Maybe she had something else in mind.

I'm exhausted. Drained of life. I wanted to smoke a cigarette at the kitchen table. I was afraid she'd stay, have one with me. I stood on the threshold. I kept waiting for her to broach the rent subject. Or for her to kiss me. Either or.

She hustled past. She flew through my flat like I wasn't there. I went to the kitchen. I sat. I shook out a smoke. I rolled it between my fingers. Flakes of tobacco looked like miniature pubic hairs on the white table beneath me. I lit up. Mrs. Horáčková came to the kitchen doorway. She had her socks and sandals on her feet. In one hand she had a mop and bucket. The bucket was full of soaked towels. In the other hand, a pile of my towels. I stood up. On top of the pile, she had my clothes. I set the cigarette down. My hand shook. Did she notice? My hands didn't look like my hands: puffy, pink, wrinkled.

I stepped toward her. I reached for the pile. She turned. She said, Zitra, zitra! Tomorrow, tomorrow! I raised my eyebrows at her. I backpedaled, I took my seat. Zitra, I replied. I picked up my pack of Marlboro Lights, flipped it open, offered her one. She said, "Not at the moment." She continued. I shook my head, tapped my ash, exhaled a lungful of smog. She said it again, then in German. I got it in German. She wanted to make dinner for me. I said yeah. I said sure. I thought whatever. Dinner.

Surrounded by water. Water everywhere. I think it means that I need to talk to Karina again. The water thing's significant, though. At least I think it is. As Markéta says, these things have power if you believe in them. It could be an illusion.

Hanging, 22.9.98

I called Božena's place. She answered brightly, "Yoselle! I'll get her for you." I heard her yelling for her sister. I heard giggles in the background. The nieces, I figured. What're they laughing at? Ilona came to the phone.

"I'm fine, Joseph. You don't need to worry. My sister keeps me busy." She lowered her voice. "She wants to invite you to dinner, but I don't want to see you right now, is that okay? I need time."

Wounded, I answered, "Yeah, no, I understand. That's okay. I like her, your sister. What does she do for a living?"

"Radiologist." Ilona was short with me.

"How's your head? How's your lady business?" Did I have to joke?

Ilona answered, "Head is fine. Cramping is better. Not much blood, few clots." She said she'll call in a couple weeks. Ilona paused. "I have to think how to tell my mother and my father. School is hard. I need some time." Ilona hushed someone in the background. I listened. I imagined Božena gesticulating in the background.

Ilona came back to me. "I call you. Don't worry about me."

"Okay. Yes. I hear you. Tell your sister I said hi. Enjoy your time with your nieces. I'm sorry. About everything."

"Goodbye, Joseph." I hung up. Things might have been different. It's just like me to fall for her after it's already over and done with.

Speaking of meeting people, I said I was going to call Jacques and meet up for a beer. I should be hanging out with painters and writers. I can't bring myself to do it.

Wringing, 25.9.98

I wasted a lot of time on Karina yesterday. I have to break that habit. Then again, she did one of the nicest things anyone has done for me lately. She made me a special Sprite.

I had been at Terminal Bar for about an hour. I had already downed two Sprites. She came and took my glass. She asked if I wanted another. I thought about it for a second. I enjoyed her attention. Before I could decide, she waved her long fingers at me, like "Okay, okay." She walked away with my glass. She set it down with the other dirty glasses by the sink. She grabbed a taller glass, one that's reserved for beer, and put ice cubes in it. She checked to make sure I was watching her. She tilted her chin and smiled as she poured Sprite from the nozzle into the glass. She topped it off, then cut a fresh slice from a lemon and placed it on the top of the ice. She put the tall glass on a plate with a paper doily. She delivered it to me, smiling, then turned back to her inventory. I couldn't believe it.

Small things make me happy. Small things make me want to put myself through the wringer. I'm falling for her more each day. I'm not sure I want to do that.

Atoning, 28.9.98

Can't get Karina out of my mind. I dreamt about her last night. Beautifully. She and I were friends like now, but this other girl got herself involved. She had a fresh look, like the beautiful girl I was dancing with one of the past Saturday nights at Roxy. Fresh, wide-eyed, the girl in the dream had curly hair. Like Dalia Babat. There's a good chance I'll see Dalia at the wedding in Barcelona. The perfect reason to go alone...

I met Dalia Babat in my freshman year at MIT. She was in one of my classes. Tall, maybe five foot, eight inches, she was thin. At the time she was too thin. I saw her running along the river a few times, her socks loose on her ankles. She was *that* thin. She told me later she struggled with an eating disorder. She told me she was doing better. She had big brown eyes and perpetually messy brown curls — a female Einstein. She didn't have time to worry about taming her locks. I invited her to one of the first formals we had at the house — she agreed to come with me, on one condition. She didn't want our first date to be in a fraternity house. Fair enough. I asked her to Harvard Square for pizza one Friday.

I showed up at her dormitory. Her roommate met me at the door. "You must be Joseph. Dalia's getting ready." I noticed a note on the whiteboard on her dorm room door — the room-mate noticed me noticing it. Like a good friend, she moved to block it — too late. It said, "Have fun, D — don't do anything I wouldn't do…" The roommate made awkward small talk until she came out. Dalia wore an Air Force jacket from WWII, slate-gray blue with square shoulders. She had on black high-waisted pleated baggy pants and a white tank crop top. Despite her dry wild hair, despite her fingernails bitten down to the quick, she was stunning. The plain roommate gave Dalia a look. The plain girl gave Dalia a hug.

We walked down the sidewalk toward the T at Kendall Square. I couldn't resist. I asked. She told me she had just recently broken up with her high-school boyfriend. "You're kind of like my first date since. No pressure." Dalia smiled. I knew right then I would get her back to her dorm early. I would be the perfect gentleman. Penance, for the jerk I had been in high school.

Dalia attended the formal with me. We didn't continue dating after that. I saw her around. Years later, she dated another guy at my house. He was a freshman when I was a junior. She made him come talk to me before she would agree to come to another formal. I smiled at the formality of it, this young hunk asking for permission. I kissed Dalia on the cheek at the dinner. She whispered to me, "I never got to thank you for that first date. You were sweet." I guess I was a little jealous of her and my housemate, as they slipped away into the party — she had put on thirty pounds. She looked good, healthy. She still ran. I tried to remember why we stopped dating. She was the It girl at the party, an elegant A-line princess V-neck, sweep-train chiffon dress in taupe, against her toned shoulders. She reminded me too much of Dani, at the time. I couldn't. I stared at Dalia across the room — me in my blue blazer with the French blue shirt and a blue and green striped tie, pleated khakis ending in brown topsiders — my date whacked me on the arm with her clutch.

The Roxy girl was dancing with me at the back of the club. I looked up. I was dancing by the stage. She was there. I don't know how these things work. I'm not sure.

Someone catches my eye. I don't know why. Maybe it's the way she dances. Maybe it's the way she looks. Maybe it's a combination of the two. While I try to figure it out, I look up. She's dancing right next to me. Coincidence? My ego says no.

I manage to say no to it, I go for something less easy and more stupid. I'm not talking about stupid girls; stupidity is the most unattractive thing I can imagine. I'm talking about stupid situations, like sitting in a bar where the girl works. From the time when she gets there in the morning and the place is empty, to the time when she leaves when the place is full. If it's easy, I don't want it. I'm not sure that's right. If it's easy, it doesn't give me time to figure out if it's what I want or not. I want to talk about Rachel here.

I want to know her now, as painful as it might be. Because then it'd be more real for me. It's not real for me to pretend she doesn't exist. I find it difficult to shut her out when she's one of the few people I know who knows me. I'm not shutting her out. I'm waiting. I'm waiting for her to contact me. She has to contact me. For our relationship to grow into the thing that it should be, she has to find it in her heart to forgive me and contact me with the will to form a relationship based on the fact that we spent five good years of our lives together. She's either angry with me or she's convinced she's over me. Perhaps she's forgiven me and has decided to keep it to herself. That's almost acceptable.

Could I do the "just hi" thing? I don't know. I don't think so. She knows better than anyone what "just hi" means. I haven't communicated with her in seven months.

I'm thinking I need to write her a long email. I should wait. In our relationship, it was important for me to wait. For her to show her feelings. I rarely had the patience for it. Having the patience is, in essence, loving her. I do love you, Rachel. That's not going anywhere. I forget about it sometimes, the way I forget about my mom or Sam. Or my dad. I have to break that. My dad's going to die one day, and I don't want to have to wait until then. That would be stupid.

I saw the Roxy girl last night. She was at the Chapeau Rouge. She may be interested in me, but I shouldn't lower myself. She's a bit fucked, I think. Judging by the crowd she runs with.

I think it's next week that I go to Barcelona. Wow. I need to figure a few things out. Like how much it'll cost to get there. On Thursday, or will it be Friday? Friday I went to lunch with Karina again. I told her I liked her. I told her that the reason I spent time at Terminal Bar is because of her. She already knew it, but she wasn't willing to let herself believe it. Next time I have to tell her that I won't stop until she wants me.

Karina, Karina, Karina. What am I going to do with you?

Following, 29.9.98

We spun last night. It's Tuesday at 1:00 p.m. I feel guilty.

Jacques and Gracie are coming apart; I'm here with them as they go through it. I could say this is bad, I could say spinning is bad, I could say that I'm bad for allowing it, but I don't think I want to go down that path. Why not? Let's go down it. Let's see what happens.

Do I need help? Why, in the end did I — after saying no two or three times — why did I end up spinning? Well, I felt good. We had a nice dinner. We came back, Gracie was here. She was writing a letter to her mom. I wanted to feel better. That's why I did it. I felt good, but I wanted more.

Did it give me more? No. Of course not. Do I feel better now? No. Now I feel guilty. I can talk myself out of that. I wonder what went wrong in my apartment while I've been away. Maybe my landlord called. I can check my messages. Maybe these guys at Identity will pull their support from me. Maybe the money I think I have from them won't be there any longer.

I should check my messages. I hope Karina called. At the same time I know she didn't. Why would she? Nothing's changed on her end.

I feel guilty.

Jacques saw Karina yesterday. Said she looks the same. He doesn't see what I see. That's cool. I hope she's good. I hope she's happy. Why does that sound cynical when it's innocent?

I invited Jacques to room with me. It's too natural not to be right. It's a good fit. I could use the help with rent. It'd make the Karina thing more difficult; might speed up the process. I'll get there with Karina.

Can I feel her? I think I can. Am I following my heart? I think I am. Let my foolish heart lead; my head will figure out how to deal with it.

I believe in the simplicity of karma. A balance; that's what's important. Do I want a meaningless job or, worse, a meaningful job? I don't. My heart doesn't. The freedom I have right now is what I enjoy. My head wants stability. Can I get that? Yes, I can. Set the example. Lead the way.

Jacques's in a bad way. Gracie's getting ready to disappear. This isn't good, folks. We have to get some light into this dark world, stop acting as if every day were the last, let ourselves be the way we need to be and enjoy the problems.

I don't need to spend the rest of the week at Identity trying to convince them to give me 10,000 CZK (329.06 USD) so that I can go to Barcelona. I'll go to Barcelona alone.

OCTOBER

Admitting, 1.10.98

JACQUES.
He's intense. Everything about him, fervid. He's a Leo, a Fire sign, the middle, the blaze. I'm a Fire sign too, the spark, the ignition, the fire starter. His eyes, viridian at the center, bordered with brown ochre, have tiny flecks of blue. They bore a hole straight through you. It can be intimidating, but like a roaring campfire he's hypnotizing. He has a mop of wavy brown hair, the color somewhere between whiskey and bark. He has olive skin, a long thin face, no facial hair, a prominent nose.

When he thinks, he sucks his cheeks in. He turns three-quarter profile. He paints. He bends to the canvas. He leans back, squints, looks for the essence. That's what it is: when he looks at you, he's looking for your essence. He dresses in dark earth tones — moss, charcoal, phthalo blue, burnt umber, Mars black. He's reedy, tall. His posture needs work. He wears corduroys or jeans, sweaters: crewneck or cardigan. T-shirts that don't say anything. No visible brands. He wears vintage French army combat boots with the lace shield and buckles at the side. He wears his wallet on a chain. All his fingers have rings. They each mean something; if you get him started, he'll tell you all about them. Most are parts from something else, never intended to be rings at all. Born on the Upper East Side of New York City, he lived in the French countryside growing up. He speaks impeccable French.

Jacques.

That's all I got to say.

Jacques needed to talk yesterday. He talked his head off. He pulled off maybe the most difficult thing he has ever done in his life. I can cut him slack.

It'll be fun to have him here. I wonder how Gracie's doing.

I love that girl, but she needs to get her shit together. Quick. She already lost Jacques. That's big. Jacques loves her. He's tough on her. She probably needs it.

Enough about Jacques and Gracie. I should talk about things that concern me. Like rent. I've been using their problems as an excuse not to face my own. I have to face the fact that I can't pay rent. I'll call the landlord today. I'll pay the rent today. I'll tell him about Jacques. About Jacques moving in.

I have to admit, of course, that there's a decent chance this won't work.

I have a long way to go in the next few weeks. I want to go to Barcelona. That means I have to get the Identity database done. I leave Friday night.

I gotta get it done for them. Four days of work will suffice. I can get my 17,000 CZK (566.86 USD). I can make it to Barcelona.

Jacques sold a painting. It's called *Winter*. At the center, a building perched on a snowy hillside. To the left and right, the trees he has interpreted as a network of tessellations, outlined in black. He paints each broken piece lovingly. They are layered over a mountain range in the distance, manganese blue mixed with Payne's gray. Maybe the best part of the painting, what holds the whole thing together, is the snowy hill in the foreground, a large unbroken field of color. He has used a black canvas, employing a dry brush technique. The black shows through titanium white tinted blue-black. Jacques says snow isn't white. It can be blue, pink, yellow, orange, depending on the time of day. It looks like the house is hiding her chin behind a snowy turtleneck. I recognize it as a scene from the Krkonoše Mountains.

It's amazing. He's in the midst of the most difficult thing he has ever done and he gets an email from Los Angeles. I wish he didn't have to send it away. I wish I could buy it. I admire the way the snow changes colors before your eyes. I am reminded of another set of rainbow bursts. A long time ago.

The email confirms. He calls me into the bedroom to show it to me. He can't let Gracie know. He's busy packing.

Krkonoše Mountains

Thinking about Jacques's painting, made me wonder about the details, especially the mountains. In English, they're the Giant Mountains, forming the border between Bohemia and Silesia, between the Czech Republic and Poland, running east to west. The picturesque range features glacial corries, barren rock faces, peat bogs, waterfalls and alpine meadows. Resplendent year-round, the Giant Mountains are the highest and most visited mountains in the Czech Republic. The River Elbe finds its source on the southern slopes. It snakes through Bohemia and arcs northward through Germany. The highest peak, Sněžka, 1,603 meters tall (5,259 feet), contains deposits of copper, iron and arsenic. Pec pod Sněžkou, roughly

translated as "furnace under Sněžka," is a small town at the base
of the tallest mountain. From there you can catch a two-sec-
tion cable car that will take you to the peak. Another ski town,
seemingly the next mountain over, but nearly forty-six kilometers (twenty-nine miles) away by car, or twenty-two kilometers
(thirteen miles) by bike, Špindlerův Mlýn, is surrounded by
four mountains on all sides. Franz Kafka wintered here in January and February of 1922. He is said to have penned the first
drafts of *The Castle* here.

It means he's on the right path. Jacques doesn't believe in
that shit. He doesn't know me well enough to know that I do.
Believe in that shit. Paths. I told him that when you're going
through something difficult and a sign comes to you, a sign of
fortune, it means you're okay. Or at least you're going to be. He
didn't buy it.

TESSELLATIONS
Siltstone forms over a period of 300 million years as silt —
fine sand carried by the force of rushing water — is covered
heavily by later sediments and compacted along the water's
edge. Local stressors crack the surface and form joints, grooves
that over time are exaggerated by the processes of erosion.
It's where geology and geometry overlap, flat rock cut to look
like tiles fitted together in systematic repetition. Without gaps,
orderly and polygonal. It has an exquisite quality, planned and
executed by a swarm of workers, like Islamic art or the work of
bees. Nature's plaid.
Prague's streets are man's plaid, cobblestones hewn from a
quarry and sorted into piles of color that workmen carefully
arrange into the patterns that pixelate the streets; in the rain, the

stones are greasy and slippery. When moonlight falls on wet cobblestones, they twinkle against the purple sky. They glisten. This day, there would be no glistening, Prague, Union Corners, anywhere. It's a New Moon.

Dani, sixteen, stands at the closet of her redecorated bedroom studying a skirt on a hanger. Tags hang from the seam. The pattern is a Black Watch plaid. Algae and midnight interlaced on a field of obsidian that teases the eyes, heavy weft, soft and fragrant. She breathes the sensuous fabric of the new skirt. The color deepens, sucking filaments of light out of the air around it. She's wearing her new Cornell T-shirt and a pair of underwear she has saved for the occasion. The space surrounding her is bright — she picked Benjamin Moore Brilliant White paint with accents of pink and chrome. It hurts the eyes. This day hewn from the calendar two months prior. The scenario plays out in her head far longer than that. She tempers the intensity of her emotions; she doesn't want to scare him away.

Cosmopolitan says to wait a year. Before a relationship gets physical. Maybe it was Oprah. A year sounds impossible. His visit coincides with the anniversary of the first kiss. One year and one day. Picture this: a trail meanders through a county park until it opens up on an olive-drab pond, covered with an unearthly foam. It happened there.

Back at the house, it's quiet; the relentless hum of the dehumidifier her father runs year-round. The scent of the lukewarm coffee pot lingers in the air. Today she'll drink her first cup of coffee.

She tiptoes into the addition. It's summer. She can feel the crisp morning air on her ankles as she passes the side door. She's in her underwear. A T-shirt over top. On a torturous sofa bed, he snores lightly. He stayed the night. They are alone for the better part of the morning: her younger brother, Charlie, is at basketball camp; her parents will be back by lunch. Gathered at the nape of her neck, her hair is like Audrey Hepburn's in *Breakfast at Tiffany's*.

She leans in. She plants her lips gently on the spot where his neck and shoulder intersect. He smells like cinnamon.

His eyes flutter. "Mmm, what have we here?"

She sighs. "Good morning, lover boy." She bites her lip.

"You smell good." He can't help but smirk.

She nestles under his arm. The yellow gingham patchwork quilt holds the heat of his torso beneath the surface. He wears nothing but his red plaid boxers. He absorbs the weight of her leg.

"What're we waiting for?" her voice full of anticipation.

He looks around. He whispers, "Here? You want to do this here?"

He radiates heat. She sits up. She places his hand on her chest. He feels her heart beating through the clean, crisp T-shirt.

She's vexed. She has an urge to taste him. Is that normal? She feels her throat flush.

She planned this. Eight weeks. Sex, for the first time, ever, on a broken-down sofa bed? "No, silly. Upstairs."

He props himself up on his elbow. He squints. He kisses her hard on the lips. Good hard.

"I'm ready. Are you?" He loves her. What's not to love?

She takes a ragged breath. "Okay." Her lips are dry. Her heart pounds. Second thoughts. She loves him. What's not to love?

They skip the three steps down to the kitchen. They run. They shuffle past the refrigerator, to the carpeted stairs. Five steps up to the landing. The squeaky step squeaks no matter where you step on it. He trips on the top step. She bounds into him. They look at each other. He's in boxers; she wears panties and a T-shirt. She pushes her elbow into his bare chest, passes him. Not about to let her win, he holds her by the hip bones. Five steps to her door. It has taken them forever to get here. They kissed until their lips were swollen and their jaws cramped. Held hands until they seeped with sweat. A year and a day. Not a second longer.

He peels back the white comforter. He slips beneath. She stops at the window. She peers down. Where her mother's car would be, a blotch on the asphalt. She holds a waist-high crystal. It hangs from a filament of fishing line. In the flood of sunlight she sets it in motion. On the walls, on the ceiling, flecks of rainbow bursts rotate.

On one elbow, he chuckles, "What are we waiting for?" She

sees his boxers on the floor. She climbs in. She lay next to him, eyes closed, tasting the salt on his skin. She isn't nervous. Is he?

"I love you." He has said it to her before, but this time, leaving his tongue, it feels different.

"I love you too." She can hear herself say it. It sounds different.

Their limbs tangle, so smooth and warm. Elbows, knees, ankles, thighs. Orderly and polygonal. He pulls her close to him against his erection. "We need to be careful."

"*Careful.*" She smirks. One eyebrow raises.

He puts his lips on her lips. Effortless, light. His hand maps the valley between her breasts. Where geology and geometry overlap. Her hands trace the contours of his arms, his shoulders. He touches the hem of her shirt. She lifts her arms. He slips it over her head. The Cornell shirt arcs across the room.

Her arms come down over his head. He kisses her ear, feeling his breath reflected on his face as he holds her earlobe in his teeth. He plucks the elastic of her waistband with one finger. He looks into her eyes, jade with hazel flecks around the edges. A snarl at the corner of her lips. She lifts her hips. That tiny movement. She digs her heels into the bed. She lifts. The twist of her body.

He reaches down under the comforter, slides her underwear to her ankles. He breathes. Is it the effort, is it something else? She scissors her ankles. She reaches down, pulls out her panties. They sail through the air.

He lays back. One arm behind his head. His heart slams against his chest. He plays it cool. She tears the foil wrapper between her teeth. She places the condom on him. She rolls it down. She's practiced, of course, on a banana. In her mind, it's a single swipe and the thing is installed. His heat and the material do not comply. She looks at him. He smiles.

Flustered, she lays back next to him. He works it on. He checks it. She would not appreciate a slipshod job. The equipment in place, he turns on his side. He kisses her frustration away.

She craves him. He touches her, as he has done before, but it's different. It's fuller, it's new.

"You sure?" he confirms.

She's pressed between the mattress and the delicious weight of him. Like a bookmark pinched halfway through a Hemingway novel.

She centers herself and nods. Her eyes devour him. The curve of his shoulder, a vein in his neck. His body twists. It's a raw sensation, carnal, possessive. They move together as if they've done this a hundred times before, as if they've always done this, as if they were made for each other.

He kisses her.

Her hands absorb the hot shape of his back muscles. She thinks of sand.

Their breathing is erratic, syncopated. Tessellated.

He buries his face in her neck. It takes her breath. The feeling of his tongue in that spot spreads through her body, down past her knees. He pushes down on her bed with his arms, looks down at her. A bead of sweat on his temple. She reaches up with her neck, pulls him down. She licks it.

He flinches. He smiles. He surrenders. The act, he recognizes, totally what she would do. She lays back, closes her eyes. She explores his taste. Pure salt, cinnamon and something older. Is it leather?

He slides his fingers under her back. His palms brush the pale flesh at the sides of her breasts.

He whispers something unintelligible in her ear.

He is heavy. Sated. Finally. Finally, she understands. She understands him.

She catches her breath, whispering near his ear, "Again."

"Your parents will be back any —" Joseph leans over the edge of the bed. He looks out the window; he's not at an angle to survey the street. All he can see are the leaves of the trees.

"It's okay. We have time." Dani has a tissue in her hand, ready for the item. She places another foil wrapper between her teeth.

┼┼┼┼┼

I need a girlfriend. Wait. I don't want a girlfriend. I can't afford a girlfriend. I'm speaking from a financial perspective here, but I guess most of the senses of that statement apply.

Poor Jacques. Poor Gracie. Poor me. This is good. Gracie needs to get real. She needs love. She has to start by loving herself. I know that. I hope I didn't push Jacques too hard to love her. He's done his share. He's done more than that. Watching her destroy herself. I don't know the nature of Jacques's love for her; I can't say as I'm able to understand the love of any person. What it is, what it was, that hardly matters; he thought he did. That's what matters.

I'm going to cut this short; I gotta work. It's up to me to fuck it up. I'm in deep. Sink or swim. Or sink.

Breaking, 2.10.98

Jacques moved in with me. It's temporary. It will be good.

I met him at the flat he shares with Gracie. It's in Malá Strana up past the American Embassy. I tapped the tops of the bollards as I passed, up the cobbled street. The road narrowed down to an alleyway and then opened out again into a square. On the left was a church with a bell tower; on the right an apartment building. I knew Jacques was on the third floor in the front; to get there I'd have to go through a passage into a courtyard, up some stairs. In one porch, I guess you would call it, an outdoor space surrounded by windows, there hung an impressive spider web. It was wet in the evening dew. Drops of water glistened from the invisible strands. Like tears, they caught the light and sparkled. Like jewels on a necklace. The shapes the web cut from the air were at once jagged and perfect, systematic and organic. I don't see the architect of this wonder, but I knew she was there.

Gracie had agreed to clear out of the flat for a few hours. That's all the time we'd have to funnel Jacques into his new reality. At the top of the stairs, I came to a crossroads. To the right, there was a door. To the left, there was a short hallway around the porch. It led to the shared toilet. It was an amazing flat they'd found, a hand-me-down from Gracie's older sister, the alleged writer I have yet to meet. Like all amazing flats in Prague, it had quirks.

I turned right. I hitched my backpack up on my shoulder, pushed my glasses up on my nose, and knocked on the door. I heard someone clomping around. The door whipped open. Jacques was brusque. Almost rude. He didn't meet my eyes. He whisked away from the entrance, manic in his sweater and jeans, his heavy combat boots. I stepped in.

Jacques yelled from the kitchen. "Paintings first. Everything else after that. Coffee's on the stove."

Jacques had prepared me for the plan last night. Over a beer at the hospoda near my flat. We sat. Jacques crushed his shoulder against the bar. He opened his chest to me. "I figure it's two trips. We'll use my car. It's not big, but it'll get the job done. Time is working against us. I don't want to see her."

I nodded. I was going to ask where she was staying, Gracie, but I knew the answer and I didn't want to remind Jacques. It was too painful.

I poured myself a small mug of coffee from the carafe next to the stove. I took a bitter sip. Jacques made a good pot of coffee, I'd grant him that. I wondered where Brad was, where Todd Lopez was, where all of Jacques's other friends were, to help us with this move. Then I realized. This was a private thing. Jacques wasn't ready, perhaps, to share his anguish with those guys, his real friends. I was a new friend; in that capacity I was helpful. A new friend for a new reality. It had to be me.

The car packed with paintings, we made the short ride to my flat. From Malá Strana to Vinohrady. I think of the doctor in one of Jan Neruda's stories, the one who is secretly in love with the younger sister, bequeathed to the older. Such a tricky thing, the human heart. The situations it got us into. Jacques didn't say anything. He maneuvered the car through the streets. It's quite romantic: two expats in a car full of paintings making their way across this ancient city. One broken-hearted, strike that, both of us broken-hearted, in varying states of disrepair. Aren't we all?

We didn't talk about the fact that Gracie can't afford the flat without Jacques, that she will have to move out soon, that she's between jobs. What that all means. At that moment, it couldn't be Jacques's problem. He had to put himself first. It was the only way, he believed, to help her. I agreed with him.

Canvases tilted against all the walls in the Laubova flat (Blanka would love that scene, wouldn't she, all that arty chaos?), we're back in Malá Strana. Lesser town. The paintings all moved, I realized that I hadn't noticed the smell before. The smell of the apartment. It was Gracie. She was not a tidy woman. It was not something that's important to her. Once the smell of oil paint and turpentine and the coffee (ah, Jacques is a sly one, isn't he?) were gone, I smelled it. That feminine smell, light, crisp, what would I compare it to? I couldn't put my finger on it, and I didn't want to leave it.

I noticed a pair of Gracie's jeans folded up on the bed. She didn't put them there. Jacques scooped them off the floor and folded them before I came in the door. Jacques burdened me with his army duffel, a heavy canvas thing. Jacques's smell was more masculine, spicy and astringent. I don't know if that was cologne he wore, or if he did his laundry separately from Gracie, but there was a difference. I wedged the heavy thing out the door and down the stairs, through the passage to the trunk of the car. Dropped it in with a thump. I wondered if my place has a smell. Of course it did, but what did it smell like? When we got back there, I'd see.

In the car the second time, Jacques talked. I reassured him that he's on the right track. I told him that Gracie was not his problem at the moment. We talked about interdependence. It seemed like he actually listened to me. Like he was open, in this moment of vulnerability, to hear what I had to say. There again, I'm useful to Jacques. He can be vulnerable with me. I reminded him this was temporary, but it was a good temporary. He could rebuild at my place.

He needed a safe place to ride out the Gracie thing. I could use some help with the rent. It's a win-win. I hope.

Jan Neruda

When I first read a few of Jan Neruda's short stories, in a book called *Prague Tales from the Little Quarter,* I could picture his nineteenth-century Malá Strana. All I had to do was imagine U Maleho Glena, the church where the Infant of Prague stands, the little road that goes up past the American Embassy to the square where Jacques and Gracie used to live. Their quirky courtyard. I could immediately imagine the setting for those stories.

Digging in, I found more and more interesting facts. I didn't know, for instance, that it's widely believed that the Chilean poet Pablo Neruda, whose love poetry I so admire, was a pen name taken in honor of Jan Neruda, an ocean and a continent away, nearly a century later.

The doctor, the banker, the luckless-in-love young man talking with his friends up on the red roofs, the beggar — they are familiar to me. Probably most of all his tales I can picture the two old men, rivals, that sit nearly back-to-back in the pub every night for decades without speaking. So right on. His work captures the everyday life of regular people right there in Malá Strana, the Little Quarter, a place that exists almost unchanged from that time. Oh you know what I mean, completely changed but unchanged as well, the space defined by its cobble and brick outlines. The colorful contents change in a time-lapse blur.

There's so much I didn't know about Jan Neruda. I didn't know about his affair with the married writer Karolina Světlá. How they supported each other's work. How they fell in love. I didn't know about the broach, a gift from her husband, she sold to give Neruda the money so he could keep on writing. When her husband found out that the broach was missing, he demanded to read all their correspondence. When he did, he forbade the relationship. The letters became a 1977 movie called *The Story of Love and Honor*. I haven't seen it, but apparently it depicts the loneliness of Neruda and Světlá, their devotion to their work, the difficult and complicated conditions of their relationship, set against the backdrop of a middle class that is petty, superficial, hypocritical and envious. I need to see that movie.

I didn't know about the May School, a group of writers in the second half of the nineteenth century. Under the Austro-Hungarian Empire, the official language at the time was German. They wrote in Czech. Their subject was the modern life of ordinary people, a revolutionary concept at the time. Writing about contemporary social problems wasn't done until this group of young writers started. Neruda and Světlá were leading voices in the May School, the name of the movement taken from the famous poem by Karel Hynek Mácha.

I didn't know about the House of Two Suns on Spur Street, now renamed Nerudova, that I have walked past countless times. It's on the walk up from Malá Strana to the Prague Castle by way of the long ascending staircases. I will have to stop by the Two Suns and see the place where Jan sat in the window scribbling down his observations as the world took place beneath him.

Could it be a subtitle for my journal, "The Story of Love and Honor"? Hardly. I would like to think it wouldn't be too facetious if it were.

Researching, 5.10.98

After all the focus on Jacques, I needed to take some time to myself. The little bit of research I did on Jan Neruda made me want to do something literary. I made my way to the Globe Bookstore. I figured I would get a coffee, a coffee all to myself. Look at books.

A beacon to expats, the Globe Bookstore nestles on a corner in Holešovice. It's an English-language bookstore that opened in the fall of 1993. In the front, a cozy bookstore, floor-to-ceiling shelves, a couple of overstuffed chairs, the floors covered in old carpets. In the back, a coffeehouse. Wrapped in a giant green logo on a beige background on the corner of a street, it draws you in. Can't talk about the expat scene without the Globe as a backdrop. I feel like I recognize the person working in the coffee shop, but I probably don't.

I selected a book on the assassination of Reinhard Heydrich. When I picked it up, I recognized the name as a topic I should know more about. I had no idea how important the name was. It made me realize how little I knew of the city I live in, how much I had to learn.

It was steep, 550 CZK (18.27 USD). A small price to pay to eliminate some of my ignorance. I might not be able to make my rent; at least I won't be so ignorant.

Check this out. Heydrich was the Nazi who was picked to lead the occupation of Czechoslovakia. Wait. That's almost correct. He was the leader of the Protectorate of Bohemia and Moravia. See, Czechoslovakia, this part I knew, was founded as an independent nation in 1918 after the end of World War I. I'd read up on Tomáš Garrigue Masaryk back in September. Interesting dude, married an American woman, spent time in the States. Seemed to me that the assassination started with the Munich Agreement. I vaguely remembered that. I would have to look it up.

The Munich Agreement

Appeasement. That was the word I was taught, the word I learned in history class. When a bully starts to make demands, it can seem like a good idea to give him what he wants. Hope it ends there. It's rarely the correct thing to do.

I have a vague memory of a photograph of Neville Chamberlain waving a piece of paper above his head as evidence of a diplomatic coup. He thought he had prevented a repeat of the Great War that was still fresh in people's minds; in fact, he had betrayed the Czechs. They called them the Sudetenlands, which is confusing. The claim Hitler made was that three million ethnic Germans lived in Czechoslovakia and those Sudetenlands should be returned to the fatherland. He was prepared to invade Czechoslovakia to take the lands forcibly if he had to. To prevent that, without a single representative of Czechoslovakia present, on September 29, 1938, the Allied Forces signed an agreement with Hitler. It effectively dismantled Czechoslovakia. Not even twenty years after the independent nation had been founded by TGM.

The Munich Betrayal. That's how to remember it. Rather than moderating Hitler's behavior, as Chamberlain had hoped, it increased his ambitions. By March 1939, just six months later, the Nazis occupied all of Bohemia and Moravia.

It reminds me. Do not give in to the beast. Stand your ground. It's good to remember.

I have the phone number for Benny Pagel's hotel. I'll get the details about the wedding reception. I don't know if I'll go.

Turning, 6.10.98

Turns out her husband was out of town on a business trip. Turns out she had no way of knowing I hadn't paid my rent; Mrs. Horáčková doesn't get involved in money matters. Turns out his plumber friend installed the hot water heater using little silver pipes that weren't appropriate for the job. Turns out the plumber spends a weekend at my place, while I'm "away." He replaced them. Turns out Mrs. Wankeova, my Blanka, died peacefully in the flat two days before I saw the place. Turns out the neighbor woman who helped me is named Mrs. Nováková. Turns out she and Mrs. Wankeova were friends. Friends and neighbors. Turns out the computer was fine; I left it for three days (magic) and it was fine. Turns out I went to dinner. Turns out I got drunk on some American whiskey Horáček bought in honor of the occasion. Turns out Mrs. Horáčková smokes American cigarettes, only when she drinks. Turns out the Horáčeks have a son who's ten and a daughter who's eight. Turns out the daughter plays the piano; she played Chopin for me, the really sad one. It was lovely. Turns out the Horáček family fell in love with my pub-Czech and my drunken antics. That night, when I left, Horáček told me that he was very unlucky as a landlord. I asked him why. He said that if his family loved me, he couldn't evict me. He said that if he couldn't evict me, he had no power as a landlord. He smiled at me like a devil. He said goodnight.

Oh yeah, and it turns out they have a cat and a dog. Deathly allergic, my ass.

Bohumil Hrabal

I wanted to read up on Hrabal. I found this bit: He had a little chalet outside of Prague. He would go there to write. The only problem was that the cottage was full of cats. The cats kept multiplying. He lamented that the cats end up preventing him from writing: when he was in Prague, he couldn't write because he worried whether the cats had enough to eat; when he was at the chalupa, he was too busy taking care of the cats or shooing them off his table to be able to write. He couldn't drive out to the cottage anymore; he worried that he would have an accident and who would feed the cats then? He took the bus, which took longer, leaving less time for writing. Instead, he wrote about the cats.

In his book *All the Cats*, he was already old. He complained that he was too bald and too wrinkled to attract a beautiful woman, but his cats still loved him the way the girls used to.

It reminded me of a Rachel story. She was allergic to cats. Unlike Mrs. Horáčková. We visited the house of a cat owner, just out of college, in the midst of trying to figure out how to cohabitate. I remembered how much I had loved my cats growing up. On the floor in the living room, we listened to music. Rachel's nose twitched. Violently. I stroked one of the cats. The cat pushed herself into my hand. It's instinctive. I had to get Rachel out of there. Later she told me she thought I would leave her for the cat. She was jealous of a cat.

Hrabal, I found, was born months before the beginning of World War I. March 28, 1914, making him an Aries, like me. He was born just outside Brno. He would not know his dad. His biological father was sent off to war before he could marry his son's mother. Here's the worst part, I had no idea: Hrabal died last year, 1997, when he "fell" from a fifth-floor hospital window. They say he was trying to feed the pigeons.

He grew up in Nymburk, a small town just east of Prague. He lived there in the local brewery with his parents and his beloved Uncle Pepin. When he died, he was buried in a casket inscribed with the words *Pivovar Polná* (Polná Brewery).

He married Eliška Plevová in 1956. His beloved "Pipsi" preceded him in death in 1987.

His most famous works were *I Served the King of England* and *Closely Watched Trains*; the latter was turned into a movie and won the Oscar for Best Foreign Film in 1967. The description of his style is very enticing: lyrical, highly visual, grandiose, energetic, diverse. I have to read Hrabal. His story gets more confounding. In 1959, his first book was withdrawn a week before it was printed. Then again in 1970, two of his books were banned, after they'd been printed and bound but before they'd been distributed. It couldn't have been fun to be a writer under the Communist regime, especially one who wasn't very much in line with the Communist ideology. He described his stylistic flourishes to one reporter as being in "defense against politics." His characters often fell into the category of wise fools. He seemed to enjoy coupling crude, sometimes lewd, humor with "a baroque imagination" — that's how Kundera put it. He was fascinated by the juxtaposition of beauty and cruelty. The adjectives abound: bawdy, explicit, morbid, eccentric, subversive and sentimental. I found myself wanting more, how did he grow up, what jobs did he have?

He studied law at Charles University, but his studies were interrupted when the Nazis banned secondary education across the Protectorate in 1939. When he earned his law degree in 1946, he never put it to use. Instead, he worked as a railway linesman, a train dispatcher, as a laborer at the Kladno iron works, an insurance salesman, a stagehand and a wastepaper baler — lines of work where he could find "reality" in the wild. He is fascinated with finding the beautiful in the mundane.

He was an epic stylist. Two of his books consisted of a single sentence. He called his lyrical, run-on narrative style *pábení*, which means palavering. I read a description of his work that said, "Some writers talk like writers; Hrabal writes like a talker." He loved to hold court in The Golden Tiger, the place I took my mother back in April when she visited. I still have that picture of President Clinton, Václav Havel and Hrabal drinking beer at The Golden Tiger.

I want to know more about what it was like to be a writer under the Communists. Censorship. That's what it was like. After the Prague Spring was crushed in the treads of Russian tanks, Hrabal's work was banned. He continued to write. From 1970 to 1976 nothing of his was published, except in *samizdat* editions. His work appeared again in 1976, even then under controversy. He had granted an interview to the magazine *Tvorba* in 1975 and it appeared to frame him as a Socialist sympathizer. It has been shown to have been heavily edited, this interview, but even so people burned his books. He was publicly called a whore. The most interesting fact I read was the view that the Communist regime had had to allow him to publish, he was a writer of such standing.

A new Hrabal quote posted in the water closet. I don't know who did it. The handwriting is Czech.

"It's interesting how young poets think of death while old fogies think of girls."
— Bohumil Hrabal

Weddinging, 9.10.98
I'm wearing a suit. I'm at the airport. I'm going to Barcelona.
Reminds me of my Tarot reading back in June with Willie. I got two horses. Now is not a bad time to go. A good time to party, a good time to enjoy friends. I can grow later.
The fog's bad. I'll be late if I get there at all. It's out of my hands now.
I don't know who'll be at the wedding. Dalia Babat? I wish.

Tad will have her email, though. Start of yet another email relationship. The plane is boarding. Here we go. This should be fun. I'm in row 14. I don't know where that is. I don't think it matters.

I think of all the people I expect to see at the wedding. Benny Pagel and Dudley Durbin are the other bachelors I know to be attending. I'm rooming with Benny, splitting the cost. I can picture him now, sitting on the floor playing his guitar, shaggy hair, woven belt, brown and white topsiders. My memory of Dudley is more frenetic. Rubbing his face, shouting, scaring girls. Then the couples and the married folk. The Reynolds, Chuck and Kristy, a year younger than me, in the same class as Tad. Chuck's forehead makes me think of Easter Island. Kristy reminds me of Mary Tyler Moore, she has the right thing to say all the time. The Foulds, Kurt and Abigail, my jock friends. I was Kurt's roommate when they started dating. I remembered Kurt as pigeon-toed and cocky. Balanced out by a down-to-earth field hockey player, Abi. Abi knew how to talk to me. She's the one who could ask tough questions. The Foulds had been at my wedding. Not the Reynolds. Not the Bettelheims, Jacob and Ryan. Jacob in med school with his suspenders and Ryan the photographer, she's pregnant, must be showing by now. Jacob and Ryan lived in New York at the same time Rachel and I divorced. Jacob had drunk a beer or two with me in those days. He bore the brunt of my sob story.

That's how it went. I was in the same class as Dudley, Benny, Kurt and Abi; one year younger were Tad, the Reynolds and the Bettelheims. Despite which classes we were in, I was perhaps closest to Jacob and Ryan. I had been roommates with Kurt and another time with Dudley. I hoped Dalia would be there.

The two Spanish girls next to me are young; one is cute. She has a deep voice, glasses.

I fell asleep before the plane took off. I had the dream again. The box was red. Without opening it, I could see seven envelopes. Each one sealed in wax stamped with symbols I don't recognize. The letters inside had not been written yet. The letters wrote themselves. I put the box on a shelf in my grandmother's attic.

I woke with a cough. I nodded at the girl with the glasses. I got out my journal.

I scribble away in my journal on the fold-down table. It occurs to me: in any other country, I'd be a star for being a writer. I'd be admired. That's the one thing about Prague that sucks. No different in America. I am not a writer. Let me not slip back into that again.

The plane descended. Turbulence started in. I had trouble journaling.

What was more beautiful? The clouds out the window, or this young Spanish girl next to me with the glasses? She held everything close to her face. She cleaned crumbs off her tray. She thumbed a paper in her hands. She let her hair down. When we landed, he girl in the glasses clapped. They all clapped. I clapped too.

The highway from the airport took us past idyllic green hills. Past the Sagrada Familia. Curvilinear, dripping-sand towers. The driver got off the highway and snaked up curving roads. We climbed higher and higher.

I snuck into a pew at the back of the church.

I saw Kurt and Abigail. They saw me. Kurt tapped Benny, and Benny slapped the shoulder of Jacob, Jacob tapped Chuck. A ripple of heads turned, smiled, waved, turned back. I sweated. Tad looked handsome, an American hero. He stood tall in his black tuxedo, black bowtie. Sofia glowed, her bronze-blond hair resplendent, her veil turned up. When she smiled, you could see her bottom teeth. A tear welled up in the corner of her eye.

Tad was at my wedding. Sofia wasn't — don't think he knew her yet. Benny, Kurt, Abigail — they were all there. No one was too surprised when Rachel and I divorced. No one showed much interest when I moved to Europe. It's the way it is when divorce hits you. Close friends get closer, distant friends get distanter. When a marriage breaks up, it's more than the CD collection that you have to split, more than the books. We were fortunate that we didn't have kids. A small blessing, covered in mess.

A church on a mountain overlooking the sea. The Temple Expiatori del Sagrat Cor, or the Temple of the Sacred Heart of Jesus, towers above the city below. With 360-degree views of the mountains and city and sea, it is an inspiring place. What events in our lives together had conspired to bring us all here?

Sofia's parents were married here. Sofia was baptized here. Father Fernández, a Catholic priest, officiated. He had baptized Sofia. He told the story of watching her grow up. In English. The flush on Sofia's face. Reminded me of Rachel flushing, for a different reason. At our wedding, Rachel was only one week out from burying her mother in the deep dark ground.

Outside the church the receiving line, held in the sun on the patio. I met Rafa, Sofia's yellow-eyed younger brother. I shook hands with Dudley. I met and immediately forgot the names of two of Sofia's three bridesmaids: the married one, the younger one. Camila, though, her name I remembered. I felt Sofia watching us as our eyes met for the first time.

A 1969 Seat 1500, a classic convertible, whitewall tires and painted a handsome off-white color. Tad and Sofia are driven away by the yellow-eyed Rafa.

Abi stood with me. She didn't say anything. So familiar how she moved, lithe and athletic. I first met Abigail Wisniewski as a freshman in college. She was dating my roommate, Kurt. Now they're married and living in Manhattan up around 34th Street. Kurt does private equity. Last time I was at their place he showed me a proposal to buy a sports team — that's what he was working on. Tall, square chin, blond hair parted on the side. He wears a cream-colored suit and a blue tie. Standing next to him in my slate-gray suit, rumpled from the plane ride, I make him look more elegant; he makes me look more shabby. Abigail is thin and sophisticated in a Connecticut kind of way.

The old schoolbus painted the classic red and yellow of the Catalan flag. Cava in a plastic flute for the bus ride — tiny bubbles tickled my sinuses. Poles are wrapped in red lights. The seats are fuzzy, yellow. Surrounded by guys I went to school with, guys from my fraternity. Four of them married their college girlfriends. Tad was marrying a woman he met after school, a woman he'd met while working.

The groomsmen, dressed in black tuxedos, with peach bow ties and matching pleated cummerbunds. The bridesmaids, dressed in tasteful peach dresses, each different from the other, sat upfront. The Cava tasted good. It was chilled and sparkling. We clicked plastic glasses. Benny met my eyes.

Divorce has a stink to it. People turn up their noses at you. Like it's contagious. I wondered for a quick second what they said about me and Rachel when I wasn't there. That's not me. I try not to care what other people think. Good friends don't judge. The ones who do aren't friends anyway.

The bus turned, groaning, into a residential neighborhood. Trees, houses, a park.

The restaurant was decorated like a treehouse.

Table 5. An archway of green leaves. I stepped through. All around the room there were arbors. Hung from the ceiling are a few swings, white rope, wooden seats. The swings were immediately overrun by shrieking little Spanish kids. A boy in a vest and clunky shoes, a girl in a dress with ribbons.

There was a lot of peach at Table 5, the bridal party seated among the guests. Tad had warned me that this wedding was going to be a little non-traditional. I didn't mind it at all.

I was across from Camila, and next to the young one. The young one was very pretty, dark hair, too much hairspray, her foundation cakey on her chin. She spoke good English. Camila had dark skin, crimson lipstick, light brown hair and light brown eyes. Her peach dress was a mermaid cut with ruffles flaring, hip and hem. The shoulders balanced at the edge. Sweetheart neckline. She removed the napkin from her lap and stood to greet me. The hip ruffle snapped. I met her eyes. My gaze dropped to her feet. Gold strappy heels. Her toenails tipped in antique white.

The young bridesmaid wore a bandage dress, a sheer cape. It made her look even younger. Tall, potted trees with braided trunks were the centerpieces. A little awkward to talk across the table. Camila leaned diagonally to catch my attention. "Joseph, tinto de verano?"

She gave the waiter our order. The sounds of children on swings.

A wistful look in the young bridesmaid's eye. "The kids should take a break. Let the adults play."

I smiled at the comment. The married bridesmaid jostled back and forth with the swing, worried that the little girl with dark ringlets would fall off.

I turned back from watching the mom jiggling in her tight dress, feeling guilty for having noticed. Camila said something to the younger one beside me in Spanish. She responded in Spanish.

Lara, that was her name, the younger one beside me. She told me that her parents, Camila's parents and Sofia's parents are all Catalonians. Their fathers are old old friends. I saw them outside smoking cigarettes. I imagine talking politics.

A sweating glass pitcher of a red drink pimpled with sliced oranges, the ice tinkling. A tray of pint glasses. Camila poured four drinks, each garnished with an orange. Cut in quarters, peels on.

Glasses eye level, she said, "Salud!" We repeated the toast and clicked glasses, looking each into the other's eyes as the glasses touched. The fizzy drink was light and refreshing despite the dark red color. Red wine and Fanta Limon, a drop of vermouth. Camila watched me as I cataloged the flavors.

I told them it was my first time in Barcelona. I had been to Madrid. Reina Sofia. Picasso.

"She is saying that we should take you to the Museu Picasso," Lara translated for me.

Rafa said something in Spanish about a fish. I asked if he was referring to paella. I had heard a lot about paella.

Camila shook her head vehemently. Was that a flirty head roll? "No! Gehry fish." She took a sip. She tipped her chin at Lara.

She reminded me. 1992 Olympics. Lara asked me if I remembered the fish? I didn't remember any fish.

Camila set her glass down, leaned around the tree. "I will take you." She winked.

We stood to welcome the bride and groom. Tad was stiff. Sofia was born to be married. Surely she had the puffy wish-list three-ring binder tied with a ribbon, the trousseau ready to go. Hand-stitched pillowcases and ironed sheets, napkins for the dining-room table. She'd made them all in her grandmother's parlor as a teenager. What is that part of me that craves formality and rigidity? Was I not a modern man?

Sofia hugged her godfather. He held her at arm's length, said something. He crushed her to his chest. He grabbed Tad by his forearm, an armlock more than a handshake, then threw his arms around him in a wild hug.

I smelled something like freshly cut cork. Camila was at my shoulder. I nodded and smiled, trying not to look at the faint smile lines around her mouth. What is it about this age, not quite young, getting older, a promise of maturity? More real and less plastic, less fleeting than youth?

Sofia and Tad did the obligatory drive-by. When Sofia hugged me, I felt the ribs of her bony dress on my sternum. Her eyes narrowed as she smiled at me. She edged around the divorce thing. Discreet, she talked privately with me. She had that effect, we were simpatico; she cut through the niceties and talked to me.

Tad said welcome in Spanish with the beginnings of the right pace and slur. He was picking it up.

Camila tagged along as we said hi to Tad's folks, looking out of place at the parents' table. She already knew them. Camila waved to the woman across the table, behind her own braided trunk centerpiece. Was she an older, more refined Camila, in pearls and a wine-colored scoop-neck dress? I got Mr. Williams a fresh drink, and a whiskey for Tad's mother. I knew he would want ice in his Coke. I asked, but the bartender forgot it.

Camila shrugged and raised a finger toward the back of the bartender. She was embarrassed by the lack of respect. So sweet.

At Table 5, I poured a little Coca-Cola into my empty glass, scooped ice from the pitcher with a spoon into the tall glass, drank the excess Coca-Cola, "Just have to improvise. Adapt. Do you know this word, *adapt*?"

Camila watched in bafflement. "Yes. I know. Like *change*."

I nodded. "Sometimes, you have to change." I could feel Ingrid sitting on my shoulder, arms crossed, shaking her long black hair at me. I remembered the cut on the white white scalp of Ilona. I would have to be a gentleman. This was Sofia's family. I couldn't be a cad. Rats.

We delivered the drinks. I thought to hold out the crook of my elbow to Camila, but we weren't yet at the arm-in-arm place. What would people think? People would think what people would think, that's what people would think. A faint whiff of that cork smell again. Clean, fresh.

"Hey, Joey, how's your mother? We really liked her, didn't we, Rebekkah? A good woman." Rebekkah nodded in the affirmative. My mother had called me Joey in front of them once; Mr. Williams didn't let it go.

I told them I had spoken to her from the airport. I didn't mention any of her troubles. I didn't mention my concerns.

Once the speeches and the first dances were out the way, the real party began. The DJ dropped "Jump" by Kriss Kross. Tad waved me onto the dance floor. The tables emptied. It was a moment. We caught the beat and the vibe. We took off. It's like electricity how it flowed across all those connections, old and new. It had been six years since I saw most of these people, but it was like we were right back there in Cambridge, like we were back on Memorial Drive dancing on the beer-sticky floors. No one was married back then, no one was divorced, we were students, we were having a good time. There was Camila. She gave me a look, this unguarded, unvarnished look. If all of Barcelona was a port opening her arms to the Mediterranean, at that moment Camila was too.

Today, Tad was the luckiest man on earth. I wanted what he had. It hit me hard. I needed a breath of air. The song changed to Arrested Development, "Tennessee." We all sung together:

Take me to another place,
Take me to another land,
Make me forget all that hurts me,
Let me understand your plan...

Sofia came to the middle of our group. A circle formed. She sang.

Take me home. Take me home.

I had tears in my eyes. I thought of Rachel. She used to love this song. Probably still does. I didn't turn away from the feeling. I didn't push it down or away. I let it be. In my chest.

In the shade of a ginkgo tree, Tad sipped his beer and looked at me. I looked over at the older men smoking cigarettes by the building. One day we would be them.

"How's Prague?"

"It's beautiful. Old, magical. The girls are…" I caught myself. Tad smiled through his beer glass. He swallowed hard. "It's okay, my man. I got married today, not you."

I kicked at one of the golden plum-sized fruits in the grass beneath the tree. A faint smell of rancid butter came to my nose.

I took a sip of tinto to replace the stink.

"We all hated that you and Rachel split up. I liked her. I liked you with her. That's over and done. Must be fun to be free." Tad raised his eyebrows at me.

I told him he was the luckiest man on earth. Tad smirked.

He told me that Camila had broken it off with a younger man a couple of months back. A few bad dates since then. She was getting her confidence back. He said it as if I could be of use in that department.

I told him that Camila might be too good for me. I asked about Dalia.

Tad shook his head.

I nodded, recalling her wild hair, the female Einstein. Just as well.

Tad put his hand on my shoulder. "What have I been telling myself all week? Remember where you come from. That's what I said to myself just before I walked down the aisle. Camila can make her own choices. Listen, you'll like this. This tree, I looked them up. Ginkgo biloba. Symbol of changelessness. A symbol of love." Tad pointed his glass at me. "This one here's a female, see the fruit?" Tad reached out a toe of his patent-leather black shoe. He kicked the thing, sent it flying. "Smells like puke."

I laughed, pinching my nose. "Fuck, that reeks."

Back inside, I danced with Camila. I soaked in the moment. A beautiful woman, in one of the great cities of Europe, celebrating the marriage of two friends.

Sitting back at our table, I looked around the room at my friends. Benny's dark suit with his trademark woven belt and topsiders. Benny rowed crew in school; these days he's working off his graduate student loans as a junior associate attorney in some DC firm. With a guitar in his lap, back in the day, we pictured him: hippie lawyer fighting for the rights of wood owls in Oregon. Here he was in debt up to his button-down collar. He worked hundred-hour weeks in international law, which sounds exciting until he explains it's mostly taxes.

Dudley held court with the wedding party and the parents. Dud would wear a tux every day if he could. Dressing casual is where he struggles. He practically performed for them.

Benny set down his drink. He started in on stories from our days in school. I watched the Spaniards soak it in. They loved the stories of these American geniuses doing dumb stuff.

Camila tipped back. Rafa was on his feet, doubled over. Now Kurt, Chuck and Jacob were with us too. Benny looked at me wide-eyed, I shrugged, Camila was laughing so hard her napkin wiped tears. Rafa was patting the hands of the woman in the flower dress. Her shoulders jerked with laughter. The waiter, a line of banquet waiters, each holding two plates, looked annoyed. Loud Americans. How embarrassing. I knew better. I had seen Real Madrid fans in the streets after a soccer match in Prague. We were no different than any drunken mob anywhere else. Despite the rolling eyes. I reminded myself to tip the waiters and bartenders. I hoped I had enough pesetas in my pocket.

I was a banquet waiter once. Serve over the left, clear over the right. There's a right way and a wrong way of doing things. The protein faced the guest. If you have the staff, plates at the table should be served simultaneously. They had enough waiters. In one of my more adventurous moments I had checked the box next to the Fish option on the RSVP card. My dinner was now staring back at me. Grilled Whole Branzino with Herb Confetti. His little mouth gaped. His eye stared up at me blankly. Garnish of grilled lemon halves. It was just that head, that disturbing eye.

I looked at Lara's plate. She got the steak. It smelled amazing. Colorful presentation, baked lemons, bell peppers in green, yellow, orange and red. A red sauce and the brown meat. Camila got the same. Rafa and I had the fish. The sommelier came around and poured Rioja for those with steak and white wine for me and Rafa. I looked up. I pronounced the Czech version of *bon appétit*.

Lara responded in Catalan, "Bon profit." Rafa and Benny responded in unison, "Servido!" Look at Benny showing off.

Rafa showed me how to eat the eyes of the fish, the cheek. The eyes tasted like the whole ocean at once. The cheek was buttery, juicy. At Rafa's prodding, I tasted the tailfin; it crunched like a seaweed potato chip. With a sip of the creamy white wine? Out of this world.

"How do you like my wine?" Sofia's father put his hand on my shoulder. I stood and shook his hand vigorously. He pulled me in for a hug. In a rush of words, Lara explained who I was. He held me by the arms. He said something in Spanish to Lara. I bowed to Sofia's mother. Square cheekbones and a pointed chin, thick walnut hair. Sofia had her eyes.

Lara leaned in. "He doesn't speak much English, He rehearsed that one line. He thinks it's funny." I looked over to where Sofia's father was hugging Camila. I smiled at the familiarity of old family friends.

Camila nodded, smiling. I admired the lanky curls of her thick, dark brown hair.

I made my way across the aisle. At Table 4, Kristy's chair was pulled back from the table. Sofia admired her baby bump. I stole a seat next to Abi. I gestured to Camila to join us. Ryan took a few candid shots with her camera.

Camila smiled devilishly. "Tell me about Joseph. What was he like in school?"

They couldn't resist.

"Quite the ladies' man, right, Joseph?" Kristy smirked.

Ryan kept on. "You know what, though? He was a good friend to Jacob. Kurt too, right?"

Abi nodded. "Yeah. Joey and I talked back then. You remember?"

"You were like a big sister to me. Mean, always hitting me when I wasn't looking." I smiled at Abi.

Abigail nodded. She looked at Camila. "He was a good friend. Joey's a good listener." Abi smiled at me. I remembered that night, sitting on a couch in the dark, talking. I was busy trying to flunk out of freshman year, Kurt was drunk and being obnoxious. I told her to be patient. I had no idea what I was saying. I could've been wrong.

Camila smiled at me. "Ladies' man, yes?" She nudged me with her shoulder. I frowned.

"That's not how it felt." I leaned forward. Abi snorted. Ryan made a pfft sound, swiveling in her chair. "Jacob, what was that girl's name who Joseph dated in school?"

"Dalia?"

Abi answered, "No, not Dalia, the other one…"

Ryan under her breath, to me, "You dated Dalia? I thought she was with…"

Jacob countered, "Kate?"

Ryan answered, "No, you know the one, beautiful, short…"

Jacob, "Marissa?"

Abi, "Gizzy? Something like that?"

Ryan, "No, I remember her, but no."

Jacob, "Suzie? Alex? Gabbi?"

"She means Heather." I looked directly at Ryan, I held her accountable. She started this horrible game.

Ryan sat forward, pumping her finger at me. "Thank you, yes. Heather. Oh, that hair? I could never get this mop to look like that. Whatever happened to her?" Ryan played humble. She had beautiful red hair. Her hair was plenty shiny.

Jacob, to himself, "Heather, Heather. Oh, yeah, I remember Heather."

Abi pursed her lips. Camila looked at me.

"She ran away. Dropped out of school."

Ryan crossed her arms. "Which is another way of saying that you broke her heart and destroyed her life."

Benny stood. "She was two-timing you, right? Didn't you catch her at a party drinking Flaming Dr. Peppers with some guy? Could not keep it in her pants." Benny had talked to her a few times. He held it against her more than I did. Benny bounced on a knee, hands in pockets. He shrugged.

Camila counted on her fingers.

What I saw was a boy lifting a young woman onto a bar, her knees on either side of him. It was a trigger for something I had witnessed a long time ago. I stopped returning her calls. I didn't want to talk about it.

Abi reached across to Camila. "Joseph's a good guy. Got himself hurt a few times along the way." Abi patted Camila's forearm.

Camila softened. She sat back in her chair. "Ladies' man," she said, smiling at me, searching my face for a hint. We'd find out about her dude later.

Later, Lara pushed Camila on the swing. They separated, they paused, they came back together, they paused. Lara beckoned to me. I stealthily replaced her. Camila had kicked off her gold strappy heels. She pumped with bare feet until she glided through the air. I ran my hands along the sides of her hips. I pushed her again. She flipped her hair over one shoulder. She spoke in Spanish. I imagined her to say, "Handsy, much?"

I grabbed one rope on her return, she spun around into me. She giggled, leaning her shoulder against my chest.

Back at the hotel, I checked in. Beaded curtains, incense burning in the foyer, thick tapestries and heavy drapes. Old books in each room, wine bottles with the wicker bottoms, tapered candles on every level surface. A fortune teller with a crystal ball would have fit right in. Benny and I had one of our epic late-night chats. Actual glasses in the room. A couple of guys who had lived together in much worse conditions. Benny sat cross-legged on his bed.

He asked me about the divorce. I told him. I rambled. I told him I had a recent incident in Prague.

Benny interrupted my soliloquy. "Think they'll make it?"

I held the glass halfway to my mouth. "If you told me one of the brothers was going to marry a Spanish woman, the last person I would've thought is Tad."

Benny asked me if I thought Rachel and I had common interests.

I told him what he already knew.

"You thought she would change. She and I talked about it.

It was something we had in common." It was a source of contention between me and Rachel. I knew she was friendly with Benny. I resented it. They both had dead parents. They thought it made them special. I resented it because it left me out.

"What about Camila?" Benny let me off the hook. I was sore about Rachel. He got up, undershirt and boxers, poured more beer. I took a swig.

Back on his bed, Benny squints. "An incident in Prague. Don't think I know that one."

I thought about leaving it alone. It would hurt to admit this one.

"I hooked up with a mutual friend. I got her in the family way." This was not me. Hooked up? So crass. I would not normally use euphemisms. In the family way? Ick. Who was this talking?

"And?"

"She had it taken care of. I went with her. It was a mind fuck." He knew my story — my parents kept it a secret from me. I figured it out when I was eleven. My mom could have chosen that. She didn't. She dropped out of school to have me. "First one in her family to make it to college, she was proud of that. Within a year she was out on her ass. One wild night with my dad."

"A mind fuck for you? You are an ass sometimes, you know? One wild night. Don't be stupid." How would Benny know? He didn't know.

Benny is the kind of friend who can call you an ass, and stupid, in the same breath. I smiled. I took a sip of my beer. I looked down at my chest. Well worth a little lost sleep.

"Don't go self-hating. Tell me."

I told him the story. Two friends in bed after a night of drinking. I told him we used up boxes of condoms. I told him she was on the pill. I told him she was hurt that I didn't argue for her to have it. I told him I thought that's what she would want; a total disregard for my opinion. I told him I missed my chance to tell her about my mother. "In the end, none of this matters. She had an aneurysm; childbirth would have killed her."

"Jesus." I got the irony, this utterance from a Jewish man. "Don't make it easy on yourself, do you? She's on the pill, you used a condom, she still got pregnant? That's bad luck. Worse, you can't tell your mom. You aren't that close with your dad. Your brother?"

I told him Sam and Gwen were trying. Couldn't tell them.

"Benny Pagel is the first person to know? I'm honored."

"Fuck you, Benny," I smiled. I drank the beer. Benny didn't question Ilona's integrity. Wouldn't think to.

Benny told me he loved me. He told me I needed to call him. "You're a good person, Joey P. Try not to forget it."

I asked if he knew about Ingrid.

"Everyone knows. We worry about you. The drugs and stuff." Benny reminded me that not everything is scorched earth, that I wasn't a miserable failure. "Look at us. This might be heaven on earth." I laughed. Benny was a rationalist to the core. He didn't believe in heaven. He certainly didn't believe in romance. Something was in the air. Even for Benny.

I thought to ask Benny what I should do if Camila wanted to have sex with me. Should I tell her no out of respect for Ilona? Out of respect for what I had done? Could I live with myself? I knew what he would say.

We went to sleep. Silently I prayed for Tad and Sofia, for Sammy and Gwen, for my mother and father. For Ingrid and Ilona.

Two-timing, 12.10.98

Sunday was a travel day. Today is Monday. I'm back in Prague. Let me finish with the weekend's events.

Saturday morning. After the wedding. Benny was already up and out, woven belt and topsiders. I showered, put on fresh clothes, a pair of jeans and a T-shirt. I headed down to find some coffee. Orange juice would be asking too much.

A small tour bus picked us up at the hotel after coffee. Kurt and Abi, Chuck and Kristy, Jacob and Ryan, Benny and Dudley, rode with me. Camila and Lara met us outside the ticket window. They had purchased tickets for us with a private tour guide. I glided off the bus with a nonchalant strut that hid my unease. Camila looked good, dressed like she was going to tapas rather than going on a tour of an unfinished Roman Catholic cathedral. The first foundation block, I had read, was laid in 1882; the Basilica had been under construction ever since. It's chief architect, Antoni Gaudí, spent his life planning this building, his magnum opus. When he died, he was buried in its crypt. The distinctive towers are said to combine the Gothic with the Art Nouveau style, but to me they called to mind the sandcastles Sam and I used to make in Cocoa Beach, Florida, on spring break with our parents; near to the ocean where the beach darkens, we would scoop up handfuls of the liquid sand. We cupped it, allowed it to drip out the crease between our hands like melting candle wax, into stalagmite piles. I imagined Gaudí had done the same on the Barcelona beaches. The inspiration for his fabulous spires. Eighteen of them, he had imagined; today eight have been built.

Camila sensed that this visit would be inspiring for me. She sidled up with a knowing smile. We stood in front of the austere Passion facade. My neck bent back to allow my eyes to take in the skeletal stone, the boomerang-shaped arch over my head. I was smitten with the place. The audacity of it, fearlessly playful and whimsical; must have been monumentally difficult to bring to life.

We rode up on a crowded elevator, Camila crushed against me, holding my hand. Only six of us could fit; we split the group. At the top, we were afforded expansive views of the sea and the east part of the city. The descent was an experience unto itself, almost surpassing the views. Spiral staircases without rails give you the impression of coming down from a very steep high indeed. The stairs themselves put you in mind of a snail's shell; you climb down into its secret whorls.

We entered the more baroque Nativity facade. It was the first one completed. We rode up the elevator into the spire. We gorged our eyes on the view of the city center. We noticed the difference: these four towers Gaudí himself built during his lifetime. The details within the towers give the impression of piles, not so much of dripping sand, but more like mounds of pottery shards, split open, spilling over.

Camila watched me. I absorbed the genius of Gaudí's creativity. Like Gaudí, she later told me, she believed that Mediterranean people were naturally gifted in creativity, originality, with an innate sense of style and taste.

Dazed, we walked back out of Nativity facade. The shuttle bus appeared, and we boarded. Lara directed the driver to our lunch plans. They had called ahead and ordered paella for ten at a place called 7 Portes. It was a good sign. My seven-letters dream from the plane. Lara assured us it was the second-best paella available in all of Barcelona; first place reserved, of course, for her grandmother. Cava Sangria at the table had been specially prepared for us. Lara and Camila related the history of paella. Near the water, the dish was prepared by the families of the fishermen with the catch of the day: fish, squid, mussels, crayfish and shrimp. Farther inland, seafood was mixed with vegetables. It's an inland Catalonian tradition to mix seafood and vegetable paella with chicken, pork, rabbit, duck or sausage.

We didn't look at menus. The center of our table was round. The air was thick with the smell of seafood and wood-fired stoves.

Ryan baited me. "What did you think of the Sagrada Familia?"

I told them what I thought. I was inspired. "I bet some people hate it." I took a drink of Cava.

Lara nodded. "It splits people. Some think it takes away from the cathedral of Barcelona. Others are convinced that since Gaudí died, 1926, his vision was lost."

Ryan said, "Compare it to Prague."

A man came through the doors with an enormous pan in his arms. A vast metal dish with wooden handles, the size of our entire table. He settled it in front of us. An old woman in a white lace head covering and long black sleeves came around to each of us, filling our plates. I looked at Camila. She grinned with her hands clasped below her chin, watching our awe. It's the kitchen-sink kind of cooking, paella. Each ingredient is cooked to perfection and added at the precise instant to achieve harmony. I took a forkful.

Camila's print top glowed in the afternoon light. She was dressed perfectly for a fall day in Barcelona: denim with a thin brown belt, matching strappy brown shoes, and her hair playfully free. I let the flavors fill my sinuses. I closed my eyes, opened them again. Ryan, stylish in her navy cardigan over a white Henley, her curly hair spilling to her shoulders, waited for my answer.

I shook my head. "Can't. In Europe, you can have both."

Jacob took a bite of paella and nodded in agreement. Lara squirmed in her chair. Camila reached for my hand under the table.

Dudley reminded them they would get to judge for themselves. He and Benny had tickets to stay at my flat. Ryan and Jake were looking for last-minute flights. When you live in America, I remembered, Europe was a week or two of vacation. My friends were now experiencing the jetlag and the compression of vacation traveling. I hadn't wanted that when I came to Europe. I wanted to stay.

From 7 Portes, the bill paid, we stepped out onto the street. We had to walk a couple of blocks to get back to the little tour bus. We were heading to a dance club. The evening had caught up with us, the night air carrying a warm wind off the water.

Camila picked me up at the hotel. I had time to shower, change clothes, brush my teeth, spritz some cologne. After what had happened with Ilona, would I be able to go through with it? I wasn't sure. It was just a few weeks back.

We parked in an empty parking lot adjacent to the boardwalk. It was the dark end of the beach. The night air was humid. There was a homeless man on the beach. He mumbled to us. Camila responded, polite but firm. We walked along listening to the sound of the waves. Camila stopped at the edge of the board-walk and took off her shoes. I took mine off too. We left them in the sand. I wondered if they would be there when we got back.

In the near-total darkness down by the water, she asked me if I had anyone back in Prague. I told her, under the light of the huge Gehry fish, sleek and modern, curved and linear at the same time. I told her no one special. The tail tipped up like hope.

Camila sat down in the sand. I sat next to her, folding my arms around my knees. The hot breath of the night held us. I asked about her boyfriend.

She told me that he was younger. Her friends liked him. "I did it for me. I needed more. Does that make me needy?"

"At our age, we should know what we want."

Camila kissed me.

We rolled around in the sand. Camila pressed herself into me. I didn't worry about the sand, didn't think about it. I undid her belt, I undid her pants. She wanted more. I whispered in her ear, "Not here."

Back at the hotel, we rode up in the elevator. Nothing had to happen. I convinced myself nothing would happen. I remembered Tad's words. I remembered Ilona. I imagined her hunched over her books.

In her jeans and T-shirt, Camila's tan skin glowed bronze. Her hair hung down straight. Those lines around her mouth. In the wavy reflection of the elevator doors, we could have been a married couple on vacation trying to rekindle a lost love.

The air-conditioning whirred. It felt good on us. She sat on the chair where I had talked with Benny the night before. Benny had made other arrangements. I sat on the edge of the bed. I kept my shoes on.

Camila unbuckled a sandal and tossed it at the door. She undid the other. She left it there, coming toward me.

She sighed near my mouth. I pulled my head back. Her forehead creased. I smiled. "I don't have a condom."

"I don't have one too."

"Give me a minute." I stood up by the bed. My erection made itself known through my jeans. Camila looked.

"I go." I sounded like Tarzan.

"I shower, yes?" I nodded, my lips welded together. I adjusted myself in my jeans.

I went down to the lobby. A convenience store with toothpaste and tampons? I hoped. Nothing. I asked the young woman at the front desk, "Condom?" She shrugged at me. "Farmacia? Too late."

I had one last resort. It was awkward, maybe even mean. I hesitated. Fuck it. I rode up in the elevator to Dudley's floor. I knocked on his door. No answer. I knocked again. His hair all over the place, squinty eyes, Benny poked his head out.

"I hate this. Do you have a condom?"

"You really are an ass, you know?" Benny said through a yawn.

Benny shut the door on me. My shoulders slumped. Camila might leave unsatisfied. Unless... Benny opened the door. He swung his arm out. "Have fun." He handed me two condoms.

I bounded up the stairs. In my haste I had forgotten my key. Stupid, Joseph, really stupid. These are the stories you hear. Foreigner brings a woman back to his hotel room, leaves her in his room with his keys, wallet, passport. When he comes back with condoms, she's gone. Stolen everything. I knocked on my door. I knocked again. Camila opened up. She was wearing my pajama top.

"Did you..."

I held one up. Camila smiled. She sat on the bed with a flounce. I said, "You know, we don't have to do this. We can cuddle." Camila stood up. She grabbed me by the belt.

"Are you afraid of me, Joseph?" I kicked off my shoes.

She scooted up the bed. I crawled to her. I hesitated. She grabbed the hem of my shirt. She pulled it up over my head. My black hair fell in my eyes. She giggled.

I looked at her. Chin, neck, shoulder, arm. I kissed her on her neck. She shuddered. She sat up. "Where is it?"

She tore the packet open. She set it on me like a communion wafer. Holding the tip with one hand, she rolled the condom down the length of me with the other. She got on top and reached down between her legs, guiding me in. Her hands held my ribs. Outside, the buskers on Las Ramblas tuned their instruments. Money rained down into their hats.

She held up one finger for me to see. She pointed at her sternum and held up the finger. The knuckles of her index finger were knobbed, the way I like. I knew she did. I wasn't sure. I liked that she told me.

She searched my face. I smiled. I nodded. On impulse, I stood up, pulled at the bedspread. It was plush, cotton, a goose-down duvet. She wiggled over it. I pulled the sheet back. I dove in. She turned her back to me. I checked the thing, tugged at the tip, smoothed the length of it.

She looked over her shoulder at me. "Is this okay? Do you like?" She led my nod. She gritted her teeth. She gripped my thigh.

Outside, a gypsy guitar, silk strings, a melancholy howl. The thin cotton sheet over us disappeared. I imagined all the buskers, out there rambling, all around us. Vast dunes of coins. Our breathing was in sync. It overlapped. It was in sync again. Like the teeth of gears knuckling together. A crescendo of cacophony. Gasping, gasping.

I let go of her. I went to the bathroom. I bounded back to her like a golden retriever with my pink tongue hanging out. She held up the sheet. I put my head on her chest. She ran her fingers through my hair.

She pouted. "Only one. Pity." Her accent, the hard *t* sound, added to the hilarity of it. She couldn't see the curl on my lips. She said sweet things. I murmured. She said, "Are you sleepy? Should I go?" I shook my head. She ran her fingers through my chest hair.

I held up a serious face. "What should we do?"

Camila frowned at me. I hesitated. I held it. I tortured her an extra second.

I jumped up. She shrieked. She clapped a hand over her mouth. I grinned like an idiot. The lights were on. The room was splayed; sandals on their sides, piles of undergarments, the shedded duvet. It smelled like sex. I found my jeans. I rummaged through the pockets. She sat up on her elbows. I held the second one up to her with a cheesy grin. She blushed. She fell back against the bed. She pulled the pillow over her face. She screamed. She kicked her tan legs against the bed. I studied her headless body a moment before I tugged at the pillow. She shook with laughter.

We climbed each other like teenagers. We hustled. We shivered with delight. Her tits bounced. I made them jump. She raised two fingers to my eyes. Wow.

She collapsed on my chest. I breathed her in. I watched the lights of Barcelona shift on the ceiling.

I gripped her to me. She held on, dangling like a monkey. I set her down and checked the condom. I pushed into her.

I locked on her eyes. I pulled all the way out. She closed them. The skin of her eyelids stretched.

A flush bloomed on her neck. She sucked air through her teeth. I pushed in hard. I pulled out partway. Couldn't hold it anymore.

I swallowed. I held up two fingers to her. Pointed to my chest, showed her again. Two fingers. She nuzzled her face into my neck. I knew exactly what she meant.

Changing, 13.10.98

It seems there's no way to get Jacob and Ryan to Prague. The plane costs 36,000 CZK (over $1,200). Each. That's double what I paid, way too much. Luckily, Benny and Dudley already had their tickets. Benny and Dudley arrive later today. I'll go and meet them at the airport.

I don't know if I'll see Camila again. Maybe not. I'd love to visit her in Barcelona. We'll see. We have time.

Horáček, the landlord, was here. Of course. The floor was an excuse. He wants me to roll up the linoleum. I can do that. That's not why he was here. I could've guessed. I could've pre-empted him. I could've given him the money. That would've been cool. I told him there was no problem with the money. That's not true. I'll send it.

I'm behind on my rent. Sorry. Sorry for living. Let him throw me out.

You wanted to be poor, big guy. You wanted "not to worry about money." Here you are, worrying about money.

I'll set dinner up with the girls. See if I can get a group of my American and my Czech friends together. I'll start making calls. I don't know if it's possible.

Touring, 14.10.98

So many people. Such a mess. Four people in my apartment; not long since there was only one. Jacques in the living room. Benny and Dudley in sleeping bags in my room. Me on the futon. Benny is threatening to get a hotel room.

I'll make breakfast for the guys.

I took Benny and Dudley to the Charles Bridge as soon as they landed. It's fun to see friends experience the awe for the first time. We stopped and got a beer at the James Joyce before heading back to Old Town Square. I showed them the Astronomical Clock and Iron Street, where I used to live. By the time I got them back to my flat, they had already seen a good bit of Prague. We came up out of the metro under the all-seeing eye. We had fried cheese, with tartare sauce, at a pub near the flat. I took them to Palac Akropolis. In the heart of Žižkov, just a few blocks from my flat on Laubova, atop a steep hill, a stately and grimy old theater. You can feel the underworldliness of the place from the street. Built at the tail end of the Art Deco period, inside it has this multi-layered, multi-chambered labyrinthian feel to it that is essential to a post-revolution cultural playground.

We found a long narrow bar under a low ceiling and ordered.

"Camila was sad when you left." Dudley was quick to share.

"Flying out Sunday after a night at the club? Not perfect."

"She'll be fine," Big Picture Benny, the rational one.

"Honeymoon Mallorca, right?" I sipped my Krušovice Světlé. The big round glasses with the oversized handle. An extra inch of foam on the top, just the way I like it.

Dudley sipped his Krušovice Dark. He wanted to try something different.

"When do we get to meet some of these Czech women you keep talking about?" Benny's question drifted. A young woman swept past us. She had her hair shaved on one side of her head and a collar with spikes. A hoop pierced in the corner of her mouth. Dudley and Benny were struck dumb.

I smiled. "Tomorrow night. You'll see."

Benny sipped his glass of wine, winced. I advised him to stick to beer, he didn't listen. He swallowed hard. "Geez," he said.

Dudley leaned in. "She could teach me how to bark. Ruff."

"What about you, Ben? Any women we should know about?" I was getting him back for our conversation in Barcelona.

"I keep a foot in the game. One woman I dated on and off in law school — we keep in touch." Benny sipped his wine. "This stuff is awful. What did I order?"

I guessed it was burčák. Young Moravian wine. Guaranteed headache for me.

Dudley looked around the bar. I could see jetlag hit him. And Benny.

Wallowing, 15.10.98
Yesterday was Agata's Name Day. I remembered!

I called Brad.

"It is?" I could hear Brad making his way to the Name Day calendar he has on his fridge, "Oh shit, it is."

"If it was me, I would get her eleven carnations and a piece of chocolate. She likes Fidorky. Is it the milk chocolate or the white chocolate she gets?" I couldn't help gloating. I know Brad's girlfriend better than he does.

"I'll get her both. Thanks, man. You saved me."

Jaroslav Seifert
My quest continues. To better understand the literary history of the Czech Republic, I checked this morning to see if a Czech writer had ever won the Nobel Prize for Literature. Yes! Jaroslav Seifert won in 1984. Born in 1901, he was contemporaries with Čapek, who was only eleven years older than he was, and Kundera, who was twenty-eight years his junior.

He was born and grew up in Žižkov in the early twentieth century. That's my neighborhood, mine and Brad's. His mother was a Catholic who attended mass daily. Seifert observed, "Religion was her poetry." His father was a staunch atheist and a social democrat. Despite the strong leadership of TGM, there was a Communist uprising of workers in 1929 that Seifert's father would have been party to. Žižkov in the early twentieth century was densely populated; squalid tenement blocks, taverns and wine bars. As a boy, he would sit on the neighborhood steps and absorb the drunken love songs and rowdy tunes. Seifert writes of his love for the dead-end streets, full of coal dust and soot. Lousy grass growing up through the cobblestones. In one poem he witnesses a white dog with a pink ribbon cut into three pieces by a tram. He prays that he does not end up like the white doggie but rather dies on revolution's rampart with a rifle in his hands.

I read his poem "To Be a Poet" and it is magnificent. I can't believe I hadn't discovered him earlier. Here's the quote I have copied out longhand to hang in my water closet:

"If love is a labyrinth full of glittering mirrors, and it is that, I'd crossed its threshold and entered. / And from the bewitching glitter of mirrors I haven't found the way out to this day."
— Jaroslav Seifert

His work has a lyrical and innocent quality to it, full of awe and wonder. It is a thrill to read. He was expelled from the Communist Party in 1929. His first books came out just as the Czechoslovak Republic was in its infancy. Just before the Prague Spring, in 1966, he was named Poet of the Nation. Then came his appointment as National Artist of Czechoslovakia in 1967. In 1969, he was elected chairman of the Czechoslovakian Writers' Union. One of the first signatories to Charter 77 along with Havel. When he won the Nobel Prize, at the age of eighty-three, he was ill and unable to make the trip to Stockholm. He attempted to send his son-in-law in his place to receive the prize but the Communist government of then Czechoslovakia denied his exit permit.

He died in Prague, January 10, 1986. I need to get my hands on a copy of his book *Sheer Love*.

Arranging, 16.10.98

I'm waiting for a call from Markéta; Jacques has been on the phone for an hour. It's fine; gives me time to journal. Time to relax.

We met up at Terminal Bar. We gathered in the yellow room at the back. Karina wasn't working. Ljuba was there. She wore a black Terminal Bar T-shirt that showed off her red hair and emerald eyes. I watched Dudley look her over as she bent to take drink orders. Agata made an appearance. Izabela stopped by too. It was good to see her. I didn't get a chance to talk to her. I saw Dudley talk to her, study her round face with all of its facets, her long brown hair. She was wearing a cute raincoat with a belt, straight from work. Agata smoked a cigarette and spoke with Benny.

A beautiful night with Jacques, Dudley, Benny, Pat, Markéta, Stella, Josh. We went to Klub Architectu, off Bethlehem Square, I discovered the place with Pat and Markéta. On the street, a chalkboard sign-next to a door. We entered and went down one staircase and another. Then a third. At the bottom a ramp that led down. The archways down here are all brick. Brick archways all around. Not red brick. These bricks were orange. They were wider than they were thick. The tables were tucked back into the carved-out spaces. A large man with greasy hair and a sparse beard came out. He took our orders. We got beer, Benny, Dudley, Jacques and me. They only serve Bernard beer here, which is a travesty. There were sconces on the wall. Lights that hang down over the tables. The place felt heavy. You expected the devil to sit cross-legged behind every pillar, grooming his tail.

The food was lavishly bland, the conversation lively. It was a reunion of sorts. Benny, Dudley and I went to school with Pat. This was their first time seeing him in a long time. I sat on the end with Stella and Josh. Stella worked for a record company and Josh ran a women's health magazine. They didn't know the others.

Jacques and I wrote a love letter to Camila. In English and Spanish. It was nice. I hope she likes it. I know she will. Maybe she'll come to Prague. Could be fun.

Remembering, 17.10.98

I haven't heard from Naked Pete. I was thinking about his story, the fight, the rugby shirt. Don't know why I didn't think of it before. I used to play rugby.

VINIFERA

A raw Western New York April day. The sky is overcast. No more than forty degrees outside.

"Daniella! Let's go!" her mother sings from the bottom of the stairwell.

Dani wears Joey's away rugby uniform jersey, a green and purple Harlequin pattern. Acid-washed jeans. Her navy-blue duck boots. A sure-footed choice for our Capricorn.

Tight ponytail, check. His class ring on a chain around her neck, check. His varsity coat, check. She grabs her oversized canvas bag. On top, a book she got from the school library. It's about the Finger Lakes. It'll take more than good looks and the right clothes to keep Joey's attention. That much is clear.

A light mist dots the windshield of the putty-gray Pontiac Sunbird. Daniella waits the requisite five minutes before she cracks her library book.

Rock weathering. Weathered rock is a combination of sand, silt and clay. The nutrients needed to support plant growth comes from decaying organic material, called humus. When weathered rock combines with humus, the result is soil. Native Americans planted and grew squash as early as 10,000 BC. Making wine from grapes is older than the written word, dates back to 7000 BC.

Joey would love these facts.

Vitis vinifera, the common grape, grew in abundance up and down the east coast of the "New" World. By the 1600s, European explorers began making inroads. Upon viewing vines overtaking a tree, Italian explorer Giovanni da Verrazzano observed that the wild grapes might result in decent wine.

The loam in the Finger Lakes is the essence of the region, the soul. A soil scientist might describe it as a sandy-skeletal, mesic

Glossic Hapludalf. Laypeople would call it Palmyra soil — a grayish-brown gravelly loam found among the drumlins of the northern Finger Lakes.

North American wild grapes grew here naturally. Wines made from these grapes were unsatisfactory. Europeans had cultivated their diverse vinifera grapevines for thousands of years. They were selected for their wine quality. On this side of the Atlantic, the imported rootstock planted in eastern North America failed to survive long enough to bear commercial crops. That is until a true believer came along.

"Please be careful tonight." Mrs. DiBenedetto keeps her eyes on the road.

Dani holds her spot with her finger. "Hmm? O h, y eah, of course."

She continues reading.

German citizen Konstantin Frank arrived in the U.S. in 1951, penniless and not knowing a word of English. Despised by the Russians because of his German heritage and suspected by the Germans of being a spy for the Ukraine, he was a man without a country. He came to America to start anew.

Though he had more than thirty years of wine-making experience in Russia and Ukraine and held a doctorate in viticulture science from the Polytechnic Institute of Odessa, Konstantin ended up washing dishes at an automat in New York City. Over a tub of greasy dishes, he dreamed of a better life. He aspired to get back into the wine industry.

He moved his family to Geneva, on Seneca Lake, to work for the New York State Agricultural Experiment Station.

Konstantin was not the first to attempt growing European grapes in this country. Others, including Thomas Jefferson, had tried, without success. It was assumed the cold winters in the northeastern United States were not suitable for the delicate European vines.

Konstantin knew better. Having grown European varieties in sub-zero climates in Russia and Ukraine, he determined it was the soil, not the climate, that killed the vines.

A pest that lived in the soil named phylloxera was the culprit. The native grapes, he found, were immune to the pest. With that knowledge, he grafted European shoots with native rootstock.

Grafting is an asexual propagation technique important to agriculture, horticulture, and viticulture. Evidence of it, some would argue, dates back to 1400 BC.

What Konstantin did is nothing earth-shattering. The difference, aside from experience, was that he persisted. When others failed, lost hope and quit, he dared to believe.

He grew Chardonnay and Riesling grapes for Gold Seal. He produced wines whose quality rivaled the Europeans. Konstantin's achievement won accolades in the wine community.

By 1962, he had saved enough money from his work at Gold Seal to open his own winery. Situated on Keuka Lake, Dr. Frank's Vinifera Wine Cellar boasts the only all-vinifera vineyard on the East Coast.

The winery business in the Finger Lakes region flourished in the 1970s. There are as many as seven family-owned vineyards and many other commercial vineyards around Keuka Lake alone. Combined with the more than twenty vineyards along the southern shores of Lake Erie, many of them producing varieties of muscadine grapes, you could say Western New York State is entwined in the grape business.

Daniella's mother drops her off in the parking lot of the elementary school. "No drinking, no drugs," her mother sings out the car window. Dani leaves the book on the passenger seat. Mrs. DiBenedetto watches her daughter get smaller in the rearview mirror. She wishes she said no sex. Would it make any difference?

Adjacent to the John F. Kennedy Elementary School, the pitch is a sunken pan of a field. It displays a series of irregular lines spray-painted in an unfamiliar pattern. To Dani, it looks like a refracted football field.

Joey kicks at the grass with his teammates on the sideline. He smiles in her direction as he jogs toward her.

Despite his wrinkled and musty jersey, he looks fresh and

clean. His raven hair catches the wind. His white cleats are too clean. She has the urge to reach under his shirt. She puts her hands in her pockets. Every word from the book is gone. She loves him. What's not to love?

"New shoes?"

"On sale. They almost fit." He smiles and leans in for a kiss. His girlfriend smells his laundry soap. She digs her nails into her palms. He jogs back to the group.

Her bag over her shoulder, she finds a place among the wives and girlfriends. They're older than Dani. The alpha introduces herself as Max's wife. She has hair the color of McDonald's french fries. Dani listens. Jobs and interest rates. She has nothing to add to the conversation.

Joey has yet to describe the game to his girlfriend; this is her first rugby match. The scrum lines up. She observes. Three large men on each team put their arms around each other. They bend at the waist. Across from them, they engage three men, like sumo wrestlers, heads tucked in. In a second row, two men place their shoulders beneath the rumps of the men in front of them. They lever themselves, cleats digging into the sod. Behind them is a third row of three. Shoulders to rumps, heads tucked into inconceivable alignment, the scrum is a raft of men. It moves as one. A man with a thick neck holds the watermelon-shaped ball, bent at the waist. He waits for the referee's whistle. He rolls the ball beneath the center of the ruck. The biggest man on Joey's team, a 320-pound, six-foot-three mound of a man named Eric who played at Syracuse, kicks at the ball. To Dani it looks like leg-wrestling. The ball rolls backward. The second line nudges it back. It comes out of the ruck. The man with the thick neck grabs the ball, then tosses it with a sideways motion. It's Michael, Joey's boss from the print shop.

They hold the ball funny. Between their upward-pointing hands. They lateral. Joseph runs along behind the ball. He positions himself for the next pass. The guy with the ball fakes. He cuts upfield in the other direction. He's tackled. But it's weird. It's like he intentionally fumbles the ball. The big guys run over and start the leg-wrestling again. The opposing team shuttles the ball back.

Dani looks over the wives and girlfriends. They talk, they don't watch. She imagines herself ten years from now, twenty, stuck here on the sidelines with the rest of them. She looks back. Joey is on the ground. He releases the ball. Eric hustles over to set up the scrum. It looks like he kicks Joey in the head. Dani winces.

The toe of Eric's boot just grazes Joseph's forehead. Up close Joseph can see the loam is sandy under the grass. The large man looks down at Joseph. He apologizes.

The ball is hooked by the opposing team. Joey jumps up. Dani exhales. He sprints for the far sideline.

The opposing team attacks. A man wearing some sort of covering over one ear is on the loose. Michael slows him down. The opposing player fakes. Michael jumps. The opposing player passes cleanly to a wiry guy with a thick mustache. Joey tries to cut him off. The mustache streaks by. It's a foot race. Joey loses ground. He lunges, catching the sprinting mustache up around the shoulders. He twists him to the ground. An awkward tackle. The ball rolls out of bounds. Michael runs over and helps Joey to his feet.

"Easy, mate. You can hurt someone." Michael recruited Joseph to be on the club team. He's not Australian, but, Joseph notes, players adopt phrases.

"Take it easy, hotshot," the mustache yells at Joseph. Michael faces the wiry man. He backs him up.

"Didn't mean it. He's a kid, he's learning."

"Learn somewheres else. Do it again, see what happens."

Joseph is shaken. He didn't mean harm, but he wasn't about to let anyone score on him in front of his girlfriend. He looks over at the sidelines. She's distracted.

Michael holds Joseph by the back of the neck. "C'mon, lover boy, to get her attention, score a try."

Joseph lines up on the far sideline. From here his girlfriend's a blip.

The scrum rucks over, the ball shuttles back, the guy with the thick neck grabs it. He tosses the ball to Michael. Michael jukes. He drives past two defenders. He scoops the ball out to another teammate. The teammate flies across the 22-yard line. He positions himself for the pass to Joseph. Joseph comes across the field. He sprints. The play opens up right in front of Dani. This is his moment. The teammate fakes, jukes inside. He hits Joseph in the hands with a crisp pass. Joseph puts the ball to his side. He veers away. There's only grass. One guy to beat. He hesitates. The defender is off balance. Joseph puts his cleat in the field. The defender, a baby-faced man, losing his hair before he should, lunges low. He catches Joseph under the knee with his shoulder, an illegal hit. Joseph buckles to the ground. A frightened scream echoes off the surrounding pines.

He knows something's wrong. It sounded skeletal, like the snap of a green tree branch. Michael and Eric run to him. He's writhing on the ground. What's his girlfriend doing on the field? Eric scoops him up and carries Joseph to the sideline. One of the wives has given up her folding lawn chair. Joseph sits in shock. This is club-league rugby. There's no doctor. The game continues.

Dani waits. She doesn't know what to do. Joey stands on the knee. To see if he can put weight on it. He can, but only if his heel is off the ground.

"I think we need to go to the emergency room."

"Concert tonight — we won't make it. Let's go to the house and get changed."

Dani stands to help him up. He gets up and she slides under his right side. He leans on her. They limp to the red Dodge, the print shop's delivery van. It's a manual transmission. It's his right leg. She's going to have to drive. She looks up at his face.

"You can drive a stick, right?" Joey's tone gets away from him.

"I can try." She practices with her father. She wishes she had practiced more.

A single incident where the van bucks. She doesn't lose heart. She closes her eyes, takes a deep breath. She slows down. They glide into the driveway, gravel crunching beneath the tires. Joseph's father is at the kitchen window. Joseph hops down from the van. His knee is gimpy. Dani hustles around to help, hauling two duffle bags over her shoulder. Joey's father frowns.

"What was that?"

Joey looks at Dani. She doesn't know that his father blew his knee out playing football.

"Whatever. My dad would've run out." Dani opens the screen door. Hinges screech.

"I bet Michael called."

Joey's mom hugs him in the kitchen. She gives Dani's hand a squeeze. She has tears in her eyes. "How bad is it?"

"The sound was awful." Joey's face goes white.

"I'll get an appointment first thing next week." To Dani, "I'm glad you were there."

Dani smiles.

"What about the concert? Sam can't stop talking about it."

Joey answers, "We're going."

"What happened to you?" Sam enters. He wears a backward baseball hat, a neon green T-shirt that says SOUL in block letters. His neon green sunglasses are flipped up on his forehead.

"None of your business, Samuel." Joey's mom turns to Dani with her eyes lidded. "What do you need to get ready? Change in my room? I'll fix you guys a quick bite before you leave." Margaret had wanted a daughter.

"Let me help Joey. Then I'll change." Joey's father turns the television up. The laugh track fades. He mutters, "Women weaken the legs."

Margaret grins a sad smile. She whispers, "He's been dreading this."

Dani is the native rootstock. She's immune to withering comments.

She guides Joey to the bathroom. He grimaces. She sets his bag on the counter and closes the door. She kisses him.

Joey whispers, "Are you going to help me undress too?"

She looks at the door.

"Bet you can't undo the buttons with your teeth."

She draws his shoulders down. She buries her face at his neck. She gets the rubber button between her teeth. She squashes it. Her neck twists. She finds the edge of the buttonhole, misses it, finds it again. Her eyes squeeze shut. She pulls her head back.

In the mirror, Joseph can see that the white webbing of his collar is wet with her saliva. He gasps. The second one, she wastes no time. She bites the button off. Joseph looks down at her. She kisses him on her tiptoes. She pushes her tongue into his mouth. His eyes pop open. His hand comes up to his lips. He pulls out the button. Dani smiles, turns. She opens the door, winks. She walks out into the kitchen.

Joseph emerges from the steamy bathroom in his socks. His girlfriend sits at the table. She bites a hummus and cucumber sandwich. Sam has one too. His mother pours glasses of milk. His sandwich is there next to Dani. He can smell Dani's perfume.

The three teenagers arrive in time for the show. A line of people snakes around the building. Joseph is gimpy on his bad leg. Dani offers her shoulder.

A black pencil skirt. Her black sleeveless tank matches. Black cowboy boots with a silver buckle. She has slung a narrow chain-link silver belt, like a vine, low on her hips. A short denim jacket over the top. Bare legs despite the chill in the air this April evening. The sun is gone, the moon waning gibbous, 93% visible. His girlfriend's hair is loose and curly. Her makeup is all eyes and lips.

Joseph tries to keep up. Khaki chinos and work boots. An overpriced black T-shirt. An olive-green jacket with peak lapels. He's in need of a haircut. He runs his hand through his inky mop.

Joseph leans. "No Sleep Till Brooklyn" to start. Adrenaline takes over. The injury is forgotten.

They get right up to the stage. MCA stands stage right in front of them. The next track is "Girls." Joseph tweaks his knee. He grimaces. He makes sure his girlfriend's not getting crushed. A bouncer offers her a backstage pass. Two, one for her and one for Sam. She shakes her head at him, rolls her eyes.

Sam protests. He can't believe she said no. They could have

met the Beastie Boys.

"You wouldn't have left your brother out here, would you?"

"He's fine."

"He's hurt."

"Whatever."

Joseph laughs, looking at his girlfriend. She was sub-zero with that guy.

Joseph leans against her. "She's Crafty" starts up. People around them shout the words. He kisses her on the cheek and takes her hand, holding it out palm up. He places something in it. Dani looks down, closing her fist over the rubber button. She smiles.

She drives them home. Joseph dozes. She and Sam listen to his Beastie Boys mixed tape as he replays the highlights. "Front row. Two encores. We could've gone backstage," he says. "That was awesome."

Eventually he settles down and dozes too. Dani sings along to the tape as she concentrates on the road.

Joseph wakes up as Dani pulls into the driveway. Gravel pops under the tires. The house is dark, except for the light by the garage. Joseph's mom left it on for them.

"Wake up, Sam. We're home." Dani's voice is sweet. Sam rubs an eye. He climbs out. He trudges inside.

She pulls Joseph into the living room. Wooden sofa, houndstooth check upholstery, mission-style end tables. A dim lamp. Oak floors, a natural sisal rug.

He stacks the sofa cushions. Dani kicks off her boots. Joseph spreads a fitted sheet over the couch. She removes her belt. Joseph smooths the flat sheet. She unzips her skirt. His father snores in the next room. Her skirt falls to the floor. Joseph plumps the pillow.

From her bag, shorts and a faded T-shirt. He memorizes her bare legs, her black panties. Joseph reaches to grab a blanket. She slips into the shorts and pulls the tank up over her head. Her black bra against her pale skin is like a shadow.

Joseph spreads the blanket. She puts the shirt on over her

bra. She doesn't put her arms in the holes. She unhooks her bra under her faded shirt, smiling at Joseph. His eyebrows raise. She pulls the front of the bra down, out through the bottom of her shirt. She lobs it at Joseph. He closes his eyes. It lands tangled in his hair. The bra is warm. It smells like her. Joseph opens his eyes. She stands close to him, lifting the bra off him. Her hand hangs in the air.

He slides his right hand under her shirt. She kisses him and drops her arm. His hand lands on her hip bone above her shorts. She kisses him again. "Goodnight, Joey," she says loud enough for anyone listening to hear. She whispers, "As you fall asleep, picture me down here all by myself."

Joseph limps upstairs, dazed. He plays back the movie of his girlfriend undressing.

My mother grew up on Keuka Lake. I spent a lot of time there as a kid. My grandfather worked at Gold Seal in the '70s and '80s. Uncles, aunts. They all did, really. I need to get back there.

Learning, 19.10.98

I have been reading more about Heydrich. Such an evil dude. A protégé of Hitler. Himmler first, but then Hitler. He helped to come up with the idea to fake the Polish soldiers' attack on a radio tower as a pretext to invade Poland in September 1939. So the Sudetenlands weren't enough; six months later, Hitler took all of Bohemia and Moravia. Then, six months after that, he is setting up to take all of Poland.

Rather than keep my notes elsewhere, I decided to take notes on my reading here. Reinhard Heydrich was born in Halle, Germany, on March 7, 1904. Makes him a Pisces, right, a Water sign, same as Karina. Interesting. He had a few nicknames, The Hangman, The Butcher of Prague. Hitler called him the man with an iron heart.

He was six feet, three inches tall. An imposing figure. People often feared him for his physical presence alone. Photos of him show a broad sloping forehead, beady eyes, liver lips; but the description of him is even scarier than that. His hips were wide and almost feminine. He had a high staccato voice.

Not a nice guy. He was found guilty of misconduct by the Naval Court of Honor for refusing to marry the daughter of a shipyard director. Soon after, he had a chance introduction to Himmler and joined the SS. Like many of the scariest people, he was involved in the Intelligence Wing of the military. It is said that he kept secret files on friends and foes alike. He was the founding head of the Sicherheitsdienst, or the SD (Security Service).

I had to look up what the SS stood for. Schutzstaffel. Translates to protection squad. Then there's the Gestapo. What's the difference between the SS and the Gestapo? Seems like the SS was more of a club and the Gestapo was an actual job. Another way to think about it is that the SS was founded by Himmler, another scary dude, only scary in a different way, while the Gestapo was founded by Hermann Göring. The name Gestapo comes from a shortening of the German words for the secret state police, or the Geheime Staatspolizei.

The question I have now is how the assassination happens. What leads up to it, how did Heydrich become the Reichfurher of the Protectorate of Bohemia and Moravia? I will keep digging.

Surviving, 20.10.98

I can't stop reading this book about Heydrich. It's fascinating. I'm obsessed. The thought that keeps recurring to me: how did I not know this before now?

The parachutists, Jan Kubiš and Jozef Gabčík. This is back before special forces were a thing. Before Green Berets, before Navy SEALs. Before training courses like BUD/S (Basic Underwater Demolition/SEAL) and SERE (Survival, Evasion, Resistance and Escape) school were dreamed up.

Survival. Resistance. These are the themes. Imagine: as your home country is being occupied by the Nazis, your mother and father, your home existing under constant threat of a foreign force, invaders, as all this is going on, you are living in exile unable to fight for your freedom. A battalion of the Czech Army was able to escape and fight with the French against the Nazis. Until the French surrender. Then the Czech battalion made its way to England. This is 1939, the Czech exiles began to gather outside London. With the help of British Secret Intelligence Service, an exile movement of Czech leadership began to take shape. With the addition of nearly three thousand Czech soldiers, maybe there was a chance they could find a way to fight for their homeland.

A handful of men were selected to be trained for sabotage and espionage missions. Among them, Jan Kubiš and Jozef Gabčík. They were hastily trained to parachute, to throw bombs, to operate radio equipment, to assemble and disassemble guns, bombs and equipment. In a matter of weeks and months, missions began flying with the British Royal Air Force.

As I read this, what stands out to me is the valor and bravery, of course, but also the luck of the whole thing. Almost all bad luck, by most accounts. The parachutists were dropped in the wrong places. The papers they were given were wrong, easily detectable by any self-respecting Gestapo agent. The equipment broke, was lost or otherwise malfunctioned. The addresses given the parachutists were based on old information, rarely helped. Worst of all, these men weren't prepared for the psychological stress and pressure of their missions. Mistakes were made. One set of parachutists visited his family; imagine the rumors and gossip he created. Heroes, it occurs to me as I read this book, do not stride in and save the day. They bumble their way through, they continue when all hope is lost, they succeed not in spite of all their failure but because of it. That, that right there, is something to which I can relate.

Visualizing, 21.10.98

Today is Wednesday. I will go to the office in the morning, I will have lunch with Patrick and Frank, I will spend the afternoon working on the visualization of the valve sensors. Then I will read. This story of Reinhard Heydrich's assassination is all-consuming. I read late into the night last night.

It was called Operation Anthropoid. Czech soldiers, hastily

trained in Great Britain, would be dropped by the RAF outside of Prague, would parachute under the cover of a moonless night and then figure out who on the ground they could trust. Who they could convince to trust them.

Gabčík injured his ankle on the descent. He couldn't walk without the assistance of Kubiš. They were not stealthy and quickly were discovered. They were lucky enough to be contacted by a sympathetic miller who put them in touch with members of the resistance movement. By this time, late December 1941, Sokol, a social athletic group, was driven underground by Heydrich and became a network for Czech resistance.

More about the athletic club later.

Moving from safe house to safe house in Prague, the parachutists obtained falsified medical leave papers, so their labor non-participation wouldn't attract attention. They schemed. They planned to assassinate The Butcher of Prague, the lead architect of the Final Solution, Reinhard Heydrich. They received help from a network of Czech patriots, all of whom were at least peripherally aware that their participation in the resistance would earn them the harshest of punishments. To complicate things, they were human, they fell in love. While in hiding, amid their efforts to plan the details of the attack, Kubiš not only fell in love but became engaged. Messy indeed.

Uncertain too. Looking back on these great deeds of great men, it's easy to think they had a mission, they prosecuted their mission, they succeeded. In fact, there was confusion and uncertainty. Some in the resistance thought it unwise to attempt an assassination on so high a leader in the Third Reich as Heydrich.

Unlucky as well. Gabčík's STEN submachine gun, the weapon of choice for insurgents, known as one of the most reliable of weapons, jammed in the very moment he stood in front of Heydrich's slowing car and pulled the trigger. Kubiš's underhand toss of the anti-tank grenade missed its mark, landing not in the rear seat of the convertible Mercedes-Benz but rolling against the right rear tire. It would be enough: the explosion ripped through the exterior of the car, blowing the passenger door open, shredding the seat. Heydrich was wounded by the blast. What ended up killing him a few days later, was septicemia, an infection caused by the presence of horsehair in his side, horsehair from the stuffing of the exploded front seat.

Bad luck even on the getaway. Gabčík ran and hid in a butcher's shop; the butcher happened to be a Nazi sympathizer. The butcher waved down the driver of the car who was pursuing Gabčík and pointed into his shop. Worse, as Klein lumbered through the shop, he ran headlong into Gabčík, who was attempting to flee on foot. Bouncing off, got away. Klein got the worst of it as Gabčík bounced off him, shooting him twice with his pistol before he escaped.

Both Gabčík and Kubiš managed to get away. Despite house-to-house searches, the parachutists were able to move from safe house to safe house for several days after the assassination. When the walls were closing in, they were forced to move to the Church of Cyril and Methodius.

Sokol

A form of group calisthenics, the Sokol movement started in Prague, in the former Austro-Hungarian Empire, in 1862. The word *sokol* translates in English to falcon or hawk. Within the first year, the movement spread beyond Prague to Moravia and Slovenia, which were also part of the Austro-Hungarian Empire at the time.

Based on the idea described as "a sound mind in a sound body," the group provided lectures, a forum for discussions, outings. Activities included marching drills, fencing, weight-lifting.

In 1882, the first *slet*, literally translated as a flocking of birds, was held. It was a mass gymnastics exhibition and festival. It became a grand tradition within the Sokol movement, and it spread the movement across many Slavic nations, including Poland, Slovene Lands, Serbia, Bulgaria, Ukraine and Belarus. The first *slet* was attended by 1,572 Sokols; at its height, attendance could be counted in the hundreds of thousands.

The movement consisted of students and professionals, but over time it would take on a working-class ethos. When Sokol unofficially attended the World's Fair in Paris in 1889, the foundation of the strong tie between French and Czech nations was built and, most importantly, the sympathy in France for the nationalism of the Czechs.

The Sokol resistance movement during the Nazi occupation was instrumental in the success of Operation Anthropoid. In particular, in the ability of the parachutists to evade the Nazi manhunt for several days and weeks after the assassination attempt and eventual death of Reinhard Heydrich.

22.10.98

The story of Heydrich doesn't end there. In fact, it gets worse. Under direct orders from Hitler, the Nazis viciously attacked the Czechs in retribution for Heydrich's assassination. More than five thousand Czechs were murdered, another thirteen thousand sent to concentration camps. They sent a squad to Lidice, eighteen kilometers (twelve miles) northwest of Prague, to kill all the adult men and burn the entire town to the ground.

In the dawn hours on June 10, 1942, ten trucks of drunken Security Police descended on Lidice. The sleepy mining village had been selected for the reprisal by the Gestapo as the result of an untimely love letter. The letter was intercepted by the Gestapo in Kladno, and upon interrogation, the Horák family of Lidice was implicated as being, among other villagers, a part of the Czech resistance that had assassinated Heydrich.

One hundred and seventy-three men were gathered into the orchard owned by the Horák family. Mattresses were rested against the exterior barn wall in order to prevent ricocheting bullets. The killing commenced at 7:00 a.m. Groups of five at a time. All the men over fifteen years of age were shot in the head. Where they stood, without blindfold or bound hands. The execution squad took two steps back, gathered another group of five and shot them in the heads. One of the German officers decided the killing was proceeding too slowly; he ordered the groups to be ten each time. The killing continued. A Catholic priest was offered mercy if he could keep the living calm as they waited for their turn with the death squad. He refused. "I have lived with my flock," he said. "I will die with them too." The bodies piled up.

One hundred and seventy-three men and fifty-three women were killed in the orchard. Another squad of Nazis with canisters of petrol set fire to all the buildings. Bombs obliterated any structure that still stood. Nazi engineers were brought in with bulldozers to knock down any stone that stood upon another. They used tractors to fill in the lake. A small stream was diverted from its course.

The Nazis desecrated the village cemetery.

While they were discreet about their various killing machines, the Nazis openly boasted about their attempt to obliterate Lidice, to eliminate it from history. Footage from the massacre found its way into propaganda films. They were proud of what they had done. The Allies were enraged. Frank Knox, secretary of the U.S. Navy, is reported to have said, "If future generations ask us what we were fighting for in this war, we shall tell them the story of Lidice." In response to the Nazi attempt to remove the name from history, a small community in Illinois renamed itself Lidice. U.S. President Franklin Delano Roosevelt was moved to praise the gesture.

Before the Americans start sounding righteous, remember that they had been slow to enter the war. Killing European Jews in concentration camps was not enough of an outrage to get them to act. They would have been accused, they feared, of sympathizing with the Jewish plight. The people of Lidice were seen as universal victims, unfreighted with the stigma of religion or race.

Lidice was not the only atrocity of its kind. Just two weeks later, on June 26, 1942, a press release announced that the Nazis had done it again. A smaller village by the name of Ležaky. A radio transmitter that had been dropped with one of the less fortunate parachutists was discovered buried in a field there. On June 24, a group of five hundred SS stormtroopers and policemen had surrounded the village and roused all the adult occupants, men and women. Thirty-three were executed. Twenty-six children were sent off to concentration camps.

So much senseless killing. So much violence.

Hosting, 26.10.98

Agata slept here last night. With Jacques. She and Brad had a fight. She came here.

It started weird. We found ourselves Friday night at Todd Lopez's thirty-second birthday party at Jo's Garaz. He's rude and dismissive, especially to women. He was abusing every woman in sight.

Jo's Garaz is an institution in Prague's expat scene. It's a bar and restaurant located in the arched walkways next to the Temple of St. Nicholas in Malá Strana. A chalkboard stands next to a heavy wooden door, arched at the top. A dozen tables line the sidewalk outside. A cramped restaurant upstairs — the ceilings are arched like a cave and the place is lit with sconces along the wall. The right side is dominated by a long wooden bar with round bar stools. Behind the bar, dug into the wall of the cave, is a shelf where all the liquor sits, back-lit for effect. Glassware stands upside down, organized by glass type, in vast waves. The bartenders are burly tattooed Czech men. They wear leather braces and speak excellent English. The waitresses are surly Czech teenagers in camisoles. They display their bra straps; their jeans that ride low enough so you can see what color thongs they are wearing. Across a narrow aisle from the bar, granite tables are arranged perpendicular to the cave. The heavy wooden benches along each side have backs, upholstered in putty pleather. Downstairs is a cave-like dance hall, empty except for a table at one end with wraparound bench seating around three sides, a pole at the other end.

Jacques and I run into Todd. He holds court with his back to the bar, a mixed drink in a highball in his hand, his forehead and nose shiny. Smirk on his face.

"Do you know how you know a Czech woman likes you?"

Todd asks the waitress in the camisole. She frowns at him and leans an ear in his direction. "She tells you she has a boyfriend." The camisole's eyes flick to Jacques and me. She walks away with an empty circular tray in her hand.

"Unoriginal. Crass. It's early for belligerence..." Jacques slides off his wool overcoat, his fingerless gloves. "Where's..."

Todd waves a dismissive hand from the end of his arm. "Happy birthday to me." He takes a sip from his drink. Jacques orders two beers from the bartender. Jacques motions to Todd to fork over the drink. Todd smiles. He complies.

Jacques takes a sip. He winces. "Any Coke in this rum and Coke?" Our beers arrive. Jacques slides Todd's drink back to the bartender. He orders a Coke. For Todd.

Watching this scene, I am transported. Rum and Coke. Dimly lit bar, pulsating music.

ANOTHER TALE FOR ANOTHER TIME

Back in March, I promised to tell the story of how Rachel and I met.

Rachel Giordano caught my eye in the freshman picture book at MIT. She caught everyone's eye in the freshman picture book. I don't know which fraternity it was that ran it, but most likely it was Foo (of course the name wasn't Foo, but I'll refer to them as Foo here), where the prevailing pastime for the brotherhood was date rape. Football too, but mostly date rape. Bunch of jocks. I digress. The Foos published annually a Top Ten list based on the freshman picture book and guess who got a nod? Yup, good old Rachel Giordano. She never got her head cracked open on a toilet seat like some of Foo's guests, but she did get her share of unwanted attention. I didn't pursue her freshman year. I hung back.

Sophomore year, after almost flunking out, I was on the comeback trail. I went to TA's office hours, I signed up for study groups, I got tutors. I survived. I partied less, buckled down more; by spring I had my shit together. That's when the alchemy happened.

See, I started to frequent a dance club called Venus de Milo on The Fens. Opposite Fenway Park. It was the more grown-up version of Axis nightclub on the same street, the sister to Jillian's billiard club, farther down. One Thursday, I was accosted by a woman with a clipboard. She asked if I would sign up for a quick survey. I laughed with my friends. I just wanted to dance. She persisted, looked at my wrist, held up a drink ticket. Of course I had a wrist band. "Twist my arm, as they say..."

The marketing woman led me to a spot on a purple couch. "A few questions," she promised.

I smiled. "Ask away," I intoned over the loud music. She asked her questions and at the end asked if I wanted to give my name and number for a chance to win a free giveaway. Free giveaway? I looked at the drink ticket on her clipboard, but she shook her head. "Something better..." She vaguely leaned in to me.

"Sure," I said. "Far be it from me to keep my number from a marketing major."

She laughed. "Not for me, of course." She tucked the ends of her bob behind an ear. "For the club."

"Ah, yes. Anything for the club." I winked at her. She shook her head and handed me the clipboard. I wrote my name and phone number. She smiled and handed me the drink ticket.

That Wednesday, I got a message at the house from Wendi at Venus de Milo. I called back on the off chance it was the marketing intern. A party. For me. Me and one hundred of my closest friends. I needed to pick up a signup sheet for the guest list.

That was it. That was how to get Rachel Giordano's attention.

I put her name on the list right under mine. I was confident. I didn't know if she knew the club, or if she liked to dance. I had a hunch it might work. I pasted it together, ransom-note style, a collage of mismatched letters from various magazines. "Rachel, are you ready for an adventure? You and a friend are on the guest list at Venus de Milo. — Your secret admirer."

I didn't know if she would show up. My plan was to have

fun with my friends either way. We got there early. Wendi met me at the coat check and gave me a raft of drink tickets. She thanked me for taking part in the survey. She said that my name had been selected. I went in and handed out drink tickets to my friends. Like I was the mayor. We danced. An hour in, Tad came up to me. Yes, Tad, Barcelona Tad, the very same. He told me she had arrived.

Rachel walked in with her Asian American roommate plus one. Rachel wore a black knee-length skirt, black suede heels and a stunning blue top, scoop neck, cap sleeves. She had a blue velvet clutch. Her plus one wore a tight miniskirt. I smacked Sam on the chest with the back of my hand. I said, "Gonna need your help here..." Sam obliged. We waited for the song to end.

Before I had a chance to second-guess myself, I walked over to Rachel. She stood at the edge of the dance floor. Her wing girl wiggled to the intro of the next song. I leaned in by Rachel's ear. "What are you drinking?" She leaned into my ear and said, "Rum and Coke." Her heat was on me. I asked, "What about your friend?" She met my eyes. She nodded her head. I saw that Sam held the friend's attention. I tipped my head at Sam. We made for the bar.

Wendi was there. I asked her for a couple of rums and Cokes. I pressed my belly against the bar. I tapped my fingers. Sam spoke to me.

"The friend seems stuck up." He frowned.

I replied, "See if you can unstick her..."

Wendi slid two clear plastic cups across to me. I handed the second one to Sam. We walked back. The girls absorbed the music. They gyrated by the dance floor.

I handed Rachel her drink. She took a sip, squinted at me. "I know you," she said. She tilted her head and blinked. "I don't know where from." I smiled and asked if she wanted to dance.

She set her drink down on a railing. Holding my hand, she led me onto the dance floor. We fell into the music. I played it cool. I kept my movements tight and understated. I watched her. She slithered vertically, if that's possible. Like she was molting. Her movements were slow. I was standing there, a foot from her. From Rachel Giordano. She was here. It was happening. Play it cool, Joseph. Keep it cool.

Sam had the friend by the hand. He brought her to dance with us. The friend could dance. She was thin, knees and elbows, she could keep a beat. Sam and me? We played off each other. We caught a wave of the music. Shared a moment, let it unravel. Rachel danced into her friend. She said something in her ear. The friend smiled, nodded and stole a look at Sammy. A hand came up to cover her mouth. Rachel came back to me. She danced close. She got my full attention. She stepped back and held her hand out to me. I took it. I looked at Sam. He shrugged. The friend danced into him.

Rachel grabbed her drink with her clutch hand and pulled me to the bar. Wendi was already there. Rachel looked at me. Wendi said, "He's having what you're having. It's on me." She slid a rum and Coke across the bar. "Your drink, my man..."

Rachel tilted her chin, squinted again. She led me over to one of the sofas. The purple sofas where this whole thing started.

"You're full of surprises, aren't you?" She asked me, "How are you doing this?"

I shrugged and took a sip of my drink. Wendi had poured it just right. It's like she knew I needed to go light and keep it cool. When love is at stake, all of heaven's angels pitch in. I thought of the marketing woman, of Wendi, of the wing girl. Any one of them could have said no, bowed out; then where would I be? In my heart I thanked them all.

"Are you the admirer, or whatever?" Rachel mimed air quotes, her clutch in one hand, her drink in the other.

"My name" — I paused, hoping she didn't note the catch in my throat — "is Joseph."

"I almost didn't come. She made me." Rachel lolled her head in the direction of her Asian housemate, who was leaning into Sam. "Don't get me wrong, I'm flattered by the invitation, but I was having one of those days, you know." I didn't know. At that moment I had no idea. Rachel smiled a forlorn smile.

I should have asked her. I should have taken the bait. I should have said, *I don't know what one of those days is like, tell me.* I was too slow. I was proud of myself or something. That momentary victorious feeling. That feeling, the high, is confusing. It blocked me. I missed the chance to ask her about her day.

I gazed into her eyes. Lights pulsed all around us. The music blared. I couldn't think of what to say. Rachel let me off the hook.

"Who's your friend?" She pointed her chin in the direction of the dance floor. Rachel's friend had folded into Sammy. They danced slowly. Sam closed his eyes.

"Not my friend. Younger brother, my." I patted my chest.

Rachel lowered her eyebrows at me. "He doesn't look younger."

"Is your friend okay? Do you think we should check on her?"

Rachel snorted. Her beauty is long and cool and sleek; you might think she's too cool to guffaw. Hardly. She's a goof; most people didn't get that far. Most people didn't get beyond the intimidating good looks, the curtain of dark hair, the eyes cast into the distance, the pursed lips. Her laugh almost doesn't suit her. She can laugh with the best of them. "She's fine."

I put them in a cab at the end of the night. It was predetermined. I knew that if the meet-up went beyond the club, I would want more and more of her time until I was lost in her. I couldn't let that happen. Say goodnight, send her home safely, get back to my friends. That's what success looks like.

Next came the hard part. Two weeks before I could contact her again. We were both busy with school, she had her own social life. I couldn't let her know how infatuated I was. Not yet. I had to be patient. It's not my strong suit.

Jacques nudges my elbow, brings me back out of my trance. I take a sip. I expected rum and Coke, but this is crispy, delicious foam, light and fragrant. It's my beer.

I follow Jacques's gaze. A tall blonde with hair the color of straw. I half expect to see a second tall girl with her. No luck.

Jacques looks at me. "Nevermind. Let's find Laura." His look is concerned. I haven't said a word since we got here.

The key for me, back then, with Rachel, the shem that made the alchemy work, was patience. Patience and persistence. It would do me good to remember that.

Todd grabs the arm of a woman. She tries to pass. She looks first at me, then Jacques. She sees Todd. A slow smile breaks. She leans in and hugs him. Kisses the air next to each ear. Her forearm blocks Todd's reach. Did that just happen?

"I know her, can't remember her name," Jacques steps away from Todd. I follow. Mid-stride, Jacques looks at me. "I saw it." Jacques looks away. "No surprise there…"

I take a sip of my beer. I know I should reply. I think of Bohdana, back in March. She told me she had a boyfriend. I believed her. I didn't consider it a come-on. I hadn't heard it put that way before. Was I naive?

We find Laura, sitting on a step drinking wine from a plastic cup. She stands up and hugs Jacques. Then me.

"I had a rabbit growing up," she says, adjusting her purse over her shoulder. She sets her cup on a ledge. She doesn't look at it. "We called her Laura the Explora. Is it weird to give a pet your own name?"

"Todd's in rare form. Are you okay?" Jacques touches Laura on the forearm.

"She liked closets. Whenever we couldn't find her, I would search the closets, Mum's room, Da's, my sister's. The hallway. Inevitably, we'd find her in the last one we looked. I'd find her, but it would always be in the last one."

"Because when you found her, you stopped looking?" It sounded witty in my head. It came out cruel.

Laura looked at me. "That's true. What was my point?"

Jacques made her sit down again. We sat on either side of her. The staircase was broad. We hunched together. The music, a second dance floor, awoke downstairs. We were at an inflection point, music upstairs, music downstairs, lights flickering. It was a trick of acoustics that we could hear each other. Jacques shot me a look. *If you don't have something nice to say…*

Laura was older than Todd. I knew that. They have lived together for some time. I guess she saw him as her young hunk, her American conquest. Who am I to judge?

"Should we help you find Todd?"

"She's in the closet. The last closet you look in." Laura veered toward me with a blurry smile. I liked her, pitied her. That's not nice. I tried to imagine the girl. She slid in her socks down the hallway, past the hallway door. She opened doors. She held a fat rabbit.

"Excuse us, coming through, coming through, Jacques..." Todd leaned heavily on Jacques. Jacques held his beer out away from himself. It dribbled. "We're parking, baby, parking on the dance floor..." Preceded by several women in high shoes and tight clothes whom Todd had chased after. One woman smacked his arm away. She half turned on the stairs, to get away from him. He must not've seen Laura. We pretended not to notice.

Jacques stood and settled his beer on the ledge. "Let's get some air." He held his hand out for Laura. She reached up. I was ready to steady her if needed. I stood last. On her feet, Laura was fine, sobered maybe. It occurred to me that she was faking being tipsy. That seemed absurd. I chased the thought away. Back through the cavernous bar. It filled in in waves, then suddenly Šárka held out a hand to me. I tried to catch Laura and Jacques. They filed toward the door. I turned.

"Look what the cat dragged in, is that the idiom?" Šárka was with friends. One guy had opened a cigarette on the table. He mixed in something else. Another friend smoked languidly. "Still dreaming your life away?"

I smiled at the attack. I leaned in to hug her, kept my hands at my sides. With her hand on my shoulder, she introduced me around. I forgot everyone's name immediately. "Are you here for the birthday party?"

"Birthday party, no. Whose birthday is it?" Šárka looked amused.

"You don't know Todd? Probably just as well."

"Everyone knows Todd. The cat who ate the canary. Studied idioms. Today was cats. Bert suggested me a teacher."

I didn't know how to work in the rabbit image. I smiled dumbly. The moment passed.

"Good to see you, Šárka. Gotta find my..."

"Of course, Joseph." Šárka leaned close to my ear. "Have you heard from Karina?" She read my face with her eyes. She saw I was not in the mood to discuss it. "You might."

Jacques stood outside, his jacket on, his fingerless gloves. He held a cigarette.

"Where's Laura?" I regretted the obvious question. I was a beat behind this evening. On my back foot.

"She left. Got a cab. Let's go."

Careening, 28.10.98

Karina was here. In my apartment. Yesterday from 2:15 p.m. to 9:00 p.m. I got a full day with her. May have been the longest time I've spent with her. Except maybe that one date we had back in July at the park, the one where I swam in the dark and she didn't.

Listen to this one:

The night before, Tuesday, I went to Klub Wakata with Ester and Agata. This place is on Malířská, Painter's Street, in Holešovice. It's a pub with a dance floor. They play a specific genre of drum-and-bass music called jungle. We call it techno, but in the States it would be filed under electronica. Machine-gun tempos and lots of breakbeats, reggae bass lines and layers of samples. Recognizable by the pitch-shifted snare rolls. The bar stools are motorcycle seats.

Agata was flirting with me all night. I didn't mind. Ester said that she and Brad are on the outs. They had a fight. Brad's still hung up on an ex, or something.

We stumbled Ester to her flat. She was the only one who was sober. We said goodnight. Agata planned to bunk up with Jacques. It was just us. I held her hand to steady myself.

We came home drunk. We were loud. The living room doors were closed. Jacques was asleep. I invited her to sleep with me. She accepted. We knew what we were doing. Thank goodness, no clothes were shed. We passed out on the futon.

I'm in bed with Agata this morning when Karina calls.

Karina was here. The best thing was not her clothes (she wore a cornflower-blue camisole, a burgundy jacket with collar and cuffs of crimped fringe, a black pencil skirt and goth black platforms that made her height more intimidating) or her black eye from wrecking her car yesterday (makes her look tough and vulnerable at the same time, how is that?) or that I could feel that she wanted to hang out someplace safe; the best thing was I got to show her a bit of me.

We ate dinner at Kojak's, the Czech tex-mex place; Jiří met us there. It's kitschy Mexican, an encyclopedic menu. Don't expect actual queso, more likely to get swiss. The guacamole comes from a jar; the parsley is powdered. Jiří was able to make Karina laugh.

I see her age in the lines around her eyes when she's tired; could've been losing her boyfriend not too long ago, her car the day before yesterday. She's not healthy right now, she's not young right now, she's not happy right now.

At the end of the night she told me that she wants to see *The English Patient* with me. It's a trap I set for her a long time ago, after I watched the movie with Brad. I told her about the Aries main character (me) and the Pisces female lead (her); how they're star-crossed, doomed, how beautiful it is, how tragic. I didn't think it registered with her. She liked that I remembered she was Pisces. When I told her I was Aries, she shrunk away. Her ex-boyfriend was Aries. She told me how pigheaded he was. She didn't make it interesting for me. She didn't tell me an anecdote or something like that; she told me flat. He's Aries. He's pigheaded, like all Aries are.

Wait until she realizes that in addition to being an Aries like her ex-boyfriend, and pigheaded like her ex-boyfriend, that I'm also divorced like her ex-boyfriend. In the end, he went back to his ex-wife. Ooh, that should be a good one...

I asked her if she has a boyfriend. She gave me the response that I guess girls must think sounds better than yes or no: she told me she has friends.

I also told her about *Good Will Hunting*. I told her I went to the school featured in the movie. I try to set up a string of movies that she'll want to see. With me. If she sees it without me, she might remember that I told her about it; she'll connect it to me. Am I really this pathetic? Am I manipulative? Ugh.

Brad wrote LAME all over a sheet of paper. I should tell Brad what happened. I should be straight with him. I leave it up to him to trust me or not to trust me. I should do it for no better reason than to be sure that he doesn't find out about it another way. Ester. She'll tell him tonight. I have to talk to Brad. Shit.

Celebrating, 29.10.98

At dinner, Jiří held up a glass and toasted Czech Independence. Karina smiled and smiled. She clinked his glass, met his eyes. She kicked me under the table. I held up my glass. I did not understand. I thought he made a comment about dating a foreigner. I held up my glass, cheap red wine. I toasted each of them. I took a sip. Karina saw my doubt. She held up her glass again. She toasted Jan Opletal. I raised my glass and met her eyes. There was a flash, a glint. She could tell I didn't know who Jan Opletal was. She took a drink.

Jiří feigned disbelief. Karina waggled a finger at me, clucking her tongue. I promised I would read up.

This morning I headed straight for the library at Charles University, the public section, the English section of the public section. I love the smell of it. Old books and dusty drapes. The sound of it. A drapery of silence. A page turns, you hear it.

Jan Opletal was a student here, in the medical faculty. Born in 1915. He took part in the anti-Nazi demonstration in Prague on October 28, 1939. It was the twenty-first anniversary of Czechoslovak independence. The crowd swelled to more than one hundred thousand people.

Nazis employed brutality in an attempt to disperse the crowds on Wenceslas Square. On Žitná (Rye) Street, Opletal was shot in the stomach. He died in a hospital bed on November 11. He was twenty-four years old. His funeral in Prague was held November 15. Black flags flew from all the dormitories. The procession quickly devolved into a demonstration against the Nazi occupation. It's what led to the brutal reprisals on November 17, nine students and faculty executed.

Yesterday, last night, October 28, eighty years ago, the Great War was coming to a close. The Czech National Committee took over the reins of power from the Austro-Hungarian Empire. TGM, technically a Czech exile at the time, had traveled more than a year all over Europe and the U.S., bolstering support for an independent Czechoslovak state that would no longer have ties to Austria or Hungary or the Hapsburgs.

Karina enjoys the process of my discovery. She guides me through Czech history.

Envying, 31.10.98

I'm sitting in Ester's kitchen. Make that Ester's dining room. I haven't seen Karina in a few days. I'm starting with jealousy. It's bound to happen. Jealousy is an ugly beast with claws and fangs to rip your heart out and feed it to you.

Speaking of, I got a chance to speak with Brad. I told him. We were outside smoking cigarettes on Ester's balcony. I told him Agata slept in my bed. I told him nothing happened. He nodded, squinting his eyes at me as he exhaled smoke.

I get to say goodbye to Gracie tomorrow. Not sure why I do this to myself.

I feel Ingrid slipping away. She's given up on me. I need a guide among the living. Like who? I could call my mom, I guess. She worries about me. What about Rachel? What about Dani? Wait — are you considering asking the women who shattered you into pieces to help put you back together again? Why should they? They left you, you left them. They have their own problems, they have their own lives.

I could call Ilona. Božena promised dinner. Ilona asked me not to call. She asked me for space. I will honor her request.

Why do I need a guide? Don't I trust myself?

I wonder what my high-school girlfriend would think, reading my side of the story. I leave her side out. What if I added her back in?

I need to write her a letter. I don't have to send it.

NOVEMBER

Holding, 1.11.98

"HEY, JOSEPH," GRACIE SAID, "YOU and I should have lunch, you know, before I blow outta here."

I should've said no. I should've said, *I barely know you, Gracie, what possible good could a lunch do?* I should have.

I said, "Yeah. We should. I'd like that." I had to be careful.

She's a good person, I think, Gracie. Lost, is all. Like me. One day she'll wake up and be like, "Shit. I had a good thing going there. I blew it." Not now. Not soon, but one day.

I met her yesterday for lunch. Right now, as I journal this, she's probably sitting in a state of ennui at the boarding gate. It probably hasn't hit her yet. Maybe it has.

Yesterday it was like the crack of two. I had been up for hours, I had done four things. Gracie was fresh like she just got out of bed, showered, towel-dried her hair and met me. At the top of Wenceslas Square. At the top of the escalator that comes up from the Muzeum metro stop, facing the big beautiful building at the top of the square. Czechs call it under the horse's ass. The statue, they mean, Good King Wenceslas, on his horse. The same place I had my epiphany about fire on my long walk home.

We met there and wandered around up through the little park. On the corner, we found a pub, brass railings, brass taps, a big copper tank to hold freshly brewed beer. We went in. The waitress hustled past us. Gracie shrugged her shoulders at me. I shrugged my shoulders back at her. Tall guy behind the bar waved us over.

I put my foot on the brass railing. I tried to make it look like I was calm and in control. I wasn't. Gracie did the talking. In Czech.

"Good day." The bartender looked us up and down. Only his eyes moved. His eyes and his hands. He polished mugs.

"Good day," Gracie answered.

"Food or drink?"

"Food."

He scanned the place, puffing out his cheeks, leaking air out his bunched lips. "Lunch rush. Kinda busy. Can you wait for the hostess?"

Gracie smiled back. "Of course." She glanced around at the empty tables, the lone waitress waiting on one couple. "Lunch rush." Gracie's Czech is good enough that she can be sarcastic. I mean, I was hungry and I would rather not be ignored or, worse, kicked out. Gracie didn't hold her tongue. It's cheeky. I like cheek.

The waitress and the female patron were talking. The couple, each with bright golden beer in mugs, each half full with crisp foam, a plate each. Looked like he got the guláš and the dumplings and she got the beef sirloin with cream sauce and cranberry. They'd been served and were now into social hour.

Gracie said to me, "I'm gonna miss this. The absurdity. The open hostility. They don't have a hospitality industry here. They have a hostility industry."

She'll miss it. It hadn't hit her yet how much. I never did get a chance to meet Gracie's sister, brief as our acquaintance was. The sister's back in the States now, a husband and a baby and you know, that American life. We think it with scorn, we expats; we live our big important European romantic adventures — and all that, all that American blight, right now to us, seems like a bunch of bills and car payments. Making ends meet. Making them almost meet. Living in Prague is closer to the metal. We don't live paycheck to paycheck, like we would be in good old Corporate America, in the suburban wastelands. We live pocketful of cash to pocketful of cash. Months in between. Hand to mouth, I guess they call it; no need for deposit slips or even a Czech bank account unless to get paid you need one. We live mostly on cash.

Gracie held out her purse to me. It wasn't a purse, more like a one-armed backpack. I held it at arm's length, but that wasn't the message I want to send. I barely knew this young woman, but I already knew I would miss her. I swung it over my shoulder. It smelled like she does: a mixture of dark perfume and cigarettes. It's nice, it's her. Gracie. She let her hair down, flipped it forward, bent over in front of me, then stood up straight, flipping that gorgeous mane back. Her sandy brown hair is like her, it has an effortless casual perfection. She probably doesn't even condition. She coiled it back up on top of her head with that flurry of fingers and hands, muscle memory to her, magical to impressionable men like me.

She took her bag back off my arm and smiled, saying, "Tell me, Joseph. How mad is he?"

"He's not mad. He's sad. He knows this is the best thing — it's not what he wanted."

"Heh. Yeah. No. No one could have wanted this. You know" — she adjusted her one-armed backpack on her jean jacket shoulder — "Jacques says it all the time. Maybe this is just the prologue. Maybe you and I will be great friends one day. Neighbors even."

"Maybe." I rocked my foot on the brass railing. I didn't believe it. I rejected it. There's this ritual, when expats leave Prague, that we do. It's a farce. We act like we'll meet up again in some fictional Prague in our futures. In my experience, it's false. When we say goodbye, we should take it more seriously. In my experience, it's for good.

The waitress came over. She was young. I mean, compared to me, Old Man Time here at twenty-eight years old. Gracie is a good four years younger. The Czech woman standing before us was probably a teenager. Gracie watched me, to see if I was going to do the typical male thing, look her up and down, start panting, tongue hanging out like I wanted to sniff her ass. I denied Gracie the satisfaction. I wondered what Jacques would do. No, I didn't. I knew exactly what Jacques would do. He'd lean back, lick his lips, raise his eyebrows.

She grabbed two menus and two bundles of cutlery and led us to the table next to the other couple.

I ordered the garlic soup and a cola. Gracie got fried cheese and french fries, a mineral water. We clicked glasses. Our eyes met. We didn't toast anything.

I took a sip and set my glass down. "When are you leaving?"

"Tomorrow morning. You know I'm not a morning person. I have someone, someone who's gonna drive me. This is between you and me, right, Joseph? None of this gets back to Jacques?"

"Yeah. No. I get it. Forgive me, but isn't this someone part of the reason you have to go in the first place? Sorry. Let me take that back. Are you sure you're gonna make the plane?"

"It's fine. I'm gonna be fine. You and Jacques worry too much. I'm a big girl. I can handle my own." The food arrived. Gracie lit a cigarette. Yeah, you can still do that here. She pushed her food toward me. I dug into the soup with a spoon in one hand, then dipped one of her fries into the tartar sauce with the other. She nodded at me, blowing out a cloud of smog. I couldn't remember the last time I saw her eat. She waved away the smoke.

"It doesn't bother me." I spilled a spoonful of the sweet and nutty soup into my mouth and bit down on one of the mini cubes of Emmental cheese. The saltiness. I would've loved a beer to wash it down. Not today.

Gracie continued. "I'm all packed up. You know, it's funny, after you get rid of all the crap you have accumulated, you can get everything that means anything to you into two medium-sized suitcases."

I nodded, took a bite of her fried cheese. It might've seemed like I was a pig eating off Gracie's plate; I'm letting her off the hook. It was okay with me if she had no appetite. If she was unsentimental. It was okay with me if she wanted to throw away whatever life she might have had here with or without Jacques in the pursuit of whatever it was she was pursuing. Was she pursued? I hadn't figured it out yet, but I wanted her to know that it was okay with me. She could be herself. Why do I so desperately need her to know that about me? Do I have a thing for Gracie? Do I subconsciously compete with Jacques to show her that she should have been with me? What kind of sicko am I?

She enjoyed my manic grunting and moaning over the pub food.

"He needs you, you know." She breathed out a nimbus of smoke. It curled and danced between us before disappearing into the ether.

I set my spoon down, rubbed the cloth napkin on my stubbly chin. "He needs me? Wait. He needs me."

"Get over yourself. Of course, he does. In a way, I need you too. Don't think I could go home if I didn't know he had, you know, someone. Ha, home. I have no home."

It's sweet that she thought she had a choice. Everyone thinks they have a choice. Especially when they don't. I looked into Gracie's eyes, see something hard there.

"Gracie, why lunch with me? We barely know each other. You've known Brad longer than me. Did you have a Last Supper with him?"

"No. I don't know. I can't talk to anyone, I feel like, but somehow I can talk to you." She took a deep pull on her cigarette.

"I'm listening." I took a drink of my cola. It was warm. I'd forgot to ask for ice. I looked up for the waitress. She was back to social hour over there.

Gracie looked into my eyes. "Shut up, Joseph. It's not like I have a confession to make." That glint of hardness. "People think you're crazy or evil if you don't want what they want. I don't know what I want, but this ain't it."

Now we were getting somewhere. She thought me and Jacques and Brad were the wise old wizards, old greybeards, ready to be put to pasture. She thought that something better was bound to come along. I knew the feeling. I could relate.

I ate. I listened. The food was good. She didn't need a response.

"I love Jacques. I do. You think I'm running away. I can't, Joseph, do you hear me, I can't."

"I hear you." I dipped a fry in the glorious white sauce. This can't be good for me. I waited for Gracie to get the lump out of her throat. If she had a lump.

"I won't cry over this, I won't." Gracie pulled a 200-crown note (10.94 USD) from her one-armed backpack and laid it on the table. "Here's what we'll do. I go to the bathroom. You get the bill. Pay with this." It was more than enough. Gracie took a drag on her cigarette. "When I get back, big hug and I'm out. I wish I met you sooner, Joseph. You might have saved me. Focus on Jacques, save him. Save yourself."

"I would say that you should call me when you get there, but with Jacques there, probably no." I wanted to say, *Be well, Gracie*. I wanted to say, *I'm gonna remember you as my friend*. I wanted to say, *Goodbye, Gracie*.

She stabbed out her cigarette. I watched the determined way she walked to the WC. I went to the bar to pay the tab before she got back, to make her wish come true. She came back. We did as she said. She was out. I stood there. I should have held her longer. I shouldn't have let her go.

Wanting, 3.11.98

I just reread a couple journal entries. I almost never do that. But I just did. A letter to my high-school sweetheart. Not a bad idea. A letter to Rachel. A letter to my mother. A letter to my father. All these letters. I'm not a writer, but I journal. Letters aren't writing. They're communication.

It's raining. Doesn't help matters. And I with a hole in my dress shoes. Water seeps into my sock. Into my soul. Water seeks me.

I conferred October 1998 to the past. I now have a full year in that folder, the past year of my life. Strong stuff. I have to clip my fingernails today.

Jacques and I went for lunch at a place near his old place. I'm sure it has a name but I don't know what it is.

Jacques said to me, "I can't stop thinking about Gracie. I can't stop worrying."

I shifted in my seat. "That's normal, don't you think? How many years together?"

"I had a chance to ask this girl out, an old friend, she called me. She threatened to visit for, I don't know, a long time. Now she's here. All I can think about is Gracie."

"Go see your friend. You need a distraction."

Jacques stirred his garlic soup. That's the thing about these places Jacques takes me to. They always have good soup and good dumplings. The meat is hit-and-miss but the soup…

Jacques set his spoon aside and looked me in the eyes. "Here's my question for you." Those penetrating eyes. "How long?"

"How long?"

Jacques picked his spoon back up and pointed it at me. "How long is it gonna take?"

"Two years." I smeared a dumpling in the light brown gravy, popping it in my mouth before I could say more. Let him marinate on that.

"You know this?" Jacques smiled with one side of his mouth. He stirred his soup, brought a spoonful to his lips, blew on it. Ripples curdled the surface.

"If you loved her and I think I can say that, yes, you loved her, even when she didn't deserve it, two years. Give or take." I whisked the fork through the gravy. I cleaned the four tines. See, you can't get any gravy that way. Hence the dumplings. *Houskové knedlíky.* The bready ones. The other ones are made of potatoes, heavier, good too, but the bready ones… Find a good little place like this one, one with no name.

"Then what?" Jacques was asking. No, like, really asking. It's a funny thing that happens. When you first get divorced, everyone avoids you. They turn up their nose. Like divorce is contagious. No, more than that, like the failure of it is contagious, like you could catch it and everything would go wrong. Then, years later, your experience is suddenly valuable to them.

You have something they need.

"Then you're free. I have this theory. It's new, so bear with me. See, I think you never stop loving someone. It's just, you turn down their volume. In the beginning, where you are, you can't hear other people. Because there are other people. You know it, even when you were with Gracie there were other people. You thought, hm, she could be interesting. In the actual breakup, you forget all those other people. You forget everything. That's temporary. You live through it. The volume decreases. The Gracie volume. It gets quieter and quieter."

"It *never* goes away?" Jacques dipped his farmer's bread in the soup, tapped it, bit it.

"Think about it. Your first love, right? If you're honest with yourself, right now, you still love her. It doesn't mean you can't love anyone else. It just means you have experience. You have loved. There's a place in your heart for her. It's over now, things moved on. If I'm honest, I still love Rachel, but the Rachel volume is lower now." I jammed half a gravy-soaked dumpling in my mouth.

Jacques's brow crinkled. "Okay, you said this is a new theory we're working out here. I kind of hate, at the moment, that I'll never get rid of Gracie completely, but go on. Run with it."

I moved the food to one side of my mouth, continued, "Hate's good. Anger's natural. You need it. One day it softens. You wonder how she's doing. You hope she's good. One day you wake up, you realize you haven't thought about her in twenty-four hours. Good or bad, your mind didn't turn toward her. The volume is down."

Jacques dipped his bread. He nodded. "Down."

"One day, there's someone new. Is she the love of your life? Or maybe, I have to admit, I haven't figured this part out completely, maybe you stop thinking like that. She doesn't have to be the girl of your dreams, she doesn't have to be the love of your life. She just has to be, I don't know, good for you. Fun, exciting, but ultimately good for you. Maybe one day you'll wake up next to her, twenty years later, and you'll have a different understanding of what 'the love of your life' means."

"Two years seems like a long time, Joseph." Jacques looked

out the window. A young woman walked by with a dog on a leash. Long legs, short skirt. Tiny backpack. Jacques raised his eyebrows at me.

"If you didn't love her, it would be shorter, I bet. Then again, if you deny yourself feelings, could be longer too."

"Hmm." Jacques wiped his bowl clean with the heel of the bread. He held his empty beer glass up for the bartender, in that efficient way that Šárka had done at the Marquis de Sade with Bert. The barkeep nodded. He put a new glass under the tap and pulled. "Sounds like you're onto something here, but you know me, I'm skeptical of wise guys who sound wise…"

"Go out with your friend. Be present, or as present as you can be. See what happens. Or don't."

Jacques blinked. He looked out the front of the restaurant. The young woman with the dog bent over. A strip of white showed between her legs. She stood up with a crumpled newspaper in her hands. The bartender arrived with Jacques's beer. He mumbled to Jacques in Czech, "Stop staring. That's my sister."

"On display for the whole restaurant?" Jacques dropped his napkin on the table.

The barkeep pointed his chin at my empty beer glass. I had to go back to work. I shook my head at him. He shrugged.

To Jacques, in Czech, "You're right. She's my girlfriend." The barkeep hustled back behind the bar. He called out to Jacques, "She just doesn't know it yet."

Seasoning, 4.11.98

I went back to the place I had been with Jacques for lunch. I got the garlic soup. It wasn't right. It tasted like dirty dishwater. I realized it wasn't seasoned. The barkeep wasn't the same either — it was a short woman with a missing tooth. I couldn't eat it. I paid and went back to work. Was I guilty of appeasement? Was I the Neville Chamberlain of soups?

BREAKING SPRING

Daniella left behind her magazine for Joseph. It's a tactic. She leaves behind pieces of herself. You get tangled up in her.

Joseph's in Florida. He reads an article in *The New Yorker*. She left yesterday afternoon. He sits in the sand.

Humans tend to settle around sources of salt. Salt mines, salt works, trade routes that are specifically designed to transport salt. Throughout history, the availability of salt is pivotal to civilization.

The importance of the white crystalline substance in history dates back to 6050 BC. People living in the area of what is now known as Romania boiled natural spring water to extract it. At the Poiana Slatinei archaeological site next to a natural spring, evidence indicates that the Neolithic people of the pre-Cucuteni culture boiled the salt-laden spring water through a process known as briquetage, or very coarse pottery, to extract salt from water.

The bulk of the water evaporates off in saltpans. Brine is transferred to thick-walled, clay salterns heated from underneath with wood and later charcoal fires. The salt crystallizes. They use rakes to collect it. More brine is added. The solution is transferred to smaller clay vessels for further reduction. To harvest the salt, the pots are smashed.

At the sites where this process was used, shards of the broken pottery are found in large mounds. The salt extracted had a direct correlation to the rapid growth of this society's population. Broken heaps of briquetage material are found at multiple sites from the end of the Bronze Age in Europe into the medieval period. Archaeologists identify the different forms of the pottery, the varied colors of red and orange, to identify trade networks.

In China, a similar shallow bed evaporation salt works dates back to about the same time period.

Prized by ancient Hebrews, Greeks, Romans, Byzantines, Hittites, Egyptians and Indians alike, wars between nations were waged over salt. An important article of trade, it was transported by boat across the Mediterranean Sea, over pur-

pose-built salt roads and across the Sahara on camel caravans.

In the Middle East, salt was used in ceremonies to seal an agreement. Ancient Hebrews made a "covenant of salt" with God. They sprinkled it on their sacrifices, a symbol of their trust in him. In time of war, it was sown around a defeated city.

Salt is also mined from ancient deposits on the earth's surface. These deposits were once underground seas, lakes, oceans.

Left behind by the evaporation of a huge sea 300 million years ago, an enormous salt reserve stretches deep underground from Syracuse, New York, west to Lake Erie, north to Canada and south over the Allegheny plateau. In Geneva, New York, salt is only two hundred feet below sea level.

During the War of 1812 with England, it became difficult to obtain salt from abroad. Commercial salt production from brine wells began on the shores of Onondaga Lake in Syracuse. Refining salt became the largest industry in Syracuse. It supplied salt to much of the country. The building of the Erie Canal allowed the bulky and low-priced Syracuse salt to flow to Chicago and beyond, buoyed on barges, by way of the Great Lakes. Although the Erie Canal was known by many names, those in Syracuse called it "the ditch that salt built."

During the Civil War, salt production in Syracuse secured the North's supply. With Yankee forces in control of salt mines in Virginia and Louisiana, those living in the South couldn't buy salt at any price. Lack of salt is thought to be one of the many reasons why the South lost the war.

She takes things. Before you know it, she has your sweater, your hat. Why does she do that?

The day before, the sky over Orlando, Florida, is pink and blue. It is pale and wan, fresh. The Bluebird bus station, in comparison, is tired, broken down. Empty. Dani's up. She's not tired. She watches her brother. He squirms in a waiting seat. The clay-colored resin forms are hooked together; a centipede. *A bottle of Clorox, and maybe.* Charlie rests on the three-hour ride. Not her.

Her brother. A last-ditch adaptation. She and Joey scheme for weeks; she'll make it happen. Six hours on a bus round trip in one day to spend five hours together? No problem. Plus, her brother has the backpack, so she doesn't have to. Her magazine, a couple of sandwiches. Bottle of water.

Joey's family drives down to Florida for spring break. Last year, the Keys; Joey talked and talked about it. This year, Cocoa Beach, north of Daytona. Joey's and Dani's dream: a few days together on the beach… One day, not even, would have to suffice.

From the bus window, ninety minutes in, Dani eyes the ocean. It's crystalline. The sun reflects sharply. To the west, over her shoulder, the faint moon, waning gibbous, 93% visible. She smiles. June 26. She has a plan. Joey has no clue.

Her favorite cutoffs. She stole Joey's Levis, button fly, paint stain near the pocket. The snick of her mother's sewing shears. She fingers the fluffy white fringe. A green Le Moyne College T-shirt over her black bikini. A gift from Joey. The green and the gold set off her eyes, he said. Her thin neck reveals the bow of her string bikini — she imagines Joey's hungry eyes.

She carries a small military satchel, olive drab; an army-navy surplus gift from Joey. Sunscreen, Chapstick, a change of clothes, her wallet. A couple of phone numbers.

She pictures Joey; he awaits her arrival. Bus trip halfway across Florida bifurcates her family's visit with cousins.

Joseph walks along the beach. It's early morning. He can't sleep. Anticipation. He slipped on red swim trunks, white piping down the side, a white cross on the thigh. He slipped out. White, V-neck T-shirt says Lifeguard on the chest. Red Wayfarer sunglasses — look-alikes anyway.

Sam's up. He rides his skateboard; driveway, sidewalk, shuffleboard courts, tennis courts. Joseph opted instead to bring *Walden* by Henry David Thoreau. His father made him choose.

Joseph lays out his towel. He opens the book. The off-white pages are painful. He turns into shadow. It's ironic; he reads about Walden Pond in winter, frozen over, on a beach. The sun glares. Waves crash and roar in the background. Joseph smiles.

Out in the woods for days at a time, Joseph's Seneca soul,

the one-sixteenth of it anyway, reinflates. A camping trip in the winter? Dani? He laughs and shakes his head; Henry David winks at him from the page.

Peanut butter and jelly. The bread translucent. She bites. With a pinkie, she dabs the corner of her mouth. Why do peanut butter and jelly sandwiches taste good when you're hungry? A small miracle. She flips through *The New Yorker*. Joey will love the piece about Truman Capote.

Joseph picks up his towel, shakes it out, gathers his book. He wonders how close his girlfriend is. He heads back to the hotel room. Sam rides up to him. Sam rolls, occasionally pushes. They find the first-floor entry, Room 117. Joseph uses his key to unlock it, drops his flip-flops outside the door. They enter the darkened room. His father snores lightly.

Dani descends the stairwell. Joseph stands across from her, his arms out wide. He can't believe it's her. She looks a little more tan and a lot more tired. She does the impossible; Joseph loves her for it. Why didn't he take the bus? She hugs him around his ribs; the thought evaporates. She looks up. Her bronze face loses contrast against her light brown hair. He kisses her.

She promised to call as soon as she arrived. She reaches into her bag. She has the phone number on a slip of paper.

"You made it." Joey is buoyant. He walks on his toes.

Sam carries his skateboard. Charlie looks dazed.

Joey holds her hand. He leads them to the beach. Joseph's mother and father are on a blanket. Big Joe wears mirror sunglasses, navy-blue shorts, no shirt. He doesn't stand. Margaret's Jackie Kennedy sunglasses are on her head. A beige halter-top bikini, denim sports shorts, piped in rainbow. She smiles. "When you put your mind to it, Miss Daniella…"

Dani greets Joey's folks. She asks if she can make a call.

"Let's use the phone in the office — I'll introduce you." Margaret lowers her sunglasses. She and Dani and Joey plod through the soft sand. Charlie and Sam make for the hotel's clubhouse, video games, snack bar. Dani listens to Margaret.

She flashes Joey a smile.

The hotel office is spartan. Orange-tile floor, grout the color of pond water. Reception desk left. A plastic ficus. Painted white brick. Someone moves behind a curtain. A short older woman emerges, smiling.

"This is Joey's girlfriend. We told you about her," Margaret says. The woman bows.

"Could we phone her parents?"

The woman guides Dani to the chunky phone. Dani dials. Someone picks up. From a bowl on the desk, the older woman gives Joseph two suckers. One purple and one red.

Outside, Margaret struts through the parking lot, spring break royalty, no in-room phone charges for her. Joseph holds out the lollipops. His girlfriend takes red.

A bulge in his cheek, Joseph says, "Come with me, I want to show you something." His voice echoes in his mouth.

Joseph is so proud of Ron Jon Surf Shop you'd think he discovered it. Through the glass doors, at the center of the place, surfboards arrayed to look like a tropical flower. T-shirts, towels, sunglasses, umbrellas, toys.

Dani to Joseph, "Need anything?"

"Pretty pricey. Just to show you, is all."

"Let's poke around."

"Ooh, bikinis." Joseph can't contain himself. "You could try some?" Joseph touches the collar of his girlfriend's T-shirt.

"You'd like that. You haven't even seen mine..."

"Dreamt of it. Check these out, ever seen these?" Joseph points to crocheted bikini bottoms. A tangle of strings.

Dani hides her horror — how could anyone wear those? She smiles. She could. Her mom would faint dead away.

Joseph keeps moving. Thongs, cheeky bottoms, boy shorts. He comes to the Body Glove bottoms. High hip cut. Yellow, hot pink, neon green and black. "These," Joseph gulps, "would look good on you."

"Get out of town." The unflattering fluorescent lights? Teasing Joey would be fun. "Beach. Back to the bus station in a couple of hours." Dani remembers the brand name, the yellow logo. Joey's right, the cut would be perfect on her.

They blink in the sunlight. They head to the beach. His folks
will be back to the hotel room for lunch soon; he'd rather have
his girlfriend all to himself. On the sidewalk, she stops. Something catches her eye. Joseph follows her gaze.

A motel adjacent, on the second-floor balcony, a woman. Her
arm splayed over the rail. Her head thrown back. She savors
something. Camel blond, dark roots. Her soft-wave permanent
grown out. Joseph steps closer to Dani. He eyes the woman on
the balcony. Above her, a young man emerges. No shirt. He's
muscled. He leans in. Her arm goes around his neck. A hand
reaches up. It traces the curve of his shoulder. The young man
sees Dani and Joseph. He winks.

"Whoa." Joseph watches. The young man lifts the woman up.
She hovers. She rocks. As if she were on a swing.

A reverend in a purple shirt stops. His back to the scene on
the balcony, he's oblivious. "You kids be careful. Do you know
how AIDS is transmitted?" He hands Dani a pamphlet and a
condom in a red package. He gives one to Joseph, a purple
package. "Read. Protect yourselves. Have a nice day." The reverend moves on. He accosts another couple.

"Let's go." Joseph laughs. He puts the thing in his pocket.
Dani looks back at the balcony. She holds the pamphlet and the
condom out in front of her. The couple are gone.

"Joey, remember the railroad tracks we walked on to get to
the falls?" Her voice takes a different tone. Joseph nods. His
face changes. His girlfriend tells a story about a boy and girl.
He, an Italian immigrant. Worked in the salt mines. Spoke broken English. He met his sweetheart on the tracks near Route 63.
A county road. They snuck around. Near the Little Italy settle-
ment.

Joseph walks. He absorbs the sound of her voice. Not sure
what she's trying to tell him, but he can tell it's important. She
looks at the ground. She says, "One night, walking home after
seeing her, he got hit by a train. Killed."

"That's horrible." Joseph imagines getting clipped by a bus.
Did the girl hear the whistle of the train? How did she find out?

Joseph looks at Dani. A tear in the corner of her eye. "At least he died happy. How did you hear the story?"

"As a little girl. It's so sad, isn't it? To finally find someone, and then… I don't want to lose you." She wipes her eye.

She leaves the rest out. She wants to tell him about the Retsof mine, near Union Corners. The largest salt mine in North America. The town was founded by a man named Foster. He reversed the spelling of his surname. Joey would love that. For years, the town was populated by Italian immigrants who worked the mines. It was a company town. The houses and the store were owned by the salt mine. The bosses lived on the Avenue in houses with indoor plumbing. She doesn't tell Joey her grandmother's name, or where she lived. The salt mine owned a small railroad, the Genesee & Wyoming, or the G&W, which was used to haul salt to the main lines in the neighboring towns. She doesn't know the name of the boy.

They descend a set of cement stairs. Soft sand of the dunes. She pulls Joey close to her. She smells hotel soap, his sunscreen, the dryer sheet smell, and something else. What is it? She searches for the name of the smell, dry, warm, fresh. Is it *summer*? "Almost a year since we first kissed."

"No way. Is it? How do you know?" Joey catches himself. "What I mean is, when?"

"June 25. Remember? First-aid training."

"Wow. That's like two months from now. Kiss me." Joey holds his lips out. She gives him a quick peck. She has more to say.

She tells him about her plan. June 26. A Saturday. Her parents won't be there. A half-marathon. Gone until lunch. Charlie, she tells him, basketball camp — same weekend. A year and a day.

"Kind of a big day, don't you think?" She looks down at the red package in her hand. She lets go of Joey's hand. She puts the condom in her pocket. Trash, first chance she gets. How could anyone trust a prophylactic given by a stranger? Man of the cloth, or pretending to be one? No way. She'll make Joey get rid of his too.

"What're you thinking?"

"You know. Maybe it's time. Take our relationship to the next level?"

"Oh shoot. Not today?" Joey jokes. She won't be deterred.

"Big step. I'm ready. You ready?" She looks him in the eyes.

Joey says something. It's after-school special logic. Boys are supposed to respect the girl in the morning, whatever that means. He tears up for after-school specials. It's sweet.

She laughs and kisses him. "Let's see the ocean."

They pile through the soft dunes. The sand changes. It's hard-packed. A gusting wind shears the tips off white caps. She tastes the brine. Dani feels their time slipping away.

On impulse, she tugs Joey's hand. She runs. He laughs. She has an idea. She stops. A spot in the soft sand. She lets go. She takes off her Le Moyne shirt. She wiggles out of her shorts. She lays them on the sand. Joey takes off his shirt. He spreads his shirt out next to her. He sits down. She lowers herself.

Her black bikini is something. She doesn't need new bottoms. Dani kisses Joseph hard. He pivots in the sand. Her hands explore his chest, his arms. His hands measure her waist, the small folds in her flat stomach. Everything is flesh on flesh, tongue on tongue, sweaty, salty lip on sweaty, salty lip.

Joseph sits back.

Dani laughs. "I know."

How did his clothes, how did hers? He's hypnotized by the pockets of her jean shorts. They tilt right, tilt left. A little hitch in between. She strides through the soft sand. The stitching reminds him of a squashed astrological symbol. Aries.

They find a place to eat. Chili dogs at a picnic table out by A1A.

Sam accompanies Joseph. He waves his skateboard goodbye to Charlie. Joseph hugs his girlfriend to his chest. Kisses the top of her head. He whispers into her hair, "I love you."

She presses her torso to his. She searches his eyes. First left, then right. The corner of her mouth twitches. "I love you too."

A small tear jumps her eyelashes.

"Call me when you get in, no matter how late. I'll answer on the first ring. I'll sleep by the phone."

Dani laughs. "Won't ring in the office?" She looks tired.

She lingers. She fills her eyes with Joey. He stands below her. His feet splay on flip-flops. A film of sand hems his shirt. She'll sleep. It was worth it.

I have to be rid of people I don't want to be involved with. Izabela's the first to go. Hold her accountable. Next Agata. Next Brad.

Jacques wants a flat of his own. I told him he can stay as long as he wants. I think he needs to be on his own to feel like he landed on his feet, not on his knees. He met his friend the other night. He said it went fine. He didn't say much more. If I had to guess, I would say he got his rebound. Cold comfort. Poor Jacques. He's a fucking mess. Can't decide where to live, can't find one of his rings, spinning on school nights (not good) and not painting. He's allowed to be a mess for a while.

So I'll wait for Karina. I hope she's healed. I hope she's got her rebound out of her system. Or was I the rebound? Not for me to decide. I won't rush her.

Singing, 5.11.98
Jacques got some sleep and found his ring. I came home from work. He washed dishes. He listened to music. I sat down and wrote a couple letters.

Letters One, Two and Three

I would copy the letters here, word for word, but after I wrote them, I realized they were too personal. Can you believe it? Your boy, Joseph over here, he might actually be maturing. Golly!

First to my mom. Here's a nice bit:

First of all, I want to say thank you for paying me back when you did. You made it possible to attend Tad's wedding in Barce-

lona. Just what I needed. I know you harbor feelings of guilt for borrowing money from your son; I urge you to forgive yourself. Waste not a second more on thoughts like those. You paid for me my whole life. You owe me nothing.

I gave her repayment more credit than it was due. Sue me. I apologized for our argument when she visited back in April. I acknowledged that I should have been a better listener when she talked to me about her life before my father. I told her about Ilona. Had to.

Next up, Dad. I invited him to come visit. He hasn't been here. I pointed out that Mom has, to appeal to his sense of competition. Then I talk about some stuff that should stay between me and him. I ended on a good note, here:

You are going to think this ridiculous. I always thought you loved Sam more. Sam made you laugh. I made you angry. I grew up hoping one day this would change. In fact, it only got worse. Except maybe now. Except maybe now when we can have a beer together and laugh.

Last but not least, for today, Sam. Told him I looked forward to his visit next year. Got in a jab about how Americans over-schedule their European visits: busy, busy, busy! Then some stuff that will stay between brothers. Settling old debts, trying to see from the other's perspective. I'll share this:

You are my brother. I will never have another. I will do my best to honor our relationship, to prioritize it over almost all others. We don't have a big family with multiple brothers and sisters like our parents do; we don't have the luxury of picking favorites. We have to deal with each other, like it or not.

It gets mushy after that. No one wants to read that.

Next stop: post office. Should be an interesting adventure into absurdity. Assorted rubber stamps will be involved.

Jacques and I had a nice moment last night in his car with

Bob Marley. We drove to Holešovice to check out a flat for him. A song came on. Before you knew it, we were singing "Everything's Going to Be All Right," over and over and over. It started with Jacques saying to me, you know, we need to remind each other. It's true.

Doubting, 6.11.98

Work. I sink myself into work. Last night I didn't get home until 9:00 p.m. because I went to Identity. I added some fields to the database, to allow them to do the reporting they've been asking for. Without the proper linkages, you can't make the reports work. Pretty reports with no data in them are not helpful. I added the fields. I got the data working. The guys were happy.

Remember the Roxy girl? The way her dark hair is bobbed makes it look like a wig. She has a round face and a rounder ass. Shiny black pants that fit just right. Legs that go all the way up. Blue eyes. Nothing like the pale blue eyes Ingrid had. Blue like denim. Fitted black T-shirt, V-neck. I danced with her. You know the way you dance in the vicinity of someone attractive, she notices you. She dances closer. She acts like she's not looking at you; she watches you the entire time. She moves like a flame, she knows how to dance, she reaches into the music with her body. That's it. We reach out to each other with our bodies. It's intense, my face over her shoulder, she lingers a second, smiles. She spins away. I go upstairs to have a smoke. She stands there. By herself. I ask her for a light though I have a lighter in my pocket. She asks me for a cigarette. She walks over. I give her one. She lights mine and then she lights hers. I ask her why she's here. She says, "It's a party." I meant to say why wasn't she on the dance floor. I tell her I don't speak much Czech. She doesn't say anything. She looks at me. She leaves.

Moments later she's back. She waits for me to talk to her. I don't. I consider offering her a drink, but I don't do that. You'd have to be an idiot, buying a girl's time with drinks. The Roxy girl watches me the rest of the night. It's ridiculous. I don't understand. Not sure I want to.

You know what I mean? It's like the realization that I could fuck Agata if I wanted to, but the second we're finished? Disappointment. It's not worth the trouble. The same is true for Karina. Without love, there isn't much to talk about. I wouldn't mind sleeping with Karina. I'd rather love her.

I can't say I think it's a game on her part. We're star-crossed. Calamity and tragedy. That's what brings us together. Like her car accident. That's what'll end it for us too.

Standing Up, 7.11.98

Pat and Markéta are in Hamburg and for the first time, I miss them. I have to reconnect with them. Jacques's right. I need to reconnect.

Vivid dreams last night; can't remember what they were.

I journal. Images flood my mind. It's Rachel and me. We lay on separate couches, end to end. Our feet touch. I slither closer. My feet are up to her knees. I touch her left foot with my left hand. Her foot is warm, soft. I run my fingers over her arch and push with my thumb into the bottom of her foot. She squeezes her legs against mine. She sighs. With both hands I pull her closer. Now my feet are by her waist and her feet mine. She wears jeans, like she just got here from a road trip. I wear pajamas, like I was getting ready to go to bed, getting ready for her not to arrive. In the dream I know that's not right. These couches are her couches, I am on her turf, it's not Boston or Manhattan, but somewhere else, somewhere I had to travel, West Coast. I encircle her right ankle with my right hand, like a cuff, like a ball and chain. Her legs are slender, I can feel the tendons and sinew. Her calves are curvy under the denim. She sits up. She straddles me. She looks down into my face.

I jolt awake right there. I don't want to come out of the trance, not yet. Her words hit me. I smile. I turn over. I try to get back into the dream. She's gone.

BACKFIRE

It was the last time we were carefree. My mouth hangs open, my eyes squint. Rachel smiles. Beatific. You can see her teeth. It's a photo. JFK International. I'm wearing a sport coat over a T-shirt. Hard reality in soft chairs. My father made us laugh. My mother snapped the picture. I didn't see it until years later.

The summer after Rachel and I began dating, I applied for and was offered a ten-week gig in Germany. Ten weeks away from a budding romance. I dreamt about working the summer abroad since we had the exchange students with the amazing accents in high school. The light grasp on American idioms. Here was my chance. I had to take it, right? Didn't I?

I don't know if I could live without taking the job, to keep my eye on a girl. I left behind my motorcycle. It was a 1981 Yamaha XS 650 Special II. It had a dark blue gas tank. I bought it from a friend the summer after our sophomore year to commute to Beth Israel Hospital for the internship I had that year. As the summer progressed, it developed a loud backfire. I conferred with a couple of motorcycle buddies. It was agreed that I needed to check the piston rings. How does one check the piston rings?

That winter, it would have been December 1990, I took the bike apart. I knew from the owner's manual under the seat that I didn't have to remove the pistons to replace the piston rings. I only had to get to the point where I could turn the crank arm by hand, with the head removed, and the wrist rings would clear the cylinder walls enough that I could release the pins.

I tore down the motor. I wondered if I would be able to put it back together again. If it would run again. I wondered what would happen if I lost one essential piece; my motorcycle, my chopper, my bike, would become for all eternity a hulk of scrap metal.

I had thought in my head that I would take Rachel for a spin on it. I had not met her yet. A dreamer. I worked and worked. I replaced the rings. I got it back together. There was a box of strange leftover parts. It was a mystery.

The moment of truth. Back parking lot, out by the dumpster. I jumped on the manual kickstart. Nothing. I jumped again. Nothing. Sweat gathered at the top of my back. I prayed. I jumped again. I jumped hard. I tweaked my knee. Nothing. Again. A little cough. A rumble. I went again. More rumble, I twisted the throttle. She coughed, rumbled, died. I jumped. Whoom. I twisted the throttle. She roared. I revved and revved.

I backed away, a grease-stained hand at my chin. I admired my handiwork. Crack. She backfired. It was disheartening.

Do you know what was not disheartening? I pulled up to the house where Rachel lived on that loud ass thing. She backfired. I ran it while she came down to meet me. She backfired again. I was embarrassed. From a third-floor window, her ex-boyfriend, the one with long yellow hair, yelled down at me. I smiled inside the helmet. I twisted the throttle in my gloved hand. I was glad I wasn't that guy.

Rachel told me she loved riding on the back of the bike with me. She dreamt of riding it herself. It was a chance to keep her occupied over the summer: maybe she would be less likely to fuck some other dude while I was off in Europe for ten weeks. A buddy of mine agreed to keep an eye on the bike for the summer. He agreed to give Rachel a lesson or two on the bike. He was my friend, he knew how much I liked this girl, he wouldn't try anything.

I lived in a workers' dormitory in Stuttgart. I read the latest letter from Rachel. In it, she told me she crashed the bike. Chris rode the bike the two blocks to her house, she got her helmet on, she threw her leg over the bike, I could picture it, in her black jeans and her black low-cut Doc Martens. She rode the thing into a curb. A nick in the front spoked rim, nothing serious, laid it down. Stood there with her fists on her hips. Chris ran over and scooped the bike up, still running. She wasn't hurt. She was embarrassed; she didn't try to ride the thing again. She ended up fucking some dude. Whatever. I'm still pissed about it, it still hurts. Here I thought I had found the love of my life. I wrote her letters every day from Germany. She knew how much she meant to me. She could not keep it in her pants for ten weeks. Less! She visited me in Stuttgart over the summer. She could not keep it in her pants for a month. Fuck. I came back from Germany and guess what? I was that guy.

She said she loved me. How could she love me and fuck somebody else? That's what I wanted to know.

Didn't she know that would devastate me? Didn't she know I couldn't look at her the same again? I guess she didn't. I guess she didn't know that for me, it was a betrayal. It told me what I needed to know about whether she loved me or not.

How is it for other people? I wondered. Can they do that? Can they go around fucking whoever they want and hold on to the illusion that they're devoted to someone? Not people, I meant Rachel. Did I mean that little to her? Did she think about me when she was with this dude? She drove around in his car. She danced to his music. She took him back to her room? No, she couldn't think about me in those moments. I was nothing to her then.

I couldn't stop thinking about it. She hadn't tried to hide it from me. She told me it was bound to happen. She expected it. She stayed at school for the summer. She worked her summer job in the math lab. Summer boarders all around her, people who didn't live in her fraternity during the semester. People could rent a room there for the summer. She said that every summer there were more than a couple cute guys who lived there. She told me she was excited to see who the cute guys were going to be this year.

What did I think? Did I think that once she met me, once she saw what was in my heart, suddenly she would become completely and utterly devoted to me? That she would give up men completely because she had met me? Yes! Yes. That's exactly what I thought. I thought if she received my letters every day, if she rode my motorcycle once or twice, I thought that I could hold her imagination. She wouldn't have time for other guys.

That's the thing. I think that exists. I believe it. Out there, there's a woman who would've been blown away by the secret admirer thing, who would've told everyone that story. Including the next good-looking guy who came along. She would bore that poor fucker with our story, how I had planned it over the course of weeks, how I had pasted that measly note together and snuck over to her room in the dead of night to slip it in through her window one early spring night when I knew her window would have to be open because the heat in the house was on too high and the night in the late winter was warm enough that she could open the window a slice. That's the thing about me. I believe that woman is out there, the woman who would've thrilled at the romance of it. Rachel, she looked the part; in the end, she was not her. Right from the first summer, I knew it. I didn't have to wait and see if our romance would grow, if her devotion would develop over time. It wouldn't. No matter how I tried to convince myself, how she tried to convince me that it didn't matter, this summer fling with this stupid guy, I knew what it meant.

Here's the kicker. While I was in Germany, I fucked someone too. I know how ironic this will sound. I know. There she was, a British woman from some obscure suburb of London, she's cute. She has this charming accent. She says adorable things.

It starts at lunchtime, I see her and her friend. Before I realize it's happening, Dudley and I talk to them. We talk and then we make plans to get together for the 4th of July. Yep, we know how ironic it is: to have a picnic with our British acquaintances to celebrate our independence. Our independence from them. On that blanket, my Brit and I, we kiss. Then we roll around. Nothing happens there, a green grassy expanse in Stuttgart outside the castle. On that blanket it's innocent enough. We neck, the Brit and I. You wonder: did I think of Rachel at that moment?

The answer is no, I didn't think of Rachel at that moment. Or maybe I did; it was a guilty feeling that I tucked away, that I tried to ignore. It wasn't betrayal. It was nothing. I did it to soak up the time away from Rachel. I wouldn't see this woman again, after this summer, I wouldn't think of her again, once I got back to reality, once I got back to school and to Boston and to Rachel.

Oh. Yeah. When I put it like that. Isn't it how it happens with me? I counter betrayal with betrayal. Do I bring it on myself? I didn't know that Rachel would fuck some dude when I made the arrangements for my British sweetheart to join me in the strictly men only workers' dormitory. It was pre-betrayal protection I provided myself. The same thing happened with Dani the summer before we left for college. She kissed Kyle and I kissed Michelle. In the short time, not ten days, we were apart that summer. I took out an insurance policy. I betrayed her first. In theory it would equal out. It didn't. It doesn't.

Maybe this is a symptom. A symptom of what's wrong with me. I'm attracted to women who will betray me, who I will betray. Is that it? That's sad, to come to that realization. I'm pre-fucked. What I needed to learn is to be devoted to people who will be devoted to me. Who are devoted to me. Maybe what I was supposed to learn is to forgive myself and to forgive my lovers. Could that be it?

My plan was to fix the rim when I got back to Boston. I would find a junkyard, I would talk to my motorcycle buddies. I wouldn't straighten that nick in the rim out: I would replace it. When I got back, the nick was minor. Inconsequential. I ignored it.

And learned exactly nothing from my own metaphor.

Snickering, 8.11.98

I had a run-in with the Snickers lady already this morning. Stupid cow. I saw her on the way in. She was in her smock, standing by the door, smoking a cancer stick. I knew it was going to lead to trouble.

I hoped I would get another cashier. Of course not. She pretended she didn't remember me. I tried to give her a mangled 20 CZK (0.68 USD) bill. She made the face — "I cannot possibly take this piece of shit" — I stood there, my arms full, *bageta* (baguette), *koblihy* (doughnuts), *vejce* (eggs), *máslo* (butter), and got another 20 CZK out of my pocket. When she didn't jump at it, I threw the Snickers on the counter. I left. She screamed out the door as I left. I turned, said, "Fuck you," and kept on walking. She didn't hear me.

I don't have to put up with anyone's shit. No more.

Jacques washes dishes. I let him, though I like to do the dishes. If he wants to get involved, he should. To replace Jacques's candy bar, I cooked him up a quick breakfast. It was good. It was all right. Nothing special. I guess it's because nobody cooks anymore. I'll cook tonight.

Knowing, 9.11.98

Yesterday was Sunday. Later in the day, I met Jacques for a beer. He said something about the Prague Uprising. I asked if he meant the Prague Spring. He was smug. Nope, he said, there's another one – look it up.

When we got back to the flat, I pulled the phone into the entryway. Jacques closed the doors to the living room. A little bit drunk, I did the predictable thing. I called Karina.

Karina answered. I sat on the linoleum and rested against the wall under the coat hooks. I settled in for a chat. It was fun. I made her laugh. She said, "It was good from you." I made a date with her for Wednesday to watch *The English Patient*.

I need to get Brad to go with me and rent the video from the English-language video rental shop in Prague 6 called Video To Go. I need to borrow Brad's flat since he has a television and a VHS video player. I plan it out. Karina's voice echoes through my head. My telephone rings.

I sit back on the linoleum floor. I answer. It's Ilona.

I try to flirt.

She's not having it.

The Prague Uprising

I found this one in the Encyclopedia Britannica in the English-language section resource room.

It was the culmination of the revolutionary democratic movement in the former Austro-Hungarian Empire between 1848 and 1849.

A Slavic conference was convened in Prague on June 2, 1848. While little was decided as to the future of the Slav states, it resulted in a peaceful demonstration gone wrong. Austrian troops of the Prague garrison fired several shots into the crowd.

The attack provoked outbursts of indignation in the layers of society, from students to artisans and factory workers, who decided to blockade streets and disrupt law and order in the city.

June 12 was the Pentecostal holiday of Whit-Monday. At the Horse Market, now Wenceslas Square, students and workers skirmished with Austrian soldiers.

The Czech liberal bourgeoisie, led by František Palacký, František Ladislav Rieger and Pavel Ŝafařík, interceded to attempt to quell any further bloodshed, but the Austrians launched an artillery attack on June 17 that led Prague to surrender.

Long, awkward pause. Ilona sighs. She invites me to dinner. At her sister's house. Tomorrow evening. Near Flora metro stop. It's one stop from the wadjet. The eye can practically see Flora metro stop where it stands.

Actually, come to think of it, everything's sure to go wrong.

Understanding, 10.11.98

Last night, I wrote a couple more letters. I love the scratch of the pen on the airmail paper. I love the light blue color, the pattern of truncated stripes around the edges. I love the airmail stamp.

Letters Four and Five

First, Rachel. Of course. I can't share much of that one. Here's a line:

I already wrote you a letter that I didn't send. I could just dust that one off and send it.

Obviously this one:

You deserved better from me.

I could have that one printed on a T-shirt. I want to let her know I think about what part of what went wrong was mine. Does she need to know?

This next one was a surprise for me. It just came out. I guess it was the mushiness; I had written to my folks and Sam, I had written to my ex-wife (whether or not I send it.) The next one starts:

Dear Future Wife,
Hello! You don't know me yet, but you will.

It writes itself from there. Here's a couple of zingers.

You have a past. Me too. You are creative. In me, you will find the ultimate champion for your passion.

My favorite line.

If I know you, you are gonna make me wait. Not to torture me although it will at times feel like torture; out of self-respect. I love that about you.

The closer.

Camping. You have to like camping. That's a deal-breaker.

Back to the post office. It wasn't as bad as I thought. Where am I sending the second one? Address: Universe.

Flora metro stop. I came up the escalator watching a young man kiss his girlfriend. He had his hand in the back pocket of her jeans.

I rang the buzzer. Up above my head, I heard a creak and a bump. I stepped back to see if I could see who it was. I heard a giggle. "Joseph, hello, is it you?" It was the voice of a young girl. The English was shockingly good if halting. She giggled with her sister, shushed her. Their mother asked them to close the window. The door buzzed. I shouldered it open.

It had been a few weeks. I'd like to say that I hadn't been

thinking too much about Ilona, but of course I had. I convinced myself that I'm still in love with Karina. I could hear Karina's laugh, distorted slightly by the phone lines.

Božena's apartment was on the fourth floor. On each landing, I clicked on the light to renew my timer.

Ilona answered the door. I held out the bottle of Bohemia Sekt. It was the bottle I'd brought with me the day I found her lying bloody on my bathroom floor. It had sat in my fridge since that day. I couldn't bring myself to drink it. She took it away into the kitchen. I shouldn't have expected a hug.

Božena barreled in for a hug. I thanked her for the invite. I admired her flat. She showed me around. The nieces were there.

Božena asked them to introduce themselves. The sisters eyed each other. The taller one, dark hair, went first. In English.

"Hello, Joseph. My name is Dorota."

Charmed, I held out my hand. "Hello, Dorota." She shook it.

The smaller one, blond, missing a few teeth in the front, stepped forward next. "Hello, Joseph, my name is Veronika."

Too cute. I held out my hand again. "Hello, Veronika." She gave my hand one hard shake. Satisfied, the girls turned to go.

"Wait. Dorota, when is your Name Day?"

The girls turned again. Dorota looked at her mother. Božena translated the question. Dorota looked back at me.

"Dvacet šest února," Dorota said, her hand coming up to her mouth. The girls giggled. Božena assisted, "February 26."

Dorota nodded once. She said to me, "February 26." Her diction was adorable.

"And yours, Veronika?" I asked the blond girl.

"February 7," she said without hesitation. She looked at her sister. Not to be outdone, Dorota turned back to me.

"Joseph, when is your Name Day?"

Ilona watched from the kitchen doorway. She crossed her arms across her belly. She leaned against the frame.

"Oh my. I don't know."

Veronika parroted, "Oh my! Oh my!"

"I look you. Name Day." She held a finger up to me.

"Drink, Yoselle?" Božena waved me into the dining room. At the sideboard, she poured me a plum brandy in a *panák*, a small shot glass. The word translated to dummy, but honestly, who's the dummy in this situation?

We ate dinner not in the formal dining room, but in the kitchen. It was a warm family kitchen. I imagined Ilona's and Božena's childhood home must have been like this. The husband is named Jan, but they called him Honza. He came out after the second plum brandy, he didn't partake. He was silent throughout dinner. He asked Ilona to translate a few times. Ilona was mostly quiet too. I caught her eyes; she was ready to talk. Božena and Ilona prepared a family favorite — duck and dumplings. I cleared the plates, Honza stepped onto the terrace to smoke, Božena poured herself and me one more plum brandy. She winked at me. We clinked dummies.

The terrace looked over a park. Honza excused himself. Ilona lit a cigarette. "I hate you, Joseph. After this night, I see you again never."

I rolled a cigarette between my fingers, smiled. "You don't mean that." I hoped she didn't mean that. I bluffed. I squinted.

"Maybe not. But feels good to say. You have to let me feel good." Ilona took a drag on her cigarette. She closed one eye as she draws it in. She smoked because she could.

I told her we could be friends. It sounded hollow. It was the first time I understood how sad it was. How permanently sad.

"We are being linked, but we are not friends." The lace of the curtains wiggled. It could have been one of the nieces. It could have been Božena.

I wanted to tell her I could have loved her. I wanted to tell her the effect her family has on me. I put the cigarette between my lips. Ilona reached out without lifting from where she leaned against the metal railing and flicked her lighter at arm's length. I tilted my head.

"You are idiot. It's okay." Ilona blew out a stream of smoke, her lips pursed. She held the crook of her right arm in her left hand. She tilted the cigarette away from herself.

I looked down at the trees in the park. They swayed. A cool

autumn wind tousled the leaves. "So what now?"

Ilona locked her eyes on me, her anger a flare that burned out quickly. "Nothing now, Joseph. I finish school. I work. You go do what you stupid Americans do, eat hamburgers and drink beer and chase girls. It is not for me to say."

I asked her about Thirsty Dog. I wanted to be able to find her. Ilona was not wrong. The words sounded hollow. Maybe it was time to fill it in. Could I tell her?

Ilona smiled. "No. No more. I said goodbye to Ingrid, over the past couple of weeks, I let her go. You will have to do the same one day. I will work for my fodder now."

What was it her father did? I remembered he had a shop, but what was it? I recalled her slurred words; she swore to me that she would rather eat shit than work for her father. I remembered that. This was it. This was goodbye.

I decided right then. I couldn't do it to her. I wouldn't tell Ilona about my mother. It would stay locked in my heart forever. I would not disgrace myself. Hurt her to make myself feel better? I decided. It was the only way.

"Can I tell you how beautiful you are?"

Ilona shook her head. "No. Now you say me how brilliant I am. What genius I possess. I want you to never forget what you lost. In me."

"You are brilliant." I told her she was right about the stories. I will finish them. Not for anyone else. For me. I told her I wouldn't forget what she did for me. I wanted to hug her. I held myself back.

Backfiring, 11.11.98

I realized this morning, in my bed, with a pillow on my head, that in the year 2011, I'll be forty-one. The date on that day, thirteen years from right now, will be 11/11/11. On the other hand, it's only numbers arbitrarily applied to the passage of time; put there to mark man's inability to cope with the void that's the essence of being.

I decided not to let myself think too much. I headed for the library. The male librarian frowned at me as I came in.

Karel Čapek

I read *War with the Newts* when I first got to Prague. Markéta
lent her copy to me. I wanted to know more about the guy who
wrote it.

He was the leading novelist, playwright, story writer, colum-
nist and critic during the first twenty years after Czechoslovakia
was founded in 1918. He is generally considered the greatest
Czech author of the first half of the twentieth century. One of
the great world authors between the wars. He was the spirit of
his country's short-lived democracy. Nominated for the Nobel
Prize seven times, he wasn't to receive it.

Born January 9, 1890, in Malé Svatoňovice, in the Bohemian
mountains. He died at the age of forty-eight on Christmas Day
1938, the result of a lifelong struggle with spondylarthritis, any of
a number of diseases attacking the spinal column, and excessive
smoking. His father was a country doctor. He was the youngest
of three siblings. His brother, Josef, was a painter. His sister,
Helena, was an accomplished pianist. He studied philosophy in
Prague at the Charles University, Friedrich Wilhelm University
in Berlin and the Sorbonne in Paris. He graduated with a doctorate in philosophy in 1915. By 1917 he had made his home in
Prague. Detective stories, humor columns, philosophical novels, apocryphal short stories and a magical biography written as
the result of years of interviews with T.G. Masaryk made up his
life's work. His most well-known work is *War with the Newts*,
a dystopian satire that skewers the twentieth century. It rings
prophetic even in the twenty-first. In it he treats subjects such
as science, capitalism, totalitarianism, fascism, nationalism,
racism, consumerism and Hollywood with his uniquely human
touch and unfailing dark humor. In his play *R.U.R. (Rossum's
Universal Robots),* he first uses the term *robot*, a shortening of
the Czech word *robota,* which means "forced labor," though
his brother, Josef, the painter probably coined the term. In his
1920 play, the word is used to describe a fictional humanoid.
The American playwright Arthur Miller wrote, "read Čapek …

for his insouciant laughter and the anguish of human blindness that lies beneath it."

The social turmoil of his time, specifically between the world wars, caused him to write many politically charged works. Inspired by pragmatic American liberalism, he believed in free expression and he strongly opposed the rise of fascism and communism in Europe. Closer to home, the threat of Nazi Germany prompted him to write several works aimed at mobilizing his countrymen. His work in 1937 and 1938, just before his death, included a novel and two plays. *The First Rescue Party* stressed the need for solidarity. *Power and Glory* expressed the plight of the noble pacifist. *Mother* sought more directly to defend the need for armed resistance to barbaric invasion. Although he was named "public enemy number two" by the Gestapo (after Alphonse Mucha), he refused the opportunity to emigrate to England leading up to the Nazi invasion. Karel died just a few weeks before they arrived. Unaware of his death, the SS came to the Čapek residence to arrest him. They took his wife, Olga, for interrogation. His brother, Josef, was arrested in September 1939, deported to the Bergen-Belsen concentration camp, where he died. Karel and Olga are buried in the Vyšehrad cemetery in Prague, with an inscription that reads, "Here would have been buried Josef Čapek, painter and poet. Grave far away."

Fictional humanoid. Ha. I am that. On so many levels.

I hurt poor little Braddie the other day at dinner. We discussed his willingness to ignore his responsibility, how he dumped his poor helpless little bunny of a girlfriend on both me and Jacques and my poor apartment. I said, "I'm supposed to take girl-advice from you?" It was funny to me; I had wanted to say it for a long time. The restraint I showed backfired; the words stewed in me. I served it to him on a cold plate of reality. The strength of it caught him off guard.

Brad had better quit with the puppy dog thing. It doesn't suit him. He's shrunk; I'm talking in actual physical size. It's as if he reversed over severe tire damage. Inviting Agata to his birthday party?

Locksmithing, 13.11.98

Yesterday I woke up with Karina.

Yep. She stayed with me. She was prepared.

She came to see *The English Patient*. I rented it. I went to work on Wednesday. We agreed to meet at Meduza at 7:00 p.m. I didn't know if she'd show.

I went there ten minutes early. I couldn't concentrate on work. Sure enough, as I stepped in, she was right there by the door. She was absolutely gorgeous.

It's the place I took my mom last Easter, the place where the waitresses were dressed as bunnies and for the first time my mom noticed the flirtatiousness.

A leafy Vinohrady neighborhood, near the Peace Square metro stop. I came up on the street from underground, next to my favorite hot-dog place where they warm the Czech rolls on hot spikes and the mustard is tasty. I crossed over the tram tracks and Vinohradska and walked up Belgicka. The names of the streets are weird here, Belgicka, like Belgium, I guess. Next one over is Londynska. Perpendicular is Uruguayska. On the other side is Americka. No kidding. America Street.

In the doorway, a black iron gate was thrown open. Cafe Meduza. Wooden door. Windows peered inside. A cozy place, five tables. Arches were green, the walls were a pale yellow. All four walls covered in framed black-and-white pictures. Two chandeliers that don't match. Burnished chairs and lacquered tables. A standing coat rack by the door. Big mirrors in ornate frames. It had the feel of an old English pub that has been antiqued to look like a grandmother's parlor. Updated with artsy stuff. It felt like a student coffee hangout.

Karina was done up. I was surprised. She was beautiful. Beautifully nervous. She was drinking red wine. I had a glass. We talked, then left in search of a pizzeria she claimed to know in some cellar. We didn't find it. We went to my local pizzeria, had more wine while the pizza was on its way. Her family wants to buy her a house. Must be strange to be a princess. She doesn't want to model anymore because she doesn't like to be in front of people. I knew that. I can see that. We stopped to get soda. Then we made our way to Brad's place.

Brad's crib's nice; way too nice for Brad. We settled in. We watched the movie. I barely watched the movie. I was busy flirting. Brad called to find out when banishment from his home would be lifted. I checked the clock. Shit. 11:05 p.m. I didn't want to tell Karina for fear she'd run out. I told Karina. She said her train left at 11:20 p.m. I said she could sleep with me. I said it like that. She looked at me.

I told her she could sleep on my futon; I would sleep on the floor. It was funny for a second. We finished off the movie. She's beautiful. She has a certain quirkiness that makes her beautiful. She has many little things out of place. She looked perfectly strange come morning. She wears too much makeup, the way that girls do when they're first allowed to wear makeup and don't know how. Either that or I usually see her with professional makeup. Her legs're more beautiful when they're bare.

I lay down with her in my jeans. She asked me if I planned to sleep in jeans. She harassed me. I changed. I let her be for a while. She came to me in her time. I started slow, but then I was all hands.

In the morning, I stepped out for cigarettes. I walked into the grocery. There she was. She saw me. I smiled. She couldn't get me down today. No way. I got doughnuts and rolls and spread butter. When she asked me about the bags, I answered in Czech. Her response was flat. Whatever. When she asked for payment, I gave her exact change.

Karina slept. I snuck into the kitchen. In the bag, the Snickers lady had slipped me a candy bar. She didn't charge me for it.

She woke up. She thought of skipping her job interview. I thought about skipping work. It would've been worth it to stay in bed all day. She got dressed.

She brushed her teeth. She wore one of my shirts. She wore a lacy pair of panties to sleep. I saw them every which way. She let me. She bent over. She stood up. She lay on her side. She sat across from me.

She put on a little skirt. She squatted. She dug in her bag. I watched her.

She leaned in at Meduza. She leaned in at the pizzeria. I let her.

There were awkward moments. As we left Brad's place, I was giddy. I let the door close. Before I noticed I didn't have Brad's keys on me. I called the locksmith. Brad was out with Ester. The Brad-whisperer. She was trying to help him figure out what to do about Agata. They had no place to go. They met Karina and me at my place. Until the locksmith came. It took about an hour. We sat there. We waited. The four of us. Cost me 760 CZK (24.75 USD).

After she left, I went to work.

I wrote her an email. It was contrived and overwrought. She responded. Cute. She couldn't wait to tell me about her interview.

Crazy. I know. It must be confusing for her too.

She told me to look up Saint Agnes of Prague. I did. Check this out.

In 1989, in the days after the Berlin Wall had been taken down, Saint Agnes of Prague was canonized by Pope John Paul II. Czechs had been waiting seven hundred years for her to be beatified. Some say it was a sign that changes were afoot.

King Charles IV originally nominated her for sainthood in the 1300s. Agnes was born in 1200, the daughter of King Ottokar I of Bohemia and Queen Constance — yes, she was a princess. And as a princess, Agnes was betrothed three times but never married. The first time at the age of three. Her marriage to the Duke of Silesia was arranged, but the duke died three years later, before she could be married off. Later she was again betrothed to a prince for political reasons; he ended up marrying another. Finally, she rejected an offer of marriage from a king, the Holy Roman Emperor himself. The Pope was forced to intervene on her behalf. In the end the emperor accepted her decision; he agreed that he could not be offended if Agnes chose, over himself, the King of Heaven.

Agnes entered the order of Saint Clare and took a vow of poverty. While there, she built a Franciscan hospital, a monastery and a convent for the sisters and monks who worked there. She was a model of Christian virtue and religious observation in her role as abbess of the monastery. God favored her with the gifts of healing and prophecy; she predicted the victory of her brother, Wenceslas I, over the Duke of Austria.

So what changed, after seven hundred years? One of the conditions of being named a saint, including documented miracles, was that the location of the person's remains had to be known. Unfortunately, it is still not clear where Agnes's remains are. Pope John Paul II abolished this rule. It cleared the way. On November 12, 1989, Agnes of Prague became a saint.

That's why Karina told me to look her up. After forty years of Communism during which religion was de-emphasized in Czechoslovakia, this event could be seen by some as a restoration of faith. Further, it was perceived as a precursor to downfall of the Communists: the Velvet Revolution.

Leaving, 14.11.98
Karina left for Italy tonight. With Phil.

Did not see that one coming.

She gave up a fashion show. She lost the opportunity to see a movie with me. To go to Italy with Phil. She must be in love. Either that, or she's fucking stupid.

Forget it. I don't want to be anyone's second choice. Don't call me. Don't bother to come back. I rehearse for the return of my self-esteem.

I'm glad I called her. She was going to skip town, like that, leave me dick-in-hand.

I guess she must've had a good night last night. She didn't mention the possibility of an Italian vacation at any time during her stay with me. You know me: I don't ask questions when I know I won't like the answers. My high-school girlfriend taught me well.

HOMECOMING

A young man and a young woman climb out of a stubby blue Chevette. A fall Friday morning, the sun has not yet risen. The moon, 47% visible, in its last quarter. It's a hole in the sky over the chilly Western New York school parking lot. The moon watches them. Joseph, a tall, slender young man in tortoiseshell glasses, one-sixteenth Seneca, shoulders her book bag. She closes the hatch. The whump echoes around the lot.

Joseph leans his hip against the crash bar. Daniella DiBenedetto steps in. She sports her cheer uniform, a white turtleneck undershirt with her black and orange skirt and vest, a white crisscrossed UC emblazoned in orange.

The hallway smells like glue and sweat. A pair of girls passes by. The strawberry blonde in a side pony; the brunette teased her bangs into a claw. They whisper behind their Trapper Keepers. Dani guides Joseph to the office. She has advised against Joseph's stained work jeans and worn-out boots. She borrowed a pair of her father's duck boots for him — he would not admit it, but Joseph likes the way they look.

The permed school secretary signs Joseph in. She gives him a visitor sticker. Joseph rakes his black hair out of his eyes. He smiles at her. His girlfriend pats the sticker on his breast.

Dani's cheer teammate, the blonde with the half-lidded eyes, sidles up. She smells of smoke. She wears a football jersey over her uniform. The waist is knotted. Number 47. His girlfriend raises her eyebrows at him. Joseph smiles.

In the auditorium, students are scattered at the edge of the stage. Football players fumble with their jerseys. They wait to see which cheerleader will wear their number.

Dani's teammates organize the jerseys, assign them to cheerleaders. Two blond guys stand by the stairs to the stage. Piggish eyes. Joseph nods. The football players laugh. The massive one with the bad haircut slaps the smaller one on his back. He shakes him by the neck. The squirrelly one stiffens. He titters.

Joseph folds down the second chair in the second row. He slumps in the seat.

His girlfriend, her eyes down, approaches him. She mirrors his posture. "I don't think I'm gonna wear one of those stinking jerseys."

"It's no big deal. Pick the number of one of the big fat guys."
Dani cocks her head.

Joseph softens. "You don't want to stand out, do you?"

"It feels wrong."

Joseph squints. "Football's wrong. Cheering for football's wrong. It's cliché." Dani's features harden. Her jaw sets.

He hears his mother's voice: *You're a guest in her school; be a gentleman. This is her world. She's excited for you to be a part of it.*

Joseph turns to face her. "That's me being bitter. I'm not allowed to play. Sorry."

After weeks of planning, after a ride home from school in the Sunbird Express, here it is. A chance to escort Daniella DiBenedetto to her Homecoming dance.

She frowns. She kisses Joseph on the cheek. She whispers, "You're the only one for me. I love you." Joseph smells her apple shampoo, feels the cold spot where her lips touched. The cheerleaders pretend not to watch.

Joseph stands. Should have taken her advice. The stained jeans stand out here. The bell rings. His girlfriend wears the number 26. The jersey is broad in the shoulders. She wrestles with excess fabric. She hip-bumps Joseph.

Homeroom is off the main corridor. Joseph hangs back. A redhead with freckles, a familiar face, greets him. Rowan wears high-waisted jeans and a black Misfits T-shirt. Her red hair is frizzy with bangs.

"Excited for Homecoming?" Joseph hangs a thumb off his back pocket.

Rowan grimaces. She makes sure none of her classmates notice. She lowers her voice. "Our team is bleak."

"Football's for meatheads. Future felons."

Rowan raises her eyebrows. "Wow. Okay. Tell us how you really feel, Joe." Rowan looks at Joe's lips, looks away. "Does she know?"

Joseph blinks. "Yes and no. I joke. She can't tell when I am and when I'm not." Joseph looks at Rowan.

"Don't joke. The girl likes you, Joe. Like, likes likes. Be nice."

"Be nice to who?" Dani adjusts the knot of her ripe jersey. Joseph turns to his girlfriend. Rowan cuts him off. "I was saying he had better be nice to the friend who introduced you two… Now, who was that again?"

Rowan brings an index finger to her chin. "Let me think. Hmm. Oh yeah, now I remember. It was me."

Joseph laughs. Dani looks around the room.

The bell rings. Joseph takes a chair-desk next to Rowan.

The homeroom teacher takes roll call. Dani turns to Rowan. "Mind if Joey sits with you while we do our rally thing?"

Rowan shrugs. "No big whoop."

Joseph follows Dani up the ramp to the English room. The posters on the walls feature some of his favorites, *Catch-22* and *Slaughterhouse Five* and *All Quiet on the Western Front*. He figures he's bound to like the teacher.

Autumn sits in the second row, one of Dani's cheer team-mates. Autumn is shorter than Dani, a different kind of pretty, with her long straight black hair, thick eyebrows and square flat nose. Her brown eyes are close-set. Autumn smiles at Joseph from her desk. Joseph turns back, his brow furrowed.

Ms. Albright is no more than five or six years older than the seniors in the school. Her terracotta hair is cut into a chin-length bob. A snowy lace collar with an amber broach, and an over-sized plaid jacket with shoulder pads. She has chubby features and glasses that are too large for her face. She looks like a cherub playing dress-up.

"The Joseph? I feel like I already know you." Ms. Albright smiles.

"I love your posters. English is one of my top subjects."

"Ugh. These posters — they come in the English teacher classroom setup pack. If you want to read a great book, I'll lend you my copy of *Fountainhead*." Ms. Albright trills in her throat. Dani rolls her eyes. Joseph blinks. You can't judge an English teacher by her posters?

After lunch, the same at his girlfriend's school as at his, up to and including the rubbery square pizza and the dry peanut butter cookies, they head toward the gym. Dani gives Joseph a peck on the cheek and goes left. Rowan leads Joseph to the right.

They find a spot up high. Students fill the wooden bleachers. Ms. Albright enters. She adjusts her glasses. She acknowledges Joseph.

The glossy floor reflects the student body in a wavy flood of colors. Black mats hang on the north and south walls of the gym with Go Braves! painted in orange and white. The cheerleaders stand at the northeast corner of the gym. They hold up a banner emblazoned with CLASS OF '87. In the southwest corner is the gym teacher, Mr. DiBenedetto. He is a tree of muscle, tanner than anyone else at the school. He wears a snug pair of black coach's shorts and a tight white polo shirt. A whistle on a lanyard. An intimidating figure — Dani tells Joseph the reason no boys from her school ask her out is that they'll have to endure his disapproval. He looks in Joseph's direction. Joseph gives a small wave. If he sees it, Mr. DiBenedetto ignores it. Joseph pulls his arm down.

His girlfriend stands at attention, her pompoms on her hips. She holds her chin at a formal angle. She wobbles on one foot, catches herself, keeps grinning. She has shared a secret with Joseph: to keep their smiles, she and her teammates smear petroleum jelly on their teeth.

Music blares, loud and garbled. Rowan grimaces, sticking her fingers in her ears.

Football players crash through the banner. They spill out onto the gym floor, center court. They wear khakis, blazers and heather-gray shirts with Homecoming 1986 on the front. They flex their muscles, howl and slam into one another like covalent electrons. Coach, a fat man in a shirt and tie, waddles out to the microphone stand. He taps the microphone. It thumps. Mr. DiBenedetto bends at the waist. He shakes his head at Coach. Rowan laughs. She cracks Joseph on the shoulder with the back of her hand.

The music fades.

Coach begins. "This year has been a great learning experience for our boys. My message is steady progress. Be the tortoise, not the hare..." Joseph loses track of what the coach is saying. He watches his girlfriend. He hadn't noticed the orange ribbon in her hair before, but it looks good on her, highlights her natural brown and auburn curls. It's evident to Joseph, if not to all present: she shines in comparison to her teammates. Her posture, her proportions, her native hometown beauty, her confidence — whatever it is, she's more colorful, more alive, more wholesome than the other girls. If Joseph were to take a picture, his girlfriend would have an aura around her. Her image would vibrate the eye at a different frequency. Autumn comes close, also a pretty girl, with her Native American beauty. The ashy blond with the half-lidded eyes has a certain allure too — but it's unwholesome, the cigarette-smoking bad girl who football players like. Maybe this glow is what accounts for Mr. DiBenedetto's frown. He holds a rolled-up piece of paper like a flyswatter waiting for something to swat.

Coach concludes, "You can't win the game in the first minute, boys. Give me your best, that's all I ask, give me the best you have to give for forty-eight minutes." The team chants, "FORTY-EIGHT. FORTY-EIGHT." The student body joins in. Joseph looks at Rowan. Rowan rolls her eyes. The cheerleaders break into high kicks and pompom raises. The football team gets together. They push and shove. The group ripples in frenetic waves. They put their hands up. Their heads jostle. Coach barks into the center of the group. His girlfriend's high kicks are getting higher.

The cheerleaders set up their routine. Joseph sits on the edge of the wooden bleachers.

"Ready? Okay!" They nod in unison. The cheerleaders project deep voices. The start of the routine is mechanical. The young women hold their arms down straight and stiff. They move into formation. Joseph's eyes are drawn, as if there is a spotlight on his girlfriend. The other young women melt into the background. The music is edgy. They work hard. They drive the routine. The crowd starts to clap along to the beat. Joseph joins in.

Dani nails her tumbling run. She punctuates with a sassy smile. She's not winded. Autumn and the ashy blond perspire.

On the downbeat, they freeze. The crowd whistles and hoots. Joseph stands. He's proud of his girlfriend. He claps. For the time being.

The assistant coach, a short man with a broad forehead, announces the senior football players. Joseph doesn't know any of these guys. His girlfriend lines up to present.

"Senior running back and linebacker, number 47, Blah-blah Blah-blah." The blond with the heavy eyelids shuffles across the gym. She offers the kid with a thick neck the rose. He takes it, doesn't look at her. He adjusts his stance. He holds the flower formally, as if he respects her. The ashy blond makes her way back with her shoulders hunched up.

"Senior offensive guard, number 26, Blah-blah-blah Blah-blah-blah!" Dani skips across the gym floor. Why's she skipping? The massive kid with the wrong haircut leers. He doesn't take the flower. He lifts her up, spins her around, sets her back on her feet. Then he takes the rose. The big kid turns to one of his teammates and high-fives him hard. She runs over to her cheer teammates. She sits down. She struggles to suppress a smile. She doesn't look up to where Joseph sits.

Ms. Albright pivots. She raises a corner of her mouth in Joseph's direction. Mr. DiBennedetto swivels his back. He talks to someone. Rowan waits for a response. Joseph stares straight ahead, his visage frozen.

Students file out of the gym. Rowan touches Joseph's arm. "Are you okay? You've gone quiet."

"No big deal, right, just a stupid pep rally?" Joseph's face contorts. It feels warm.

"You gonna tell her?"

"What's there to say?" He stares at the hallway floor. His fingers are splayed. The smell of gym mats hangs in the air.

"Oh, okay," Rowan hisses. "You're good with some jerk flipping your girlfriend around? You're fine with that?"

Joseph's voice quavers. "What can I do? Being jealous and weird ain't gonna help. Can't go down that rabbit hole."

"Talk to her. Tell her how it made you feel. If you don't, she'll never know." Rowan has known Dani since grade school. His girlfriend might not realize it happened. That it might uproot her boyfriend.

"Why should I? Shouldn't she know? My girlfriend's a cheerleader. I have to suck it up, right?" *If that's what happens, right in my face, what happens when I'm not around?* Each of the football players spins his girlfriend around, one by one.

"You two have this picture in your minds of this perfect couple, but guess what? You aren't. If you want to get closer to her, here's your chance, you gonna take it?"

Joseph drops his chin, whispers. "I can't. I don't know how." Something deforms.

"Figure it out, Joseph. If you don't, you'll lose her. Maybe not tonight, maybe not next year, but one day, it'll happen again, you'll see it. You'll wish you had told her. I won't be there to tell you I told you so." Rowan waits for Joseph's response. He has none. She turns into the crowd, looks back. Dani reaches Joseph. She has a rose in her hands. Rowan shakes her head, waves. She heads for her locker.

His girlfriend holds a rose beneath her chin. She gives Joseph a cheesy grin.

"Already gave yours away, didn't you?" His shoulders slump. Joseph takes the rose. "Can we get out of here now?"

His girlfriend smooths his visitor sticker on his chest. "Study hall next. In the library. It's your favorite…"

Joseph sucks an icy breath through his teeth, holds it in, then exhales. "Okay. Let's go."

Dani pulls a black Canson sketchbook from her book bag. She slides it across the table to Joseph. He can't resist.

He flips it open. Her i's are dotted with circles. Her capital letters are oversized and swirly.

At the dawn of the last ice age, 2.6 million years ago, the area that is now New York State was covered by a vast glacier. An ice sheet thousands of feet thick welded layers of ice and snow by cycles of freezing and thawing. The glacier was so massive it deformed bedrock. Melting glacier ice scatters tons of rock, soil and sand. Nature's conveyor belt. Think of the outcroppings that form Central Park in Manhattan, Joey, imagine the schoolbus-sized rocks tumbling, time lapse, through miles of translucent ice, flipping, coming to rest where they now lie.

I wish I could shrink you down and fit you in my pocket. You would love NYC!

Joseph borrows a pen from her pencil case. His scrawl is urgent and scratchy. He bends to the page.

My great-aunt told me this story when I was a boy. One day, during the Great Flood, a woman, daughter of the Great Chief of the Sky, awoke above where birds fly. She burned with fever. She vomited. The Great Chief remembered his dream: heal her with tea from the roots of the Tree of Life.

To harvest a fiber, he dug a hole in the shadow of the Tree. His daughter sipped the tea. She lay back in the divot. Her fever cooled. While his sister slept, her brother, thinking her father meant to uproot the Tree, dug the ditch deeper. The Tree of Life tipped over. The sky was rent. She slid through the hole. Waking, she grasped at the roots of the Tree with both hands. Brother covered the hole and ran away before his father saw.

A woman tumbles across the vast blue sky. She plunges into the sea. Turtle swims to her. The woman climbs onto Turtle's carapace. She lays there gasping. She fit him, he was meant to save her. She falls into a deep sleep. She wakes matted in sweat. Her fever breaks. Her belly swells. She finds four seeds in her fist. Turtle calls Toad. Turtle instructs Toad to swim down to the bottom of the sea and retrieve rock, soil and sand to build land. Toad dives. The earth becomes what is New York State today. Sky Woman plants seeds in the north, south, east and west. In the spring, in the shade of new leaves, Sky Woman gives birth to a girl.

September 1986, Joey

Joseph closes the sketchbook. Dani slides the book into her book bag. She would read it days later, after Joseph went home. She zips her pencil case. She smiles. Writing in the sketchbook perks him up. Joseph leaves the rose on the table in the library. Dani doesn't notice.

Joseph finds the Chevette. Each Sunday after church, even during the blustery winters, Mr. DiBenedetto cleans three cars:

an ugly brown Buick nicknamed the Toad; Mrs. DiBenedetto's car, a gray Pontiac with red pinstripes, dubbed the Sunbird Express; and the Chevette, which doesn't have a moniker. Most weeks, the Chevette doesn't come out of the garage, unless Mr. DiBenedetto drives it on an errand to keep the battery up. He's had the car since college. It's his baby. He saves his baby for his baby girl. It's a manual transmission. His daughter works on achieving facility with the clutch.

Dani snaps the radio off. She's deliberate, all Capricorn. Despite her sure-footed pride, she's slipping.

Joseph says, "I could drive if it'd be easier."

His girlfriend frowns. "You'd love that. You could tell my dad you bailed me out on the stick. No way." She rolls to a stop after the bridge. She flicks the right turn signal.

Joseph remembers what Rowan said. "You're doing great." He hears Rowan's voice. He's not ready to talk.

She lets out the clutch. The Chevette bucks. She accelerates to smooth it out. A squirrel in the street in front of them freezes. The car careers forward. Joseph seizes the headliner. He ducks his head. He watches in the side mirror. The squirrel pirouettes and falls to the pavement.

"Stop!" Frantic, shrill, adolescent. It's not him. She jams on the brakes, holds down the clutch. She takes the car out of gear.

"What happened?" She leans over to look at Joseph's legs, look at the passenger door. Joseph follows her eyes. Is she thinking she somehow ran him over, snapped his ankle, maybe? Doesn't make sense.

"The squirrel. We hit him. We have to make sure he's okay."

"If we hit him, he's not okay."

"Go back!"

"Joey, calm down," Her hands shake. "What are you gonna do? CPR?"

"We need to make sure he's out of his misery."

"It's a squirrel. There's a million of them. What's the big deal?"

"Did you do it on purpose?" It's not fair. He can't help it. "Here's how it goes. Squirrel dies in the street. Buzzards smell him. Vultures feed on him. He doesn't have any dignity. Is that what you want?"

"Okay, okay. What should we do?"

"We need to bury him," Joseph says. He doesn't know what it means. "We did this to him. We need to make it right."

She swings the car around. Joseph gets out to inspect the squirrel. She puts her forehead in her trembling hand. He's dead. Joseph can't believe it.

She lets out a controlled sigh. "We're a couple of blocks from the house. Let's go home, get what we need and come back." She sits up straight. Her hands are at ten and two.

"Thank you. For understanding." Joseph knows he's being weird. The thought of the squirrel's body lying there on the tree-lined street in the valley, his guts running across the asphalt, until there's nothing left... They need to put nature back the way they found it. Is he trying to make his girlfriend feel guilty? Is that it? If it had been him at the wheel — would he still want to bury the squirrel? It wasn't her fault. It was an accident. Why did he feel like this?

In her parents' driveway, Dani sets the parking brake. Joseph gets out. He looks up at the trees. A redwing blackbird flutters across the frame of blue sky. The leaves are peaking; rust, gold, orange, yellow. She retrieves her bookbag. Joseph holds out an arm to carry it. She speaks, "Mom's home, you can get what you need from her. Let me change. I'll help you."

In the kitchen, Dani brushes past her mother, "Joseph needs help. He'll explain."

Mrs. DiBenedetto's confused gaze follows her daughter. Joseph stands in the kitchen entry. The tall young man takes in the kitchen in the daylight. Apple magnets on the fridge, a picture of apples on the wall, apples on the tablecloth, an apple clock. Mrs. DiBenedetto collects apples. She's not ashamed of it.

"Do you have an old shoebox that we could borrow?"

"Is everything okay?" Mrs. DiBenedetto rests her hip against the counter. Wearing one of her favorite twin sets, candy-apple red, she folds her arms into each other.

"We hit a squirrel. It was an accident." Joseph chokes up.

He's surprised.

"Seat belts?" Mrs. DiBenedetto straightens pearls on her neckline.

"Always. Dani'd never." Joseph waves a hand, catches himself. "Didn't feel a thing. Saw him in the rearview mirror. Car's fine. It's just… the squirrel."

Mrs. DiBenedetto can hear her daughter open and close her closet door. She's trying to figure out how she's going to talk to the two of them about being responsible, about being careful, about drinking and drugs. And sex. She's fond of Joseph, such a smart young man, polite, caring, but she can tell he's upside down. She doesn't need to read their notes to each other to know that they're in love.

Each morning she transports the Canson sketchbook — 5" x 8", black, hardbound — to her classroom in Joseph's school. Joseph's there early, anxious to gobble up his girlfriend's words. Each afternoon, Joseph stops by her classroom with the sketchbook, a new message scribed for his sweetheart. Mrs. DiBenedetto places it in her canvas tote to drive home. It's why her car is called the Sunbird Express.

"I think we should bury him, don't you?"

Mrs. DiBenedetto pushes her cat's-eye glasses up on her nose. A tear collects at the edge of Joseph's eyes. A rope of phlegm forms in his throat. Over a squirrel? He's a sensitive boy, she's aware, but this...

"I figure put him in a container, bring him home. Bury him in the backyard. The flower beds, maybe. Don't want to mess up Mr. DiBenedetto's lawn."

Rather than judge, she guides. "Who knows what squirrel diseases there could be. How will you get him — it — into the box?"

Joseph shrugs.

Mrs. DiBenedetto hands him one of her prized apple dish towels. It's yellow, decorated with Red Delicious apples, whole round apples and apples cut in half with their seeds showing. "How are you getting him home?"

"On my lap while Dani drives?"

"What if it drips? Mr. DiBenedetto won't care, but you never know with that car. Have to walk it back here." Or you could come up for air, Mrs. DiBenedetto thinks. She looks over her glasses.

"He — it — could drip on me, right?"

"Keep an eye on the box. Shovel's in the garage. A lot of work for a dead squirrel, isn't it?"

Joseph looks at Mrs. DiBenedetto. He's like a turtle on his back in the road, kicking in slow motion against the sky.

"Is everything okay?" Mrs. DiBenedetto takes a step forward. She reaches as if she were about to put her hand on his fore-arm. She feels a pang of guilt. It was her idea to introduce her daughter to Joseph. Her daughter was spending too much time with boys in town. At the pizza place, at the park. She thought if Dani had a chance to meet a nice boy, from outside Union Corners, she might slow down. "She'll listen if you want to talk. You should talk to her."

"I can't stand the thought of that squirrel rotting there in the street, getting run over again and again and again."

Dani comes down the stairs. Joseph lowers his head. She stands next to Joseph. She changed into a pair of tennis shorts and a rugby shirt. "Come on, Joey," She touches his hand. "Let's give Mr. Squirrel a proper send-off. Have you thought about the eulogy?"

Joseph laughs. A bubble of snot shoots out his nose. Embar-rassed, he wipes it on the dish towel. Dani shoots her mother a look. Mrs. DiBenedetto holds her hands palm up. Dani acts, "Let me take this. I'll get you a proper burial cloth."

As if on a conveyor belt, his girlfriend drops the apple towel on the washing machine. She grabs one of her dad's old rag-gedy running towels from the hall closet and is back around to Joseph. He smiles at her. "What?"

"Are you always this cute, or is it just when you're rescuing your crazy boyfriend?"

"I'm always this cute. Wait until you see the dress."

Joseph takes the towel and the Reebok box. They stuff their feet into their shoes. Joseph neglects to tie his work boots. The laces dangle. His father hates that. He scuffs around the stubby

Chevette. Joseph takes a hard look. He squats down. He can't find a scratch; he can't see a spot of blood or a piece of fur. Was the squirrel faking it?

Dani rests the shovel against the garage. Joseph stands, "Can we talk about Homecoming? What if we didn't go?"

She pirouettes. She catches his eyes. "Seriously? I thought that's why you came. To go to the dance together?"

"I came to be with you. We don't need any dance to have some fun." Joseph pushes his glasses up on his nose.

"You love to dance. You brought your suit. It's gonna be fun. You love this stuff. Is it the squirrel?" Dani ambles down the driveway. She's trying to get a read. It would be fun to hole up at the house too, that's not a bad option. It's not like they would be alone.

"I don't know. I don't feel welcome." Joseph looks down at the sidewalk. She can see his mind at work. He's thinking it's not his sidewalk. Not his trees, not his street. What it must feel like to have eyes on him from all the windows. She's used to how it is here. But him? He's the outsider who's come to town to corrupt their daughters.

"You *are* welcome. People are jerks. They're jealous. I love you, Joey. My mother brought you here herself, didn't she?" Dani wraps Joey's arm, the one with the running towel, around herself. She breathes him in — cinnamon, wool, cologne, sweat. How is it that his sweat smells good? He smacks of something she craves.

They keep walking. He's thinking. It's like he wants to ask her a question but can't figure out how. Spit it out already, Joey. What're you waiting for?

Dani's eyes smile. The way the wind catches his black hair. It can't be easy. To be a star athlete, an ace student, to be a leader in his own school; here, to be a foreigner, an outsider. To be judged by people who don't know you, who don't know your folks, who don't know where you live. She blinks. Her lips tense against each other. It's not easy to fit in. She knows it herself when she watches him play basketball. The cheerleaders call out his name. It stings. To think one might throw herself at him. To think he might let her.

She doesn't normally notice the crickets, cicadas, the sounds around her. Is it always this beautiful? She hears the same sounds outside Joey's house twenty-six miles away when they sit out at the picnic table. Here in the valley, things are different. Like the way people treated Joey at her school. They were backward, but no one not from here could say it. For her, it was nice to spend time with a boy who read books, a boy who wrote letters to her. With a boy who wasn't all hands and heavy breathing.

"About this dress of yours..." Joey finally asks. She knows it's not the question his mind gnaws on. A boy who liked to talk about clothes. He didn't dress fancy, mostly those old work jeans and boots. He'll be dashing in his suit and tie.

She can see a small brown shape on the road. She dreads the smell.

She looks at the sidewalk in front of her. "Don't know if I should. We might not be going to the dance, in which case I can save it. When's the next dance at your school?"

Joseph turns. He drops the box and the towel on the sidewalk. He grasps both her hands and looks into her eyes. She looks back at him. She's glad she brushed her teeth when she changed.

Her hands come up to his face. She thumbs his chin. A fine stubble grows there like sandpaper. If he were pure Seneca, there would be no stubble. She closes her eyes. She kisses Joseph. She searches him. Her lips pulse. They soften. They harden. She draws him in. She pulls him closer. Her tongue darts in, touches his tongue. To let him know it's okay. She wants to devour him. She presses her body into his. His arm slides around her waist. They fit.

He tastes the toothpaste on her breath. She brushed her teeth when she changed. He loves her for that. He notes the color of her lips with nothing on them. It's not pink and it's not red. It's fainter, more human and beautiful, a color that defies description. Why paint over perfect? He leans in close. He can see the lines in her bottom lip. He wants to feel the texture with his tongue. Their foreheads meet. He pulls back to study her faint freckles. They fade away.

They kiss. He's surprised by how good it feels to relax.

Joseph blinks hard. He shakes his head. "Whoa."

"Spaghetti straps."

"What?" Joseph's eyes droop.

"Blue taffeta. Sweetheart bodice. Slate blue, stately and mature. Not shiny. I didn't want shiny."

Joseph murmurs. He looks in the direction of the house across, but that's not what he sees.

He loves her attention to these things. "Mid-calf. The shoes are blue too, matte satin pumps, kitten heels. You wrote me about kitten heels."

"More."

"I'll show you. Right after we get this squirrel memorial over with. I feel bad that I killed your friend."

"He wasn't my friend, we crossed paths." Joseph smiles.

She's serious. "Does this count as my first accident? What do you think?"

"Doesn't count. I think the squirrel's playing possum. He's gonna stand up and say, 'April Fool' and run away."

"April Fool in September? Did that kiss melt your brains or what?" She bounces.

"You're an awfully good kisser. I won't ask where you learned it from."

"My hand. I read it in *Cosmo*. I used to practice it in seventh grade. It's kind of fun."

"Practice on me anytime." Joseph drapes the towel over the squirrel. He rolls the thing, still warm, stiffening. Dani opens the shoebox and steps away. She turns her head. Joseph catches a whiff of death.

"Whew! In you go, little buddy. Sorry about your luck. We didn't mean it. You weren't quick enough." Joseph shuts the lid. He inspects his hands. He wishes he'd thought about plastic gloves. He picks up the Reebok casket by the edges with the tips of his fingers, cranes his head around. He inspects it for wet spots.

"Stay upwind."

Back at the house, Dani stands by the back edge of the garage in a flower bed. She hangs on the handle of the shovel. Joseph rests the squirrel coffin on the grass. He takes his pullover off. His T-shirt comes up around his neck. He can feel his girl-friend's eyes on his torso. He pauses a full second, letting his shirt fall down slow motion. She's frozen. She holds the handle of the shovel like it's her only chance of staying upright. He takes the shovel from her and holds out his sweater. He lets go. It falls to the grass. Joseph looks from the raglan on the grass to her, to her face. Her expression hasn't changed.

Dani's eyelids close. "I, uh, I didn't know." She lowers her-self to pick up his shirt, her face tilted in the same direction. She opens her eyes. She laughs. "I mean, I knew, but I guess I didn't know, uh, how good, um, shape. You are in. I assumed, baggy pullover..." She buries her face in his sweater. It's warm. She can smell Aqua Velva, wool, that cinnamon note she knows is Joseph.

"Over summer, Coach, my dad, had us get our base miles early." Joseph jumps on the edge of the shovel. The blade knifes into the dark topsoil. "I have to eat better."

"It's getting hot out here. Let me get you a glass of water."

Dani goes into the house. She hugs the pullover, then lays it across the scratchy plaid back of the sofa in the addition. She gives it a pat. She floats into the kitchen, forgetting to take off her shoes. She stares. She washes her hands before grabbing an apple tumbler from the cupboard.

Mrs. DiBenedetto stands next to her. "Is he okay?"

"He's fine." She doesn't break her stare. She fills the glass, laughs to herself. "He's fine." She gulps the glass of water, doesn't take a breath. She fills it. The water tastes sweet and fresh, cool but not cold.

Mrs. DiBenedetto picks lint off her daughter's shoulder. "Did you guys talk?"

"About what?" She sets the glass on the counter and scratches a spot on her knee. She clears her stare with a shake of her head.

"I don't know. About anything?"

"We talked. I think Joey overreacted. He's paying for it now." Dani's eyes go distant. "We must be having our Indian Sum-mer."

"Do you think it's about the squirrel?" Mrs. DiBenedetto's hand comes up over her mouth. The Canson sketchbook had been her idea.

"Definitely not the squirrel." Dani picks up the glass of water and heads for the door. "Thanks, Mom. Love you." She doesn't look at her mother. The door slams behind her. Mrs. DiBenedetto decides it's about time she gets the water on for noodles. The kids should have something in their bellies before they head over to the game.

Outside, Joseph stands over the hole with his fists on his belt. The box juts out of the small pit. It mocks him. Dani hands him the glass of water. He takes a deep drink. Out of the corner of his eye, he detects a devilish look in her eyes. She steps toward him, slips her hands under his shirt.

"I'm sweaty." Joseph lowers his arm, spilling.

"I don't mind." She bites her cheeks. She runs her hands over Joseph's skin. "I want to taste you."

Joseph tips his head down. Careful not to touch her with his hands, he kisses his girlfriend. Joseph looks up. He stiffens and steps back, tripping on his laces.

"Hello, Daniella. Joe." Mr. DiBenedetto stops in the driveway. He gives them a stern look, holds it. He sighs. "You digging up my yard, Joe?"

"No, sir. Just a spot in the flower bed. Burying a squirrel, sir. He's dead." Joseph stops talking.

She skips to her father. She throws her arms around his neck. She gives him a kiss on the cheek.

"Why are you burying a —?" Mr. DiBenedetto holds his arm out. "Don't answer that. Don't want to know." He kisses his daughter on the top of her head. He gives her a squeeze. He eyes Joseph. His frown deepens. "Run in the morning?"

Joseph swallows hard. He nods, then nods again.

Mr. DiBenedetto nods. He pauses before continuing on into the house.

She whispers, "Keep digging, Joey. Picture me in my dress."

Joseph pulls the box out of the hole. A freshly turned earth smell seers into his nostrils. With each bite of the shovel, he pictures himself getting closer to Dani's heart, closer to understanding himself. Either that, he smirks, or he's digging his own grave.

"Close your eyes," Daniella sings from the kitchen. Joseph alights on the sofa in the addition. He paws through his duffle bag. He sits up. He closes his eyes. He sings back, "They're closed."

He hears a rustle behind him. A suppressed giggle. He keeps his eyes shut. He smells apple soap on his hands. It mingles with his own musk. He can't wait to take a shower.

"Okay — open." Her voice is full. Full-throated, full of energy, full of anticipation. She stands with her toes almost on Joseph's toes. The dress sweeps against his knees.

She towers over him. Her slender shoulders and arms are bare, the blue dress resplendent.

Joseph, "Wow."

She swivels her hips. His eyes absorb her transformation. Gone is the orange ribbon; her curls hang free, loose, wild. She fills up the dress in the right places without divulging any of her secrets. The spaghetti straps frame her collarbones, her elegant shoulders.

Joseph croaks, "Turn." She smiles. Her eyes darken. She takes a step back, aware of the coffee table behind her. She doesn't want to go crashing ass-over-teakettle. She turns half-way around. Naked shoulders and back, zipper halfway up.

"Help me." She pulls her hair to one side. Joseph stands, unsteady on his feet. His fingers entice the zipper to the top. He breathes her in, a light floral scent and something like a creamy rose musk. He aches to put his arms around her, his mouth on her neck. Her mother's in the kitchen. The pass-through window is to their left. She could be watching.

"Mmm." It's the only word Joseph can muster from his considerable vocabulary.

"You like?" Dani giggles. A warmth pools below her belly. It's delicious, and sort of thrilling.

"What's not to like," Joseph murmurs, his breath hot on her neck. Joseph coughs. He remembers himself. "You're right, not shiny is way better."

She faces Joseph. Her fingertips press into his chest. She pushes. Joseph falls into the couch. He pictures her hitching the dress up. He imagines her straddling him on the scratchy sofa. She looks toward the kitchen. She sings, "He likes the dress."

Mrs. DiBenedetto sings back, "I knew he would."

Dani sets herself sideways into a chair. She lowers her voice. "You said you weren't allowed to play football?"

Joseph feels Mrs. DiBenedetto listening from the kitchen. He tells the sob story, old as time. Father meddles with his son. He thinks he can control fate. Son gets his fate anyway. "Coach saw me on the track. Talked to my dad. Dad didn't care. No football."

She whispers, "You'd look good in the uniform. Not quarterback, though — too many hits. Wide receiver."

Her voice has a romantic drooling quality to it. It's adorable.

"Didn't know you were a fan of the sport."

"I carried water for a couple of practices, watched some drills."

"Drills, huh? That's what you were watching?" It's Charlie, Dani's younger brother. He comes in uninvited, plops himself down between them. "From what I heard, you were cow-eyed over the guys." Charlie crosses his eyes. He sticks out his tongue at Joseph.

Joseph smiles at the undermining. He wonders if his girlfriend will fall for it.

"In their dreams. Never seen a bunch of slower, more uncoordinated, less disciplined bunch of boys. I felt bad for Coach. I suggested that we reserve water for the ones who could catch a ball. Coach thought I was too hard on them."

Charlie turns to Joseph. "It's lucky you live halfway across the state. You don't have to witness my sister's interest in the game, if that's what you call it."

"Joseph knows he's the only one for me." Her cheesy grin.

"Ugh, I gotta get out of here. Good luck to you lovebirds. I might vomit." Charlie stalks out. He receives a scorching look from Mrs. DiBenedetto.

At halftime, the crowd gets up to procure refreshments. Joseph and his girlfriend's parents stay glued to their seats. The night is cool, the air smells of twig fires, popcorn and apple cider. The lights on the field have a saturating effect; the only redeeming quality of the game. That and maybe the cheerleaders. They line up on the field and hold. They wait for the music to begin. Dani breaks form. She catches Joseph's eye. She shoots him an exuberant little wave. Joseph summons a smile to his face. He holds up a hand. It's pathetic. She shows her teeth.

Someone stares at Joseph. He looks in the direction of the consignment hut. In line, a redhead with freckles. She wears a black Union Corners shirt with white and orange rings on the sleeves. Rowan turns her head a quarter. She holds her hands out, palms up. Joseph crinkles his brow at the gesture. Then he shakes his head, No. Rowan's shoulders collapse. She turns back in time to step up and place her order.

The routine concludes with a pyramid. The dead-eyed blonde forms the foundation on hands and knees, Autumn spots the lift. At the center, Dani rises, her fist in the air. She holds the pose and then twists. She flips through the sky into her teammates' cradle. They set her on her feet. Together they take one step forward. They fist-pump the air, their pompoms splayed around them on the ground, as if discarded. Mrs. DiBenedetto stands. She claps wildly. She tugs at Mr. DiBenedetto, who rises and adjusts his belt. Joseph stands and claps. He keeps on clapping.

Saturday morning, Joseph and Mr. D go for a run. Mr. D is no slouch, he ran Division 1 cross-country. Joseph likes to push him. A wily veteran, Mr. D; calls for a break in the middle to "stretch" and then he asks a bunch of questions about training. Joseph knows he's buying time. Right at the end, before they wear themselves out getting back, he says something strange. He says something about hairy-legged boys sniffing around. Joseph looks down at his hairy legs.

"Not you, Joe. Mrs. D says you're okay," Mr. D let it drop.

The Homecoming dance is in the gym, the scene of his humiliation. Thankfully the dimensions of the place feel different now. The bleachers have been stored away. It's darkened, but not too dark, as the chaperones have specified. There's a medium-sized disco ball in the center of the ceiling. The feathered-haired disc jockey has set up on a cafeteria table commandeered for the occasion. The music is cheesy: "Heat of the Moment" by Asia and "Cold as Ice" by Foreigner.

Joseph's caught in the middle. On earth, he worries that they'll run into the massive kid with the unfortunate haircut; up in the sky, he's thrilled to be here with his girlfriend. He wears his grandfather's wingtips, a navy suit, a white shirt and a green tie. Freshly moussed hair, he escorts her on his arm. She glows, her hair up. It showcases her pale neck and shoulders. She doesn't look like a junior tonight.

Dani grabs his hand and pulls him onto the dance floor. Joseph is stiff. He feels the six-mile run. He begins to thaw. He's grateful for the warmth of her hand in his, soft and smooth, the thin wrist, her arm, her shoulder.

On the dance floor, she closes her eyes. She smiles to herself. She enjoys the music, the attention, the thrill of the night. That, or she's laughing at him, thinking about some other guy. Joseph looks around to see if he can find anyone else he knows. They talked about this night for weeks; Joseph thought it might never come. But here he is. She smiles, her lips together. She opens her eyes. He's mechanical, but the moment warms him up. She mirrors his movements for a couple of bars. He dances closer to her. The office secretary comes by. She tightens her lips. Joseph smiles, backs off. The office secretary continues her patrol.

"She chaperones a lot. I think she likes the music. I'd like to catch her dancing," Dani breathes on Joseph's ear. It's hot. His face flushes.

Joseph and Dani wait in line for a cup of punch. She says, "It isn't easy, I know, this isn't your Homecoming." She takes a cup, sips. The bottom half of her face disappears behind the cup. She sips again, hands it to Joseph. He takes a sip.

Before he can answer, the lights go down, the disco ball lights up. Specks of light rotate on the walls, across the floor, across his girlfriend's raised eyebrows, her round eyes, her parted lips. The song is Madonna, "Crazy for You."

Joseph steps away. She follows. She readies herself to concede the night. He dumps his cup in the trash and turns. They run into each other. Startled, they jump apart. She takes a step forward, pressing herself into him. She looks up. He holds his left hand out. He says, "May I have this dance?"

She tips back. Her limbs spark. She feels the difference between his heat and the cool air between them. She looks up into Joseph's face. Her expression brightens. She puts her hand in his and follows him to the dance floor.

Joseph mouths the count. He leads his girlfriend around the dance floor. She rests her head on his shoulder. Joseph wonders how long it will be before they run into the massive kid with the bad haircut. He makes up his mind to focus on the young woman in his arms.

Back at the house, Dani's parents have already gone to bed. Joseph and Dani kiss on the couch in the addition. She stops, reclines, touches Joseph's lips with her thumb.

"I better go. My parents won't let you stay again if they think they can't trust us. You okay with this?" She stands, her knee touching Joseph's knee. She waves her hand in a circle,indicating the sofa bed. Warmth comes off him, up her thigh.

"Wait." Joseph reaches for her hand, folds her wrist up and, palm to palm, aligns her fingertips with his. "I know what we should call your dad's car."

"Please don't say 'Squirrel Killer.'" She nudges his knee with hers. She considers mounting him. She has to get out of here. Before she does something she shouldn't.

"Ha. No, get this: the Turtle." Joseph slides his fingers in between hers.

"You saying I drive too slow?" She tries to cool herself down.

"More like slow and steady wins the race."

"The snub nose, the hatchback. I like it. Let's see if it sticks. G'night, Joey." She speaks a little louder than necessary, in case anyone's listening. She lets go of his hand and recedes into the darkness.

He stacks the cushions into a wobbly tower. He unfolds the

bed. Down to his boxers, Joseph dives into the pillow face first. All he can smell is Dani. She tumbles and zooms through his dreams.

Communing, 15.11.98
Working that story through made me realize that the letter to my high-school sweetheart, where this whole seven-letters exercise started, was maybe the most important one. They are all important, but for me, for growth and healing, this is an inflection point. Ilona, just like you said, I did it for me. You were right!

Letters Six and Seven

A letter to Ingrid. This one I will burn up by the High Castle. In the garden, near the cemetery. In its entirety.

Dear Ingrid,

I will never know what happened to you. I am beginning to come to terms with that.

You must know that your death will affect me the rest of my life. Ilona feels the same way. Others too. You won't be soon forgotten. I appreciate your advice now and then, although I would be bullshitting you if I didn't admit that I know the Ingrid in my head is not you, but only a symbol of you, my symbol, a part of me.

I don't know if you believed in heaven or God, we didn't talk about it. Wherever you are, I hope you are as happy as we were in our best days, the best days you had with Lars, with your family. I thought about writing your father a letter, but I don't know what I would say. I could tell him how much I miss you, how much I miss you singing on your guitar, how much I miss the anticipation I used to feel going over to your flat for a dinner party among friends. I will always remember the impact you had on me. I will use it to become a better human being.

I would say a prayer for you, but you wouldn't accept it.

Instead, I raise a glass in your memory.
Miss you,
Joseph

Finally, Letter Seven. Dear Dani. Excerpts. I start by leveling the playing field. I make a confession to her. I go on to confess that I know more than I probably should have. More than I needed to know. This:

...we were cagey. You hoped I wouldn't bring it up; I hoped you wouldn't. Our wishes came true...

I tell her about the stories, how they're meant for me. I make the point that for two overachievers, neither one of us would admit defeat. Then at the risk of going saccharine:

I think of you fondly. I hope you found whatever it was you were looking for. My best to Mr. and Mrs. D and Charlie.

Time-traveling, 16.11.98

Markéta and I met for tea. She told me to meet her under the horse's ass. Seems to be a pattern.

We went to the same teahouse where I went with Ilona. It was uncanny. Markéta followed her intuition. She could detect the emotion I had connected to this spot, she followed the thread to the exact place.

There is a lot I didn't know about Markéta. She told me about the nude sculpture of her out there somewhere. I knew about that. I wondered about it at odd moments. This time it was even weirder.

"My ex, the one I told you about. He wrote a movie. About me. He asked me to play the lead role. I didn't think I was right for the part. You know? How can you play yourself?"

I drank my tea. I tried to absorb.

"He had a casting call. He invited me and Patrick to attend, to help him decide. Patrick went. I couldn't do it. Patrick described it to me, a line of dark-haired women, like different versions of me in a row. My ex asked each one to cry on cue. Most couldn't do it, or couldn't do it and be believable. Can you cry on cue?"

I shook my head. I had taken acting lessons, but we never got to the lesson on crying on cue.

"Me too. No way. But this one woman, Patrick described her as very pretty and very intense, she did it. Almost immediately, a tear gathered in her eye, jumped off her eyelash onto her cheek and ran down in a straight line." Markéta drew the line on her cheek. It was like time-travel, I was there with Patrick. I watched the woman audition for the part of his wife. Strong tea.

"Anyway, my ex and the actress live together now. The movie is done. I don't want to see it. Would you want to see it?"

I nodded my head. I paused. Would I? I nodded my head again. How many times in life do you get to see a movie about one of your friends played by a woman who can cry on cue?

"Patrick wants to see it. He said when she stopped crying for the audition, she cackled. Snapped right out of it, wiped her face, back to normal. Freaky, right?"

I told her about Karina. She said there are some things we can do to improve my chances. I'm manipulative, I've come to realize. Not sure I want to use dark arts to conjure a future with her. Not sure I'm ready for that particular step.

My head spun. We re-emerged into the battleship of the day it was.

Josef Václav Myslbek

With all my focus on Czech literary tradition, I wondered about Czech artists. Like the statue of Saint Wenceslas at the top of Wenceslas Square — who did that? The answer is Josef Václav Myslbek. The pre-eminent academic sculptor of the Czech Nationalist Revival. Born in 1848, just weeks after the Slavic Council held in Prague was cut short by the Prague Uprising. The Austro-Hungarian Empire began to crumble. The seed of national pride germinated. Imagine living in a place where your native tongue was not the national language — I guess it's not that unique — thinking of Cherokee or Apache. Or Seneca.

Plays were written in Czech, Czech poetry surged into people's consciousness, Czech music flooded taverns and homes. It set the stage for Czech sculpture.

Myslbek's parents imagined a more practical life for him. They encouraged him to study shoemaking, they apprenticed him to a printer. Josef had other ideas. He began spending all his free time in an art atelier. When he chose a course of study, no sculpture program existed at the Academy of Fine Arts; he studied painting and portraiture. When he got out of school, he created his own studio. His sculptures depicted all the traditional Czech legends. His work was realistic and historically accurate. He studied ancient texts to ensure that he costumed his figures correctly. You can see those statues today in Vyšehrad where they now stand. They originally lined the Palacký Bridge.

Later in life he led the Prague School of Applied Arts. The interesting fact about the statue of Saint Wenceslas for which Myslbek is perhaps the most famous: conceived in 1887, when Myslbek was thirty-nine years old, it would not be completed until 1923, a full thirty-five years later. It was installed after Myslbek's death. The public reception for it was chilly; by the time it was finished it was already outmoded.

I guess I had better finish these stories off. Can you imagine dying before your masterwork is done? Or, like Gaudí, being buried in the unfinished cathedral of your masterwork?

Emptying, 17.11.98

It's my mom's birthday. I should find a way to call her. I don't think I can. Email will have to do this year. I could call her on her own calling card. She'd love that. I should put some water on for coffee.

I emptied myself out for Rachel; she wasn't able to fill me up. I needed to be filled.

Jacques took a few of my power lines pictures. He says it's about connection, those pictures I took. When I call my mother, does my voice travel on those wires?

I called Markéta yesterday. She was in the bath. In the bath with the phone.

It went something like this:

Me: In the bath with the phone?

Markéta: I knew I would get a call. I needed a bath. I smelled like an onion. I set the cordless by the tub. I didn't know it would be you. It's not like I'm psychic.

Me: How did you know you would get a call?

Markéta: I knew. I could feel it.

Me:

Markéta: Can you imagine otherwise? Naked, dripping all over, bubbles on my bum? Fumbling for the phone, the phone ringing, ringing…

Me: Just don't drop it.

Markéta: Drop what? I won't.

I told her about Karina. How she stayed, how she left. I asked her what she thought. She said we should have tea.

Jacques claims he saw Karina in Prague after she was supposed to have left. He said he thinks he saw her at Le Clan on either the 15th or the 16th, he wasn't sure. He said she was with the photographer guy, Guillermo. Can't be. She hopped a train with Phil. He must be mistaken. I won't worry about it.

Le Clan is the after-party place in Vinohrady. It opens at 2:00 a.m. I was only there once. I missed the live lesbian sex show that Brad and Jacques talk about.

Protesting, 18.11.98

I started out at Albertov, nine years after the fact, where the students began to congregate, on that fateful day, November 17, 1989. Just nine years. I brought my leather messenger bag with a notebook, pens and the reading material I had printed out at the library for the occasion. One page was a map of where the student protestors had gone. I got there at 3:30 p.m., just as the description of the protest had said it started. I was not the only one there. I might have been the only expat. One girl I saw, red hair, glasses, she wore the plaid frock of a school uniform. I smiled at her.

In 1989, the crowd had been fifteen thousand strong. I looked around. I would guess we were no more than a hundred. The solidarity felt good.

People gathered in front of a bronze plaque. One by one they touched it. I took a picture of it with my camera. I touched it myself. It said, "When — if not now? Who — if not us?" These words were spoken, I found out, by a famous actor and dissident who spoke on Wenceslas Square with Havel in the days following the Velvet Revolution. Translating them later that night, a chill ran up my spine. Nine short years ago!

People chanted in Czech. I scribbled them down. They were "Freedom" and "Dialogue." This one I knew without translating: "Long live Havel."

I stood at the fateful spot where the leaders of the protest had to choose. Go right, in the direction of Wenceslas Square, or go left, in the direction of the High Castle. The group began to meander to the left. According to my watch we were ahead of schedule. It would be dark soon; being ahead of schedule wouldn't hurt anyone.

People brought flowers and candles, as the students had in 1989, to lay at the grave of the famous poet, Karl Hynek Mácha. I saw the red-haired schoolgirl lay a flower down and say some words to herself. I forgot to bring flowers. I retrieved my printout of the poem. It's called "May." I read it out loud in English. I looked up after the last line of the first canto, "Like burning tears the lover weeps." This time the red-haired schoolgirl in her glasses smiled at me.

The crowd did not pay me any mind. It's a poem about May 1, the day of love. I wondered how good the translation was. I would have a look at the original Czech one day. To see if I agreed with the English words chosen.

The description of the protest march I had read said that only a few of the protestors had come to the grave of Mácha. To me, it was a highlight not to be missed.

I stowed the poem in my bag. The chants changed here. I wrote them in my notebook. Something about the wrong castle.

Should have protested in front of the Prague Castle. The humor of it.

The parade of patriotic Czechs and I made our way back to Albertov. We continued from there up Peel Street and High Castle Street to Charles Square. On High Castle Street, protestors first ran into a blockade of riot police. They did not yet engage. Instead they turned toward the river. Our little crowd grew. Just like in 1989, when people see our group, people wave from their windows and hop off passing trams to join us. I saw a familiar face, couldn't be sure it was her, needed to get a look. Coca-Cola jellybean eyes.

People swarmed across the street to the bridge. We were right under the Dancing Building. I took pictures of the river. People stopped traffic. They blocked the trams. The Dancing Building danced in the background. The protests in 1989 arrived here around 6:30 p.m. We were early. It was already dark. We were under the amber streetlights. The bells of the trams rang and rang. Czech people danced on the tracks. The conductor hung his head out the window. He howled with the patriots.

I saw that Penny and her friends had a two-liter full of an amber liquid in a backpack. Several in the group carried plastic cups. A towheaded blonde, one of the Lisas, if memory served, squatted on the cobbles. She filled cups. I knew it was Penny when I saw the paint on her hands.

The crowd moved along the river. The group had formed into two columns: one closer to the river, and one on the opposite side. Tram tracks divided the road. We moved in the direction of Cafe Slavia and the National Theatre. Penny and presumably the rest of the teachers from the international school were on the river side; I noticed the red-headed student with the glasses was by the buildings, with me.

We made the right turn after the National Theatre. The numbers in the group swelled. The protest description mentioned here that the riot police that night in 1989 managed to separate the crowd here; I saw how that would be possible. The two groups nearly fifteen meters (fifty feet) apart, two lanes of traffic and a tram line separated us. That is if the terrain hadn't been altered. It says that actors and musicians cheered from the windows and doors as the crowd passed here in 1989. Chants started up again. I got out my pen. "Freedom for artists" and "Freedom for culture" were prevalent. I stowed my notebook. I chanted along. I stood on the curb, the side where passengers wait for trams. I shouted. It felt good. I could imagine in this space, how it must have felt with ten thousand people, maybe more. The three-story buildings on either side. The river and the green hill behind it to our backs; patina-green spires and red-tile roofs in front. It was here that the protest was cut off from both sides. The protestors were pinned down.

I read that there was a moment of panic, in 1989, cut off by riot police in front, sealed from behind by riot police. The police shouted for people to leave — the protestors were cut off from leaving. The protestors nearest the riot police sat down. What else could they do? They sat down. They formed a line. People laid flowers and candles and flags down to fill the lane formed between the sitting protestors and the riot police. In 1998, along what I assumed to be a similar spot, people laid flowers and flags and candles. It must have been about 6:30 or 7:00 p.m. by now. One of the Lisas brushed past me.

I stepped in front of Penny. "Remember me? Buck Green's birthday party?"

Penny tilted her head. The other Lisa said, "Oh yeah, the guy at the door. Pain in the ass. You remember, Lisa?"

The first Lisa came back. "Starts with a J. Justin? Joshua?"

"Joseph."

Penny smiled. The paint on her hands was white and red and blue. "I think I would have remembered you."

"Nah, I was on my way out, you were on your way in. Penny, is it?"

Penny turned to a tall guy with a goatee. "Get my friend Joseph here a drink. His hands are empty." Tall guy handed me a cup. Lisa 1 poured from the two-liter.

I took a sip. Gambrinus. These folks liked the same beer as me.

A guy with a bull horn spoke up. First in Czech. Then, some-how, in English. "Moment of silence at 8:45 p.m. A few minutes away." I read that it was at 8:45 that the violent repression of the peaceful student protest started. Batons flying, blood flowing. Tear gas canisters deployed. I held my cup out to Penny, Lisa and Lisa. "Long live the revolution." They each met my eyes. We touched plastic cups.

At 8:45 p.m. the crowd fell silent. No one died in the Velvet Revolution, but it wasn't bloodless. The violent suppression didn't quell the protest. It fanned the flames. Regular citizens were outraged that their sons and daughters were savagely beaten; it had been a peaceful protest.

The chants started up again. I got out my notebook.

Penny saw me struggling. She offered to hold my drink. I gave it to her. I scribbled down the chants in Czech.

"What are you writing?" Penny took a drink from her cup.

"I want to see if I can translate what they're saying. My Czech isn't great."

I wrote and would translate later "Let us go!" and "Our hands are bare!" I thought it might be more like "Our hands are empty!"

My notebook stowed, Penny handed me back my drink. Lisa topped it up.

I took a sip.

Penny said, "When you had that notebook out, I was gonna give you my number. But I can't."

"Can't?"

"On probation. I have to wait three months. It's a long story."

"Who says you can't?"

"The only person who matters, as far as my number is concerned. Me."

I was emboldened. "Can I give you my number?"

"No."

"Why not?"

"Probation. Goes both ways. All ways." Penny waved her paint-stained hands. "If you tell me, I won't remember."

I smiled. I told her my number.

"See? It's already forgotten."

Inspired by the moment of silence, by the enormity of the night, the echo of history, the banter with Penny, I thanked the tall guy, the Lisas. "I should get going."

In unison, the Lisas, "So soon?"

"School night," I smiled. "Thanks for the camaraderie."

I made my way toward Iron Street.

Giddy, I drank a glass of mineral water and translated my notes at the kitchen table. By candlelight. I got out the Czech translation dictionary. The kitchen table shakes as I write. The flame from the candle shakes, the shadows on my walls vibrate. Three months is not that long.

Clearing, 19.11.98

I ran into them last night at the Little Goat. Ilona and Lars. Seems they are a thing now. It suits them. It honors Ingrid that they got together.

Ilona didn't say much to me. She hugged me but it was a distant hug. A hug to prove to Lars that things weren't weird between us. I hugged Lars. He slapped me on the shoulder and shook my hand, holding it for an extra second. He seems happy. I asked Ilona about school. She said it was fine. Lars proudly explained that she had finished her oral exam. Ilona would graduate in the spring.

He talked. The idiosyncratic grammar. I noticed his glasses. No smudges. Maybe it was the lighting in the underground cavern that is the Little Goat. We sat at the back bar. His glasses were spotless. Maybe he had just cleaned them. Ilona asked me about Peter. Naked Pete. I told her about the Knowledge, how he had gone home, cleaned up his act. She smiled. Our eyes met for a second. That was it.

It was like she said. I drank my beer. We were linked, forever; we would not be friends. I couldn't tell if she had filled Lars in, but from the hug alone I guessed she hadn't. Probably just as well.

The Prague Autumn

I studied up on the debate between Havel and Kundera. That's it. Kundera called it the Prague Autumn in 1969 in an essay published in the journal *Listy*: "I would venture to say...the significance of the Czechoslovak Autumn may even surpass the significance of the Czechoslovak Spring." Havel's response is scathing: "The world is not composed of big dumb superpowers that can do everything and clever little ones that can do nothing." Kundera called Havel's boundless optimism a form of "moral exhibitionism," while Havel challenged Kundera's fatalism.

The debate raged on. Kundera wrote essay after essay. A book called *The Curtain* explored the vulnerability of small nations with larger neighbors. Havel wrote a play in 1978 called *Protest*, which is a fearless examination of the decisions oppressed people are forced to make: to fight back or not to fight back. I think back to Operation Anthropoid. The decisions the leaders of the Czech underground had to make, whether to subject their families to Nazi reprisals or not. I think back to the decisions Milada had to make.

Karina called. From Italy. She was sweet. Too sweet. She said she sent me a postcard. She said I would like it. I didn't ask her about Phil. I held my tongue.

What's Karina up to? I think I know. Keep me warm, make sure I remember her and don't stray too far. It could mean that she didn't know she'd be out of town this week. Everything's all right. Everything's gonna be all right.

Silencing, 20.11.98
Last night was crazy. I left work at 6:30 p.m. I re-installed a computer. It was frustrating. To be visible on the NT network, peer-to-peer, I had to reinitialize the hard drive. Maybe that's what I need.

I got the postcard from Karina. I hung it in the water closet. A quote.

"Be ahead of all parting, as if it were

Behind you, like the winter that's on its way out.
For among writers, one is so endlessly winter that
Having made it through winter, your heart survives after all."
— Rainer Maria Rilke

I suppose she thinks it makes up for the fact that the night after she stayed with me, she left for Italy with Phil. I suppose she likes the "For among writers" bit since I'm adamant that I'm not a writer. Is she saying that if we make it through winter, we will survive?

I had another dream last night. Rachel sat next to me at a table, like a lab table. We watched a movie, a training video or something. She didn't say anything. She leaned into my shoulder. I looked behind me to see if anyone noticed. She lifted her legs onto my arms. White jeans, no shoes. I kiss the bottom of her left foot. She stands on my face.

It's about travel, about running, about my inner self, these dreams. Like I am about to disturb the part of my unconscious where she dwells. I need to think about this more.

Rainer Maria Rilke

After I hung the postcard from Karina in the water closet, I decided to do some research. First, was this guy Czech? Yup, born in Prague. His full name was René Karl Wilhelm Johann Josef Maria Rilke. That's a long name. The "Karl Wilhem Johann" part sounds awfully Austrian, which he was, officially Bohemian-Austrian, I think. The Josef part was after his father. I recognize myself there.

Who was contemporary to Rilke? Born December 4, 1875, in Prague and died December 29, 1926, in Valmont, Switzerland. His birthday is coming up. His closest contemporary was Kafka. Rilke was eight years older. When Rilke left Prague, Kafka was struggling with his sums in a classroom behind the Týn Church. By the time Kafka's work was first published,

Rilke was already an established poet. I don't know if they met face to face, but I found this: after reading *The Metamorphosis,* Rilke said, "I have never read a line by this author which did not concern or astound me in the strangest way."

What did Rilke write? The *Duino Elegies* and the unplanned *Sonnets to Orpheus.* He is known as one of the most lyrically intense of the German-language poets. Kafka wrote in German too. What is Duino? It's a castle in Italy. Not just any old castle. A seaside castle, on the northern coast of the Adriatic. I had to look up the Adriatic — it's the part of the Mediterranean Sea that goes up the back of Italy's boot, between Italy and the Balkan Peninsula. The old castle is set atop a pile of rocks; it juts out into the sea. The new castle, where Rilke probably stayed, is inhabited to this day. He stayed there for six months, between 1911 and 1912. It's where he started the cycle of poems. As a thank you to Princess Marie von Thurn und Taxis, the patron who had hosted him in the castle, he named his work the *Duino Elegies.* He wouldn't finish the cycle until 1922, a full decade later. In an attempt to understand his "creative crisis" I dug into his childhood.

Rilke was the only son of an unhappy marriage. His father, Josef, was a railway officer after a failed military career. His mother felt that she had married below her station; her father was a merchant and an imperial councilor. Sophia Entz, known to all as Phia, was the daughter of the Entz-Kinzelbergers. They lived in a house on Panská 8, near the base of Wenceslas Square. On top of her poor selection, she also mourned René's older sister, a baby who had died one week after being born.

Phia and Josef insisted that at the age of eleven their artistically and poetically talented son attend a military school in Austria. As a result of illness, he left military school and later attended a trade school, from which he was soon expelled. He prematurely returned to Prague at the age of sixteen; with the help of a tutor he managed to pass the university entrance exams. He studied art history, literature and philosophy in Prague and Munich. While in Munich in 1897, at the age of twenty-one or twenty-two, he met and fell in love with Lou Andreas-Salomé, a widely traveled and intellectual woman of letters. She urged him to change his name from the effeminate René to the more Germanic Rainer. In 1898 he traveled to Italy, where he stayed for several weeks. In 1899 he made the first of several trips to Russia with Salomé and her husband. While in Moscow, he met Leo Tolstoy, Boris Pasternak and several other writers and poets. While he had an unhappy childhood and an unsuccessful career at school, ultimately, he had found his way to meet with great writers of his time, even at an early age.

He continued his self-imposed internship in the arts. In 1902, Rilke traveled to Paris to write a monograph about the famous sculptor Rodin. He had a difficult time in Paris, although he did get to meet post-impressionist painter Paul Cézanne and he was inspired to write his only novel, *The Notebooks of Malte Laurids Brigge*. I will see if I can find a copy at the Globe.

Earlier, I found a reference to the *Sonnets to Orpheus,* calling them, as I noted, accidental. Let me figure out what that means. Rilke struggled with depression and other psychological issues for most of his life. Perhaps most acutely, in 1915, following his conscription into the Austro-Hungarian army, he went silent. He didn't speak for several years. Only in 1920 did he finally decide that he needed to finish what he had started in 1912 at the Castle Duino. In 1922, in the midst of a self-described "savage creative storm," not only did he finish the *Duino Elegies*, but in a matter of three weeks, he wrote all fifty-five sonnets. Let me break that down. In three days, allegedly from February 2 through 5, Rilke completed the first twenty-six sonnets. Then, by February 11, he had completed his unfinished manuscript that he had started a decade earlier, the *Duino Elegies*. Two weeks after that, he finished the remaining twenty-nine sonnets. Within three weeks, the forty-six-year old poet had done his best-known work. Writing to his former lover, Lou Andreas-Salomé, in the midst of the creative outpouring, Rilke described it as this: "...a boundless storm, a hurricane of the spirit, and whatever inside me is like thread and webbing, framework, it all cracked and bent. No thought of food." He considered the two works "of the same birth."

Why Orpheus? The mythical god carrying everywhere his lyre and charming all fauna with his song? Rilke, it seems, considered Orpheus the original poet. In the symbol of Orpheus, he discovered what he, Rilke, was meant to be. Like he had followed the thread into himself. He found there the thing he had been seeking.

As to my own seeking, to following my own thread, I have added two more quotes to the collection in the water closet.

"Have we learned that? Or have we yet
To learn? Both. Hesitating between
Is what gives our faces character."
—Rainer Maria Rilke

"Here in the kingdom of decay, among what's wasting
Be a tinkling glass that shatters itself with sound."
—Rainer Maria Rilke

Translating, 23.11.98

I wonder how *Mila* Karina's doing… I have to admit. When I wrote about Rilke's weeks-long stay in Italy, the dagger in my side twisted.

Jacques did a painting based on the Batavia powerlines pictures I took. Out on 63, as it leaves Batavia. Amazing. The painting is great.

Kundera pulls it off. I should study how he does it. Learn (then steal) his technique. Jacques's having a hard time. At least he paints. It's good he does.

Milan Kundera

Born April 1, 1929, in Brno, Czechoslovakia.
Emigrated to France in 1975. Stripped of his Czechoslovakian

citizenship in 1979 by the Communists. He became a naturalized citizen of France in 1981. He claims his work should be judged alongside French writers and his books should be shelved in the French authors section.

Prior to the Velvet Revolution, his books were banned in Czechoslovakia. He's been nominated for the Nobel Prize in Literature several times, but he hasn't yet won.

He studied literature and aesthetics at the Faculty of the Arts at Charles University. He started out following in his father's footsteps to become a pianist. While he was in school, he found his way to writing. By 1952, he was teaching literature at the Academy of Music and Dramatic Arts in Prague.

While he was a member of the Communist Party, he was kicked out on two occasions. He attempted to reform the Czechoslovak Communist Party. He argued bitterly in print with Václav Havel about the Prague Spring and the Prague Autumn. He joined the Communist Party in 1948. He was expelled in 1950. He was readmitted to the Party in 1956 and remained in the Party until 1970. The straw that broke the camel's back, so to speak in Kundera's case, was his active participation in the liberalization of the Czechoslovak Communist Party in 1967 and 1968, the Prague Spring. He refused to admit his political digressions, and in retaliation, he was attacked by the Party. They banned his books, ousted him from the faculty and expelled him for the Party for the last time.

He initially wrote his novels in Czech. From 1993 onward, he wrote his novels in French. From 1985 to 1987 he translated all his work into French.

His work deals with erotic comedy, political criticism and philosophical speculation. That might sound like an odd combination, but he successfully brings it all together in his masterwork. His most well-known novel, *The Unbearable Lightness of Being,* was published in 1984. The novel enjoyed international acclaim. It was accelerated by a 1988 film adaptation directed by Philip Kaufman, starring Daniel Day Lewis as Tomas, Juliet Binoche as Tereza and Lena Olin as Sabina. The book was originally published in Czech, but not in Czechoslovakia, where it was banned. Rather than be thought of as a political dissident, or a dissident writer, Kundera has asserted that he should be thought of as a novelist, a French one at that.

I first read The *Unbearable Lightness of Being* in college. I remember the mention of that country with the name spelled funny. I remember the mention of the Prague Spring, and the Soviet tanks.

Esteeming, 25.11.98

Brad called this morning. He needed to borrow my camera. I accompanied him. We ran a few errands. That's cool. Kept me out of my head. Need to stay out.

Prague is a playground for men with low self-esteem, he said.

Brad needed dead pine trees. He designed a Christmas card. A picture of Christmas trash. On the sidewalk. Before Christmas has even come.

I dreamt about Karina last night. She called someone. I helped her. It wasn't my phone. It belonged to an older guy. We weren't lovers or anything. Me and Karina, I mean. We were like now. Nothing.

That's the way it'll end too. She'll end up in some Amerika; I'll stay here. We'll have crossed our stars. I don't care. She disappeared on a trip with some guy the night after she spent a night with me. She didn't call.

Bedřich Smetana

What about Czech music? Everyone knows Dvořak, but no one is more Czech than Smetana. Talk about Czech national identity; you have to listen to him.

Bedřich Smetana was born in 1824. At the age of six he played concerts. As a youngster, he went to live with relatives. He fell in love with his cousin Louisa. He wrote a song for her,

"Louisa's Polka." His music captures the essence of Bohemia, seemingly of what it is to be Czech. Probably most familiar is his song "Vltava." It has a sound that came to be identified with the nation's dream of independence.

While Myslbek was born seemingly of the Prague Uprising, Smetana preceded it a bit. His résumé describes the inflection point: from the Austro-Hungarian Empire to an independent Czechoslovakia. Check this out: While he was briefly the Court Pianist for former emperor Ferdinand in Prague, his submission for the royal wedding of the current emperor Franz Joseph was rejected because it did not pay enough homage to the Austrian national anthem.

Smetana has this delicate, crystalline tone that captures the natural beauty of Bohemia. He was peer to the Austrian pianist Franz Lizst and sought his guidance. The life he led was far from charmed. He lost a wife and four daughters to tuberculosis. While he remarried, his career was marred by conflict. He left the Czech National Theatre at the age of seventy-four. It could have been his biggest downfall, but in fact, his work blossomed after that, even as his hearing failed. He lost all hearing in both ears, yet continued to compose, not unlike Beethoven before him. He wrote a letter to Jan Neruda. In it, he feared that he might go insane; later in life he was committed to an asylum, where he later died.

It's Thanksgiving. I thought, up until now, I didn't care. I do care. I wish I didn't.

I know people who are hosting Thanksgiving-type things; I'm invited to none of them. It's okay. Sometimes, when you're convinced that you have friends, you find out that you don't.

Cleaning, 27.11.98
It's been eight elephant months now; every morning I wake up and roll around the bed. I think of her.

"I wonder you. You're on my mind." — *Prince*

You know what I need to do today? I need to clean. That's what I need today. Four hours. Place'll be like new. It'll be great. I can do some work before. Give my mind grist to chew on.

Synchronicity has been strong these past few weeks. Strings, threads, I don't know what it means. The water of course, but I know what that is.

It's 3:00 p.m. I just woke up. I was worried about Thanksgiving; it turned out fine. Brad, Chris, Jacques, I, Ester, and a few other girls ended up at Todd Lopez's house. Todd and Laura from the birthday party? They entertained friends at their tastefully decorated flat. The dinner was gorgeous. Afterwards, Todd got up and went outside. One of the girls went with him. To smoke a cigarette? They were gone thirty minutes or more. Laura prattled on and on. Everyone pretended not to notice. When he came back, I said, "There he is, the man of the hour." Ick.

Living, 30.11.98

Strange to write the date here and not know if it's right. Correct. Accurate. It's stranger still when you consider that I've been living like this for the past however-many months and I've only screwed the date up once or twice. That's crazy.

Karina hasn't called me. I can't wait for her to call. I have to move on.

Jacques and I tore at each other yesterday. I see now why. Jacques thinks he needs me to do that to him because he's scared to do it himself.

Jacques sees through my weakness and into my strength. He sees through my strength, back into my weakness. Markéta too. I have good friends. I have plenty else. Of course. Elijah's a good kid.

DECEMBER

Blanking, 2.12.98

WHAT IS IT? THE DATE. I'm forgetting something. A surprising gift journaling has given me. I have these strange moments, almost like déjà vu. I write the date and it triggers.

I went to the Name Day calendar I keep on my fridge, Blanka's fridge. There it was, plain as day. Blanka. My dear Blanka!

The only thing written on the page was the date. I dropped the pen. I threw on some clothes. I glanced in the mirror. Bedhead be damned. I put on my boots and lumbered out the door. It's a fine crisp day out there, cold. I made for the fresh fruit and vegetable stall up the street. I knew they had carnations. I picked out eleven red carnations. I got one of each of the Fidorka, the circular chocolate wafer goodies. I guess the plural would be Fidorky. My hands shook. I paid the man. He wore a dirty blue smock. Red, blue and gold. How will a ghost eat chocolate, you ask? I had a plan.

Wednesday, 9:30 a.m. I figured the neighbors might not be in. Carnations and Fidorky in hand, I stopped on the floor beneath my own. I knocked. Mrs. Nováková answered.

She was getting ready for work. I said good day in my best
formal Czech. I said, "Happy Name Day." I held out the three
circular chocolates. She smiled at the carnations under my arm.
She chose the red one. Dark chocolate, my favorite too. Mrs.
Nováková smiled at me. A tear gathered in the corner of her
eye. I said goodbye in Czech. I came back here.

In a crystal pitcher, the carnations sit before me. I journal. I
fill the page with my scribble. All the best to you on your Name
Day, Blanka. I eat the blue Fidorka. I push the foil back. Milk
chocolate, not my favorite. I'll leave the white chocolate one
for Elijah.

I should explain. Jacques got his own place. I found myself
alone in the apartment again. The walls of the water closet are
covered with quotes we have collected there. Elijah's contribu-
tion is a longhand transcription of "If" by Rudyard Kipling. He
was hinting. He needed a place to stay. I had the keys returned
from Jacques in my hand. I told him the amount. His contribu-
tion to the rent will be a help.

Doubting, 4.12.98

With people, or without them, I'm utterly alone. Stuck in my
head. No one is able to reach in and touch me anymore. I bid
farewell to the best of my friends. I'm left with nothingness. I
can't help but think that Elijah, my Canadian rube flatmate, is
not worthy of my time. I'm sorry. I hate to be judgmental. He's
not. Neither are blue-haired Bostonian Sadie Mae or the Mon-
tréalaise sisters, Meg and Ashley. Three short girls, smart, fun,
a good distraction — they're not what I am looking for. Dark,
mysterious, painter Jacques is worthy, at least his myth is worthy. At times I see through the legend I have built of Jacques.
Jacques plays the intellectual. We all do, I suppose, but there are
holes. Gaping holes.

I'm not satisfied with anyone right now because I'm not satisfied with myself. I'm not unaware of it. I run a hand through
my gloomy hair. I push my tortoiseshell glasses up on my nose.

I think like this. It keeps me from worrying about my ex-wife
Rachel or Karina, my ten-month obsession, or any of the girls
who're ersatz for what I want. What I want is connection, a

sense of wholeness. What I want is the sound round fullness of completion, a validation of love. I have plenty of love, true love, good love, warm friendly love, but it isn't that fleshy exhortation, it isn't the celebration of existence that is sex. I need sex. I need a companion. I need a mate. I don't have one. The problem is not my obsession or my ex-wife or my two-timing twenty-one-year old or my dead mermaid or the first girl to break my heart or anyone. The problem is I need someone.

She's out there. I eclipse her. Karina eclipses her. She's not worth my time or effort. I thought maybe she was, I thought I saw something; I was wrong. Five weeks now she hasn't called or written. She doesn't know who I am. That's fine. That's dandy.

Doesn't get me any closer to what I want. Or need. Karina will go to the States with her English tutor for the holidays. She'll not come back. At least not to me. Can I accept that? Can I let it go?

Warming, 6.12.98

Elijah and I headed out to Old Town Square around 5:00 p.m. to participate in the Svatý Mikuláš festivities. Saint Nicholas in English. We left the flat on Laubova. It was already dark. We got on the metro at George of Podebrady. Below the all-seeing eye. It is a straight shot on the Green Line, just four stops away. Elijah had a monthly pass, I stopped to buy *jízdenky* (metro tickets) at the NonStop Tabák (newsstand) on the way. On the magazine racks, the cover of *Czech Elle* magazine featured a gorgeous brunette with pale skin in a red velvet hooded jacket bordered in ermine, at her waist a thick black leather belt. Elijah held up the magazine to me. "Look familiar?"

I knew about the photo shoot for *THINK* magazine. Karina had told me about that one. I knew that she was getting more work. The cover of *Elle*? Why hadn't she told me?

"I'll buy every copy they have left when we get back." I was half kidding. She looked good. Her eyes locked, a curl on her lips, the glossy sheen of her hair.

On the metro, above the dangling straps, there was an ad for *Elle* magazine. It was Karina, magnified, a new pose from the

Mrs. Claus photo shoot, in this one she's laughing, her head tossed back, a carefree gesture, like someone whispered to her the funniest thing she's ever heard. I can't describe the feeling. I wanted to hate it. I knew it was fake, a manufactured moment. The more I looked at it, the more believable it was. In my heart, I was glad she was happy, that she could be that happy. The red red lips, the bright white teeth, the color of the inside of her mouth, her gums. Her relaxed tongue. She might actually be laughing. Could I make her happy? Could I be happy? Elijah smacked me on the shoulder. We were at our stop.

We came up out of Staroměstská metro station at the Kaprova exit. The air was clear and cold. A light snowfall had just started. Elijah and I were accosted on the sidewalk by three characters. The tallest one was dressed like a pope; tall red bishop's hat, long white robe with red silk stole to match. He carried a crosier with a curved top like a question mark. He rang a bell. Saint Nicholas, obviously, the Greek bishop upon whom the Santa Claus legend is based. Another character was dressed all in white with a coat-hanger halo; she was the angel, I am told. She looked familiar. Maybe one of the topless dancers at the place by the Charles Bridge. Or a waitress at the Chapeau Rouge. Perhaps she just looked like one of them. The last character was the best — soot-covered face, his hair sticking in all directions. He limped along on a cloven hoof and a foot. He wore a matted brown fur jacket. He dragged a chain. He carried a burlap sack. That is Čert or Krampus, a polymorphic figure, half-goat half-demon. The angel beamed. A bad girl. She hooked a sweet smile into us. I wondered if her blond hair was a wig or not. I couldn't tell. Krampus shouted in my face, "Bububu!" He rattled his chain at me.

Mikuláš asked me a question in Czech. I told him I didn't understand. Elijah translated, "Have you been a good boy this year?" I put my hand on my chin. I rolled my eyes heavenward. If I was not good, legend had it, Čert would take me in his sack and deliver me straight to hell. Krampus held his burlap sack open. He waved a piece of coal in my face. The angel in the push-up bra pushed forward. She held, her hands folded together, a basket of rock candy. A lace dress, sky-blue eye-shadow and giant wings on her back. I took a piece of candy. Krampus rattled his chains in anger. They waited for me. I looked at Elijah. "Sing a song or recite a poem." he said to me.

I said, "Kolo, rovno, hovno." It's a Czech rhyme. It translates to "Bicycle, straight, shit." Čert hopped up and down, one paw and one hoof. He rattled his chains in glee. Mikuláš dismissed us with a wave of his holy hand. The angel took a long look before retreating.

"I don't think they were impressed." Elijah said. I unwrapped the hard candy and popped it in my mouth.

I should have said "Strč prst skrz krk," a vowel-less Czech tongue-twister that translates to "Put your finger through your throat." That would not have impressed either.

At Old Town Square, we watched the scene play out in the Christmas Market. Multiple trios wandered the edges of the square. We watched a Krampus with elaborate horns and heavy black gothic boots run up and scare two children. The little boy jumped straight up and shrieked, while his sister shrunk away, crying. The parents cackled with glee. The angel and Mikuláš tried to settle them down.

The Jan Hus Memorial dominated the square. Two boys in matching brown plaid jackets, one a head taller than the other, probably four or five years old, were reciting a poem in unison. In tears. A group of three teenagers passed beside them. They acted unimpressed. One turned and said something, the others collapsed with laughter. Elijah and I paused at one of the wading pools. The fishmonger, his apron covered in blood and fish guts, paused. His square knife hung in the air. He smiled a greasy smile. At me. The cleaver came down with a thump. A dozen huge carp were in the water. They wriggled against one another, submerged beneath a thin film of oily water.

"Going for a swim, jako?" Karina stood next to me. She was with Ljuba. I looked at Elijah. He had on a sly smile.

"You should swim with me this time. Did you bring your plavky?" I hugged Karina. Six feet, one inch tall. I had to crane my neck. I had to stand on my tiptoes to kiss her on both cheeks.

"Asi ne, prostě… Příliš studená." I didn't show any signs of comprehension. She translated. "Too cold. I know how to warm your heart, jako." Karina smiled at me. She removed a gray cable-knit fingerless glove from her right hand. She shoved it into her tiny backpack. I watched the large snowflakes fall on the top of her downturned head, the flakes perched on her glossy hair the color of a seam of coal. She looked fresh, innocent, like a coal-haired angel. Was it a dream?

I pushed my tortoiseshell glasses up on my nose. I adjusted my heather beanie. Karina looked in my eyes. She grabbed my hand. Her long cool fingers intertwined with mine. As if we had held hands a thousand times before. Her fingers were tapered, her fingernails narrow and elegant. I was in shock. Elijah followed along beside us. He talked with Ljuba. Ljuba's red hair bounced on her shoulders as she walked — I knew her boyfriend. She smiled too much at Elijah.

Karina led me up to a wooden stall in the Christmas Market. The crude sign nailed to the awning read, "Tajemné Elixíry." I looked it up this morning. It means, "mysterious elixirs." Karina asked the attendant for a *horká medovina*, a hot honey-wine. I ordered a *svařák*, hot mulled wine flavored with cloves and orange. Ljuba's green eyes glittered. She ordered a Czech coffee, an instant coffee with a shot of Becherovka. The drinks came out, one by one. We inhaled the warming aromas.

"Do you, jako, know? Have you had till now?" Karina asks. I shake my head. Elijah, wearing a red parka with a white maple leaf emblazoned on it like a badge, had been here longer than me. He was less embarrassed to play the tourist than I was; he nodded his head.

"Here, jako, Joseph. You must." Karina gave me her *horká medovina*. I took a taste. It was hot, it burned my tongue. I waved my hand in front of my face. It's sickly sweet, like a white wine port. I nodded my head. I handed it back to her. She gave me back my steaming cup.

"Maybe I'll stick to this," I said. I got a good whiff of cinnamon and cloves. The wine was hot too. My tongue was numb.

Elijah said to me, "Czech rum. You have to try it." The hot water and the lemon and the sugar cube — they soothe on a cold night. Ljuba hunched her shoulders. She held her coffee in both hands. She wore black leather gloves. Her red felt jacket showed off her copper hair. I wondered if she'd smell like apple shampoo, like that day at the club months ago, or something different.

I sipped my wine. I watched people. They basked in the glow. Stalls overflowed with Christmas trinkets. Ornaments, wooden tops and trains, hand-knitted lace; Bohemian crystal, of course. Karina stood next to me. Her breath steamed. She held her drink with both hands. I kept the cinnamon stick out of the way. I sipped my mulled wine. I studied her in profile. Why was she being kind to me? Where was this coming from? Perhaps in the spirit of Christmas, her gift was to pretend that we are an item. It didn't make sense. The way her blood-red lips pout, the graceful swoop of her long nose, her pale skin against her sable hair. So tall and thin and fragile. Like a dream. I was afraid I might wake up.

I teased her. "Karina, are you going to drink your medovina or just hold it?"

"Jako, to warm my hands." Karina held up her bare hand. She looked at my chin. "Already, this one is cold." She stepped away a few paces, chucked the plastic cup into the trash barrel. Like a runway model, she turned back to me. She put her hands in pockets and stomped her model walk back toward us. She lowered her eyes, looking up through her eyebrows. She made sure everyone watched her. She caught the attention of a tall Mikuláš; he adjusted his pants under his robes.

I held out my hand. Karina smiled, her eyes dancing. She took the miniature backpack off one shoulder and took out a striped coin purse. Her long thin fingers unzipped the purse. She dug through layers of paper money to find a couple coins. She zipped the bulging coin purse back up, coins pinched in her knuckles. She leaned down to kiss me. Just like that. On the mouth. As if we were boyfriend and girlfriend, as if it was the most natural thing in the whole wide world. She stood up straight. She was proud of the effect she had on me. She put the coin purse in the mini backpack and slung it on her back. She stomped her model walk to the mysterious elixir hut and handed her coins to the vendor, a man in a felt hat. He looked at her for an extra few seconds. He had seen her somewhere before.

Elijah and Ljuba huddled around me. Elijah smiled. "Surprised?" He told me Karina had called the flat this morning while I was at work. He'd asked her to bring a friend.

"I am agog," I said. I looked into Ljuba's green eyes. They twinkled like the lights buried in garland that outline the huts of the Christmas Market. I thought better of it. I pointed to Elijah's drink, steaming in his gloved hand, "I am a-grog…"

Ljuba laughed. She leaned into Elijah. He put his arm around her. He flicked his eyebrows at me. He got the better deal in this configuration. She held her drink out for Elijah. He took a sip. He elided, "It tastes like Christmas." I knew what he meant. Out here on the square, the flavors explode. Pine, cinnamon. A hint of licorice.

"Hmm, Beton." I could taste it. A splash of tonic, on the rocks? Perfect after work. "Let's walk around, maybe get one later."

Elijah asked Ljuba what she wanted for Christmas. Karina came back. I held up the cinnamon stick. I sucked the wine out of it. I placed it back in the cup with the remnants of cloves and orange zest.

"Shall we?" I held out the crook of my elbow to Karina. She hooked her arm through and tossed her hair over her shoulder. She replaced her hand on the warming cup.

"Will you go home for Christmas, Joseph?" Karina asked me about my family.

I told her I decided to stay here. I have the money, if I wanted to go. If I go home for every holiday, am I getting the most out of my expat experience? I debated it. Lots of expats stay here for the holidays. I wanted that too. "My mother's not happy with it. She'll be okay." I hadn't spoken about my family to Karina. It was a first.

"Maminka would not hear of it." She had one Christmas away from family. Thailand, a few years back. With her ex. He didn't talk to her for two days. They were staying in a tiny thatched hut. Stuck together, silent. "It was, jako, awful. Never again." Karina paused. She pursed her rosebud lips. Parentheses of wrinkles formed around her mouth. "Go home, fast all day, clean the house. The sun sets, we eat like pigs."

I rankled at the thought of Karina with her big dumb golem of a boyfriend. "How was Italy?"

"It was, jako, nice. Phil is sweet. Total different from my idiot ex." She told me Phil paid for an extra room. "It was sweet." The cobbles beneath my feet sparkled. They reflected the lights from the giant Christmas tree on the square beneath the spires of the Týn Church. The tree, near the Jan Hus Memorial, is thirty-one meters tall (over one hundred feet), taller than the tree at Rockefeller Center in New York City. Between the two is a stage for live music. A group of middle-aged men in period costume play medieval music. I was dubious. It was platonic? Please.

"He's back in St. Louis now, vlastně. Haven't heard from him. He was getting back with his ex-wife."

Terrible idea. There was no going back. I pasted a smile on my face. I tried to focus. On Karina. I looked back. Elijah doubled over laughing. Ljuba shook, her fingers by her mouth.

It had to be a romantic night. The falling snow, the mulled wine, the cheerful spirit of the people on the square. We walked arm in arm. Under the Christmas lights and decorations. It was too much. It didn't match the place where I and Karina were. The trajectory of our relationship. As in, no relationship at all. I had two choices. Either accept the night for what it was, enjoy the company and the scenery. Or reject it as false. Wait for our relationship to catch up.

We left the Christmas Market behind and snaked our way through Prague. I guided Karina down Iron Street. Across from the Astronomical Clock. The street I used to live on.

A shop assistant worked a marionette outside his storefront. It is Hurvinek, a famous Czech character, a boy by turns hyperactive and lazy. Karina and I stopped to watch. The puppet brought one hand to his face. Hurvinek looked up, pointed to Karina. By degrees, his head turned to the puppeteer. The shopkeep murmurs to Hurvinek, an accented mix of Czech slang and English, "No yo, very pretty girl." Hurvinek does a spastic dance. Karina pulled me away.

"I saw your cover." I congratulated her. I said we should celebrate. I tried to keep it crisp. I had questions. I didn't want to scare her away. Not just yet anyway.

"Tata called me in Florence. To tell me about it. He is proud of it, jako. Don't you think I look stupid?" Karina's confidence was gone. Her face is plastered all over the city; she's feeling self-conscious?

"You know how to keep a secret…" I bit my tongue. I couldn't spill my insecurity. My inner crazy.

She got the call. Holiday photo shoot. "I had to stop my ticket. Phil left without me. He was angry, vlastně." At the studio, she told me, five models showed up. Five. All dressed the same. They did a bunch of shots, with props, etc. She said it was all very stupid. "If Guillermo was not there, I would leave."

Guillermo. The photographer, the guy from Ingrid's memorial service, who shot her back in the spring. I could picture him. Italian guy, short, leather jacket, long hair.

"They chose you… Your picture, I mean, for the cover." We pass by Můstek, at the bottom of Wenceslas Square. I glance up at Baťa. I pictured my two-timing Izabela. Her round face, her high cheekbones. Her short skirts and wedges.

"Tata hired agent. He said I have to protect myself. I don't know — seems, jako… too soon? What you think?"

Karina, supermodel, cared what I thought? She looks up to me. Like I'm some globetrotting entrepreneur. "Listen to your tata." I told her to make sure the agent is reputable. I told her people will try to take advantage of her. "Don't do anything you don't want to do."

"That's what my tata says." Karina stood tall. She leaned on me. We turned onto Štěpánská. "Agent can be accountant too."

I told her the accountant should be separate from the agent. She needed a team, checks and balances. I looked back to make sure Ljuba and Elijah made the turn. "What about Šárka?" We passed by the Lucerna Passage.

"Hele, vlastně, good idea." Karina leaned over. She nuzzled just below my chin with the bridge of her nose

From the street, Karina and I descended seven steps into a strange vestibule. Advertised as the best pub in town, an expat pub extraordinaire, Jama (which translates to "pit" or "hollow") is a tavern. The vestibule contained a table to hold fliers, free circulars and periodicals. Above it, a pin board with advertisements for roommates. An ad for the *Jama Revue*, a literary magazine. It was already defunct by the time I arrived in Prague.

Through an arched doorway, the main room. The ceilings arch. The room contains three structural arches, painted orange underneath. The arches end on each side in rough-cut paneling. Tables to the left and the right. Centered under the arches, a bar. Framed rock posters cover the walls. They creep up the ceiling. David Bowie. Bjork. A cover of *Rolling Stone* magazine featuring Britney Spears. A poster of Yoda. Ric Ocasek of the Cars. John Lennon, Bob Marley, Jimi Hendrix. The Ramones. The Bee Gees, Guns N' Roses, the Eurythmics. A framed article from *Playboy* magazine.

We took seats at the bar. It was empty. The bartender was a short bald Czech dude wearing a white suit, miniature wings and a coat-hanger halo.

Toward the entrance was a table with a built-in wooden bench and a high back. Elijah and Ljuba sat. A waitress in a fur dress, her face smeared with black coal, chains around her slim waist, burst through the two swinging doors leading to the kitchen. She grabbed four menus, dropped two at the table, brought the other two to Karina and me.

Adjacent to the kitchen doors was a high wooden shelf where extra condiments, napkins, spare table tents were stored. The female Krampus stopped there. She grabbed flatware, napkins and a condiment centerpiece for each couple.

The food in Jama was not great. People used to talk about the chicken wings; they were awful, like every other place in Prague — oversauced, undercooked, soggy, gelatinous.

I unbuttoned my jacket. I tossed it over the stool next to Karina. It reminded me of the way Naked Pete had taken off his jacket and sat on it that day back at Little Glen's. Karina unzipped her coat. She removed her gloves. She dropped her jacket over mine. Our coats spooned. She tossed her hair forward and back. Her cheeks were red. The tip of her nose was blue. She caught me looking at her.

I ordered a Becherovka. Karina got a Beton.

I shot the first one. I winced. It burned going down. I tasted anise. We sat there, our wet clothes on the bar stool next to us.

My brow furrowed. I could feel myself changing. A few months ago, a few days ago, I would have given anything for a date with Karina. Now that she's here, I've lost interest? She's beautiful. She's tall, thin. With all the attention she's been getting lately, her hair, her skin, her clothes have never looked better. On balance, she didn't get my sense of humor, she hadn't read my stories. I knew next to nothing about her family.

Is that it, then? Was this the end? Was it the end before the beginning?

"Joseph." Karina drained her highball, sucking at the ice. "Can I stay at your place?" She told me the last train home from Smíchovské nádraží left in a few minutes. To get it, she'd need to go now. Karina leaned in. She placed a hand on my chest.

Tell her no. Send her home. It's okay. What would Ingrid say?

"I thought you'd never ask." It was an out-of-body experience. I watched myself deliver the line. "We won't be alone. Elijah lives with me now." There may yet be a saving grace.

Karina brought both her cold hands to my face. She pressed. I allowed my face to be turned. Karina giggled. Elijah and Ljuba were on the high-backed bench, at the table by the entrance. They were a writhing lump of flesh. They hungrily attacked each other. Elijah came up for air, stood up from the bench, wobbled. He came around the table, tucking in his shirt. He sidled over to us. Ljuba sat back. She touched her mouth, adjusted her hair.

"We're gonna take off. Might not be home soon." Elijah grinned at Karina. Karina tipped her chin. She blushed. It was cute. "Maybe not until tomorrow. Have fun..." Elijah strutted back to the large table. He finished his Pilsner Urquell. He signaled the she-Čert waitress. He turned to Ljuba. Ljuba looked around the bar, convincing herself she didn't know anyone there. She dove back in. She kissed Elijah.

Karina sipped her refilled Beton. She smiled at me. "You were saying?"

What was the harm, I figured. So she stayed at my place. Didn't mean anything had to happen...

Back outside, our jackets were on. My heather hat and her fingerless gloves in place. The snow continued falling on Prague. It's a peaceful feeling. Snow falls. There's silence. That is the thing about winters in Prague. It is cold and dark. You feel hemmed in. The short days. The sun comes out. It's set low in the sky. At night, the snow brings lightness back. It's orange under the streetlamps. Large flakes accumulate on the sidewalk, against the buildings, over the cobbles. There is a comfort to it, a welcoming feeling. It was too cold to walk home. I hailed a cab on Wenceslas Square.

In the cab, Karina slid across the seat. She curled into me. I wanted it to be real. I have dreamt of what it would have been like for us to be girlfriend and boyfriend since she was a barmaid at Terminal Bar. I remembered the red sweater, the red wine the night I missed the tram home on purpose. The night I wrote about one of my high-school girlfriends. That last kiss. It felt like years ago. Ten months? Had it been that long?

I put my arm around Karina. I held her. I stuck my nose in her hair. It was that smell again, cedar and ambergris. Mixed with the sweat from her scalp, her hair smelled like a damp forest floor sprinkled with cedar shavings. There is something herbal too, a heady whiff of witch hazel.

The cabbie looked at me. In the rearview mirror. I looked away. I watched the National Museum pass beside us. The majesty of it at the top of the square.

I looked at my watch. There was still time.

I redirected the cabbie to Smíchovské nádraží. Karina sat up. "You don't want me to stay?" Karina pouted.

"We need more time. You just got back from Italy..."

"Is it Phil? I don't love him. We had fun. I don't love him."

I smiled. I put my hand on her hand. "I think this is about me."

My heart swelled. It had to be right, wrong as it felt. Could have been the only chance I'd ever get with Karina. It was a risk I had to take.

At the train station, I asked the cabbie to wait. I said, "Počkejte, počkejte." He nodded. I got out. I held the door for Karina. She emerged from the cab like she was about to saunter down the red carpet. The train was in the station. We could see it. Karina turned to me. "When you are ready, jako. Goodnight, Joseph." She kissed me. It was tender, generous. She lingered. She smiled at me. I watched her walk toward the train station.

I held my ground. I couldn't see her anymore. I got back in the cab. I asked the cabbie to wait. The train lurched into motion. I told him to go. It's what my mom would have done. I said, "Tak, jdeme."

I came home to my empty apartment. I was alone but I didn't feel lonely. I wonder how long self-satisfaction will keep?

Rebounding, 9.12.98

I had a dream last night. I was getting on a tour bus to go snowboarding. I saw a tall young woman with black hair and gray cable-knit gloves. The smoke from the bus's exhaust pipe curled around her thick boots. Her thin calves encased in tight indigo denim. I touched her under her bent elbow. She turned. It wasn't her. I was shocked. I said, "My mistake." I tried to laugh it off. I was crying. At the back of the bus, I found Ingrid. She was drunk already. Black hair, under a thin blanket. She held out a bottle of tears to me. I wiped my face. I took a sip. I handed it back. Ingrid was not Ingrid anymore. She was Rachel. She was sober. She reached out to me from under the thin blanket. She beckoned me in. I crawled in with her.

I woke up. I went into the kitchen. Ljuba was there. She made tea for her and Elijah. They have been spending a lot of time together. She was in a pink short-sleeved shirt and black panties. She didn't cover herself. She's confident. No bra. I had on short pajama bottoms. I had a V-neck T-shirt. I felt like I should go, put on some clothes, come back.

"Dobré ráno," she said in a sweet voice. "Nechceš nějaký čaj?" I replied good morning in Czech. I politely refused her offer of some tea. I told her I would get a cup of coffee. I sat down. I tried not to stare at her shapely pink legs. She giggled at me, over her shoulder. She switched to English. "Did you sleep okay?"

I didn't tell her about my dreams. She sat across from me at the table.

"Have you talked to Karina?"

I told her I hadn't.

"I thought you two should be together. I didn't like Phil. He's not... simpatico. Rozumíš?" I nodded. I did understand.

The greasy daylight streamed in through the kitchen windows. Her emerald eyes illuminated. "I'm happy Phil sent her home." Ljuba lengthened her back.

"Sent her home?" I thought he went back to the States.

Ljuba said it was stupid. She said Karina could be difficult. She said the word *sulky*. "I thought she told you."

"She didn't mention it," I said. Sulky? Why was she sulky? She's in Italy, Phil's paying, she just got the cover of a magazine. What's there to sulk about?

She said Karina didn't know what she wanted. She said Karina didn't know what was good for her. She said Karina came back from Italy smarter. "Ne, not smarter, that's not the word. You know what I mean, wiser. Like owl."

"Ah, like owl." I nodded. I processed. Phil sent her home. I was picking up the rebound from Phil's rejection. Great. Can you imagine if I had let her stay with me? Humiliating.

Ljuba stirred milk into her tea. I tried not to watch. The way her tight T-shirt moved. I got up. I turned the burner on under the red kettle. I got a cup from the cupboard. I spilled some instant coffee in.

"She's not a bad person, Joseph. Her heart is broken." Ljuba told me Karina's ex was mean, a jerk. Ljuba said she'd told Karina a long time ago but Karina didn't listen. She'd told her to pay attention to me. She'd told Karina to notice. Ljuba stretched her arms above her head. She yawned. "Now, she listens."

Might be too late.

Connecting, 16.12.98

I called my brother to wish him a happy birthday. I used the call-back service. It was easy. Once I got through, once he picked up the phone and said, "Hello?" I did it the way my mom would do it — I started singing. I could hear him sigh, hold the phone away from his face. The way he thanked me was annoyed. It's natural, it's the way I act when my mom calls and sings me "Happy Birthday." It's the way I respond when my brother calls me and does the same thing.

Christmas birthdays are tough. My brother hated it when our aunts and cousins would combine his birthday and his Christmas gifts. My mother made it a point in our family to put up the Christmas tree *after* my brother's birthday.

Sam's twenty-seven now. My younger brother's old. That's cool. I hope this year will be a good one for him. Twenty-seven's a rough one. I should know. Jimi Hendrix, John Belushi, Jim Morrison, they all can testify. As if twenty-eight's any easier...

I work on the stories. I put in the trick. I learned it from Ilona. The geology. I'm not a writer. I have these stories. I have these journals and these stories, but that's it. I'm a database guy. I need to stick to that. I store data. I provide the basis for understanding things. I analyze patterns, I collect information. I organize it. It can be used to remember.

I got the special Czech open-faced sandwiches and jelly doughnuts for my breakfast yesterday. It was bone-chilling cold. I stopped in the hardware store. My hands shook. I handed the clerk my keys. I wanted to make a copy — one for the outer door and one for the flat. Elijah has a set. The ones that Jacques had made back in November when he moved in. I have my keys. I need the copies in case, as I fantasized all the way back in March, I ask Karina to live with me.

The fantasy has expanded. I know how I want to do it — if I want to do it. Imagine: I open the door. I step aside. There is a note at the front door. It says, "Follow me." A thread disappears into the flat. She follows. Down the length of the hallway, into the kitchen, back across the entrance to the living room. Around the living room. Into the bedroom. Around the bedroom, to the futon to the bed to the wardrobe. To the desk. Into the hallway, across to the bathroom. To the washing machine, to the clothes drying rack, to the shower wand, hot and cold, to the sink, hot and cold. Up to the mirror. A note, "Open me." Inside the medicine cabinet — keys.

A key ring with a fob, maybe a heart on it? I haven't found the fob yet. Now I have the keys. I don't know if I will give them to her. The fantasy is fully formed. My hands might have been shaking from excitement. Or cold.

I already have the thread as well. I'm string boy, after all. Ingrid shakes her head at me.

I called my dad. I used the call-back service. I figured why not, I'm on a roll. I didn't know what I was going to say.

Panicking, 21.12.98

Jacques wants me to give Karina up. I should. He was excited to see her. I stop waiting. I have other things to do. I walk into a party. And there she is.

I panicked. I talked to her. We didn't say much. She reached in her purse for a tube of lip balm. It was La Bello Yellow, a Czech brand. She took off the cap. She smeared it on her lips. It set something off in me. I left. It was awkward. Jacques waved for me to stay. I didn't. She saw that. She went there to find me. I'm sure of it. I didn't come back.

THE POND

Position yourself to be successful, his mother's words. Her voice resonates. Sounds good, but what could he do?

Joseph shakes his head. He jumps down from the cab of the Canyon Red Ford F-150. Borrowed it from his cousin. Today is not the day to break down. Daniella DiBenedetto's on her way.

It's a brilliant June morning. Temperatures predicted to be in the low eighties. Too brilliant. The sky is blue zircon fringed above the trees in cherry wine. Like a stain in the bottom of a glass.

Joseph, clad in a black polo and a pair of khaki cargo shorts, worries he wore the wrong clothes. Despite a temperate spring, it's humid. He wipes his brow with the back of his hand. He doesn't dare use his shirt for fear it will leave behind salt residue. They haven't seen each other since December. He intends to make an impression.

The Saturday morning is fraught with opportunity. If he doesn't blow it, he will be certified in first aid and CPR. It would qualify him for resident camp counselor. To complicate matters, Daniella takes the class too.

They write letters back and forth. An occasional phone call to hear her voice. Five months. He doesn't know if he's up to the challenge. He likes her. Does she like him?

He arrives at the county park fifteen minutes early. Too early. Cut grass. The softball field is freshly mown. A tang of yesterday's charcoal flavors the breeze.

A family unloads their minivan. Two adults, two boys and a girl, an Igloo cooler and a bocce set.

Under the shade of a pavilion, the first-aid session coordinator prepares materials. You might think it was a birthday party. On closer inspection, the party favors are of a different sort: rubber gloves, triangular bandages, bag-masks. An armless, legless torso.

He has a few minutes to burn. A sign out by the road caught his eye.

Joseph reads:

Genesee County Park and Forest was the first county forest established in the state of New York. The land was originally purchased in 1882 to supply wood to the County Poorhouse for cooking and heating.

Genesee County's Poorhouse for the care of indigent people opened in 1827 with a home and farm consisting of 108 acres on the corner of Bethany Center Road and Raymond Road.

"Hey!" She waves from the lot. She's punctual.

She marches in his direction. She's dressed like she couldn't make up her mind. Her navy-blue Canisius T-shirt; a pair of athletic shorts embroidered U.S. Naval Academy. Her legs have a dewy sheen. Her hair is a knot of curls; she pulled it through the back of a baseball cap.

"Did you know this was a poorhouse?" Joey swipes his upper lip with lip balm.

"And an asylum." Maybe even a portal to other worlds. She leaves that part out. She doesn't want to freak him out.

"Geez. Really?" His voice cracks. It's cute.

Dani checks the time on a gold pocket watch. Two inches in diameter, the face ambered with age. The numbers and hands are a deeper shade of bronze. A small diamond glitters in the center.

"It's my grandfather's. Listen." She holds it up to his ear. The sound is like a drip down a deep well. The drip echoes. It hesitates. Time bends. A flash of warmth rushes over him. He's afraid. If he falls in, he might never find his way out.

"Phases of the moon, see, waning gibbous." Her voice brings him back. It's about abundance. She doesn't tell him that. She doesn't want to sound like a lunatic.

The shade of the pavilion, the cool concrete refreshes them. The first-aid class begins. The medical technician is a woman in her late twenties, cute in a utilitarian sort of way, but Joseph doesn't notice. He's bewitched.

They practice. They put on rubber gloves. They take them off. They learn how to properly dispose of them. Joseph refrains from snapping his glove on Daniella's thigh.

Joseph compresses the chest of a baby mannequin with his thumbs. Daniella holds the nose of the adult mannequin. She leans down to put her mouth on the disinfectant-reeking device. Her eyes flick to Joseph. He squeezes the bag-mask. He doesn't notice it has fallen off his patient. The MT concludes the activity. The instant before Daniella's lips land.

They both ace the quiz. A rivalry sparks between them. They fill out each other's name, mailing address and home phone number. Like it's a competition. He got the house number wrong. She fixes it on the picnic table.

The MT signs a slip of paper for each of them. Certificates will be mailed. "Enjoy the rest of your day, you two."

Dani conjures a picnic. Tricolor noodles, black olives, grape tomatoes, cubes of ham, grated Parmesan, shredded mozzarella, Italian dressing. Two bottles of water, freshly cut strawberries and an unopened bottle of Hershey's syrup.

Near the playground, Joey finds a table in the shade. Dani

watches him. The way he walks. His calves flex. He runs cross-country. She likes him. What's not to like?

"Open your mouth," she prompts. In one motion, chocolate, strawberry and the tip of her finger go into his mouth. She remembers the young family next to them. The baby girl watches.

He jogs down the embankment to the pickup.

Dani stands at a sign. It reads, Memory Lane. She raises one eyebrow without the other. He looks at her eyes. They flash. They were green but now they're hazel.

He positions himself beside her. He's vexed.

Memory Lane bisects the park. Hand in hand, they amble.

They talk college, plans for the summer, music. They spar.

"Everything, as long as it's not country."

"Ever heard of George Jones? Johnny Cash?"

"The guy on Hee Haw?"

"I'll play it for you. In my room." A knot forms in her stomach.

His hand sweats. He hopes she doesn't notice. He lets go of her. He leads them off the path.

His sense of direction is patchy, like a quilt. He remembers how to get from one place to another by feel. It's discontinuous.

She walks behind him. She enjoys the view. He's a Boy Scout, a Counselor-in-Training; Joey'll be a lifeguard. In his red shorts with the white piping.

They talk fashion.

"I like classics. L.L.Bean."

"That preppy stuff?"

Dani pops his collar. She tells him he's cute.

Before he can blush, "Expensive. Teachers' kids shouldn't expect stuff like that."

"It's guaranteed for life. Quality."

"With a body like yours, Guess? jeans."

"L.L.Bean is too expensive, so designer jeans?"

He doesn't answer.

She wants to ask if he believes in spirits, if he has weird

dreams. She saves that for another day.

"Orange is my least favorite color. I look horrible in orange. My skin turns green." Her school colors are black and orange. "A color reserved for beach towels and creamsicles."

"Prison uniforms. Traffic cones."

He stops. Their shoulders brush. He looks confused. They stand at the end of a clearing. A pond covered in a thick layer of foam. It tucks in a corner. The foam is neon green. Viscous as frog spawn.

"Do you have Chapstick?"

He pats his pants. He squeezes his cargo pockets. He locates the lip balm. The thought of her lips makes him frantic. He digs two fingers into the pocket. He can't get it. He feels inadequate. He jams his fist in. A beige button goes flying. It disappears into leaf litter. He sighs. She maps where she last saw the leaves wiggle. He holds the tube out to her.

"Not like that." She takes off her cap. An abundance of curls cascades over her shoulders. Her arms hang. She closes her eyes. She tilts her face up. Does she want him to draw it on her?

He slathers his lips. She opens one eye. She closes it. He caps the tube. He slips it in his pocket. He steps closer. Their lips touch.

He skips ahead. Two days. Can't stop thinking about the poorhouse. His mother jokes about it. If they had those today, most of his family, the whole Snipe clan if not the entire Seneca tribe, would be in one. He looks it up in the library.

An announcement in the *Batavia Times*, dated December 9, 1826:

Notice is hereby given that the Genesee County Poorhouse will be ready for the reception of paupers on the first day of January 1827 ... The Overseers of the Poor of the several towns of the County of Genesee are requested, in all cases of removal of paupers to the county poorhouse, to send with them their clothing, beds, bedding and such other articles belonging to the paupers as may be necessary and useful to them.

With a little digging:

Eligible for assistance included: habitual drunkards, luna-
tics (one who has lost the use of reason), paupers (one with no
means of income), state paupers (one who is blind, lame, or
otherwise disabled) and vagrants.

In 1828 the County constructed a stone building attached to
the Poorhouse for the confinement of lunatics and a repository
for those committed for misconduct. The insane were housed
at the County Home until 1887 when the Board of Supervisors
agreed to send "persons suffering with acute insanity to the
Buffalo State Asylum and cases of violent, chronic insanity to
Willard."

A list of those who died while living in the County Home was
compiled from information in the registration records, receipts
for coffins purchased, mortuary listings, and reports from the
Superintendents of the Poor. Information on the cemetery
located at the County Home is almost nonexistent. The 1886
Proceedings stated, "The burying ground we have improved by
building a fence in front and grading and leveling the ground
as much as could be done without injury to the graves." A cem-
etery register or plot map has yet to be discovered.

In 1867 the Superintendent of the Poor reported that of the
1,018 poor, 706 had become paupers by intemperance.

He found this too:

Rolling Hills Asylum is a nationally known center of super-
natural activity. Spirits roam the grounds passing between this
world and the next.

Dani was not kidding.

Joseph got out a map. On a hunch. He drew a straight line
between the house on South Main Street Road and the house
in Union Corners. Chills ran along his arms. It goes directly
through Genesee County Park. The abandoned building on the
corner is the midpoint. It bisects the distance.

It's their first kiss. He tilts his head. She holds her head still. He exaggerates the motion. He gets the balm all over her. They come apart. She laughs. She wipes her bottom lip. She's on her toes. She's light-headed.

"Missed a spot."

She's flat-footed. He's grateful. He had no idea how he would get her to do it. She cast her spell. She moons, playful. He laughs. Their lips meet.

He goes slow. He feels. He touches her tongue with his. He backs off; their top lips touch. They breathe the same air. They touch noses. He rotates his head to the left. He leans into the feeling.

She comes up for air. "Let's find your button." She's not going to let it go. He looks around near his feet. He feels drunk. He processes: the imprint of her body on his. If he thinks about it, he can feel her breasts, her belly.

She steps back. She zooms in. She stands. She's triumphant. She holds the button between her thumb and index finger.

"Any idea who belongs to this?" she says.

She puts it in his pocket.

They hold hands. They leave the pond behind them. The knot in her stomach returns. The whole way back to the parking lot. She tastes him. Chewing gum, sweat, salt. She breathes in his laundry soap. She thinks about when he will kiss her again.

I left the party. I went home. I came up out of the metro at George of Podebrady, under the all-seeing eye. There she was. Sat on a bench. Karina laughed with Ljuba. They smoked cigarettes. Laughter somehow broke the spell; the all-seeing eye went back to just being a big stoic brick church with a clock on top. Elijah left for Canada last night.

Do I want her to be my girlfriend? I don't know.

Am I ready?

I know Karina's not the one for me. We can have sex if she wants, but it won't make any difference. Or will it?

Ljuba jumped up and hugged me. She kissed me on both cheeks. She said she had to go. I asked if she wanted to come upstairs and hang out. She politely declined. She said good night to Karina. They exchanged looks. I tried not to notice.

"Do you want to hang out?" I asked Karina. She nodded once slowly, then again. I grabbed her hand. Nothing had to happen.

I led her down my street. I asked her how long she had been there. She said, Not long. It was Ljuba's idea, she said. To wait for me.

"How'd you know I wouldn't bring someone home?"

Karina shrugged. She smiled.

Upstairs, Karina asked me for a towel. I found one for her. She took a bath. I tried to read *Doctor Zhivago*. I couldn't. I put on some music. I got a glass of water.

Karina came out of the bathroom. She wore the towel. The music was Jamiroquai. A song called "Cosmic Girl." It's danceable, vaporous. It's the only music I have that I know Karina likes. She asked, "Aren't you tired?"

"I am."

"Should we lie down?"

"We should." I left the music going.

She pulled back the duvet. She laid down. The towel around her. Her wet hair on my pillow. She reached out to me. I stripped down to my underwear. I climbed in with her.

I kissed Karina. My hands searched the length of her. She kissed me back. I unwrapped her. Her soft skin. Warm and supple. I explored. Her breasts, her nipples, her sternum, her ribs. I vowed to feed her in the morning. Her hands were on me. My arms, my wrists, my back. My hips. My hands found her pelvis. So angular. I couldn't picture it. It didn't seem possible, this impossibly tall, impossibly thin woman held together by fashion. I felt between her legs. She sighed. It wasn't true. It sounded false. She turned into me. She held me. I held her. I waited for it to feel real. I fell asleep, waiting.

I went to the post office. For presents this year, I have decided to send things I made myself. To my mother, I sent a story. Not one of the stories I have been working on, a different story. A story about a young woman at the beginning of her college career who meets this dashing young man. She falls madly in love. She becomes pregnant. She had not received proper guidance at home. She's the first to take a shot at high education. She has a choice to make. She chooses the baby, a boy. She builds her life around him. She's going to like that story.

To my brother I sent ten pictures of places in Prague that I love. I wrote a piece about each. He'll probably hate it. He'll think I'm bragging about my charmed life in Europe. I don't mean it as a brag. I want to share it with him.

For my sister-in-law, Gwen, I did five drawings. I'm no artist, she's the artist; I hope she'll like them. I did the illustrations in the places I photographed and wrote about for my brother. A companion piece.

Karina swaddled herself in the blankets off the bed. She hunted for her clothes. I made her tea. She didn't drink it. She came into the kitchen in her underwear. She picked up the cup. She sniffed it. She set it down. She went looking for her pants. I watched the way her hips and ass rotated against the fabric. She left. I sat down to journal.

Dreaming, 22.12.98

Karina and I spoke this morning. She had a deep voice. She didn't say *jako, prostě, vlastně* (as in, simply, actually) once. How about that?

I called her. I sent her an email. The email got through. She replied. Karina took the time to tell me at what time she'd be where. She wants to see me. She's lonely. Her man rejected her. Ljuba told me. I don't know if Karina knows I know. I'll see her soon. I need to stop by work to retrieve the packages from my mother and my brother.

I don't want to have a girlfriend. I don't want to fall in love. Not with her. It's been too long. It's been too stupid.

Today is Dani's birthday. Happy birthday, Dani.

I had a dream about Karina last night. We were getting mar-

ried. I thought, "Do I really want to marry her?" Karina had
braces. She was too careful. She wore an ice-green metallic slip
dress with a low scoop back. She wore a dandelion crown.

Wondering, 24.12.98

Avi sent around an email invite to come to his house for the
Christmas Eve feast. He and Barbora will throw a traditional
Czech Christmas for all the expats, whatever that means. I
suppose there will be carp. He said to bring anyone who was
around, in the spirit of the *Štědrý den, Štědrý večer*, which literally means Generous Day or Generous Evening. In his email he
said that no one should be alone and no one should go hungry. I
forwarded the invite to Pat, Jacques and Brad. Pat will be with
Markéta's family, but I think Jacques and Brad will come with
me.

Karina stopped by on her way home. My flat's not on her way
home. I'm lucky I hadn't started with my project to put up the
thread yet. She came in for a minute. I asked if she wanted some
tea. I asked if she wanted something stronger. She refused. She
asked me what the packages were on the floor in the living
room. I told her presents from America, from my mother and
my brother. A smile curled on her lips. "I wonder what is in
them," she said. She gave me a kiss. She gave me a warm hug.
She gave me a slow kiss. Her hand on my chin. She had to run.
Her mother expected her. We will see each other after Christmas. I figured as much. I walked her out. I watched her go down
in my elevator.

Carping, 25.12.98

I wake up. Christmas morning. I go for the packages. I'm
alone.

I chose to be alone this year. I could be at home. I could wake
up in my mother's house like the year before, like the year after.
I could wake up in my brother's townhouse. Not this year. I
commit to Prague. I commit to the future. I unwrap, ready for
whatever comes next.

Now, in the bleak light of my first Christmas morning alone,
I stand here with the boxes opened and undone, I sip coffee. I

write in this journal.

I called my mom. Call-back service again.

"Thanks for the sweatsuit. I love it. Black on black." There is a rasp in my voice. I try to sound cheerful.

"I knew you would love it. Could it be any darker?" I could hear her smile through the receiver.

"Did you get the story?"

"I got it." My mom paused. I waited. "Oh, Joseph," she sobs. "I love it." She wipes tears. I can hear her. "You know, I wanted to write a book once."

"I know. That's why I wrote it for you." I choked up myself.

"It's Bohemian, a story as a gift. I can't wait to show my sisters. Joseph, have you been keeping up on your dishes? Have you been eating? You know I worry. Especially after what happened to Ingrid..."

"I know, Mom. Try not to worry."

I must have said goodbye three times. We finally let go.

I should call my dad. I should call my brother and my sister-in-law. The phone rings. It's Karina. She asks me what was in the boxes. I tell her. She thinks it's sweet. I think it's strange. Karina calls me Christmas morning. The word *sweet* from her? I ask about her Christmas Eve. Czechs feast on the eve. She tells me her mother is crazy. I tell her all mothers are crazy. They spent the day cleaning, she says. She says it was "like punishment."

Her brother got her a present. She tries to describe it; she doesn't have the words. Doesn't matter, I can picture it — it is a trend in Prague at the moment. Digital, chunky, red or white or blue or yellow. She tells me you can't get these watches in the Czech Republic. Her brother drove to Austria. For her.

Dinner at Avi's place was fun. Barbora met me at the door, around three in the afternoon. The house was dark. No lights were on. Barbora told me we had to wait for the first star to come out. Then we could turn on the lights and dinner could be served. Looks like I am the first to arrive. I hand her the bottle of wine I brought.

Even in the dark, the table in the dining room looks amazing. One end of the table is covered in *obložené chlebíčky*, open-faced deli-style sandwiches. I know what they are because Avi has made cards in both Czech and English. It's cute. The other end of the table is covered in powdered cookies, *vánoční cukroví*, the card says. There are probably a dozen different kinds. Barbora says they are all homemade, but she didn't make them. We have her *babička* (grandmother) to thank. I notice a rope tied around the legs of the table, noticeable under the festive red tablecloth. I ask about it. Avi bounds over to tell me. It is a superstition. Tying the legs of the table will protect the house from thieves and burglars in the coming year. Avi asked me if I wanted a beer. "On *Štědrý den*, we're supposed to fast and abstain from alcohol. You are fasting, are you not, Joseph? You won't be able to see the *zlaté prasátko*."

Avi uncaps a bottle of Velkopopovický Kozel and hands it to me. I take a sip, squinting, "The golden pig?" The beer with a goat on the label is a crisp pale lager.

Avi's eyes widen. A big smile spreads across his face.

"If you are able to fast all day, in the evening you will see the *zlaté prasátko* on the wall." Barbora nods behind Avi. I guess it's no different than thinking a fat man in a red suit lands on your roof and slides down your chimney, right?

"I already ate. I can pretend." I take a sip of my beer. I pick up a Prague Ham *chlebíček*. I take a bite.

Buck comes in. He carries his guitar over his shoulder. He has a bag from Bakeshop Praha. He speaks perfect Czech to Barbora. I feel a pang of envy wash over me. He hands the *vánočka*, braided Christmas sweet bread, to Barbora's grandmother. He wishes her Merry Christmas in a Prague accent. I hate that he picked it up quicker than me. Buck and I shake hands. I wish him a Merry Christmas. He wants to ask me about Ingrid. I look into his eyes. He knows.

Brad and Jacques came shortly after that. I introduced them around. We sit in the living room. We drink beers together. I ask Brad about Agata. They are back together again. It never ends with them. "She's home with her family. I was invited, but I know better. Her uncles and cousins just try to see how much slivovice I will drink before I throw up. Happens every holiday. Did Elijah go back to the motherland for Christmas?"

I tell them the Canadian rube did go back. I want to tell them about Ljuba, but I think better of it — they might be connected to her boyfriend. I let it go.

"How's Karina?" Jacques can't help but needle me. I nod. "Saw her on the cover of the magazine."

Brad piles on, "And on the metro. And on a billboard in Vršovice. She's everywhere. I have to say, I never saw what you see, Joe, but she looks damn good in the photos."

"Yeah." I empty my beer. I have no more to say on the topic. "I'll get another one. You guys need anything?" Brad and Jacques shake their heads.

In the kitchen, I offer my help to Barbora. She and Avi move the platters of cookies and open-faced sandwiches into the kitchen. She asks me to set the table. "An even number of place settings, with at least one extra. Oh and here," Barbora holds out as plate of fish scales to me. "Put a scale or two under every plate. For health and wealth in the coming year." I take the plate, wrinkling my nose.

I set the plate of scales on the dining-room table and grab a stack of plates. I set ten places, scales under each plate, green cloth napkins, flatware. Jacques comes in. He asks Avi a question.

"Sure, man," Avi directs. "In my bedroom, make yourself at home." Avi comes over to me. "Oh, dude, we need to move this one place setting. No one can sit with their back to the door. It's bad luck." Avi takes the Christmas tradition all the way. I move the place setting. And the fish scales. Jacques appears back in the living room with a guitar. He sits down next to Buck. They tune. I grab another goat beer. I join Avi and Brad in the living room.

"It's part of it, man," Brad says to Avi. "A Czech woman means multiple Christmases forever. If only Agata's family were atheists..."

"Nah, they would still celebrate Christmas," Avi says under his breath. Buck's teaching Jacques a song. Jacques says, "No, that's good, I'll follow you. You know the songs."

Buck laughs. "Learned them yesterday." He reminds Jacques that Barbora and her grandmother know all the words.

Avi sighs, stands and gets back to work. "Dinner in a few, gentlemen. Freshen up your drinks. We'll step outside to see the first star."

Brad looks at me. "You know, an American would be much easier. I mean, think about it, if I had kids with Agata, we'd ping pong back and forth across the Atlantic for life. Holidays are a hassle. Sucks that Czech women are so hot, doesn't it?"

"I said I would never date another American ever. I meant it. What's this about you and Agata and kids? Didn't you guys break up like a few months back?"

"Theoretically, my man, theoretically. Never say never, you know?" Brad holds out the bottom of his brown beer bottle to me. I clink it.

"To theoretical children." I drink my beer. I think of the keys. What should I do?

Avi, Barbora and her grandmother come into the living room. They have their coats on. Buck and Jacques place their guitars aside. We grab our coats and head outside. Brad comes out without his jacket. He lights a cigarette.

We see the first star. I don't point out that it's probably a planet. It's cold. We go back in. Brad stabs out his cigarette on the side of the building. Back in the flat, Avi ushers us into the dining room. He lays down the rules. "Once we sit down, we can't get up from the table until everyone is done. If you have to use the restroom, do it now." Avi explains that we'll sing carols. He asks the guys to bring their guitars in. "The first one to get up from the table will die within a year." Avi catches my eyes, then Buck's. "Forget that — let's just stay until the end." He had the beer crate next to him, he said. In case we needed more.

Barbora and her grandmother serve the first course, *česnečka polévka*, garlic soup. It is topped with cubes of Emmental cheese and rye bread croutons. Potatoes, onions, tons of garlic. Garnished with dill and parsley. Once everyone has a bowl in front of them, Avi says, "Dobrou chuť," which is the Czech equivalent of *bon appétit*. We all wish each other *dobrou chuť* and dig in.

We eat soup. We have Buck's *vánočka*, sweet bread with apricots and raisins that have been soaked in hot brandy for days.

Not a huge fan, but I have a taste. To prove that I'm game. Fried carp comes next. With *bramborovy salat*, potato salad. Avi tells a story. An earlier expat Christmas at Beth's apartment. The same one that Kamil took after she left.

"I walk in and there she is, Beth, on her knees." Dressed in a white plastic apron, he said, dish gloves and lab goggles. The gloves were purple. On the floor, a rubber mallet, various rusting knives with wooden handles. A pair of yellow gardening shears. Laid out on newspaper. Blood all over. She dug out guts. She clipped off fins. She severed the tail. Bits of guts and fish and blood were everywhere. Splattered all over the white tile. It looked like a massacre, he said. She stuffed the offal in a plastic bag. It said Kotva on it, Avi told us. She stood up — bag in one hand, carp head in the other. She slipped in the blood on the floor. She caught herself. The head kept mouthing. It looked down. Beth looked at Avi. His mouth hung open. "She said, 'What?' I told her I would help her clean up. It was hilarious." The potato salad is tasty. The carp is pungent. It is cooked to perfection. Nothing that could have been done better; it's a dark and smelly meat. I eat a couple of bites. I wash it down with beer. I move on. Whew.

Brad speaks up. "Barbora, why carp for Christmas? I know it is a tradition, but why?" Barbora smiles. She translates for her grandmother.

Barbora relays, "For good luck." She told us in Slovakia and Poland they have the same tradition. Buy a carp at the Christmas Market. It becomes a family pet for a few days. It swims in the bathtub. Some people ask the fish monger to cut the filets right there on Old Town Square, she said, but the authentic way to do it is to bring it home and butcher it personally.

Buck wipes his hands on his napkin. He nods to Jacques. They reach for the guitars. Buck strums. Jacques follows along. Buck hits a rhythm.

Barbora and her grandmother come in from the kitchen. They start singing. I don't recognize the tune, but they obviously know it. I assume it is a traditional Czech Christmas carol. It was "*Nesem vám noviny*," which translates to "We bring you good news." I don't need to understand the words to enjoy the mood. Same with the next song, "*Půjdem spolu do Betléma,*" or "Let's all go to Bethlehem." Buck plucks the melody. Jacques strums the chords. Around the table, full of good food and Czech beer, the effect is amazing. I scrape my plate for the last of the *bramborovy salat.* At the end of the song, Buck smiles at Jacques. He counts out the beat. It's an American Christmas song, "Rockin' around the Christmas Tree." Avi doesn't miss a word. He passes me a fresh beer. Before I can react, Brad opens it with a bottle opener on his keychain.

Barbora and her grandmother duck back into the kitchen. They bring back the platters of Christmas cookies. I could burst. I grab a couple of *sušenky* anyway. There's a knock at the door. Blue-haired Sadie Mae and her Canadian friends, Ashley and Meg, arrive. We get up from the table to welcome them. I intro-duce them to Avi, Barbora and her grandmother. I tell them they missed the carp. Ashley says, "Timed it perfectly," as Babička drags the girls into the kitchen to make plates. Brad steps out-side for a smoke. I accompany him.

"Good thing the girls showed up — turning into a sausage party there."

I laugh. I rub my belly. "Do you think they'll let us off with-out Becherovka and slivovice?"

Brad takes a long drag on his cigarette. "Fat chance," he says.

Pressing, 26.12.98

I received two voice messages yesterday on my machine.

The first was Naked Pete. He said, "Happy Christmas, Joseph. You were right. I am back on the Knowledge with the help of my uncle. Spent the last two days on the scooter with my maps. The old brain may change yet. Thank you."

The second was my dad.

"Joe. It's your dad."

Ha.

"I need to come see you. Never been to Europe. Call me back, would you?"

I called him back. I told him to come. I told him I would help him arrange it. I told him he could stay with me.

I have to decide what to do about Karina. I need to see her. I should call her.

Waffling, 28.12.98

Karina invited me out to her parents' house. I make my way to the metro station George of Podebrady. On the way, I buy metro tickets at the NonStop Tabák. From the magazine racks, Karina looks up at me. I haven't bought a copy of the magazine. I catch the metro to Můstek, change to the B line and catch another to Smíchovské nádraží. I'm half an hour early to catch the train. I sit down on a bench. I wait under the mural.

Pictures of people. People work, people harvest. A man carries a basket of fish. A woman carries a hoe over her shoulder. Another woman holds a baby. People file past. There are men, there are boys, there are women, there are girls. Ten months I have been chasing. I sit in a train station. I watch girls walk past.

I stopped at a kiosk. A rack of keychains. A little dog. A red glitter high-heeled shoe. My train would leave in a few minutes. I spun the carousel of keychains. A heart. A red plastic heart, with a gold chain and a gold key ring. It was perfect. I snatched it off the carousel and paid the clerk. I tucked the heart in my pocket and ran down to the platform.

At her house, Karina tells me her parents are out for the evening. I half thought I would get to meet them. Karina had another plan. She led me into her room. She sets me down on her bed. I take a look around, getting a read on this young woman. She strips off her sweater. I sit back. It feels rushed. I don't know what I'm supposed to feel, what I'm supposed to do. She wiggles her shirt off. She's in her bra. I want to talk. Not sure what the hurry is. I never thought I would be that guy.

Headlights sweep her bedroom wall. She clasps her shirt to her breast and pushes me out of her room. She kisses me, then rushes me down the backstairs. From the top of the stairs, she points in the direction of the train station. The way her hair swings. I hear her father open the door. He calls her name. I walk out into the dark. I wonder what the hell just happened.

On the train, on the way home, I pull out the keychain. I look at it. It is perfect. Exactly what I needed. I would pour a glass of wine. I will string up the flat. My vision comes together.

Starting, 30.12.98

Karlův most, the Charles Bridge, was chilly this morning. I ran there. To truly enjoy the bridge, you have to go when no one else is around. A low fog skirted the bridge, drifting between the statues of Saint Vitus and Saint Joseph. Saint Joe holds the hand of Jesus as a young boy. The streetlights were on.

It was dawn. The heavy black lamps cast off spheres of yellow-orange radiance. I came from the Old Town Square side. The tower looms large. It is dark. Mossy green against the purple sky. The sun peeks over the horizon.

I had some thinking to do. I found Saint John of Nepomuk, the relief. I touched the bright spot of brass that everyone touches. I faced upriver, crossed myself, said a prayer. The story started with me on that very bridge. I bridged from my past into my future. It was the day I met Karina for the first time. I bet she doesn't remember.

I shivered. I put my hands in my pockets. I felt something in there.

I pulled my hand out of my pocket. My breath billowed out in front of me, crystallizing in the air. In the palm of my hand sat the keys. The fob I found, the one with the plastic heart attached, it had seemed perfect in the train station. I looked down at it in my hand. It seemed cheap. Cheap and vulgar.

I thought about the stories. They are fiction. None of them are what happened. There are shards of the truth. Pieces of reality mixed in with the misty romanticism. I want to believe the fiction — but it's just that, fiction. The distant past.

I thought about Rachel. How I tortured myself, how I obsessed over her, how I couldn't let her go long after she was gone. Day after day, I woke in a pool of sweat, in a pool of Rachel, unable to get my mind off her. Until I stopped. It was an act of will. It was pure determination. She was long gone. In my mind, she was as present as if she woke up next to me.

All the others. I sell myself short. I ask too little. Content with the dust, when I'm after diamonds. It was time. Time to put all that behind me. It was time to open up.

I don't know why. I kissed the keys. A prim peck. I reached

back. I chucked them. Over the wall, between two statues. I threw them as far as I could. No one will understand, but in that moment, watching the little splash, breathing my heavy breaths, I felt whole. First time in a long time. I will take down the thread throughout my flat. It's embarrassing. What if Ljuba or Elijah catch me? I will chuck the whole ball of mess, happily. I will start again.

CONNECT WITH RICK

https://www.rickpryll.com/

FACEBOOK
facebook.com/rickpryllauthor

TWITTER
twitter.com/rickpryll?lang=en

INSTAGRAM
instagram.com/rickpryll/?hl=en

PINTEREST
pinterest.com/rickpryll/_saved

GOODREADS
goodreads.com/author/show/7908009.Rick_Pryll

Lightning Source UK Ltd.
Milton Keynes UK
UKHW041520251120
374080UK00014B/806/J